DETROIT PUBLIC LIBRARY

P9-DMU-923

A MIDSUMMER'S EQUATION

CHASE BRANCH LIBRARY
17731 W. SEVEN MILE RD.
DETROIT, MI 48235

JUN -- 2018

CH

BY KEIGO HIGASHINO

The Detective Galileo Novels

The Devotion of Suspect X
Salvation of a Saint
A Midsummer's Equation

The Kyochiro Kaga Mysteries

Malice

CHASE BRANCH LIBRARY
17731 W. SEVEN MILE RD.
DETROIT, MI 48235

A MIDSUMMER'S EQUATION

Keigo Higashino

TRANSLATED BY ALEXANDER O. SMITH

MINOTAUR BOOKS
NEW YORK

This is a work of fiction. All of the characters, organizations, and events portrayed in this novel are either products of the author's imagination or are used fictitiously.

A MIDSUMMER'S EQUATION. Copyright © 2011 by Keigo Higashino. English translation copyright © 2016 by Alexander O. Smith. All rights reserved. Printed in the United States of America. For information, address St. Martin's Press, 175 Fifth Avenue, New York, N.Y. 10010.

www.minotaurbooks.com

The Library of Congress has cataloged the hardcover edition as follows:

Names: Higashino, Keigo, 1958– author. | Smith, Alexander O., translator.
Title: A Midsummer's equation : a Detective Galileo novel / by Keigo Higashino ; translation by Alexander O. Smith.
Other titles: Manatsu no Hoteishiki. English
Description: First English-language edition. | New York : Minotaur Books, 2016. | Series: Detective Galileo series ; 3
Identifiers: LCCN 2015038889 | ISBN 9781250027924 (hardcover) | ISBN 9781250027917 (ebook)
Subjects: LCSH: Physicists—Fiction. | Murder—Investigation—Fiction. | Japan—Fiction. | Mystery fiction. | BISAC: FICTION / Mystery & Detective / Police Procedural.
Classification: LCC PL852.I3625 M3613 2016 | DDC 895.63/6—dc23
LC record available at http://lccn.loc.gov/2015038889

ISBN 978-1-250-14542-0 (trade paperback)

Our books may be purchased in bulk for promotional, educational, or business use. Please contact your local bookseller or the Macmillan Corporate and Premium Sales Department at 1-800-221-7945, extension 5442, or by email at MacmillanSpecialMarkets@macmillan.com.

First published in Japanese under the title *Manatsu no Hoteishiki* by Bungeishunju Ltd.; English translation rights arranged with Bungeishinju Ltd. through Japan Foreign-Rights Centre / Anna Stein.

First Minotaur Books Paperback Edition: November 2017

10 9 8 7 6 5 4 3 2 1

A MIDSUMMER'S EQUATION

ONE

Kyohei found the transfer gate from the bullet train to the express line without any difficulty, and by the time he ran up the stairs to the platform, the train was already there. The sound of people talking inside the car spilled out through the opened doors.

He stepped on at the nearest door and immediately frowned. His parents had said it wouldn't be that busy, now that summer was almost over, but most of the four-person booths were already full. He walked down the aisle, scouting for that elusive booth with only one or two people in it.

Most of the passengers were here with families. He saw a lot of kids his own age, all looking far too happy.

Idiots, Kyohei thought. What was so great about going to the ocean? It was just a lot of salty water. It was way more fun to play in a pool, especially one with a waterslide. They didn't have those at the ocean.

At last he spotted an empty seat way in the back. There was someone sitting across from it, but he would have a whole two-person bench to himself.

Kyohei threw his backpack down on the empty seat and glanced at the man sitting opposite him. He was wearing a dress shirt and blazer and didn't look much like a tourist. His long legs were crossed, and he was reading a magazine through rimless glasses. The cover of the magazine had some complicated pattern on it and a bunch of words Kyohei didn't know. Nose buried in his reading, the man hadn't noticed him.

Across the aisle, a heavy, older man with white hair and an old woman with a round face were seated across from each other. The woman poured from a plastic bottle into a cup and handed it to her husband. He took it from her with a scowl and drank it down, mumbling something about her giving him too much. These two weren't dressed like tourists, either. They looked like old folks from the country, going home.

The train lurched into motion. Kyohei opened his backpack and took out a plastic bag with his lunch inside. The rice balls wrapped in aluminum foil were still warm. A small Tupperware container held some fried chicken and grilled egg, both favorites of his.

He drank some water out of a bottle and crammed one of the rice balls into his mouth. He could already see the ocean outside the window. There was a blue sky today, and sunlight glittered off the waves in the distance, beyond the white spray closer to shore.

"It'll just be for a little bit, while we're in Osaka," his mother had told him. That was three days ago. "You'd rather go play in the ocean than stay up here alone, wouldn't you?" Until then, Kyohei had never considered the possibility of going all by himself to stay with relatives so far away.

"You sure he'll be okay?" his father had asked, tipping back a glass of whiskey. "Hari Cove's a long way away."

"He'll be fine. He's in fifth grade already. You know, I heard that the Kobayashis' little girl Hana went all the way to Australia by herself," his mother had replied, her fingers typing away at her computer. His mother made a habit of tallying sales for the day in the living room each evening. "Hari Cove is only in Shizuoka. That's practically next door."

"Yeah, but her parents took her to the airport, and her relatives picked her up at the other end. All she had to do was ride on the airplane. That's easy."

"It's the same thing. He only has one change off the bullet train. And they're not that far from the station once he's there. I'll give you a map." She said this last part to Kyohei directly.

"Sure," Kyohei said, his eyes glued to the game in his hands. There was no point in protesting. No matter what he said, his fate was sealed: he would waste away in the boring countryside while his parents were in Osaka. The same scene had played out many times before. Back when his grandmother was still alive, they'd send him to her house west of Tokyo. But she'd passed away the year before, and now it was the same deal, only he had to go further to stay with his aunt and uncle.

Kyohei's parents ran a small clothing boutique. It kept them busy, and they were forever running off to this place or that, trying to sell their latest designs. Sometimes Kyohei would go with them, if he didn't have school. He was fine spending a night alone by himself, too.

This time, they would be gone all week. They were going to Osaka to open a new shop.

"I guess you are in fifth grade already," his father had said with a shrug. "Listen, Kyohei, have fun at the ocean. You get a whole week. The food's great down there. I'll tell your aunt to stuff you full of fresh fish." His voice was a little slurred with the whiskey. And that was the end of it. His parents might have given the appearance of having an actual discussion, but its conclusion was set in stone from the very beginning.

Like it was every time.

The express train cruised down the coastline. Kyohei finished his rice balls and was playing his game when the cell phone in his backpack began to ring. He paused his game and fished around in his backpack until he found it.

It was his mom. Kyohei sighed inwardly and answered.

"Yeah?"

"Kyohei? Where are you?"

Now, that was a stupid question. She was the one who checked the schedules and bought his ticket for him.

"On the train," he said, keeping his voice down.

"Glad you got on all right."

"Yeah." *What were you expecting?*

"Be sure to say hi to everyone for us when you get there. And give them the presents, okay?"

"Yeah, fine. Bye—"

"And don't forget your homework, Kyohei. Do a little every day. If you let it build up, it'll only be worse."

"I know, Mom," he said quickly and hung up. Why did his mother always feel the need to tell him the same things over and over? She had already given him the speech about the homework before he left the house that morning. Maybe all mothers were like that.

He threw the phone back in his backpack and was about to restart his game when he heard a low voice say, "Hey."

He ignored it.

"Hey, kid." The speaker sounded irritated.

Kyohei looked up from his game and across the aisle. The white-haired man was glaring at him with a frightening scowl on his face. "You're not supposed to use cell phones here," he said in a rasping voice.

Kyohei blinked, surprised. No one ever complained about cell phones in Tokyo. *Wow, I'm really out in the boonies.*

"But they called me," he said, pouting a little.

The old man glared with anger at Kyohei and pointed a wrinkled hand over the boy's head. Kyohei turned around, looked up, and read the small plaque: "Courtesy seats. Please turn off your cell phone in this area."

"Oh," Kyohei said.

"See?" the old man said, victoriously.

Kyohei pulled the phone out of his backpack and showed it to the man. "I can't turn it off. It's a kids' phone."

The man frowned, not understanding. His bushy white eyebrows drew closer together.

"Even if I press the button it just comes back on by itself. There's a code you can put in to make it really shut off, but I don't know it."

The old man considered this for a moment before saying, "Then move to another seat."

"Oh, leave the boy alone," the old woman sitting across from him said. She smiled at Kyohei. "I'm sorry, dear."

"No, no, no." The old man growled. "The boy needs to learn his manners. There are rules that must be followed." His raspy voice was growing louder. A few of the other passengers craned their necks to see what the commotion was.

Kyohei sighed. *Just my luck to sit next to a grumpy old man.* He grabbed his backpack and a plastic baggie he'd been using for a trash bag and was about to stand up when the tall man sitting across from him put an arm on Kyohei's shoulder and pushed him back down into the seat. Then he snatched the cell phone out of his hand.

Kyohei looked up at the man in surprise. A blank look on his face, the man thrust his hand into Kyohei's trash bag and pulled out the aluminum foil.

Before Kyohei even had a chance to say something, the man spread the aluminum foil out on his knee, then crumpled it in a ball around the cell phone.

"There," he said, handing it back to Kyohei. "You can stay in your seat."

Kyohei took the phone in silence. He felt like he was watching some kind of magic trick, but he wasn't entirely sure what had happened.

"What's that supposed to do?" the old man asked.

"Aluminum foil blocks cellular signals," the man said, his eyes back on his magazine. "He won't be able to send or receive calls. It's the same as if it were off. Society lives to see another day."

Kyohei gaped in shock between the two men. The old man looked a bit confused, but when he saw Kyohei looking at him, he coughed loudly and closed his eyes. His wife was grinning as if this were the funniest thing she'd seen all year.

A short while later, many of the passengers started getting up and pulling luggage off the overhead racks. An announcement indicated that they would soon be stopping at a popular destination for beachgoers.

The train stopped, and about half of the passengers got off. Kyohei considered changing seats, but the man across from him stood before he did. Pulling a bag off the rack, he moved to another seat further up the car.

Kyohei frowned. He couldn't move too. He glanced across the aisle. The old man was snoring.

The coastline here was dotted with beaches, and at each station, the number of passengers on the train grew fewer and fewer. It was still a ways before Hari Cove.

The old man's snoring grew louder, though his wife didn't seem to notice. She was looking out the window at the view. Unable to concentrate on his game, Kyohei finally stood, picking up his backpack and bag of garbage.

There were plenty of empty seats to choose from now. He walked down the aisle, thinking to get as far away from the old man as he could, when he saw the man who had wrapped the aluminum foil around his phone. His back was turned, and he was crossing his legs and reading his magazine. Kyohei glanced at it over his shoulder. He was on the crossword puzzle page. Several of the blanks had already been filled in, but he wasn't writing. He looked stumped.

"Temperance," Kyohei muttered.

The man stiffened in his seat and looked around. "What did you say?"

Kyohei pointed at the blank line in his crossword puzzle. "Five down. 'Who reads the bones?' I think it's Temperance."

The man looked down at his puzzle and nodded. "It does fit. Is that someone's name? Never heard it before."

"Temperance Brennan. She's the lead in *Bones*. She looks at dead people's bones and figures out all kinds of things from them. It's a TV show."

The man narrowed his eyebrows and looked at the cover of his magazine.

"You can't put fictional characters in a science magazine's cross-word puzzle. It's not fair," he grumbled.

Kyohei sat down across from the man, who had already returned to his puzzle. His pen was moving rapidly now, its previous hurdle cleared.

The man reached for the bottle of tea on the seat next to him. But when he lifted it up, he noticed it was empty and put it back down.

Kyohei held up his bottle of water, still half full. "You can have some."

The man looked at him with an expression of shock on his face, then curtly shook his head. "No."

Somehow disappointed, Kyohei was putting his bottle back into his backpack when the man added, "Thanks, though." Kyohei looked up, and their eyes met for the first time. The man quickly looked away.

They were getting close to Hari Cove now. Kyohei pulled a printed map out of his shorts pocket with a marked location that read "Green Rock Inn."

He'd been here two years ago, but that time, he'd come by car and with his parents. This would be his first time walking there from the station. He spread out the map and traced the route with a finger, when the man asked, "You staying all by yourself?"

"My aunt and uncle live there," Kyohei said. "They run the place."

"Oh? What's it like?"

"What do you mean?"

"I mean, is it a good hotel? Are the facilities new, are they clean, does it have a view, is the food good, is there anything to recommend it?"

Kyohei shrugged. "Only been there once, so I dunno, but the building's really old, I remember that. And it's a little ways away from the ocean, so the view's not very good either. I don't know about the food. It's okay, I guess."

"I see. Could I have a look?"

Kyohei handed him the map, and the man wrote the name of the hotel, the phone number, and the address in the corner of his magazine and tore it off.

"Interesting name. Are the rocks green?"

"Not really. There's a big rock out in front with the name carved on it, though."

"I see," the man said, returning the map.

Kyohei stuffed it back in his pocket, then looked out the window. The train was just emerging from a tunnel, and it seemed to him that the sea on this side sparkled just a little bit brighter.

TWO

By the time she had both sneakers on, the hands of the old clock on the wall were at half past one. *Right on time*, Narumi thought. If she took her bike, she could be there in fifteen minutes. That would leave her plenty of time to talk with the others.

"I'm heading out, Mom," she called over the counter.

Setsuko came out through the long curtain hanging in the doorway to the kitchen. She had a handkerchief tied around her hair, a sure sign she was the middle of prepping dinner. "How long will you be?" she asked.

Setsuko looked young for a woman in her midfifties, Narumi often thought, and if she ever bothered to put on makeup, she would probably look even younger. But the most she could be bothered with in the summer was some sunscreen and foundation.

"I'm not sure. Maybe two hours?" Narumi said. "There's a couple of guests coming in tonight, right? Know what time they're getting here?"

"They didn't say exactly, but in time for dinner I should imagine."

"Well, I'll try to be back before then."

"Don't forget that Kyohei is coming tonight, too," her mother reminded her.

"Oh, right. Is he coming by himself?"

"That's what they said. His train should be getting here anytime."

"I'll stop at the station on my way," Narumi offered. "I'll pick him up. I don't want him to get lost."

"Thanks, dear. I don't think my brother would be happy with me if I lost his only son."

Narumi nodded, thinking that was hardly likely in a small town like theirs. Outside, the sun was beating down. The large piece of polished obsidian engraved with the name of the inn reflected the sunlight, making it almost too brilliant to look at.

Slinging her bag over her shoulder, Narumi got on her bike and headed for the station. The roads in the area were hilly, but Green Rock Inn was up on a bluff, so she could coast all the way.

She was there in under five minutes, and passengers from the train that had just arrived were already coming out—only a dozen or so of them in all.

Among them she spotted a boy in a red T-shirt and khaki shorts, wearing a backpack.

The boy's sullen expression looked familiar, but Narumi hesitated a moment before calling out to him. The reason for her hesitation was twofold. For one, it had been two years since they'd met, and if that really was he, he was a lot bigger than she remembered. Two, he was talking familiarly with the man walking next to him, but her mother had just told her he was coming alone, and she knew this man wasn't her uncle.

Thankfully, Kyohei noticed her and, after a parting word to the man, came running up. "Hi!"

"Hey there, Kyohei. You've gotten big."

"You think?"

"You're in fifth grade now?"

"Yeah. Did you come down to get me?" He looked up at her, his eyes squinting in the sun.

"I just wanted to make sure you got here in one piece. I actually have someplace to go, but I have a little time, so if you need help finding the inn, I can show you the way."

The boy shook his head and waved his hands for good measure. "Nah, I'm fine. I got a map, and I've been here before. Just up the road, right?" He pointed to the slope Narumi had just descended.

"You got it. Look for the big rock out in front of the house."

"Yeah, I remember." The boy started to walk.

"Hey, Kyohei," Narumi stopped him. "Do you know that man? The one you were talking to." She pointed toward the station where the man who had been walking with Kyohei was talking on his cell phone.

"Nah, I don't know him. We were just on the train together."

"Do you always talk to strangers?"

The man didn't look particularly suspicious, but Narumi felt a certain responsibility to instill a little common sense in her cousin.

"Some old man started yelling at me, and he helped me out, that's all."

"Oh," Narumi said, wondering more about why the old man had been yelling at her cousin than anything else.

"Okay, so, see you later?"

She smiled at him. "I'll be back in a couple hours, we can catch up then."

Kyohei nodded and started walking up the hill. Narumi watched him go for a bit, then got back on her bike. She saw the man from the train waiting at the taxi stand. *Too bad for him*, she thought. The taxis came whenever a train was due, but there were only two or three of them in town. If there wasn't one waiting there now, it would be a good thirty minutes before the next one showed up.

Narumi pedaled along the road paralleling the train line, enjoying the sun on her face. The sea breeze was tossing her hair around, but she didn't mind. She'd kept her hair short for most of the last decade. It was a lot less trouble that way. Sometimes after a dive, she'd walk over to the bar and have a beer without even taking a shower. *Guess I can't really fault Mom for not wearing any makeup, can I?*

Eventually, the road took a turn away from the coast and began to climb. Here there was a shopping center and a bank and a few other buildings, making it more of a proper town than the area near the station. A little further on, she came to the gray building which served as the local community center and the site of a very important hearing that day.

She parked her bike outside and took a look at the large tour bus sitting in the parking lot. She walked over until she could see the name by the bus's door: "DESMEC." That's what everyone called them, but their official name was the Deep Sea Metals National Corporation. To Narumi, they were the enemy.

No one was on the bus, which meant they had already arrived and were getting ready. *It's on*, Narumi thought, making a beeline for the entrance.

An official from city hall was checking people in at the door. Narumi showed her admission badge and walked to the lobby, where a large number of people had already gathered. Her eyes scanned the crowd until she heard someone calling out her name.

Motoya Sawamura, weaving between people, was striding toward her. His face and arms were darkly tanned. Since moving home from Tokyo last spring, Sawamura had been working at a home appliances store in town, and he did some freelance journalism on the side.

"You're late," he said as soon as he got close enough to be heard. "What were you up to?"

"Sorry. Is everyone else here?"

"Already inside. Come on."

Narumi followed Sawamura into one of the waiting rooms off to the side of the main hall. She wondered what strings he'd pulled to reserve a whole room for their group on a day like today. There were already a dozen or so familiar faces gathered. Half the people were the same age as Narumi, while the others were older, in their forties or fifties. They came from a variety of occupations, but all were local residents. Some she had known from before, but most she only met through Save the Cove.

Sawamura took a deep breath and looked over the room. "The pamphlet I passed around has everything we've discovered through our research, and you can be sure that they're going to say some things that disagree with our findings. That's going to be the battle-field this war is fought on, so look out, and take notes, but keep your comments to yourselves. The real fight's tomorrow. Today we listen to what they have to say, and tonight, we talk strategy. Any questions?"

"There's nothing in here about the money," one of the men said, holding up his pamphlet. He was a social studies teacher at the local middle school. "I'm sure they're going to make a big point of the economic benefits their proposed development is going to bring to the community."

Sawamura smiled at the teacher. "I didn't feel the need to put it in there because that argument's already so full of holes, we hardly need to poke new ones. The story changes every five minutes depending on who's doing the talking. Yeah, they'll bring it up again today, and I'm sure they'll make it sound sweet, but anyone who thinks those benefits are coming their way is a fool."

"The money's not what's important here," Narumi chimed in. "Protecting the natural beauty of our coastline is. Destroy the environment, and you can't put it back the way it was, no matter how many millions you throw at it."

The social studies teacher shrugged at that, but was silent.

There was a knock, and the door opened. A man who worked at the community center poked his head in. "It's almost time. If I could get you to move into the meeting hall?"

"Let's go," Sawamura said, sounding every bit the leader.

The chairs in the big hall were tiered, like bleachers. If they filled all of them, they could get four or five hundred people in here,

Narumi thought. It had been built with the idea of welcoming speakers from other parts of the country, but as far as Narumi could remember, no one famous had ever come to give a talk in Hari Cove.

Narumi and the others from the group sat up front. She set her pamphlet on the table in front of her and got ready to take notes. Next to her, Sawamura was checking his audio recorder.

The seats in the large auditorium slowly began to fill. The mayor and a few other local officials were in attendance. She'd heard there would be people from the neighboring towns as well. The buzz had been building for days. Everyone was interested, and nobody knew anything—the perfect combination to fill a room.

As she was looking over the crowd, her eyes met a man's eyes. He was probably a little over sixty, with gray hair parted down the middle and a white, open-collar shirt. The man smiled and nodded curtly in her direction. She nodded back, wondering who he was.

A narrow conference table had been set up on the stage, with a line of folding chairs behind it. Small nameplates in front of each seat listed a name and credentials. Most of the people were from DESMEC, but there were some independent scientists, too—an oceanographer and a physicist. A large screen hung on the wall behind the chairs.

Now the doors to the front of the hall opened, and men in suits came filing in, their faces hard. Someone from city hall silently led them to the stage.

A short distance away from the table was a chair for the emcee. A man with glasses, about thirty, picked up the microphone.

"It's time, so we'd like to get things started. We're still missing one participant, but he should be here any moment—"

The side door opened with a slam, and a man came dashing in, carrying his suit jacket over his arm.

Narumi noted with surprise that it was the man she'd seen at the station, the one talking to Kyohei. Sweat glistened at his temples. *He must have given up on the taxi.* It was a short distance from the station by bicycle, but quite a journey on foot.

The man sat down behind the nameplate that read "Manabu Yukawa, Assistant Professor of Physics, Imperial University."

"Well, now that we're all here," the emcee resumed, "I'd like to begin this informational hearing concerning the development of undersea resources in the Hari Cove area. My name's Mr. Kuwano. I'm in the Deep Sea Metals National Corporation's public outreach office, and I thank you for your interest in our project. We'll start with an overview from our technology division."

A man whose nameplate announced him as a manager in DESMEC's technology division stood as the lights in the room darkened. The words "Developing Undersea Resources" appeared on the screen in giant, bold letters.

Narumi straightened in her chair, not wanting to miss a word. She knew that protecting the ocean was *her* job. No one would do it for her. And if she failed, the natural jewel that was Hari Cove would be torn apart in the name of economic progress.

It had all started with a report from the committee of natural energy resources at METI—the Ministry of Economy, Trade, and Industry—that had shocked Hari Cove and the surrounding towns. The report stated that the region of the sea beginning a few dozen kilometers to the south had been selected as a top candidate for testing the commercial viability of developing hydrothermal polymetallic ore.

This ore was found in lumps of rock that formed in the sediment around hydrothermal vents on the seabed. They contained copper, lead, zinc, gold, and silver, as well as rich deposits of the rare metals germanium and gallium. Were it possible to recover these rare metals, then Japan would go from resource-poor to resource-rich overnight. The government was putting a lot into the development of the necessary technologies, with DESMEC leading the charge.

This latest finding had generated such excitement because it was at the relatively shallow depth of eight hundred meters. The shallower the water, the easier and cheaper recovery would be. That it was only a few dozen kilometers from land also improved the viability of the site.

When the report made the rounds, Hari Cove and the towns nearby had erupted—not with anger over the coming destruction of the natural habitat, but with excitement at the prospect of a new industry and the jobs it would bring.

THREE

I don't remember this hill being this long, Kyohei thought with a sigh, stopping to look around. The best swimming in the area was down by the station, so he'd been up and down this road a hundred times in a car, but this was his first time walking it.

The scenery hadn't changed much in two years. A large building—a former hotel—squatted at the bottom of the hill. The roof and walls were a sooty gray, and all the paint had flaked off the large sign out front. His father liked to call it "the ruins of Hari Cove."

"Why isn't anyone living there anymore?" Kyohei had asked once as they were driving by.

"It used to be a fancy hotel," his father had told him. "But people stopped coming, and they couldn't keep it open."

"Why'd they stop coming?"

His father shrugged. "Probably because there were better places to go."

"What kind of better places?"

"You know, fun places. Like Disneyland, or Hawaii."

Kyohei had never been to Hawaii, but he was a fan of Disneyland.

People got jealous when you told them you were going to Disney-land. No one got jealous when you were going to Hari Cove.

Kyohei resumed his climb. He started to wonder why anyone had ever built such a big hotel in a little town like this. He wondered if it had ever really been as popular as his dad claimed.

Finally, he spotted the inn. It was only about a quarter the size of the ruins below, but it wasn't any newer. Kyohei's uncle, Shigehiro, had taken it over from his father fifteen years ago, but he hadn't done any renovations in all that time. "I got a renovation idea," Kyohei's father had joked. "Tear the place down. No one ever comes here any-way."

Kyohei slid open the front door and stepped inside. The air-conditioning was running full blast, and it felt good. He shouted, "Hello?"

The curtain behind the counter moved, and his aunt, Setsuko, emerged with a big smile. "Kyohei, you made it! My, but you've got-ten so big!" she said, echoing Narumi's greeting. *Maybe they think that makes kids happy*, Kyohei thought.

"Thanks for putting me up," Kyohei said, remembering his manners.

His aunt chuckled. "Now, now, none of that. You're family. Come right on in."

Kyohei took off his shoes and put on a pair of the guest slippers they had lined up at the entrance. The inn may have been small, but there was a lobby, complete with a wicker bench.

"It must've been hot out there! I'll get you something cool to drink. Juice? Tea? I think we have some cola. . . ."

"Cola!"

"Thought so," Setsuko said, giving him another smile and disap-pearing behind the counter.

Kyohei dropped his backpack and sat down on the bench. His eyes started to wander around the room. There was a framed painting of the sea from what looked like the nearby coast. Next to it was a map with little illustrations showing local spots of interest, except the map was faded so badly he could barely make anything out. An old clock on the wall showed the time was two o'clock.

"Hello there, Kyohei," came a gravelly voice, and his uncle Shigehiro appeared. "Good to see ya!"

His uncle hadn't changed much in the last two years either. He was still plump as a Buddha, but his hair was thinner now, making him look even more like a Buddha. The only real difference was that now he was sporting a cane. "Because he got too fat for his knees to hold him up," Kyohei's father had said.

Kyohei stood and said hello.

"Sit down, sit down. I've got a mind to sit down right there with you," Shigehiro said, sitting down across from Kyohei and chuckling. He had a big grin on his face. *A happy Buddha*, Kyohei thought. "So, how're your parents?"

"Busy, like always," Kyohei said.

"Busy's good."

Setsuko came out with a tray carrying a teapot and three glasses, one already filled with cola.

"Hey, no cola for me?" Shigehiro asked with a frown.

Setsuko shook her head. "It's barley tea for you, mister. You have to watch your sugar," she said, pouring him a glass.

Kyohei drank his cola, grateful for the cool sweetness after the long climb.

Setsuko was Kyohei's father's older half-sister. Setsuko's mother had died in a car accident when she was still little. Her father later remarried and had Kyohei's father, hence the nine-year difference in their ages.

"I saw Narumi at the station," Kyohei said. "She said she was going someplace?"

"Eh? Where's Narumi off to now?" Shigehiro asked his wife.

"Oh, you know," she said, "that thing about the cove. They're talking about digging up gold and silver and the like out there."

"Oh, right, that," Shigehiro said, utterly uninterested. "Sounds like a bunch of hogwash to me. Digging up gold from the ocean."

"I wouldn't know about these things," Kyohei's aunt said with a shrug. "Narumi was pretty worried that if they started working out there, the sea would get all dirty, you know."

"Well, she's right to worry about that," Shigehiro said, a bit more seriously. He took a long sip of his tea.

"Oh, I almost forgot," Kyohei said, opening his backpack and taking out the paper-wrapped package inside. "Mom wanted me to give you this."

"Oh, she shouldn't have," Setsuko said, smiling even as she furrowed her eyebrows. She began opening the package immediately. "Look at this, tsukudani beef jerky. Oh, I've heard of this shop. It's famous! She really shouldn't have. I'll have to call and thank her."

Kyohei finished his cola, and his aunt immediately asked if he wanted a refill. "Yes please," he said, and she swept his glass away. That was a nice change of pace. At home, he would've been told to get it himself, if they let him drink cola in the first place.

Maybe spending the rest of summer vacation in Hari Cove wouldn't be so bad after all.

FOUR

A manager from DESMEC's development division stood next and began to talk about their coming plans in detail. First, they would conduct a survey of the seabed to determine the amounts and densities of the various ores, as well as their metallic content. At the same time, they would be working on specific new technologies for extracting and removing the ores. There would be more investment into smelting technology as well, up until the point at which they were ready to assess the site for potential commercialization within a ten-year time frame.

Narumi felt somewhat relieved, if only because they were avoiding the kind of vague, saccharine promises they had heard too often. Things about "new industry lifting up the local economy." To the contrary, the development manager's talk made it clear there were still many unknowns, and they were proceeding with care.

Yet there was a magic to the words "undersea resources" that made people dream big, as if gold and silver really would come erupting out of the sea to shower the community with riches. To those primarily concerned with invigorating the local economy, it seemed like a godsend at a time when the town sorely needed one. Year by year,

Hari Cove had been slowly falling apart. The tourism industry, their main source of income, had been in recession for some time and showed no signs of picking up.

Yet that didn't mean they should give carte blanche to some unknown technology. Hari Cove lived and died by the ocean. And if that ocean wasn't brimming with beauty and life, neither would the town. Sacrificing the ocean in order to save the town was a fool's bargain.

Narumi realized early on there wasn't much she could do about it all by herself, so she launched a blog, becoming the unofficial spokesperson for the sea near Hari Cove. One of the first people to e-mail her after the blog went up was Sawamura. He had been focusing on articles about natural preservation efforts in the area and had reached out to his environmentally minded friends. Save the Cove was their idea. Narumi had been invited along for the ride.

She had responded almost immediately. If anyone was doing something to save the cove, she wanted in.

So began long days of exchanging information and research. Sawamura sold his apartment in Tokyo and came back home so he could be on the front lines. Drawing on his connections, they found more people willing to help their efforts, but things really took off when their central message, that the mining would disrupt the cycle of life in the nearby ocean, struck a chord with the local fishermen. After that, the fishermen started showing up to meetings in larger and larger numbers.

Finally, the government took notice. METI directed the organizations involved with the mineral surveys to hold an informational hearing—a huge coup for the Save the Cove movement, and Narumi's big chance. She could get the word out officially now.

Up on stage, the DESMEC engineers were still talking. They explained at length the measures they would take to protect the environment, but nothing passed the sniff test for Narumi. It took two hours before they were finished with their presentation, after which there was a Q and A.

Sawamura's hand went up immediately. He took the mic that was passed to him and began to speak.

"As the name would suggest, hydrothermal ore deposits form around hydrothermal vents on the seabed. These vents have a very specific deep-sea ecology, providing a home for many species that do not, and cannot, live elsewhere. You spoke of trying to predict the effect of mining operations on these ecologies, but there's nothing to predict. Everything living around these vents will die if you mine there. To put it in perspective, some of the creatures living in these environments take several years to grow to a size of only a dozen or so centimeters. But they only take an instant to kill. How will you protect them? If you have any ideas, I'd like to hear them."

My thoughts exactly, thought Narumi.

The development manager stood to answer. "As you say, some damage to the life around the vents will be unavoidable. Uh, due to this, we're proposing a genetic survey. That is, we will analyze the genetics of the organisms living near the vents to ascertain whether or not the same organisms live anywhere else on the seabed. If we find a species that does not exist elsewhere, then we will make preservation of that species a top priority. Exact methods will depend on the species in question, I should think."

Sawamura held his mic back up. "In other words, if you find the same kind of organism living someplace else, you're fine with killing the ones you find near the vent?"

The manager frowned and said, "Erm, essentially, yes, that's right."

Sawamura pressed on, relentless. "Can you *really* do a genetic survey of every single organism living in the area? There is a lot we don't know about deep-sea ecologies. How will you know for sure what exists where? How do you propose to find everything?"

"Well, all I can say is that we're prepared to do what we need to do to make it happen."

"That's not going to work," interjected a new voice, joining the conversation. Everyone on stage tensed as they turned to look at the one who'd spoken. It was the physicist, Yukawa.

"Not even specialists in the field profess a full understanding of deep-sea life, so I don't see how any of us can," the physicist added. "If there's something you're not going to be able to do, you should just be honest and admit it."

The development manager fell silent, a look of chagrin on his face. The emcee took a step toward the mic to say something, but Yukawa beat him to it. "What we have here is a very basic problem. The only way to make use of underground resources is to mine them, and if you mine them, they're going to damage the local flora and fauna. That's as true under the water as it is on land, but it hasn't stopped us— that is, mankind—from doing it over and over again. That's a fact. You just need to make a choice." He put down his mic, closed his eyes, and leaned back in his chair, oblivious to the stares of the entire room.

It was after four thirty when Narumi left the hall with Sawamura and the others.

"That went pretty much like we thought it would," Sawamura said. "Though with less grandstanding than expected, thankfully."

"I thought they were pretty transparent, considering," Narumi agreed. "It sounds like they're really just putting out feelers at this point—and at least they are considering some measures to protect the environment."

"Don't relax just yet. Once they get a whiff of the money to be made, they're going to charge full speed ahead. Nothing's going to stop them, certainly not concern for the environment. That's the way it's always been. Look at what happened with nuclear power in this country. We can't let ourselves get tricked like that again."

Narumi nodded. He was right, of course. The hearing had lulled her into a sense of accomplishment, but that was an illusion. The real work was only just beginning.

"I was surprised at the range of people they brought to the meeting. When that professor butted in, telling them they should just admit it when they couldn't do something? That was impressive."

"Him?" Sawamura frowned. "Bet you ten to one he's a corporate shill. They put him up there to make them look like they're not all about the money."

"I don't know, I thought his heart was in the right place, at least about not trying to pull the wool over our eyes. You never hear that kind of honesty from most officials or politicians."

"Maybe," Sawamura said with a shrug.

They left the community center and went their separate ways. "See you tonight," Sawamura said as they left. They would gather again after dinner to prepare for tomorrow.

Narumi got on her bicycle, waved, and pedaled off. Past the station, she dismounted and began to walk. It was much easier pushing her bike up the long slope than trying to ride it.

A taxi passed her just as the Green Rock Inn came into view. She watched it pull up at the inn. That would be their one reservation, arriving for the night.

It wasn't unusual for them to only have one reservation a night these days. Summer hadn't brought an increase in guests. In fact, there were fewer each year, and not just at the Green Rock Inn. Several inns and other businesses serving the dwindling tourist industry had already gone belly up, and Narumi knew it was only a matter of time for the inn. They already couldn't afford to hire any help except in the busiest months, and the only reason her parents were able to run the place by themselves the rest of the time was that there were so few guests. It had only gotten more difficult when Shigehiro hurt his knee.

The taxi passed her again on its way back down. She recognized the driver. He nodded as he passed—the kind of courtesy you only see in a small town.

She stepped inside the inn to find Setsuko greeting the newly arrived guest at the front counter. He was writing in the guest book.

When he finished and turned around, Narumi was surprised to see he was the man she'd noticed at the hearing, the one wearing the open-collar shirt. He smiled warmly to her and nodded, almost as if he'd been expecting to see her here.

"I'll show you to your room," Setsuko said, key in hand as she stepped out from behind the counter. A small travel bag in one hand, the man followed her in silence.

After they were gone, Narumi went behind the counter and checked the guest book. The man's name was Masatsugu Tsukahara. Not a name she recognized.

Maybe it's nothing, she thought. He might have nodded to her at the hall because their eyes happened to meet, a friendly gesture of solidarity. But then she looked back at the guest book and frowned. The man had listed his address as being in Saitama Prefecture. Why would someone from north of Tokyo come all the way down here just to attend a hearing?

"Hey, Narumi, welcome back." She looked up. It was Kyohei, looking out the door by the front counter.

"Hey. Were you down in the basement?"

"Yeah, with Uncle Shigehiro."

She heard the sound of a cane striking the steps leading to the boiler room underneath the inn.

A few moments later, Shigehiro appeared at the top of the stairs.

"Oh, welcome back," he said to her. "How was the hearing?"

"Good. I'm glad I went. There's going to be a debate tomorrow—sorry I'll be out again."

"Not a problem," her father replied. "You do what you need to do."

"You're protecting the environment, right?" Kyohei asked. "That's cool."

Narumi lifted an eyebrow. "You think so?"

"Totally! So do you, like, get on a boat and ram whaling ships?"

"Hardly," she said. "But what we do is very important. We're trying to stop people from wrecking our ocean. If they start mining the seafloor, it might hurt the local fishermen."

"Oh," Kyohei said, clearly having no interest in anything that didn't involve fierce battles on the high seas.

Setsuko returned and announced, "He says he'll eat at seven."

Narumi looked at the clock. It was almost five.

"Also, we had a last-minute reservation, a single," Setsuko added. "The call came in right after you left, Narumi."

Last-minute cancellations happened too often, but last-minute reservations were a new thing, Narumi thought, just as she heard the front door slide open behind her. "Hello?" said a familiar voice, and Narumi nearly jumped. She turned to see the physicist Yukawa standing in the doorway of the Green Rock Inn.

FIVE

The Green Rock Inn had a few private dining rooms on the first floor, where guests came for their meals. Kyohei was supposed to eat dinner with Narumi's family in the little room next to the kitchen, but when six o'clock rolled around he snuck out to take a peek at the dining rooms where their new guest, Yukawa, would be eating.

The sliding doors to the first dining room on the hall were open, and a serving cart had been left in the hallway outside. Aunt Setsuko would be in the middle of serving dinner.

Kyohei peeked inside. Yukawa was sitting alone in the middle of a room big enough for ten, watching as Aunt Setsuko arranged dishes on the tray in front of him.

"So places in town are open pretty late, then?" he was saying.

"Well, late for the countryside, maybe. But that only means ten or ten thirty. I'd be happy to show you," his aunt was telling him.

"I'd appreciate that. You go out drinking often?"

"Oh no, I certainly wouldn't say 'often.' It's much more of a 'rarely,' if that."

"That's a shame," Yukawa said, suddenly looking toward Kyohei.

Their eyes met, and Kyohei jumped and shrank back away from the door, out of sight.

"Is something wrong?" he heard his aunt ask.

"No, nothing. This looks delicious," Yukawa said as Kyohei snuck away, treading as lightly as possible on the floorboards.

He had his own dinner soon afterward. His aunt and uncle had pulled out all the stops for their guest, and the table was loaded with sashimi and all kinds of homemade dishes.

"Eat up," his uncle said, pushing a plate of sashimi toward Kyohei. "We can't send you back home skinny, or we'll never hear the end of it." He laughed, his belly sticking out like a giant, quivering watermelon.

"And thanks for snagging a customer for us," his aunt said. "That was unexpected!"

"All I did was show him the map," Kyohei explained. "He was the one who wrote down the number and everything."

"Well, you did just the right thing. He must've figured that any hotel good enough for you was good enough for him."

Kyohei shrugged, pretty sure that had nothing to do with it.

Close to seven, Narumi stood from the table, saying she had a Save the Cove meeting and wouldn't be back until late. Kyohei left to go back to his room. There was a TV show he wanted to watch.

He'd just reached the elevator when the doors opened and an older man with short hair stepped out. He looked like he'd just been in the bath. He was still wearing his robe, and his face had a ruddy sheen to it. The man looked at Kyohei a little curiously, then walked off in the direction of the dining rooms.

Kyohei took the elevator to the second floor and walked down the hall to his room. He'd been given a room big enough for four. His aunt was worried that he'd feel lonely in such a big room all by himself, but Kyohei wasn't a little kid anymore, and it didn't bother him in the slightest. He spent some time stretching out on the tatami mats, enjoying the space, then reached for the remote control.

After about an hour, he got up and took a look out the window. He knew the ocean was in the distance, but it was too dark to see anything but the spot between the inn and the road where the floodlights by the front door lit a circle of pavement.

He'd been standing there for a while when he heard the sound of the front door opening. Two people walked out: Yukawa, and his aunt. He wondered where they were going at this time of night. He didn't see his uncle anywhere.

The phone in his room began to ring. Startled, he hurriedly picked up the receiver.

"Yeah?"

"Kyohei? It's Uncle Shigehiro. Were you asleep?"

"Nope. I was watching television."

"Right, well, how about you and me set off some fireworks? I've got some left over from last summer."

"What? Now? Yeah, okay!"

"Good, come on downstairs."

"Be right there."

His uncle was waiting for him in the lobby. He had a bucket and a sizable cardboard box at his feet.

"Since everyone's decided to head out, I figure now's our chance to have a little fun for ourselves," his uncle said.

Kyohei looked inside the cardboard box, his eyes going wide. It was an impressive collection. There were fistfuls of sparklers, and even some bigger fireworks, the kind you stuck in the ground and shot up into the sky before they went off.

"No time to waste! You mind getting the box?" Uncle Shigehiro asked, picking up the bucket and beginning to walk with his cane. Kyohei lifted the cardboard box in both hands and followed after his uncle.

SIX

It was a little before nine when Narumi, Sawamura, and the others left the meeting hall. "How about a drink?" Sawamura offered. Two of the younger members immediately agreed.

"How about you?" he asked Narumi.

"For a little while, sure."

They said good-bye at the station to the people who had to leave right away, then headed to the usual bar, the one that stayed open the latest.

They had just reached the door when Narumi spotted her mother standing next to the seawall, staring out toward the dark ocean. She called out, and Setsuko turned as if she had just been woken from a dream. Her lips curled in a vague smile, and she walked across the road toward them.

"Good evening," she said to Sawamura and the others before turning to Narumi. "You finish your meeting?"

"Yeah, but what are you doing out here, Mom?"

Setsuko nodded in the direction of the bar. "Oh, I brought one of our guests down. You know, Mr. Yukawa."

"Let me guess, you joined him for a drink or two?"

"Just a wee bit," she said, holding up her thumb and index finger a little way apart.

"Again? Mom, you know you're not supposed to drive after you have a drink."

"Mr. Yukawa's going to take a taxi home, and it was just a little."

"Even after just a little, Mom. The law's the law."

Ever since her father hurt his knee he'd stopped drinking, but her mother had always been overly fond of alcohol. Even if she didn't come down to the bar, a whiskey before bed was her nightly routine.

Narumi sighed. "So that's why you're out here, trying to clear your head?"

"Something like that," Setsuko replied, a bit mysteriously. "You need to watch how much you drink, too, young lady."

"I'm hardly a young lady, and you're not one to talk, Mom," Narumi said with a smile.

"Then I'll stop now while I'm ahead. I suppose I'll walk home. Have a nice evening," she said to Sawamura and the others.

"Wait, I'll give you a lift," Sawamura said, looking toward Narumi. "I came here in the pickup from the store, and I'm parked right by the station," he explained. "I was wondering what to do with it anyway. This way I can take your mom back and leave it at home so I don't have to worry about drinking too much."

"Oh, you don't need to go out of your way for me," Setsuko said, waving her hand.

"It's no trouble at all. And I can't have you walking up mountains in the dark."

"Are you sure? Well, thank you."

"No need to thank me," Sawamura said. Then, to Narumi, "I'll be right back."

"Right, thanks."

After seeing Sawamura and her mom off, Narumi went into the bar with the other two from the meeting. Her eyes darted quickly over the place. Yukawa was sitting at a corner table, reading a magazine.

"Isn't that the physicist from earlier today?" one of the two—a girl still in college—whispered in Narumi's ear.

"Yeah, I think it is," the guy agreed.

Narumi told them that Yukawa was staying at her family's inn, and they nodded, making the connection. The three of them sat at a table across the room from Yukawa, who was still absorbed in his magazine.

They drank beers and chatted for about half an hour, at which point Narumi excused herself and walked over toward Yukawa's table, announcing herself with a "Good evening."

Yukawa looked up from his magazine and blinked. "Oh. Hi," he said, unsurprised to see her. *He must've noticed us earlier*, Narumi thought.

"I heard you shared a drink with my mom?"

"I believe we had a round, yes. I hope that's not a problem?"

"No, not at all. Actually, I was wondering if I could join you for a moment." She pointed to the chair across the table.

"I don't mind, but what about your friends?"

"They'll be fine." Narumi glanced at the two, deep in some conversation, punctuated by occasional laughter. She leaned closer to Yukawa and said more quietly, "I was kind of a third wheel anyway."

"I understand."

Narumi called over the bartender and ordered herself a shochu on the rocks.

"Your mother tells me you were at the hearing today."

"Yes, you remember the man who asked about DESMEC's plans to protect deep-sea organisms? I was with his group."

"I see," Yukawa said, nodding. "Then please apologize to him on my behalf for butting in on the conversation."

"You can tell him yourself. He should be here any moment. But I don't think there's any need to apologize. It sounded like a very honest opinion."

"Too honest, I'd say. I just can't abide people making vague, illogical statements."

The bartender brought Narumi's drink. Yukawa raised his and they clinked their glasses together in a toast.

"From what your mother was saying, you're quite the activist."

"I wouldn't put it that way. I just think I'm doing what I should be doing."

"And what you should be doing is opposing undersea resource development?"

"I'm not against development per se. But I want to protect the environment, particularly the ocean."

Yukawa rattled his ice in his glass and took a slow drink of his shochu. "What exactly does it mean to protect the ocean? Is the ocean such a fragile thing that it requires our protection?"

"It wasn't, but we've made it fragile. In the name of science, and progress."

"Science?" Yukawa set down his glass. "You sure you want to go there?"

"The ocean is the source of all life. Over millions of years it's given birth to all kinds of species. But did you know that in just the last thirty years, the ocean has lost more than thirty percent of those species? Coral reefs are a prime example," she said, the words spilling out with practiced ease. She'd been saying the same thing in a lot of places recently.

"And this is somehow science's fault?"

"Scientists are the one who conducted that hydrogen bomb testing over the Pacific."

Yukawa lifted up his glass, but before he drank, he looked up at Narumi. "It sounds like you've decided that this plan to develop the hydrothermal ore deposits off your shores is another example of us scientists making the same mistake we've made in the past. In other words, destroying the seabed without concern for the resulting devastation of the environment."

"No, I think there is concern for protecting the environment. But how can you say what will happen for sure? No one predicted when we started using oil that it would raise global temperatures, did they?"

"Which is why surveys and research are so important. DESMEC isn't saying they're going to start digging up the seabed and commercialize those resources right this moment. It's precisely because they don't know what will happen that they're trying to find out as much as they can before they start mining."

"But as much as they can won't be everything, will it," Narumi pressed on. "Isn't that exactly what you said at the hearing today?"

"I believe I said we had a choice. If getting those rare metals isn't important enough to warrant digging holes in the seabed, then there's no point to this operation."

That was the question here: how much did they really need this undersea mining operation, and what sacrifices were they willing to make for it? That would be the central point in the debate tomorrow.

"Well," Narumi said, "I suppose we should save the rest of this discussion for the community center tomorrow."

Yukawa smiled. "Playing your cards close to your chest? Very well," he said, ordering another round before looking back at Narumi. "But you should know, I'm not technically a supporter of the mining proposal."

"You're not?" Narumi asked. "Then why were you on stage today?"

"Because DESMEC asked me to be there. They thought they might need someone to explain electromagnetic surveying."

"Electromagnetic surveying?"

"It's where you use a large coil to measure magnetic fields in the seabed and analyze them. It allows you to determine the composition of the substrate for about a hundred meters beneath the seabed. In other words, you can find out how metallic deposits are distributed without digging holes."

"Which is environmentally friendly? Is that your point?"

"That's the largest merit of the technology, yes."

Yukawa's shochu on the rocks arrived. He glanced at the menu and ordered the squid shiokara. The pickled saltiness of the dish was a popular choice to offset the sweetness of the shochu.

"Doesn't your involvement in that kind of research make you a supporter?"

"How does that follow? It's true that I proposed a new method of electromagnetic surveying to DESMEC, who is clearly a supporter of the mining. But only because it seems to me to be the most logical choice both financially and environmentally, should the plan be approved. It makes little difference to me, however, if the plan doesn't go ahead."

"But won't your research have gone to waste, then?"

"No research ever goes to waste."

His shiokara arrived. "Now, this looks delicious," Yukawa said, peering through his glasses at the dish just as the front door to the bar rattled open.

Sawamura walked in and took a look around the place. He hesitated when he saw Narumi sitting apart from the others, and with the physicist, no less.

He walked over to them, a perplexed look still on his face. "Well, what do we have here?"

"I believe you know Professor Yukawa from Imperial University? I might not have mentioned that he's staying at our place," Narumi explained.

Sawamura's mouth opened in an "ah" of understanding, and he nodded. "That explains why your mother was talking about bringing Mr. Yukawa to the bar."

"Care to join us?" Yukawa asked, indicating the chair next to Narumi.

"Why not?" Sawamura sat down and ordered a beer.

"You were gone longer than I expected," Narumi said once he had settled in.

"Yeah, well, there was a bit of excitement at the inn."

"What kind of excitement?" Narumi frowned. Excitement and the Green Rock Inn were not things she normally associated with each other.

"Well, calling it 'excitement' might be a bit of an overstatement. It sounded like one of your guests went out and didn't come back when he was expected, so your father was worried. Anyway, I had my pickup there, so I drove around a little bit to help look."

"Did you find him?"

"No, actually," Sawamura said. His beer arrived, and he took a swig before continuing. "He wasn't anywhere near the inn. I was going to look a little longer, but your parents said not to bother. They told me he'd show up sooner or later, and I should get back down here or else I'd miss the party."

"Maybe he's out night fishing," Yukawa suggested.

"I don't think so," Narumi said. "I saw his luggage when he arrived, and he didn't come prepared for anything like that. I don't think he's a tourist."

Narumi explained that she'd seen him at the community center earlier that day. This confused Sawamura even further.

They drank a bit longer before leaving the bar. Narumi and Yukawa decided they'd walk back to the Green Rock Inn together.

"Well, I drank too much, but that was a good place. I might end up there every night," Yukawa said as they walked.

"How long will you be in town?"

"I'm not sure. I was supposed to go out on the DESMEC survey boat and instruct them in how to test the electromagnetic survey equipment. Which would be fine, except the survey boat has yet to arrive. Apparently there's some red tape holding it up. But I suppose if you work with a government agency, you have to expect to deal with a little bureaucracy," Yukawa said.

Not the words of a strong DESMEC supporter, Narumi thought.

The front light at the inn was still blazing. Inside, they found Shigehiro and Setsuko in the lobby, both looking distraught.

"Still no sign of him?" Narumi asked

"Nothing," her mother replied. "We were just talking about what to do."

"Well, we could call the police," Shigehiro said, "but I doubt they'd do much about it at this time of night. Let's wait till morning, and if he's still not back yet, we'll give the station a ring."

"Sorry to hear about the trouble," Yukawa said. "Please let me know if there's anything I can do to help."

"No need to worry yourself," Shigehiro said. "He'll turn up any moment now, I'm sure."

"Right, well, good night," the physicist said, heading for the elevator.

SEVEN

The scene was about two hundred meters south along the coast from the main harbor in Hari Cove. A uniformed officer was standing in front of the seawall, next to a parked police van. *Probably forensics,* Tsuyoshi Nishiguchi thought. It was still too early in the morning for onlookers.

Nishiguchi stopped his patrol car and waited for his supervising officer and the captain to get out before opening his own door and catching up with them. The uniformed officer greeted them as they arrived.

Captain Motoyama was standing on tiptoes, peering over the seawall at the other side. A frown spread across his round face. "Well, he couldn't have picked a more inconvenient spot," he said.

Hashigami walked over to take a look for himself. Hashigami was five years Nishiguchi's elder, but much taller. "Yeah," he said, agreeing with the captain. "No kidding."

Nishiguchi gingerly approached the seawall, fearing the worst. The worst, in this case, was a drowned corpse. He'd seen plenty of them since transferring to his current post, but something about the way they looked got to him every time.

He swallowed and looked down four or five meters to some rocks by the water where a few guys from forensics were already milling around.

The body, a man's, was lying atop a large boulder, facing upward. He was wearing a bath yukata and a quilted vest over that, except *wearing* might not have been the right word. It was more like the clothes were wrapped around him. He was a little on the overweight side, but there was none of the distinctive swelling of a drowning victim. Instead, his head had been split open, spilling blackish-red blood over the nearby rocks.

"Hey down there," Motoyama called out. "How's it look?"

An older forensics officer looked up, putting a hand to the rim of his glasses in greeting. "Can't say just yet. He probably fell."

"You find a wallet or anything?"

"Nope. Some clogs though."

"You know what inn he was staying at?"

"No. There's nothing written on either the clogs or the yukata."

Motoyama turned to the uniformed officer behind them. "Who found the body?"

"A local resident, sir. She rents parasols down at the beach during the summer and was on the way to work. She should be at the beach now, but I have her number if you want to talk to her."

"No thanks," Motoyama said, waving his hand dismissively. He pulled out his cell phone, punched buttons with his fat fingers, and put it to his ear. "That you, Chief?" he said. "This is Motoyama. I'm down here at the scene. It's not a drowning—looks like he fell from the seawall. We think he's staying at one of the inns around here. Still got his yukata on." He paused, listening to the chief on the other end of the line. "Right, we'll pay them a visit," he said. "The what Rock Inn? Green? Got it."

Nishiguchi stepped over to the captain and gestured to get his attention.

"Hang on a second, Chief," Motoyama said, putting a hand over the phone. "Yeah?"

"I know that place. The Green Rock Inn," Nishiguchi said.

"Right," Motoyama said, bringing the cell phone back to his ear. "Nishiguchi says he knows the place. Right, I'll get him on it."

Motoyama hung up and looked between the other two. "Turns out the inn phoned in a report that one of their guests went missing after he went out for a walk last night. Go check on it."

"Mind if we take the cruiser?" Hashigami asked.

"It's walking distance from here," Nishiguchi said. "Which means it probably *was* their guest."

"Right, that settles it," Motoyama said, looking back over the seawall. "You get a picture yet?" he called down. "Just the face. Nothing too gruesome, if you can. Thanks."

One of the younger forensics officers climbed up a ladder to the top of the seawall and handed a Polaroid to Motoyama, who held it out to Nishiguchi. "Take this."

The face in the photo was a little pinkish and expressionless as a mask. He didn't look too bad from the front. The gaping hole in his skull was on the back of his head, which meant they could show it around without anyone fainting on them.

The Green Rock Inn was less than a kilometer away. The two detectives walked up a winding slope, which got much steeper about halfway along. Hashigami started muttering that they should've taken the cruiser.

"So what's the deal with this inn? You said you know it?" he asked Nishiguchi.

"Yeah. One of my old classmates' parents run the place."

"Great, you can do the talking."

"Sure, but I doubt they'll remember me. I haven't seen the family since I graduated high school."

Nishiguchi remembered the daughter's name: Narumi Kawahata. Most of the kids in his high school had known each other since middle school, but not her. She had transferred from a school in Tokyo just before high school started.

Narumi was a quiet girl at first, spending most of her time alone.

There was a small observation deck near the school where you could look out over the sea, and he spotted her there often. She would just stand and gaze out at the water, seemingly lost in thought. She always got good grades, and Nishiguchi always imagined that she was going to be a writer or something like that.

But eventually, an entirely different side of her came to light. In the summer, she would help out at the inn and work down at the beach. Not at one of the vending stalls or cafeterias, but picking up garbage. The money wasn't very good; it was practically volunteer work. Nishiguchi worked for some of the beachside stalls, so he saw her quite a lot. He asked her once why she chose that particular job. "What's the point of having a beautiful ocean if you don't keep it clean?" she asked, her face tanned a deep brown. "You locals don't appreciate what you've got."

She wasn't exactly mad at him, but her comment made it sound like he wasn't doing his part. It left a bad taste in his mouth.

His reverie was interrupted by their arrival at the Green Rock Inn. They'd both taken off their jackets on the climb up, and the underarms of their dress shirts were stained with sweat.

Nishiguchi slid open the front door and called in. "Hello?" He was greeted by a welcome blast of air-conditioned air.

"Come in," a woman responded, and the curtain behind the front counter moved. He immediately recognized the woman, who came out wearing a T-shirt and jeans, as Narumi, but he hesitated a moment. He wasn't used to seeing her as a grown woman.

"Wait, is that you?" Narumi's eyes went a little wider, and she smiled. "Nishiguchi, right? Long time no see. How've you been?" Even her voice sounded grown-up. Which was obvious, given that she would be thirty, like him.

"Hey, I've been well, thanks. You look good."

Narumi smiled, then her eyes went over to Hashigami, and she bowed a little, not entirely sure what to make of him.

"Actually," Nishiguchi said, "I'm here on work. I'm with the Hari Police Department now." He showed her his badge.

Narumi blinked. "Police? You?"

"Yeah, I know, it's funny how things turn out." Nishiguchi held out his business card to her.

"Wow, a detective," she said.

"We got a call from your inn this morning saying that one of your guests had gone missing."

"That's right. Oh, so that's why you're here?"

"Yeah. Actually, this morning a body was found down near the harbor."

A look of shock came over Narumi's face.

"He was still wearing a yukata, which is why we thought he might be your missing guest."

"Wait, I should probably get my parents out here," Narumi said, disappearing behind the counter.

Hashigami stepped up and gave Nishiguchi a jab in the ribs with his elbow. "She's not bad. When you said 'classmate,' I was thinking a guy."

"She's your type, is she?" Nishiguchi asked quietly.

"Oh, she'll do. Put a little makeup on her and she'll be a real beauty."

"If you say so." Nishiguchi didn't know about the makeup, but he had to agree that Narumi had grown into an attractive woman.

A short while later she reappeared with her parents, whom she introduced as Shigehiro and Setsuko Kawahata. From the looks on their faces, Nishiguchi could tell that she'd already told them about the body.

Shigehiro had filed the report that morning, so Nishiguchi showed him the photograph first. He took one look and grimaced, then passed the photograph to his wife. She grew a little pale, and put a hand to her mouth. Narumi looked away.

"Well?" Nishiguchi asked.

"That's him, no doubt about it," Shigehiro answered. "Was it an accident?"

"We're not sure yet. It looks like he fell onto some rocks and hit his head."

Setsuko pulled out the guest book and register, identifying the deceased as Masatsugu Tsukahara, 61, from Saitama Prefecture.

"Around what time did he leave the inn last night?" Nishiguchi asked.

"I'm not really sure," Shigehiro told him. He explained that he had been out in the back garden with his nephew setting off some fireworks from around eight o'clock the night before. It had been about eight thirty when he realized that their guest hadn't signed up for breakfast the next morning. He went back to the inn and phoned the man's room from the front desk, but there was no answer. Thinking he was probably either in the bathroom or down in the bath on the first floor, he went back out and lit a few more fireworks. They finished a little before nine, so he tried calling the man again, but there was still no answer. He went to check the big bath on the first floor, but he wasn't there either. So, he went up to the man's room on the fourth floor. There was no answer when he knocked, and the door was unlocked, so he went in and found the man's things, but their guest himself was nowhere in sight.

Around that time, Setsuko had come back from town, having shown one of their other guests to a local bar.

Narumi explained about Sawamura and about running into their mother in front of the bar.

"Mr. Sawamura said he wanted to say hello to my husband, so he came in, but when he found my husband worrying about his missing guest, he offered to help look," Setsuko said, continuing the story. "While he and Mr. Sawamura were driving around in the pickup, I took a look around the inn."

"Of course, in these parts after nine, it's pretty dark, so unless he was walking on the road or standing someplace out in plain sight, we didn't have much of a chance of finding him," Shigehiro added.

Nishiguchi nodded. There were no streetlamps anywhere along the hill up from the station.

Hashigami took his cell phone out of his pocket and stepped outside to phone in a report.

"Still, I never imagined he'd turn up like this," Shigehiro said, putting a hand on his head. "Where was he found?"

"The seawall right around where the Headland Restaurant used to be," Nishiguchi said, referring to a place that had closed three years earlier.

"With all the rocks around there, that would be a pretty nasty place to fall," Shigehiro said.

"I wonder why he was down there in the first place," Narumi said.

"Out for a walk, most likely. Maybe wanted to see the ocean at night. Or maybe he just wanted to walk off dinner and the drinks."

"So he climbed up on to the seawall and then fell off?"

"I suppose so."

Narumi's eyes went to her old classmate. "Is that what happened?"

Nishiguchi shrugged. "We can't say for sure. The investigation's only just started."

Narumi grunted, unimpressed.

Hashigami returned from outside and whispered, "The bags," into Nishiguchi's ear.

"If you don't mind, we'd like to check Mr. Tsukahara's belongings. Could you show me to his room?" Nishiguchi asked.

"Happy to," Setsuko offered.

The two detectives got on the elevator with her. Nishigami pulled on his gloves while they were riding up.

There were eight guest rooms on each floor, each with its own name. Masatsugu Tsukahara had been staying in one called the Rainbow Room. The room was large, with a low table and floor cushions pushed off into one corner and a futon laid out on the tatami mats. There was a strip of hardwood flooring over by the window with a chair and another smaller table.

"Who spread out his futon and when?" Nishiguchi asked.

"It was a little after seven, I think. I came up while Mr. Tsukahara was at dinner. My husband doesn't do the futons anymore on account of his knee, so when we don't have any part-time staff around, me and Narumi handle things."

The futon looked untouched. Tsukahara must have left the room right after coming back from dinner.

His luggage was a single, old traveling bag. Hashigami examined the contents, finding a cell phone. It was a simple one with only a few basic functions, designed for elderly users.

His clothes had been neatly folded and placed in a corner of the room: an open-collar shirt and gray slacks. Nishiguchi fished in the pockets and found his wallet, with a decent amount of cash inside.

He checked the driver's license. Both the name and the address were the same as in the ledger downstairs. Then he pulled another card from the wallet.

"Uh-oh," Nishiguchi said.

"What you got?" Hashigami asked.

"A union member's card. To *our* union. He's a cop."

EIGHT

Kyohei woke up from a dream of someone shouting. He looked around. The ceiling and the walls were unfamiliar.

It took him a moment to remember he was staying at his aunt's. The train ride down, the fireworks with his uncle the night before—the events of the day before came filtering back slowly. But this room wasn't the one they had brought him to when he arrived. He didn't see his backpack anywhere, either.

Then he remembered his uncle suggesting they go eat watermelon. This room was his uncle's living room, then. He had been eating watermelon, and his uncle left to call one of the guests. He remembered starting to watch TV, but nothing after that.

Kyohei got up and looked around. The table he had been eating his watermelon on had been pushed into the corner. He was wearing the same T-shirt and shorts from the night before. *I must've fallen asleep watching TV.*

There was a clock on the television stand that read 9:20.

Kyohei opened the sliding door and went out into the hall. He heard voices from the lobby and went out to find two men standing there. One was middle-aged, short, and heavyset. The other one was younger and looked pretty fit. Uncle Shigehiro was out on the wicker bench, talking to them.

"Hey there, Kyohei. You just get up?" his uncle said.

The man looked in his direction, and Kyohei stopped abruptly.

"This your nephew?" the middle-aged man asked his uncle.

"Yes, my wife's brother's kid. He's here for summer vacation."

The man nodded at that. Behind him, the younger man was writing something down on a notepad.

"Anyway, if you wouldn't mind leaving the room exactly as it is?" the man asked.

"No problem," Shigehiro replied. "I'm sure we won't need it with summer break gone. It's not like people are breaking down the doors to get reservations," he added with a chuckle.

Kyohei wondered what had happened and what room they were talking about.

"Uncle Shigehiro?" he asked. "Can I go to my room?"

Shigehiro looked at the middle-aged man. "He's on the second floor. That's not a problem, right?"

"Of course, not at all," the man said, smiling at Kyohei. "Think I can ask you to stay off the fourth floor, though? There's something up there we have to check out."

"They're the police," his uncle said, and Kyohei's eyes widened.

"The police? What happened?"

"Well, that's probably best left for another time," his uncle said, nodding his head toward the men.

Kyohei knew this particular routine well. It was just another case of grown-ups keeping secrets from kids for *absolutely* no reason whatsoever.

It used to annoy him so much that he would start asking questions, but he'd given up trying. Instead, he grunted and headed back to the elevator.

He was about to press the button when he had a thought and glanced toward the dining rooms. There were slippers in front of one of them.

Walking quietly, Kyohei approached the room. The sliding doors were wide open. He peeked in and saw Yukawa sitting exactly where he had the night before. He was stirring something on his tray, but his hand stopped abruptly, and he said, "Do you like peeking in on other people eating?"

Kyohei reflexively drew back from the door, then gave up and walked out into the open. Yukawa was draping sticky beans over his morning rice. He hadn't even looked in Kyohei's direction.

"I was just wondering who was in here," Kyohei said.

Yukawa answered that with a snort and a slightly derisive smile. "That was a waste of your time. If you'd thought about it, you would've realized that this is a dining room expressly for the use of guests. Which makes it likely anyone in here was a guest. Given that there are only two guests staying in this entire inn, and that one of them is no longer with us, that leaves only one person it could've been. Namely, myself."

"What do you mean, 'no longer with us'? Did the other guy leave?"

Yukawa's chopsticks stopped in midair. His eyes met Kyohei's for the first time. "Oh," he said. "You haven't heard."

"I know something happened. The police are here. But they didn't tell me what." He looked down at his feet. "Typical."

"Don't sulk. Usually when grown-ups hide something from you, it's because knowing it won't do you any good." Yukawa took a sip of his miso soup. "They found his body down by the harbor."

"His body? What, he died?"

"Apparently he left the inn last night at some point and never returned. This morning they found him on the rocks by the seawall. They think he might've fallen by accident in the night."

"Oh, wow. How did you hear?"

"The girl who works here. Narumi, was it? My breakfast was late, so I went to find out why, and she told me the whole story."

"Ah," Kyohei said, looking down the hallway. He wondered where Narumi was now.

"I believe she's at the police station," Yukawa said, seeming to read his mind. "Along with the woman who runs the place."

"Why did my aunt have to go down to the police station?"

"So that they can write up an official report. Your aunt was the only one who spoke with the man. They probably want to know whether there was anything unusual about his behavior yesterday."

"They have to go through all that trouble just because he fell on some rocks?"

Yukawa's chopsticks stopped again and he looked at Kyohei. "You should consider the feelings of the deceased's family. Do you think they'd be satisfied if the police just told them, 'Oh, he fell on some rocks'? No, they probably want to know how it came to pass, in as much detail as possible. Personally, I would hope the police take their investigation very seriously."

"What's that supposed to mean?"

"It's not supposed to mean anything beyond what I said," Yukawa said, eating some of his rice with sticky beans and reaching for a teacup.

"Can I ask you something?" Kyohei asked.

"If it's about what happened, I've already told you all I know."

"No, not about that. I was just wondering why you decided to stay here. There are lots of inns in town."

Yukawa picked up the cup and shrugged. "Should I not have stayed here?"

"No, but didn't you have reservations somewhere before you came?"

"I did, but not my own reservations. Somebody at DESMEC arranged them for me."

"Hey, I know them. They're the ones that want to dig up the seafloor, right? Narumi doesn't like them."

Yukawa chuckled. "Right. Well, I'm not exactly allies with DESMEC either. Mostly because I don't have a position on their undersea resource development proposal. This is why I want to avoid being in their debt as much as possible. One might think it only natural for them to provide lodging, since they asked me to come down and help with their informational hearing, but it bothered me nonetheless. That's why, when I met you, I decided on this place. That seems like as good a reason as any to me."

"I guess. You're pretty strange for a professor."

Yukawa furrowed his eyebrows. "Professor?"

"You teach science at a university, right? Doesn't that make you a professor? Or are you just a teacher?"

"Either one is fine. I do have my doctorate, but I doubt you're that interested in my credentials."

"I'll call you Professor, then. It sounds better."

"As you like. So, exactly how am I strange?"

"Well, if it was me, I would've stayed at the place they got for me. I bet it's a better inn than this one."

"I heard it was the fanciest resort hotel in Hari Cove."

"See? They've got money. I bet they'd pay you a lot if they go through with this undersea mining thing, too."

Yukawa finished his tea, then, shaking his head, set down his cup. "Scientists don't make decisions based on potential profit. What a scientist must consider foremost is which of the many available paths will lead to the greatest benefit for humanity. Even if said path doesn't result in any personal gain, it's still the one to pick. Of course, ideally, we hope that the most beneficial path also results in personal gain."

Kyohei decided that the professor was a bit of a talker who liked making things sound more complicated than they really were. Who used words like *humanity* in a sentence like that?

"So scientists aren't interested in money?"

Yukawa shook his head again. "No. We are interested in money. I want money, myself. If you're offering me some with no strings attached, I'll be happy to take it. My point is, I don't conduct research for the sake of money alone."

"But studying science is your job, right? And they pay you to do your job, don't they?"

"I receive a salary from the university, yes."

"Then you should think more about making money. If Mom and Dad hire somebody to work at their shop, and that person doesn't make money for them, that person needs to be fired. They say that all the time."

Yukawa scooted back from the table, crossed his legs, and turned to face Kyohei straight on. "We seem to have a misunderstanding on some basic things here, so let me explain. I receive my salary in exchange for teaching physics to university students. I conduct my own research as well, of course, but no matter what great papers I might write, the university won't give me any more money for them. They do pay any expenses incurred by the research, but you can consider that more of an investment. Should one of my papers win an award, like the Nobel Prize, that would confer a good deal of prestige on the university."

Kyohei stared at the professor. "You're gonna win the Nobel Prize?"

"It was merely an example," Yukawa said, pushing up his glasses with his finger. "Scientists want to uncover the truth. You understand what the truth is?"

"Like true or false? Sure."

"I'm talking about a deeper truth. For example, a lot of physicists are very interested in how the universe came to be. Have you heard of neutrinos? They're particles released when a star goes supernova. By analyzing these particles, you can understand things about the nature of stars an almost unimaginable distance away, but if you ask what sort of benefits that kind of research brought society, I'd have to agree that the benefit to our daily lives is practically nonexistent."

"So why do they do it?"

"Because they want to *know*," Yukawa said. "You used a map to get to this inn yesterday, did you not? Because of that map, you are able to find your way up the road without getting lost. Likewise, in order for us as a species to walk the correct path in life, we need a very detailed map that will tell us what the world is like. Except our map is incomplete, almost entirely useless. Which is why, even now, in the twenty-first century, people are still making mistakes. War and the destruction of the environment and countless other things persist because the only map we have is woefully lacking. It's the mission of scientists to fill in those missing pieces."

"I don't know. It sounds kind of lame."

"What's *lame* about it?"

"Well, the not getting paid part, for one thing. Why do it if you don't get paid? Anyway, I don't much like science class in school. Most of the stuff we learn there is totally useless. What's so fun about studying science?"

"Everything. You just don't know it yet. The world is full of mysteries. And the joy of uncovering even the slightest mystery is incomparable to any other joy you will ever know."

Kyohei shrugged. "If you say so. It's not my thing. I'm not sure me worrying about humanity taking the right path will mean much of anything unless I become president of America or something."

Yukawa chuckled. "My fault for taking the big example. But we can narrow our focus down to the choices a single person has to make. Whenever you take an action, you have to make a choice. What are you going to do today?"

"I haven't decided yet. My uncle said he'd take me down to the ocean last night, but after that guy dying, I'm not so sure that'll happen."

"Let's assume that your uncle is available to take you down to the ocean. You'll have a choice: to go to the ocean as planned, or put it off for another time."

"That's not a choice. If my uncle could take me, why wouldn't I go?"

"Well, what if it were raining?"

Kyohei looked out the window. "Is it supposed to rain?"

"I have no idea. But even if there are blue skies now, the weather could take a turn for the worse, couldn't it?"

"Well, I could check the weather before going."

"Ah, yes, the weather. And who do you have to thank for the

weather report? Scientists. Except, modern weather reporting is not entirely accurate. You probably want a weather report that's going to tell you exactly what it's going to be like on the beach when you go today—specifically, what it's going to be like an hour from now, and for another hour after that. Wouldn't you?"

"If they had a weather report like that, sure."

"You say *they*, but what could *you* do about it?"

"Um, nothing? I don't know how to tell the weather."

"You could ask someone who does. Say, one of the fishermen down at the harbor. They'd probably be able to tell you. Every morning they get up and judge the weather before they go out fishing. They have to, because it could cost them their lives if the sea got too rough. They can't just rely on the weather reports, they have to rely on what they know about the weather the day before—the color of the sky, the direction of the wind, the humidity, et cetera—to get the most accurate prediction possible. That is science. What you're studying in school science isn't helping you? Fine. Try learning how to read a weather chart, and then tell me if science still isn't helping you."

Kyohei was silent. Yukawa stood, a satisfied look on his face. He started to leave, but then he stopped and looked down at Kyohei. "It's okay if you don't like science," he said, "but that doesn't mean you can just ignore things you don't understand. It'll come back to haunt you."

NINE

Central Hari was the largest train station on the local line and the closest to the police department. There was a rotary out front for buses and taxis. Still, to anyone coming from Tokyo, it would look like the sticks, thought Nishiguchi. He headed up to the city himself a few times a year and was always a little awestruck by the size and complexity of the stations.

"Anytime now," Motoyama said, looking down at his watch. Nishiguchi checked the time. It was 2:20 p.m.

The two detectives were standing just outside the gates at the station, waiting for an express train. They'd both been on their feet since the morning, and their shirts were soaked with sweat. Both of them were wearing jackets, however, and their ties were tied tight and straight.

Masatsugu Tsukahara's widow, Sanae Tsukahara, had answered immediately when they called the number he had left in the guest ledger. When Nishiguchi explained why he was calling, she fell silent, a long silence that spoke volumes. When she eventually asked what had happened, her voice had been shockingly calm.

Nishiguchi had laid out the facts as plainly as possible, and the widow had listened in silence. Nishiguchi left her his cell phone number so she could call when she knew what train she would be arriving on. The plan was for him to pick her up at the station by himself, but about an hour after the phone call, Motoyama called to tell him he'd be coming along. Apparently, a man named Tatara, a director in Tokyo Metropolitan Police Department's homicide division, had called their boss saying he wanted to accompany Sanae Tsukahara. The deceased had been in the same department as Tatara at some point before he retired last year.

Though the union card had told Nishiguchi that Tsukahara was a former cop, the revelation he was in Tokyo homicide came as a surprise. Yet it did make one thing clear: now he knew why the widow had sounded so collected on the phone moments after learning of her husband's death. She'd probably spent many long years anticipating that very call.

With a director from the Tokyo Police Department arriving, they couldn't just send one of the rank-and-file to greet the train—thus, Motoyama's addition to the welcoming party.

"There it is," he said, peering through the gates. Passengers were starting to come down the stairs. The number of tourists had dropped sharply after the weeklong holiday in August. Everyone they saw was identifiable at a glance as local, if not by their clothes, then by the size of the bags they carried.

One couple stood out from the crowd as clearly different, however. The woman was slender, wearing a gray dress and lightly tinted sunglasses. She looked to be about fifty. The man was on the short side but broad shouldered and looking smart in a black suit. His salt-and-pepper hair was neatly combed, and he wore wire-rimmed glasses.

"And that's them," Motoyama whispered. "Look at those eyes. That's a detective who earned his rank."

The man spotted them immediately and strode over, the woman following closely behind him.

"Director Tatara?" Motoyama spoke.

"Yes, and you are?"

"Motoyama, Captain, Hari Police Homicide. This is Detective Nishiguchi."

Nishiguchi bowed his head as he was introduced.

Tatara nodded back, and indicated the woman standing behind him. "This is Mrs. Tsukahara. I believe you've already spoken."

"Yes. I'm sorry to meet you under these circumstances, Mrs. Tsukahara," Motoyama said, turning to face the widow and bowing deeply. "You have our condolences."

Nishiguchi bowed too.

"Thank you for your concern, and for handling this . . . matter," she said, her voice a shade deeper than it had sounded over the phone.

"And thank you for allowing me to accompany her," Tatara added.

"Of course," Motoyama said.

"When I heard what had happened, I knew I wasn't going to get any work done today anyway. Detective Tsukahara was more than a colleague to me. I owe him a great deal."

"I see," Motoyama said, taking out a handkerchief and wiping the sweat from the side of his face. "I regret not having known him."

"Where's the body?" Tatara asked, straight to the point.

"In the morgue. Forensics should be finished by now, so I can take you there immediately."

"Thank you," Sanae said, once again bowing deeply.

Nishiguchi drove them all to the Hari Police Department, where Okamoto, head of Criminal Investigation, was already bowing deeply at the entrance when they arrived.

"Please don't hesitate to let me know if there's anything you need, anything at all," Okamoto said, looking as though he might commence wringing his hands at any moment. A director from Tokyo homicide essentially outranked even the commissioner at a small station like theirs.

Nishiguchi and Motoyama led their two guests downstairs to the morgue. The body had been laid out on one of the beds in such a way as to conceal the crack on the back of his head as best as possible.

Sanae took one look and said, "That's my husband." Her face was pale, but she gave no outward sign of emotion.

Nishiguchi and Motoyama left the two of them in the room and waited in the hallway outside. Five minutes later, the door opened, and Tatara walked out.

"All finished?" Motoyama asked, as gently as possible.

"I thought I'd give her a little time by herself. And, I was hoping that might give me a chance to hear some of the details?"

"Certainly," Motoyama said. "There's a room we can use." He looked over at Nishiguchi. "You stay here and bring the widow to room number two when she comes out."

"Yes sir," Nishiguchi replied.

He waited for about ten minutes in the dimly lit hallway before the door quietly opened and Sanae emerged. Her eyes were red, but there was no trace of tears on her face. She must've already touched up her makeup, Nishiguchi thought.

The meeting room was on the second floor. When they arrived, Motoyama was pointing at a map spread out across the table, indicating the location where Tsukahara had been found. Okamoto was there, as well as Commissioner Tomita. Tomita stood up from the table with surprising swiftness for someone so overweight. He immediately bowed and offered his condolences.

"They found him in a place called Hari Cove," Tatara said, turning to the widow. "Ever heard of it?"

She shook her head and sat in one of the chairs.

"Director Tatara informs me that your husband left the inn without indicating exactly where he was going," Motoyama said. "Was that typical of him?"

Sanae's hands clutched the handle of the bag on her knees tightly. "He had been taking trips to hot springs and the like on occasion— by himself, as I usually work on the weekdays. Sometimes he'd have a particular destination in mind, but other times he would just have a general idea, like he was going to see the foliage, or the ocean. I knew he was headed in this general direction this time, but not precisely where he was going."

"Had he ever mentioned Hari Cove before?"

"I'm not sure. I don't think so," she said.

Motoyama picked a travel bag up off the chair next to him and placed it on the table. "Have you ever seen this bag?"

"That's his, yes."

"Would you mind checking the contents and letting us know if there's anything in there that looks unfamiliar to you?"

"Is it all right to touch it with my bare hands?" Sanae asked—the kind of question only a detective's wife would think to ask, Nishiguchi mused.

Motoyama nodded.

She checked the contents and told him that everything inside was her husband's, as far as she knew.

"And the cell phone? As far as we could tell, he hadn't used it much recently. We see the last call as having been made three days ago, to the Green Rock Inn. Probably when he made his reservation."

Sanae picked up the phone and checked recent calls. "That would be pretty normal," she told them. "He's had the phone for a while, but he rarely used it. He spoke of not having many people to call since retiring . . . and he never sent text messages or e-mail."

Motoyama nodded. Next, he pulled a plastic bag containing a single piece of paper from the inner pocket of his jacket. This, too, he placed on the table.

"Are you familiar with this? Feel free to pick it up."

Sanae took the plastic bag and examined its contents. A frown spread across her face.

It contained a piece of paper that Nishiguchi had discovered folded into the pocket of Masatsugu Tsukahara's shirt. It was printed with the words "Informational Hearing and Discussion on the Proposed Development of Submarine Hydrothermal Ore Deposits" and was marked with an official DESMEC stamp.

Sanae shook her head and set the plastic bag down. "I've never seen this before."

"What is it?" Tatara asked.

"It's an attendance voucher for a hearing in town," Motoyama explained, filling them in on the proposed development and the local reaction.

"And Mr. Tsukahara attended this hearing?"

"Yes, we have a witness who saw him at the meeting hall yesterday, and it's our opinion that he came to Hari Cove with the express purpose of attending that hearing."

Tatara frowned and looked over at Sanae. "And you never heard anything about this?"

"Not a word. I'm not even sure what these ore deposits are."

Tatara shook his head and rested his elbows on the table. "Well, that's odd."

"We talked to some of the people involved with the hearing, and they did indicate that there were people there other than locals or those directly related to the development project," Motoyama said. "Since it is the first proposal of its kind in Japan, they opened attendance to anyone in the country who wanted to come. Could Mr. Tsukahara have had an interest in resource development? That voucher was only sent to people who specifically requested one."

Both Sanae and Tatara nodded at that, though neither looked convinced.

Commissioner Tomita spoke. "Could it be possible that in his travels after retiring he developed an interest in the environment? Environmental groups have been talking quite a bit about the proposed development and the risk of damage to the ocean around Hari Cove. That might've led him down here."

It was an almost flippant theory, Nishiguchi thought. Tomita clearly wanted this case to go away quickly. There was no sign it was anything other than an accident, and he couldn't have appreciated the presence of a Tokyo Police director on his home turf.

Tatara didn't respond, instead pulling the map over toward him.

"How do we get from here to the place where it happened? I'd like to see it for myself, if that's all right."

"We'd be happy to give you a lift," Motoyama offered.

"Great, then, let's go."

"Right. . . . Er, about the body. I assume you haven't made funeral arrangements yet?"

Tatara looked slowly between Motoyama's and Okamoto's faces before turning to Commissioner Tomita. "I gather, then, you don't have plans for an autopsy?"

Nishiguchi stiffened in his chair. Having a director from Tokyo homicide even mention the word *autopsy* made everything seem more serious.

"Er, well, no. I mean, based on all the reports we've had so far, there's really no need," Tomita managed, casting a look at Okamoto that screamed *help me.*

"The local physician's opinion was that death was due to cerebral contusion," Okamoto said, his tongue tripping over his words. "Right?" he said, looking at Motoyama.

Motoyama nodded, and added, "We also analyzed his blood for alcohol content. He had been drinking, but not to the level of impairment. It might have made him a little unsteady, however. Our working theory is that he went for a walk to clear his head, climbed onto the seawall, slipped, and fell down on the rocks."

Tatara looked down at the table in silence for a few moments before looking back up. "Let's go take a look at the scene first," he said. "We can consider the remains later. If that's all right?" The last question he directed toward Sanae.

"Of course," she replied.

They arrived at the scene about half an hour later.

Getting down to the rocks themselves was too much trouble, so they settled for looking down from the seawall. They could still clearly see the blood splashed on the rocks below. Sanae put a hand over her mouth as a choking sob escaped her lips. Tatara held his hands together in silent prayer for a moment before he began scanning the scene.

"We've been questioning people in the area since this morning, but nobody spotted Mr. Tsukahara down here last night," Motoyama explained, his tone apologetic. "Out in the countryside, few people go outside after eight o'clock."

Tatara looked around. "Must get pretty dark at night."

"Pitch black, yes."

"And this was about four hundred meters from the inn? I'm surprised he managed to walk that far in the dark. Or was he carrying a flashlight?" Tatara muttered, half to himself.

"Well, maybe I shouldn't have said pitch black," Motoyama corrected himself. "Er, that is, it gets pretty dark, but he would've been able to see enough to walk. The moon was out last night," he added, a little meekly.

"But you didn't find a flashlight?"

"No, well, that is, it might've fallen into the ocean," Motoyama stammered, his eyes wandering toward Nishiguchi.

"Since the proprietor of the inn didn't even know that Tsukahara had left, I'm sure they didn't loan him a flashlight," Nishiguchi said. "However, these inns usually have a flashlight in every room for emergencies, which he might have taken. I'll check in with them and find out."

Tatara stared down at the rocks, not even nodding in acknowledgment. Eventually, he looked back up, turning his sharp eyes toward Motoyama. "I'm sorry, but can we return to your station immediately? There's something I need to discuss with the commissioner."

TEN

Sweat trickled down the DESMEC development manager's face despite a blast of cold from the air conditioner right above him. He wiped at his forehead with a handkerchief before lifting the microphone again. "Like I said, we need to do more studies before we know what effect this will have on the plankton. Admittedly, if we dig into the seafloor, it will affect the food chain. What we need to do is find out exactly how large an effect it will have, then—"

"But what if your survey has an effect? What then? That's what I want to know. Who's gonna take responsibility if we can't catch any fish?" The man shouting at the stage was a local fisherman, thick arms protruding from his T-shirt sleeves.

"I'm sorry, if we could all calm down," said a haggard-looking man off to the side of the stage. Today, they had a public relations manager from city hall acting as emcee, and the two hours of heated debate that morning had already worn his voice down to a croak. "DESMEC hasn't finished explaining their position here, so let's hear what they have to say, and then raise hands to speak. Please? I hate to repeat myself, but I really need everyone to follow these basic rules of order."

The development manager from DESMEC brandished his mic

again. "We've already done a little excavation, and, thus far, have seen no significant effects. Of course, we will be slowly scaling up operations—"

"What do you mean, already started? Who gave you permission to do that?" another voice shouted.

"What are you talking about?" a man in a suit sitting near Narumi said, standing. "Of course they already started their survey—that's how they knew there's rare metals out there in the first place. You don't need permission to do a survey."

"Hey, whose side are you on?" the man in the T-shirt growled back.

"No one's side. Not until I hear more. That's why I came. Enough with the fish, already. I want to hear what DESMEC plans to do for local business."

"Enough with the fish? Enough with you! You ever—"

"Excuse me, people, please!" the emcee spoke loudly into his mic, his eyebrows furrowed into a consternated V. "If we could stop right there. Raise your hands, people. Then talk. That's how this works."

The first public debate on hydrothermal ore mining in Japan wasn't going smoothly. With the exception of a handful people, no one in the room really knew enough about the topic to have a meaningful conversation. Even Narumi was frustrated with how little she understood of the issues, despite weeks of research.

That, and she was finding it difficult to focus on anything being discussed. Her mind kept wandering back to the day before, when her eyes had met Tsukahara's. Had he nodded to her? Was she just imagining things? She'd hoped to learn something about him when she went to the police station with her mother the day before, but the police only asked them questions and told them nothing.

Narumi's eyes went to Yukawa, sitting up on stage with the people from DESMEC. He had several papers spread out on the table in front of him, but the look on his face said he wasn't paying attention to any of it. *He's not even wearing his glasses.*

The meeting finally adjourned forty minutes past schedule.

Everyone on stage stayed in their chairs, looking stunned with exhaustion. Everyone except Yukawa, who quickly gathered his things and strode from the room.

"Well, I guess that's that," Sawamura said, standing up and stretching. "At least we got them to agree to another hearing. I'll consider that a victory."

"But they're not going to release any of their data on deep-sea organisms," Narumi complained. "I don't buy that they're still 'prepping' it, whatever that means. I was hoping you'd say something during the Q and A."

Sawamura slid his informational handouts into his bag and shrugged. "I thought about it. But then the topic shifted to fishing. I guess I just missed my timing."

An unusual slip for someone like Sawamura, a veteran of this kind of debate, Narumi thought. She took it as a sign that this issue was far more complex than anything they'd dealt with before.

"By the way," Sawamura said, turning to her and lowering his voice as they left the auditorium. "How are things at the inn?"

"What do you mean?"

"I heard about your guest. Small town, word travels fast."

"Oh, that. It was such a surprise."

"The police have anything to say about it?"

"Not much. They don't really know what happened yet. Other than the obvious, that is—that he got drunk and fell."

"Huh. You gotta wonder why he climbed onto the seawall in the first place. You think it was suicide?"

"Not really. I mean, it's only a drop of five meters or so there. If you were going to commit suicide, wouldn't you jump from someplace a little higher?"

"Yeah, good point," Sawamura muttered back.

Outside the community center, Narumi said good-bye and got on her bike. Shortly after she began pedaling up the coastal road, she spotted a tall man up ahead, walking along the side of the road. She slowed down and called out, "Too quick, Mr. Yukawa."

He stopped and turned around. "Hey," he said, a little weakly. "What's too quick?"

"You, standing up and leaving the stage before anyone else."

"You noticed."

"I also noticed that you weren't wearing your glasses. It looked like you'd pretty much checked out."

"I was mourning the loss of a perfectly good day spent listening to that pointless debate." Yukawa started to walk again, so Narumi got down off her bicycle and starting walking alongside him.

"Going back to the inn? Why not take a taxi?"

"Because I've decided that the taxis in this town are useless. You see them drive by all the time when you don't need them, but when you need them, there's not a single one to be found."

"I'm surprised you thought that debate was pointless," Narumi said. "I thought everyone was very engaged."

"The DESMEC people just wanted to have on record the fact that they held a hearing, and the opposition was just whining. That's not a debate. It's a waste of time."

"You think asking that the environment be protected is whining?"

"It is when you expect them to adopt some mythical flawless plan offering perfect environmental protection. Nothing's perfect in this world," Yukawa said, his pace quickening. Narumi had to trot to keep up.

"We're not asking them to *do* anything. We're asking them to not destroy the environment. It's not like they have to go out of their way to help. They just have to avoid doing anything stupid."

"And who decides what's stupid? You?"

Narumi stopped in her tracks, but Yukawa kept walking. She stood there glaring at his back for a moment before getting on her bike again. Jamming down the pedals, she sped past him, then stopped up ahead, turning back to look at him.

The physicist met her eyes. "Still eager to debate?" he asked. "The meeting's adjourned."

She glared at him a moment, then sighed and made a big smile. "You're still in town for a while, aren't you, Mr. Yukawa?"

"Until I'm done helping with the survey boat, yes."

"Then, there's a place I want to show you. Can you dive?"

"Excuse me?"

"Scuba diving. Ever been?"

Yukawa stiffened, a look of alarm in his eyes. "It might surprise you, but I do have my license."

"Excellent," Narumi said. "Then let's go diving, soon."

"Is that the place you want to show me? The ocean?"

"Is there any other place we've been talking about all day?"

"No, now that you mention it. I'd be happy to go if the opportunity presents itself."

"It will. That's a promise." Narumi put her foot on one pedal and began to push. She couldn't wait to see the physicist's face when he saw what was out there under the waters of Hari Cove.

ELEVEN

Kyohei was just looking in the window of a small gift shop close to Hari Cove Station when he heard someone calling his name. He turned to see Narumi approaching on her bike.

"What you up to? Buying souvenirs for home?"

Kyohei shook his head. "I just ran out of things to do, so I came here looking for something fun."

"Ah, I guess the beach plans fell through?" Narumi asked, a frown passing across her face.

"Yeah, pretty much."

"Are the police still up at the inn?"

Kyohei shrugged. "They were there most of the afternoon, so I don't know. How was your meeting? You have fun?"

Narumi chuckled dryly. "Fun isn't exactly what I'd call it. Are you heading back to the inn?"

"Nah," he said. "I think I'll walk around here for a bit more first."

"Okay, well, don't stay out too late," Narumi said. She got off her bike and started the long walk up the hill.

Kyohei bought a cola from a vending machine and sipped it, considering his next move, when he spotted Yukawa walking down the road. He had his jacket slung over his shoulder.

"Looks like you didn't make it to the beach after all," Yukawa said.

"How do you know?"

He pointed at Kyohei's face. "You aren't tanned one bit."

Kyohei sighed. "My uncle was too busy with all the police."

"That's unfortunate. I wonder what they're hoping to find."

"How should I know? I checked out the rocks a little while back, but they'd already cleaned all that up, mostly."

"The rocks?" A glimmer of interest shone in the physicist's eyes. "You know where it happened?"

"Yeah, sure. My uncle told me. Right before he told me to stay away."

Yukawa nodded. "Show me."

"Who, me?"

"Do you see anyone else here?"

"Well, okay, but there really isn't anything left."

"Doesn't matter. Let's go," Yukawa said, stepping out ahead of him.

Several minutes later, the two of them were standing by the seawall. Yellow tape had been stretched out in front of the wall, but there were no policemen in sight. Yukawa ducked under the tape and kept walking, so Kyohei followed suit. Reaching the seawall, he jumped up and lifted himself to the top in order to look over.

"I think that's where he fell," Kyohei said, pointing toward a rock with a reddish stain. "They couldn't find one of the sandals. Probably dropped into the sea."

"One of the sandals? So he was wearing the other?"

"I don't know. Probably."

Yukawa nodded and adjusted his glasses with his finger. He was staring down at the rocks with great interest, as though there was something there to see.

"What is it?"

Yukawa blinked, shaking off whatever thought he had been lost in, and said, "Nothing. It's nothing." His eyes went out across the water. "Quite the view of the ocean from here. I can see why Narumi is so taken with it."

"It looks even better earlier in the day. Do you know why this place is called Hari Cove?"

"I assume because of volcanic activity in the area," Yukawa replied.

"Volcanoes? What do they have to do with anything?"

"Well, *hari* is an old word for the amorphous substances found in volcanic rock."

Kyohei furrowed his eyebrows. "No, that's not it," he said. "Here, the word *hari* means 'crystals.' You ever hear of the Seven Treasures? Buddhists say there are seven great treasures in the world, and one of them is crystal."

Yukawa slowly turned to face the boy. "Is Buddhist trivia a hobby of yours?"

Kyohei grinned and scratched his nose. "My uncle told me last night when we were shooting off fireworks."

"I see. So what about this crystal?"

"Well, when the sun gets to the middle of the sky, it's supposed to light up the sea and make it look like there are a lot of colored crystals at the bottom. So, Hari Cove."

Yukawa's mouth opened partway, and he nodded. Then he turned back out toward the water. "I see," he said after a moment. "The water here must be very clear, then. Thanks for telling me that. I'll definitely try to come back here at noon one of these days."

"Yeah, except you can't really see it from here. It's too shallow. You have to go out about a hundred meters first."

"A hundred meters? No problem, I'll swim it."

"Yeah, except you're not supposed to swim around here."

"Then I could go to the swimming beach."

"Yeah, but then you'd have to go even further out from the shore till you got to the place where it's really pretty. Like two or three hundred meters. Past the buoys that mark where you're allowed to swim."

"Right, then I just need to go on a boat."

"Yeah, that's what I figured," Kyohei said, his shoulders drooping.

"What, is there something wrong with that too?"

Kyohei leaned against the seawall, folding his arms and resting his head atop them. "I can handle big boats, but not the little boats around here. I get sick right away. My mom says it's because I'm a picky eater, but I don't believe that for a second. I'm pretty sure it just has something to do with my body. I've got friends who are way pickier eaters than I am, and they don't get sick."

"You're correct. It does have something to do with the body. It's because your semicircular canals aren't functioning properly. But there are techniques you can use to remedy it, sometimes completely. How do you do in cars?"

"I'm okay in the car with my dad, but I get sick on buses sometimes. That's why I sit toward the front whenever I can—it shakes less up there."

"It's not just the shaking, it's where you put your eyes that's important. For example, if you're on a very curvy road, inertia forces your body toward the outside of the curves, correct? If you allow your eyes to look toward the outside of the curve at the same time, the information coming from your semicircular canals and the information coming from your eyes don't line up, your brain gets confused, and you feel sick. But if you fix your eyesight in the direction the car is moving, the effect is far less. That's why most people who get carsick don't have a problem when they're actually doing the driving, because when you drive you're always looking forward."

Kyohei lifted his head and looked at Yukawa. "You study that too, Professor?"

"It's outside my specialty, but I have looked into related technology."

Kyohei grunted. "Sure sounds busy being a scientist. But I'll try that next time I'm on a bus. Still, that's not going to help with the boat."

"Why not?"

" 'Cause I want to see the ocean. That's the whole point of going out, right? If I'm always looking forward, I won't be able to look down."

"That is true."

"My mom doesn't let me take medicine for seasickness 'cause of allergies, so that's pretty much that." Kyohei stepped away from the seawall, heading back to the road.

"You're just giving up?" Yukawa asked behind him. "You don't want to see the crystals at the bottom of the sea?"

"I do, but I don't want to get seasick even more," Kyohei said, walking a little further, then stopping. He looked around. Yukawa was still standing by the seawall. "You're not going back to the inn?"

Yukawa took his jacket off his shoulder and put it on. "You go on ahead. I'm going to be here for a bit, working on my plan."

"What plan?"

"My plan to show you the crystals at the bottom of the sea, what else?"

TWELVE

Yukawa had requested a seven o'clock dinner, but the hour had come and gone with no sign of the eccentric physicist.

Narumi was wondering what to do, when he appeared, drenched in sweat, carrying a large paper bag in each hand.

"Mr. Yukawa. I was just about to phone you."

"Sorry. Couldn't get a taxi to save my life."

"Will you be heading up to your room first?"

"No, I'm fine like this."

His dishes were already laid out. Throwing his bags and jacket off to one side, Yukawa sat down at the table.

"I see you paid a visit to the hardware store," Narumi said, pouring him a glass of beer. She recognized the logo on the paper bags. It was a small place, but vital, as it was the only one of its kind in town.

"I required some materials for an experiment," Yukawa said, lifting the glass to his mouth, but before he took a sip, he turned to look at her. "Actually, there's something I want to ask you for, if it's not too much trouble."

"What's that?"

"I need some empty plastic bottles. Preferably something designed to hold carbonated water."

"I should have some two-liter cola bottles in the back."

"Perfect. I'll need five or six. I'll come down for them later."

"What are you going to use them for?"

"Ah. You can ask the resident stubborn preteen that tomorrow."

Narumi narrowed her eyes. "I take it you're referring to my cousin?"

"Yes. I don't think I've had the pleasure of meeting a boy with his particular brand of obstinacy before."

Yukawa took a drink of his beer, then looked up, noticing Narumi's eyes on him. "Is there something on my face?"

"No," she replied, stifling a laugh. "Enjoy your meal."

Leaving the dining room, Narumi grabbed the master key and got on the elevator to go to Yukawa's room on the third floor to lay out his futon.

The first thing that caught her eye when she entered the room was a cardboard box in one corner—a package that had arrived earlier that day. He must have had someone express ship it to him, since he hadn't known he was staying here until just the day before. She glanced at the packing slip and saw that it had been sent from Imperial University's Physics Laboratory Number 13. It had a large FRAGILE sticker on one side, and the label read "Contents: Bottles."

Narumi laid out his futon and went down to the living room, where her parents were drinking tea after dinner. Kyohei was nowhere to be seen.

"I put out the futon," she announced.

Setsuko nodded. Both she and Shigehiro had sour expressions.

"What is it?" Narumi asked, looking between her parents' faces.

"It's nothing, we were just talking," Shigehiro said slowly. "Thinking it might be time."

"Time?" Narumi echoed, though she knew immediately what they meant. "Time to close the place down?"

"Not sure as we have a choice, with the way things have been. Yeah, the holiday season is over, but even still, one guest? That's not going to pay the bills. And after what happened . . ."

"But that wasn't our fault," Narumi countered.

"Not sure we can say that. If we'd had someone on staff, we might have known when Mr. Tsukahara went out, and there wasn't anyone to send out to look for him when he didn't come back. His widow came by today around lunchtime, and she didn't have one mean word for us, but I could hardly meet her eyes. She even said she wanted to pay for his night's stay. . . ."

"You didn't take it."

"Of course I didn't," Shigehiro said, shaking his head. "I told her we couldn't possibly accept that, and even then she insisted, saying it was the least she could do for all the trouble. Took quite a while to talk her down."

Narumi sighed.

"I don't know," her father continued. "It just feels like it's about time. Fifteen years. I think that's a pretty good run, all things considered." He folded his arms across his chest and looked around, as if he was already saying good-bye.

Narumi's own mind traveled back to when she first came here, still in middle school. Her father had left his job at a company in Tokyo to come back to his hometown and take up the reins at the Green Rock Inn. It had already been several years since his father, Narumi's grandfather, had been crippled by a stroke, and people had started wondering openly when Shigehiro would come.

She could still remember vividly the day they arrived in town. She had visited several times before, but for some reason, just knowing that it was going to be her home made everything look different. What struck her first and strongest was the beauty of the sea. Her current devotion to its protection was an outgrowth of that first impression.

The sound of a hushed buzzer brought her back to the present. Someone was pressing the button on the front desk.

"Who could that be at this hour?" Setsuko wondered, looking up at the clock.

Narumi shrugged and stood. Out in the lobby, she found Tsuyoshi Nishiguchi standing by the shelves where guests put their shoes upon entering the inn.

"Hey," he said, raising his hand in greeting. "Sorry to bother you again."

"It's no bother," Narumi said. "I'm sorry you have to work so late. It must be rough being a detective."

"We're usually not this busy, but when something big happens, well, you know. Can't really loaf around when there's been a, er, a loss of life."

Narumi raised an eyebrow but nodded. "So what have you found out? Do you know how it happened yet?"

"Still can't say for sure. We're not even sure it was an accident now."

Though his tone had been casual, Narumi stiffened at the words. "Wait, what does that mean? If it wasn't an accident, what was it? Suicide?"

"Like I said, we don't know. I'm pretty sure it wasn't a suicide, though. Still, other possibilities have come to light. . . . That said, we'll probably wind up filing it as an accident after all," Nishiguchi stammered.

Narumi narrowed her eyes at her old classmate. "You're saying there's a possibility it was murder?"

Nishiguchi blanched and scratched his forehead. "Look, we don't know. Just, it turns out that Mr. Tsukahara was a detective in the Tokyo Police Department. Homicide."

"Whoa."

"Anyway, when the widow came down today, she brought a guy who used to be Mr. Tsukahara's subordinate. He's a director in Tokyo homicide now. You know what that means? That's only one rank below commissioner, which is the person who's directly in charge of investigations. Anyway, that had the local brass sweating bullets."

"Did he have something to say about what happened?"

"Yes, would be my guess. I wasn't there, but we showed him the scene, and then he started talking about having to see our commissioner right away. They were in there for about an hour, then the director and the widow went back to Tokyo with orders to send the remains back after them. Not for a funeral, either."

"For what then?"

"An autopsy," Nishiguchi said in a hushed voice.

Narumi swallowed.

"If it looks like murder, you know Tokyo's going to get involved, even if it isn't their jurisdiction. That's got everyone at the station on tenterhooks. Which is why I'm trying to get everything squared away before the end of the day." Nishiguchi leaned toward her and added, "And everything I just said, that's just between old friends, okay? Don't tell anyone else."

"Yeah, sure. No problem. So, how can I help you?"

"Right, I almost forgot," Nishiguchi said, straightening his back and clearing his throat. "Actually, there's something I wanted to borrow from you, if I could? Your, er, guest ledger, I think it's called? We need a record of people who stayed here."

"What are you going to do with that?"

"Well, it's a bit of a sensitive subject," Nishiguchi began, glancing around before continuing, "but people were wondering why Tsukahara chose this place to stay."

"You mean why'd he pick an old, rundown inn like ours?"

"I didn't say that! I'm just saying, well, he might've had a specific reason. Like someone recommended it to him. That's why we need to know who stayed here in the past."

"Oh, I get it. How many years back do you want?"

"As many as you got."

"Okay, I'll ask my folks." Narumi went back to the living room, mulling over what Nishiguchi had said. It was a good question. Why had Tsukahara chosen the Green Rock Inn?

THIRTEEN

Kyohei finished breakfast and was on his way back to his room when he spotted Yukawa in the lobby. He was sitting on the wicker bench, staring at the framed painting of the ocean on the wall.

"Did someone in your family paint this?" he asked as Kyohei was walking by.

"I dunno. Something wrong with it?"

Yukawa pointed at the painting. "You can't get this view of the ocean from this inn, no matter where you stand. It made me wonder where it was painted from."

Kyohei looked between the physicist's face and the painting. He shrugged. "Does it matter?"

"Very much. This town prides itself on the beauty of its seascape, and this inn was built to cater to people lured here by its beauty. If we find a painting of the ocean in such a place, we would expect it to be a local scene. If the ocean in this painting were actually the ocean from an entirely different area, or something the painter just made up, well, that's a kind of fraud, if you ask me."

"Fraud sounds a little strong," Kyohei said.

Yukawa stared at the painting a few moments longer, then turned to him. "What are your plans today?"

"Nothing."

"Perfect," Yukawa said, looking down at his watch. "It's eight thirty now. Meet me here in half an hour."

"Huh? Why?"

"I believe I mentioned I was working on a plan to show you the bottom of the sea. Well, my plans have taken shape, and I'd like to put them into action as soon as possible," Yukawa said, standing.

Kyohei looked at the physicist in surprise. "I told you I don't like boats."

"And I heard you. We're only talking about one hundred meters here. We don't need a boat." Yukawa made his hand in the shape of a pistol and pointed the barrel at the painting of the sea. "Let's hope it works."

Roughly thirty minutes later, Yukawa showed up in the lobby carrying two large paper bags. He handed one of the bags to Kyohei, but the top was folded shut and he couldn't see inside. It wasn't as heavy as he expected it to be, judging by the size. When he asked what was inside, all Yukawa said was, "Don't get your hopes up. It's not lunch."

"By the way, did you bring your cell phone?" Yukawa asked as they were walking outside.

Kyohei fished the phone out of his shorts pocket and showed it to him. Yukawa nodded approvingly and started to walk.

The physicist wouldn't tell him where they were going, so all Kyohei could do was follow. He thought they might be going to the place where the guest had fallen the night before, but Yukawa showed no signs of stopping as they passed by the rocky shore.

Past the harbor, they came to a breakwater extending out into the ocean. Yukawa began walking down it toward the end, his pace quickening.

"Are we going to do something at the end of the breakwater?"

"That's why we're here."

"Well, what are we doing, then? Tell me already."

"Don't be impatient, you'll see soon enough."

Yukawa finally stopped when he reached the very end of the breakwater. "Open your bag," he instructed, "and spread out its contents on the ground."

Kyohei opened his bag, finding a plastic bucket, some plastic string, and what looked like a long tube made out of cut plastic bottles.

"We're making a bottle rocket. Sometimes called a water rocket. Know what those are?"

"Yeah, we made them at school once. They shoot water out of the back, right?"

"They most certainly do."

"Is it going to take a long time?"

"Don't worry, it's already nearly finished. I did most of the work last night in my room and then dismantled it to fit in the bags. It will be easy to reassemble." Yukawa worked while he talked, sticking the various pieces together with practiced hands. Kyohei watched as the rocket gradually took shape. It was easily over a meter tall, considerably larger than the ones they'd made at school.

"You made this in your room?"

"It was the easiest solution to the problem, believe it or not. It should provide an interesting lesson in physics, too."

"How is firing off a rocket going to let us see the ocean floor?"

Yukawa's hands stopped their work. He pushed up his glasses with the tip of his finger. "Ever hear of Yuri Gagarin? He was an astronaut—the first man in outer space, and the first man to orbit the earth. He did that in a rocket. Without rockets, mankind would never have been able to see what the earth really looks like. We need a rocket."

FOURTEEN

In the homicide division of the Tokyo Police Department, Detective Shunpei Kusanagi was in the middle of laboriously typing up a report when he sensed someone standing in front of his desk. He looked up to see Division Chief Mamiya glaring down at him.

"Don't tell me you can't touch type, Kusanagi."

Kusanagi narrowed his eyes. "What about you, Chief?"

"You know I don't have time for that crap," Mamiya said. He glanced around the office and leaned in a little closer. "Speaking of which, got a moment?"

Kusanagi chuckled. "Didn't you just tell me you needed this report done on the double?"

"It can wait. Come with me, Director Tatara's waiting."

"Tatara?" Kusanagi immediately began thinking back over the last couple of days, trying to figure out what he could've messed up badly enough to get the director's attention.

"Don't worry, he's not going to chew us out. Come."

Mamiya walked off without waiting for an answer. Kusanagi got up from his desk and hurried after him. They reached a small meeting room, where Mamiya knocked on the door. A voice from inside said, "Enter."

The two detectives walked into the room to find Tatara, his jacket off, sitting in one of the chairs. He had spread several papers out on the conference table, along with some photographs. Kusanagi spotted a photocopy of a map, though it wasn't an area he was familiar with.

"Have a seat," Tatara said. "I called you both in here because I have a somewhat irregular request for Kusanagi." The director's face was calm, but there was a serious look in his eyes.

Kusanagi straightened a little in his chair. "Yes, sir?"

"I assume you've heard about Masatsugu Tsukahara's death?"

It took Kusanagi a moment to reply, "Yes, yesterday, but only a rumor. They said he died on a trip somewhere?"

Masatsugu Tsukahara had left the homicide division ten years ago. He'd been transferred to another department, apparently due to ill health. They hadn't even been on the same squad when he was in homicide, so Kusanagi barely knew the man. He didn't even know he'd retired when he heard about the death.

"Well, it's a long story, but basically, I owe a lot to Tsukahara. My entire career, really."

Kusanagi nodded, unsure whether he should offer his condolences.

"Yesterday, I went with his widow to visit the town where it happened," Tatara continued. "This is where they found him." He placed a photograph in front of Kusanagi, showing some rocks on the coast somewhere, photographed from above. "He was lying on these rocks. The local physician's assessment was cerebral contusion."

A wrinkle formed between Kusanagi's eyebrows. "So he slipped and fell, something like that?"

"That's how the locals are calling it. They weren't even planning an autopsy."

Kusanagi raised an eyebrow. "But something was off, I take it?"

"As soon as I saw the body in the morgue, I knew this was no simple fall on the rocks," Tatara said, looking between the two detectives. "I've seen plenty of accidental deaths by falling. Even when we're only talking about a few meters, if he hit hard enough to cause cerebral contusion, there should have been internal hemorrhaging throughout the body. But he was hardly bruised at all. Which says to me Tsukahara was dead *before* he hit those rocks.

"Once I had a chance to examine the scene, I felt even more sure foul play was involved. Tsukahara liked to drink as much as any of us, but I never knew him to drink to excess. I don't buy for a second that he scrambled drunkenly up on that seawall, then slipped off the other side."

"Is that what the locals said?" Mamiya asked.

Tatara chuckled and shook his head. "If we leave this case in their hands, it will die a quick death. No, we need to requisition the body and perform an autopsy here."

Mamiya's eyes widened. "And we're going to do that?"

"The Hari police commissioner's already signed off on it. I had our chief of detectives give the local station a call. If we find reasonable evidence of murder, we'll get their homicide people on it—after sharing our findings with them, of course. That should keep the locals happy."

Kusanagi nodded, duly impressed. He examined the man across the table, his neatly combed hair making him look more like a banker than a cop, remembering the stories he'd heard about Tatara back when he was a detective, not an administrator, and working actual cases. Tatara was rumored to have been a loose cannon who kept everyone on his team guessing what he'd do next. *Guess the rumors had some truth to them.*

"So when's the autopsy scheduled?" Mamiya asked.

Tatara grinned. "It's already under way. They brought the body in last night, and started the autopsy this morning. We don't have an official report yet, mostly because they haven't determined the cause of death."

"Am I to take it that means it wasn't cerebral contusion?" Kusanagi said.

"No. The injury on his head was most definitely inflicted *after* death. Nor were there any signs of natural causes, like a cerebral hemorrhage or heart attack. In other words, he didn't keel over on top of the seawall and then fall onto those rocks."

"So he wasn't sick, and there weren't any injuries other than the one to the head," Kusanagi said, choosing his words carefully. "Poison?"

"Probably," Tatara agreed. "They're running a bunch of tests right now. It's only a matter of time before we nail it down. The real question is, why did a dead man end up on those rocks?" Tatara tapped the photograph on the table.

Kusanagi raised an eyebrow. "I assume we'll be setting up a task force in Hari?"

"Sooner or later, yes. I expect we'll get a formal request for assistance from the Shizuoka Police. Problem is, if we wait that long, we might lose our chance to pick up the trail. Also, I doubt the locals will give us jurisdiction on their turf, so we might end up getting only part of the full picture." Tatara took a breath. "We need to move on our own on this one."

"You mean the Tokyo Police Department will be effectively taking over the investigation?" Kusanagi asked.

The director shook his head. "No. I'm not trying to shove the local police out completely. I'm happy to have them conduct their investigation. That said, I'm not going to go to Tsukahara's widow or, for that matter, Tsukahara himself when we meet in the great beyond, and say we couldn't find his killer because of inept police work. That's why we need to conduct our own investigation. And if we find anything of value, we'll bring it straight to the local prefectural headquarters."

"And you want me to conduct this investigation?" Kusanagi asked.

"That's right," Tatara said, his eyes shifting to Mamiya. "How about it? You just wrapped up a case, probably won't have anything for a while, right? Think you can loan me your detective until the next case starts up?"

"Well, it's fine with me, but . . ." Mamiya's words trailed off as he turned to look at Kusanagi.

"Why me?" Kusanagi asked.

Tatara's eyes glimmered. "You don't want to take this on?"

"No, that's not what I'm saying. But assigning me to the case doesn't make much sense. There are a lot of other people, high-ranking people, in the department who knew Tsukahara a lot better than I did."

"Like me, for instance," Tatara said. "You're right."

"Of course, I'm not suggesting that you go out there yourself, Director," Kusanagi quickly added.

Tatara shook his head. "I don't think anyone else in the department knew the deceased like I did. Which pretty much leaves everyone else but me on equal footing."

Kusanagi frowned. "I guess what I'm asking is, was there any particular reason you picked me, other than the fact I'm not currently on a case?"

"Hey, Kusanagi," Mamiya grumbled. "Don't get me in trouble here."

"It's fine," Tatara said. "You have every reason to wonder why we picked you." A smile played across the director's face as he picked up a piece of paper from the table. "Like I said, we haven't received a formal request for assistance. Which means we can't do anything too heavy-handed, without pissing off a lot of people and making things harder for us down the road. Still, we need to know what's going on down there, or our hands will be tied. It's a sticky problem, so I started thinking about how we might solve it." He pushed the paper across the table toward Kusanagi. "I asked if anyone else was staying at the inn where Tsukahara spent his last night. Turns out, there was only one other guest that night at the inn. And it's someone we know."

Kusanagi looked down at the paper. It was a copy of a page from the guest ledger of the Green Rock Inn.

Kusanagi looked up from the paper. "Yukawa? What the hell was he doing out there?"

"What *is* he doing, you mean. He's still in Hari Cove," Tatara said, a smile spreading across his face. "You can ask him yourself."

FIFTEEN

With a *whoosh* of compressed water, the rocket soared into the distance. Kyohei frowned. He'd missed the moment of launch again. The rocket was flying across the water too fast for his eyes to follow, with much more power than he'd expected.

Yukawa held up a small pair of binoculars and watched as the rocket splashed into the ocean.

"Distance?"

Kyohei checked the reading on the electric fishing reel they had stuck into the ground. They had attached a fishing line to the back of the rocket, and Kyohei was in charge of checking the distance of each launch.

"Uh, 135 meters. A little less than last time."

"Right. Reel her in," Yukawa said. He was sitting cross-legged on the breakwater and typing on his laptop, using his satchel in place of a desk.

Kyohei watched him out of the corner of his eye as he reeled the rocket back in. This was the seventh time in a row they'd performed this exact same procedure. Yukawa clearly loved firing off the rocket, but he hadn't done anything about showing Kyohei the bottom of the sea yet. Kyohei was starting to wonder what the point of all this was.

Yukawa squinted at the screen of his laptop and folded his arms across his chest. "I think we have the results we need. I've determined the source of the variation between our simulated results and the actual launches. We should be able to achieve perfect conditions for our launch."

"You mean we have to shoot the thing off again? How many times are we going to do this?"

"As many times as possible," the physicist answered. "With water rockets and manned rockets alike, it behooves us to test our equipment as many times as possible. In the case of an actual rocket, however, there are budgetary constraints that prevent unlimited testing. In our case, the main constraint is time: the sun is starting to get pretty high in the sky, and if we don't hop to it, we're going to miss our chance to see these so-called 'crystals' on the seafloor. So, the next launch is for real."

Yukawa stood and tossed the plastic bucket into the water. The bucket had a line of nylon rope tied to the handle.

While Kyohei continued reeling in the rocket, Yukawa deftly manipulated the bucket at the end of the rope, scooping up seawater as he had done six times previously.

Yukawa's rocket was remarkable not only because of its size, but also the curious shape of its fins. Yukawa claimed they were his own original creation, but Kyohei couldn't see what was particularly creative about them. Another unusual feature of the rocket was a weight he placed inside, about the size of a pack of cigarettes. He would adjust the position of the weight very slightly each launch. The weight measured in at almost one hundred grams, which Kyohei thought had to be cutting their distance by a lot, but according to Yukawa, the weight was a vital component.

Not for the first time, Kyohei wondered who exactly his strange professorial friend was. Yes, Kyohei had expressed some interest in seeing the crystals that gave Hari Cove its name, but it wasn't like he'd asked anyone to go to such lengths. Lengths he didn't even understand, because Yukawa wouldn't explain anything to him. All he could do was watch in silence as they performed one test launch after another.

Not that he was upset. To the contrary, it was exciting. He had the sense they were doing something important, even if he didn't know what that was.

"Ready for the real thing?" Yukawa asked, reaching into the rocket and pulling out the weight he had carefully placed inside.

"Huh, you're taking it out?" Kyohei grunted. "I thought that was *vital*?"

"It was vital, but it was just a stand-in for testing purposes. We'll be using something else for the actual launch."

Just then, a cell phone rang. Yukawa reached into his satchel, pulled out his phone, and checked the display. A cloud came over his face as he answered. "Yukawa speaking."

The person on the other end was saying something Kyohei couldn't hear. He watched Yukawa's eyebrows move.

"Sorry, but I can't make it today," Yukawa said. "Anytime after tomorrow would be fine. Yes, I'm in the middle of an experiment. Good-bye." He hung up.

"Work?" Kyohei asked.

"It was DESMEC, telling me to come to a meeting," the physicist explained. "That is, they call it a meeting, but all they really do is eat and waste my time. That hardly qualifies as work."

Yukawa began pouring a carefully measured amount of seawater into the rocket tank through a modified water valve at the rocket's base. After setting the rocket on a homemade launch pad, he attached a bicycle pump and began filling the tank with air. Kyohei could see the bottle expand. They knew from the previous testing exactly how much seawater to use, how much air to pump, and what angle to set the launch pad. The only difference this time was that the testing weight was gone.

"There," Yukawa said, removing the pump from the rocket. He

pulled his cell phone back out and punched at it with his thumb before putting it into the small chamber where the test weight had sat.

"What? You put your cell phone in there?"

Just then, Kyohei's own phone began to ring. He fished it out of
his pocket.

"Answer that after the launch," Yukawa said. "Now, on the count
of three. Three, two, one, liftoff!"

Yukawa pressed the switch attached to the launch pad and the
rocket took off, blasting water behind it with impressive force. Kyohei's eyes darted forward, following the semitranslucent rocket as it
caught the sun and glimmered against a backdrop of blue sky.

The rocket landed in the sea a considerable distance further than
their previous launch. Kyohei checked the reading on the fishing line.
"Wow, 225 meters! A new record!" he shouted in excitement.

"Good," the physicist said calmly. "Now answer your phone."

Only then did Kyohei realize that his phone was still ringing. He
fished it out of his pocket and noticed the incoming call was a video
call. He pressed the button to accept and stared at the screen.

"Hey!" On his screen he could see a glimmering undersea world
of reds, blues, and greens. The seafloor looked like a massive stained-
glass window. The water was perfectly clear, and light from the sun
above refracted in a hundred different angles, each creating a different color.

"Well?" Yukawa asked.

Kyohei showed him the phone screen. The faintest hint of a smile
came to the physicist's face. He gave a satisfied nod. "I'd say our experiment was a success."

SIXTEEN

Detective Isobe from the prefectural police's homicide division had a face permanently set to scowl. He had square, blocky features, with plenty of padding at the cheeks, and both his eyebrows and eyes were thin as threads. On the rare occasions when he did crack a smile, it carried the promise of reckless ambition and cunning schemes.

Isobe had arrived at the Hari Police Department with three of his subordinates, "For the time being," he announced. "If we do set up a task force here, I'll be bringing in at least fifty others," he said, his chest puffing out a little, though, at his rank, the chances that all fifty of them would actually be under his command were slim.

Okamoto merely smiled and promised they would be ready.

Isobe's advance group had arrived with orders to ascertain the details surrounding the discovery of the body. Motoyama, Hashigami, and Nishiguchi were all summoned to the meeting room to deliver the briefing, though Motoyama did most of the talking. He explained the ins and outs of the case and gave them an idea of the overall timeline of events following the discovery, while Isobe listened, arms folded tight across his chest. The narrowness of Isobe's eyes made it difficult to tell whether he was sleeping or not. Only his occasional nod gave any indication he was listening.

"We're still unclear what the connection between Mr. Tsukahara and Hari Cove might be," Motoyama concluded. "Nor are we entirely sure of the reason behind his interest in the undersea mining talks."

Isobe groaned and his eyes opened wider as he scanned the faces of the three detectives. "So, how sure are they about this?"

"Sorry?" Motoyama asked. "How sure is who about what?"

"The widow and this director from Tokyo. How sure are they that it was murder?"

"Well . . ." Motoyama began, shooting a look at Okamoto, whose eyes were fixed firmly on the floor. "We didn't find anything particularly suspicious in our examination of the scene," Motoyama continued. "There were no signs of a struggle, nor any other visible evidence of injury."

"But this director noticed something you didn't, right? That's why he ordered the autopsy?"

Okamoto looked up. "We're not entirely sure that's what happened—"

"Then what happened?"

"Well, the deceased, Mr. Tsukahara, was the director's superior officer in Tokyo. So, I think he just wanted to double check everything, you know."

"Which is why we're here," Isobe growled. "Just to get this straight, you didn't order an autopsy yourselves because you didn't think you'd find anything, correct? You think it was just an accident."

Okamoto and Motoyama sat silently.

Isobe shook his head and muttered under his breath, "Great."

"That Isobe guy's got a bad reputation," Hashigami said, leaning on the window as he looked outside at the passing scenery.

"How so?" Nishiguchi asked, fiddling with the tab on the can of a vending machine coffee.

The two detectives had boarded at Central Hari Station. The train car was empty, so they were sitting across from each other in a booth seat meant for four.

"Let's see, he's ambitious, a bit of a manipulator, and a brownnoser to boot. The whiff of homicide in this case has got him all excited. Great chance for a promotion."

"That was him excited? He looked pretty grumpy to me."

Hashigami waved a finger. "He was just putting that on. I bet you ten to one he's back at the prefectural office right now, delivering his report so energetically the spit's flying out of his mouth."

If Isobe wanted this to be murder, that explained why he'd been so irritated with Okamoto and Motoyama's insistence that it was an accident.

The train made its way along the coastal line, arriving at Hari Coast Station. Neither of the detectives moved to get up. They would be going one stop further, to East Hari.

The day Tsukahara attended the DESMEC hearing, he'd taken a taxi to the community center. They'd since tracked down the taxi driver, and he said he'd gotten a call from the dispatcher for pickup at East Hari Station, despite the fact that Hari Cove Station was much closer, a fact that had been written on the attendance voucher in Tsukahara's possession. So Nishiguchi and Hashigami were on their way to do some questioning and find out exactly why he'd been way out in East Hari the morning of his death.

East Hari Station had been built a ways inland, with a straight road leading from the front of the station toward the coast. A few side streets led off to local points of interest: a rose garden, a music box museum, a museum of curios and trompe l'oeil paintings—all attractions planned in previous decades to make up for the town's distance from the seashore. Few had been successful. Most of the small shops along the main road had their shutters closed, making it hard to tell which were open.

"Compared to this place, Central Hari's a metropolis," Hashigami commented as they walked. "At least there you see people on the street. This is a ghost town."

Still, they were successful in finding a few shops that were open for business. They split up to ask questions, each carrying a photograph of Tsukahara. Nishiguchi was the first to catch a break: an old woman who worked at a shop with rows of dried seafood on display recognized Tsukahara's face. She said he'd stopped by the day before.

"He wanted to know the way to Marine Hills," she told him.

"Marine Hills?"

A smile formed in the wrinkles of the woman's face. "The summer resort place. They built it some time ago. Don't think many people are up there now."

Nishiguchi got directions and gave Hashigami a call. They took a side street and began heading up a long, gentle slope.

"Come to think of it, I've heard of this place," Hashigami said. "Some big real estate place threw down a bunch of homes. Only ended up selling a few of them. It was a big loss."

"Do you think Tsukahara had an interest in failed real estate deals?" Nishiguchi wondered out loud.

"Everyone's got to have a hobby."

Eventually, the first of the homes came into view. No doubt they seemed like the peak of luxury at the time they'd been built. Now they looked painfully run down and dilapidated.

A man in his fifties wearing a straw hat was clipping grass by the side of the road. Hashigami called out to him, and he introduced himself as an employee of the real estate company.

"All the homes are for sale as far as I know, not that anyone's buying. Guess they figure they at least need to keep the grass cut, just in case."

Hashigami showed him the photo of Tsukahara.

"Oh yeah, I seen that guy just the other day," the man said immediately. "He was checking out Senba's house. That's why I noticed him."

"Senba's house?"

The man pointed off into the distance. "See that white one there, up on the slope? That's Senba's old house." He turned back to face the detectives, and added, "You know—Senba, the murderer."

SEVENTEEN

"Hey, Kusanagi, I found it."

Kusanagi leaned back and swiveled around in his chair. Kaoru Utsumi was approaching, a folder in her hand.

"Oh, thanks. What was the case?"

"Wouldn't it be quicker to read it yourself?"

"I'll look over the details later. Give me the short version."

Utsumi leaned on a nearby desk, staring down at Kusanagi. "You're feisty today," she said.

"Of course I'm feisty. This is on orders from the director."

"I understand, except for the part where I'm your assistant all of a sudden."

"They said I was allowed to deputize whomever I needed."

"So why me?"

Kusanagi grinned and looked up at her. "I told you Yukawa was there, didn't I?"

"Which is why they've picked you. Still missing the connection to me."

"It's pretty obvious. He's not going to drop everything to help us with the investigation, so your job is to win him over."

Utsumi scowled. "I'm not sure I'm qualified."

"You'll be fine. He won't listen to me, but if you come crying to him, he'll fold. I guarantee it."

"I have to put on a show, now?"

"I'm sure you'll do whatever the situation demands. Now, please, the case? We don't have a lot of time."

Utsumi sighed and glanced down at the folder in her hand. "Name: Hidetoshi Senba. Arraigned on charges of murder sixteen years ago, and sentenced to eight years in prison. The murder took place on a street on the west side of Tokyo."

"On the street? Was it a fight?"

Utsumi shook her head. "The victim's name was Nobuko Miyake, forty years old at the time. She'd worked for years as a nightclub hostess but was unemployed at the time of her death. Senba was an old acquaintance, and they went drinking the night before he killed her. Apparently, he asked her to return some money he'd loaned her, and she played dumb, saying she didn't remember any loan. The next day, he went to meet her and threatened her with a knife, saying he'd kill her if she didn't return the money. Instead of getting scared, she laughed at him; he lost his temper and stabbed her. That's the digest version."

Kusanagi crossed his arms behind his head and leaned back in his chair. "Seems pretty clear-cut. Nothing too newsworthy there. Did he go on the lam or something?"

"No. They arrested him two nights later."

The report of a woman found lying on the street in a residential area of Ogikubo had come in at around ten o'clock on the night of March 10. By the time the police arrived, she was already dead. She had multiple stab wounds to the chest. She was carrying a driver's license, making identification easy. Some simple canvassing revealed that she'd been drinking the night before at one of her usual hangouts with a middle-aged man who hadn't been there in several years. That was Senba.

They discovered an old business card of his upon searching the victim's apartment. Apparently, he'd been a regular back when she was a hostess. After suffering some business losses, he'd moved back to his wife's hometown for a period of time before returning to Tokyo. His residence at the time was a two-story apartment on the east side of Tokyo.

The detective who'd paid Senba a visit noticed something odd about his behavior and asked if he might look inside his apartment. Senba refused, so the detective left, but lingered nearby in order to keep an eye on Senba's apartment.

Eventually, Senba emerged with a small bag in his hand. The detective followed him, and when Senba paused by a nearby river and looked around, the detective approached and called out to him. Senba immediately broke into a run. Though it was close, in the end the detective caught up to him, and he was put under arrest.

A bloody knife was found inside Senba's bag, and it didn't take long for the labs to confirm that it was a match for the one that killed Nobuko Miyake.

"The detective that caught Senba by the river that day was none other than the late Masatsugu Tsukahara, the subject of our current investigation."

Kusanagi shrugged. "Any detective who was refused entry to someone's apartment would suspect something was up. So, was Tsukahara in charge of the interrogation, too?"

"Yes, according to the record."

"An eight-year sentence . . . which means he's out by now. The real question is why Tsukahara went to his old house."

The call had come from a Detective Nishiguchi in Hari about an hour earlier. Nishiguchi found out about the house and its former occupant, but they had no files for the case in their local offices, thus the request.

"You think he just stopped in on his way?" Utsumi wondered out loud.

"What do you mean?"

"I mean, maybe he was on his way to the hearing in Hari Cove, and just decided to take a little detour to see where the man he'd once arrested used to live?"

Kusanagi groaned. "It's a bit of a stretch. I can understand if the man was living there, or maybe his family, but an empty house? That, and it was already for sale at the time of the murder. Hardly seems worth a visit."

"Yeah, you're right," Utsumi agreed, letting go of the theory with uncharacteristic ease.

"Anyway, send those files on to them, and let's get that address."

"Hidetoshi Senba's current address, I take it?"

"You're on the ball, Detective."

Kusanagi's phone rang. It was an unregistered number. He answered.

"It's Tatara. Got a moment?"

"Sure, of course," he said, straightening a little in his chair.

"I got a call from the lab. They found a cause of death."

"Yeah?"

"You're going to be surprised. It was carbon monoxide poisoning."

Kusanagi gasped, despite himself.

"Apparently, it was really hard to pin down, so they ran every blood test in the book. That's when they discovered levels of carboxyhemoglobin well above the lethal amount. It would've taken him only about fifteen minutes to die after he hit saturation. Also, they found traces of sleeping pills."

This fit a common suicide profile, of course, except people who committed suicide by carbon monoxide poisoning rarely then jumped off of a seawall.

"I'll inform the guys at the Shizuoka PD. And I've had them send a copy of the report to the locals, too. If anyone calls, be sure to tell them," Tatara said quickly. Kusanagi could hear the sound of people in the background—the buzz of another police station, perhaps.

"Can I ask a question, Director?"

"Sure. Make it quick."

"You were in the same division with Tsukahara sixteen years ago, correct?"

"Yeah, what about it?"

"Do you happen to remember a murderer you picked up around then, a man by the name of Senba?"

"Hidetoshi Senba?"

Kusanagi was startled by the director's quick response. Of all the cases he must've seen in the intervening time, something about this one must've stuck in his memory.

"Yes, he killed a former hostess."

"What about him?"

Kusanagi related what he had heard from Nishiguchi. Tatara was silent for a moment. "Listen," he said, "I'm over at the Shinagawa Police Department. You mind coming down here?"

EIGHTEEN

Narumi was getting the dining room ready for Yukawa's dinner when Kyohei showed up.

"Can I eat out here too?"

"In the dining room?" Narumi turned to face her cousin. "You want to eat with Mr. Yukawa?"

"He said he didn't mind. And I'll carry out my own food."

"Well, I guess it would be okay."

She'd heard the two had been out somewhere playing together most of the day, and they both had bad sunburns to prove it.

She'd just finished putting out Yukawa's trays when he showed up with a plastic bag filled with fireworks.

"Looks delicious," he said, looking at the cold vegetables with shrimp. He sat down at the table.

"I'm sorry we don't have more to offer."

"Don't be silly. I'm starting to think I might need to go on a diet after this trip." The physicist smiled.

Kyohei arrived, carrying his own tray with some egg over a ball of rice. He carefully set it down on the table across from Yukawa.

"That looks pretty good too," the physicist remarked.

The front desk buzzer sounded, so Narumi said, "Enjoy your meal," and excused herself.

Nishiguchi was in the lobby. He raised a hand in greeting, though he didn't smile.

"Something more about Mr. Tsukahara?" Narumi asked.

"Something I need your help with, actually," Nishiguchi said, licking his lips before continuing. "I was hoping I could look inside the building a bit?"

"You want to see Mr. Tsukahara's room?"

"Er, no, actually, the entire building."

"What for?" Narumi asked, a wrinkle forming between her eyebrows.

Nishiguchi grimaced and glanced outside. Her eyes followed him out to the front and she stiffened. There was a line of men outside in dark blue police uniforms.

"Who are they?" she asked, her voice a little quieter.

"The forensics team from the prefectural police. I'm sorry, I can't go into any more detail about this. If now doesn't work, I can't force you to let us in, but we'd just be back later with a warrant. But if we could just get this finished with now . . ."

Nishiguchi was clearly uncomfortable. Narumi gave him another look, then said, "I'll go talk to my parents. Hang on." She disappeared into the back.

Shigehiro and Setsuko were just sitting down to dinner in the living room. Their chopsticks stopped in midair when Narumi told them what was going on.

"What's left to see? Weren't they all over the place yesterday?" Shigehiro asked, disgruntled.

"He won't tell me. What should I say?"

Shigehiro looked at his wife, then got to his feet.

"I'll go too," Setsuko said, and so the three of them went back out front to talk to the detective.

Back in the lobby, several of the officers had come inside. They were all wearing their hats and carrying bags of various equipment.

Shigehiro asked for an explanation, and Nishiguchi said more or less exactly what he had just told Narumi moments before. The other men were already looking around, scanning every visible inch with their eyes.

"Might you be more specific about where you want to look? I'm just worried about disturbing our guest," Shigehiro said.

One of the men in the hats took a step forward. "We'd like to see the kitchen first, if possible."

"The kitchen's back there," Shigehiro said, pointing past the counter. The man nodded and began taking off his shoes. Immediately, the others stepped in beside him and took off their shoes. A few went into the kitchen, and Setsuko followed after them.

Another of the men from forensics looked between Shigehiro and Narumi. "Can I see the boiler room?"

"That's downstairs," Shigehiro said, walking ahead with his cane. "This way." He went behind the counter and opened the door to the stairs.

Another man approached Narumi. "Mind showing me the room the victim was staying in?"

Narumi nodded and fetched the key from behind the counter.

NINETEEN

"There are essentially two kinds of fireworks, but while they operate by the same basic principles, the method of propulsion is slightly different. The first, called an aerial shell, works a bit like a cannon. For example, take that straw." Yukawa paused here to point at the straw in Kyohei's glass of cola. "If you stuck a wad of tissue paper into one end of that straw and blew on the other, the wad of paper would go flying in the opposite direction, correct? With aerial shells, you place them onto a mortar tube launch pad, then stick a lifting charge underneath. The force and the gas pressure from the lifting charge is what sends the firework up into the sky. With the second type, a skyrocket, the rocket itself explodes, sending a spray of sparks beneath it, vaulting it into the air. It's just like the water rocket, except with gunpowder in place of water and air pressure."

Yukawa ate while he spoke, barely pausing for bites. The smoothness with which he was able to give his explanation even while swallowing impressed Kyohei more than what he was actually saying.

"So the fireworks you brought are skyrockets, not the aerial things?"

"Shells, yes. Real aerial shells aren't purchasable without a license, and you need to be a registered pyrotechnician to get one of those."

They had stopped by the convenience store on the way back from the ocean to buy the stash of fireworks. It hadn't been Kyohei's idea— he had only mentioned setting them off with his uncle the night before.

Kyohei had just finished his rice and was drinking his cola when one of the doors to the dining room opened and a man wearing a blue uniform and a hat poked his head in.

"Oh! Excuse me," he said, immediately leaving and closing the door behind him.

Kyohei blinked. "Who do you think that was?"

"With that uniform, he's in forensics. They must be back to do more investigating," Yukawa said.

A few moments later, Narumi came with some tea. She apologized to Yukawa for the intrusion.

"Any idea what they're looking for?" he asked.

"I'm not sure, but they seem interested in anything that can generate heat."

"Such as?"

"Well, they wanted to make sure that all the burners in the kitchen worked, things like that."

"That's odd. I fail to see the connection with an accident down by the ocean."

"Well, the police say it's related, but they won't tell me more than that."

Yukawa sipped his tea and said only, "That *is* how they operate."

They left the dining room after dinner and ran into several men dressed like the one before, wandering around the halls of the inn. Kyohei and Yukawa were stepping out the front door when the doorway to the basement stairs opened and Shigehiro appeared. "More fireworks?" he asked.

"Yeah. Mind if we borrow your bucket?"

"Not at all," Shigehiro said, his eyes going to the plastic bag in Yukawa's hands. "Looks like you got some shells in there," he said.

"Technically they're skyrockets—I hope it's okay?"

Shigehiro grinned a little sheepishly and scratched his bald head. "Well, we got away with it last night, but really, the fire department only wants you to set off fireworks right by the ocean. Guess they're worried about brushfires. Normally I wouldn't give it a second thought, but with our guests tonight . . ."

"I understand completely," Yukawa said. "Wouldn't want any flying into the inn by mistake. We'll hold off on the skyrockets tonight," Yukawa said. Kyohei nodded.

They stepped outside and went around to the back of the inn where there was a small clearing between the building and the woods.

Kyohei was about to light a sparkler, but Yukawa stopped him. "Can you explain the basic principle of how fireworks work?"

"Well, it's just gunpowder stuck on a stick, right?"

"If it were, it would explode as soon as you lit it." Yukawa pulled something white from his pocket—a ball of cotton, which he placed on the ground. From his other pocket, he took a nail and some sandpaper. He began sanding the nail above the ball of cotton, so that little black specks of metal began to accumulate below.

"Now we light it," Yukawa said, touching the flame of a disposable lighter to the ball.

The ball caught flame immediately, sending up tiny sparks. Kyohei shouted with surprise.

"Even metal that doesn't normally burn will ignite under the proper conditions. Fireworks are essentially metal, several kinds mixed together."

"Why do they use different kinds?"

"Good question. Let's try lighting one of the sparklers," Yukawa said, holding out his lighter.

Kyohei lit the sparkler in his hand and watched as multicolored sparks began to fly from the tip. As the sparkler burned, the color of the sparks changed.

"The blue sparks are copper, green is barium. Red sparks are strontium, and yellow are sodium. All metals. As you can see, each metal and metallic compound gives off a distinct color when it burns. This is called a flame reaction," Yukawa explained, his quiet voice at odds with the noisily burning sparkler. "Fireworks use this effect to—" Yukawa's voice trailed off as his eyes went upward.

Two forensics officers were coming down the fire escape on the backside of the inn. They looked in Kyohei and Yukawa's direction and nodded their heads.

"I wonder where they were. I didn't see them until just now."

"Probably up on the roof. There's a chimney up there."

"Oh?" said Yukawa, raising an eyebrow.

One of the men, the one wearing glasses, walked over to them.

"Sorry to interrupt you. You're the guest staying here?" he asked Yukawa.

"Yes, I am."

"I was wondering if I could have a few words," he said, pulling something out of his breast pocket.

"You don't need to show me your badge, I know you're a police officer. How can I help?" Yukawa asked.

"You've been staying here for the past two days?"

"That's correct. I checked in the night before last."

"Right. Has anything unusual happened during your stay at the inn?"

Yukawa made a face as though he didn't understand the question. "If you mean what happened with the guest falling on the rocks, I did hear about that."

"Not that, I meant anything unusual happening in the inn itself. Did you experience any strange physical sensations, smell any odd smells. Anything like that?"

"Sensations? Smells?" Yukawa shook his head. "I can't say I noticed either of those, sorry."

"I see. Thanks for your time," the man said, turning to walk away.

"Aren't you going to talk to him?" Yukawa said. The men turned and saw Yukawa pointing at Kyohei.

"Er, right," the man said, looking a little bewildered. He took a step toward Kyohei. "How about you? Did you notice anything strange?"

Kyohei shook his head without saying anything.

The man nodded, bowed curtly to Yukawa, and left.

Yukawa looked back up at the inn for a moment, then turned back to Kyohei. "Where was I?"

"You just told me why fireworks change color."

"Right. Let's discuss the physics of the black snake firework, then," Yukawa said, reaching back into his bag.

TWENTY

It was a little after eight o'clock when Narumi got to the bar. Sawamura was already waiting for her, his laptop on the table in front of him.

"Sorry I'm late," she said, sitting down.

"No worries. The police still there?"

"They only just left."

"What are they looking for, anyway?" Sawamura asked with a frown.

Narumi gave him the same explanation she had given Yukawa.

Sawamura's frown deepened. "But why? Didn't he fall off the sea-wall and hit his head? Doesn't seem like that would require a whole lot of investigation."

All Narumi could do was shrug.

"I'm just as confused as anyone, really," she said. "Still, I have a feeling things will just blow over."

"How's that?"

"Well, it wasn't meant for my ears, but—"

Narumi had just collected Yukawa's tray from dinner and was heading back to the kitchen when she overheard several men inside talking. She couldn't hear everything they said, but the general consensus appeared to be that there was nothing out of order in the inn whatsoever. As the police made to leave, Nishiguchi had whispered in her ear, "Hopefully we've put this thing to rest for good."

Sawamura gave a sigh of relief, even as he shook his head and muttered, "Who knows what the police are thinking? I sure don't."

They began going over their notes from the hearing the other day, but neither of them was able to put their heads into the work. Eventually, Sawamura said, "Let's call it a day," and closed his computer. "What do you do at your place once the summer is over, anyway?" he asked. "I know a lot of the inns close for the season."

Narumi told him that her parents were considering shutting down for good, and he didn't seem surprised.

"Times are tough, huh. Now what are you going to do for work?"

"I'll find something. I figured I'd have to search for a job come fall at any rate."

"I have an idea," Sawamura said, a serious look in his eyes. "How about working as my assistant?"

"What? What do you mean?"

"Well, my writing gig keeps me on the road a lot, but my position with Save the Cove means I also need to be near my base of operations to keep in contact with everyone. Basically, I need someone to hold down the fort when I'm out. I'm thinking I'll convert a part of my house to an office, and if you could come work there, it'd be a big help. I should be able to pay you enough to make it worth your while."

Narumi's eyes dropped to the table. She hesitated, uncertain what to say. It wasn't a bad offer. In fact, she was immensely grateful. She wouldn't have to leave town, and she could devote herself to protecting the ocean. But she was worried about what might be behind the offer.

"Well? What do you think?" Sawamura asked with a smile. "I know I've said this before, but I think you and I could be great partners. An unbeatable duo!"

Narumi smiled but her eyes wandered.

Sawamura had a way of keeping things vague. When he talked

about partners, did he really mean just work partners, or was there a more personal agenda as well? It was hard to tell. No, he *made* it hard to tell.

They'd only been working together for a short while before she had sensed a personal interest from him. She'd pretended not to notice. She respected him as a journalist and an activist, but she just couldn't see him as a romantic partner.

Time had passed, and Sawamura had begun saying things that, depending on how you interpreted them, could be taken as a kind of confession of his interest in her. Maybe he thought that by dropping little hints, he could get her to start thinking of him not just as a friend, but as a man.

"I'll have to think about it," she said.

"Of course, take your time."

He smiled, but Narumi could feel the added weight in the air.

Back at the inn, she found Yukawa pacing in the lobby. He was carrying a bottle of red wine in his hand.

"Ah, you've come at the perfect time," he said. "I was hoping I could borrow a bottle opener."

"Where'd you get the wine?"

"I had it sent from the university. Looks like I'll be here a bit longer."

That explained the box with the FRAGILE sticker she had seen in his room.

She returned with a bottle opener from the kitchen and handed it to him.

"Care to join me?" he invited her.

"Sure, why not?"

"Good wine loves good company."

Narumi went back to the kitchen and took two of the few wineglasses they had down from the shelf.

They sat down at the table in the lobby and toasted each other.

She took a sip, detecting an oaky fragrance as the flavor spread through her mouth. She swallowed, leaving only a faint, pleasant sweetness on her tongue that made her want to take another sip.

The label on the bottle read "Sadoya"—a winery in Yamanashi, Yukawa informed her.

"I didn't think any Japanese wine tasted this good," Narumi said.

"Japanese people are oddly uninformed about what is good about Japan," Yukawa said, swishing the wine around in his glass. "There are a lot of people out in the countryside doing their darndest to make amazing things, but no one notices. Tokyoites write off this wine as 'too local' without even tasting it. Much like you've devoted your life to protecting Hari Cove, when an outsider might say why bother when there are plenty of other beautiful coastlines around?"

"So what we're doing here doesn't mean anything? Is that what you're saying?"

"Not at all. To the contrary, it's quite important, and should be recognized as such. In fact, just today at noon Kyohei and I saw the sight that gives Hari Cove its name. The sparkling formations on the seafloor—it was remarkably beautiful."

Yukawa's words sounded heartfelt. Narumi made another mental mark in his favor.

The phone behind the counter began to ring. Narumi stood up, glancing at the clock. It was almost ten at night. They rarely received calls this late.

"Hello, Green Rock Inn."

"Sorry to call so late," said a man on the other end of the line. "I was hoping I could talk with one of your guests, by the name of Yukawa? Tell him it's Kusanagi."

TWENTY-ONE

"So we've concluded that none of the heating or cooking appliances present at the Green Rock Inn were malfunctioning. Though everything we saw had been in operation for some time, some of them more than twenty years, we found nothing out of order. A thorough search of Masatsugu Tsukahara's room also revealed no traces of anything having been burned, such as charcoal briquettes, making the possibility of carbon monoxide poisoning slight in the extreme."

The man dispassionately giving his report on the team's findings was the chief forensics officer from the prefectural police. Nishiguchi sat in the corner of the conference room, rubbing a hand over his chest. He had been too worried to sleep much the night before. Though he had been with the forensics team at the inn until nearly eight, they hadn't told him anything, leaving him to infer everything from their tone of voice. Not that anything they said made him think they'd found a problem. His main cause for worry was that he had stupidly confided this to Narumi, which meant he had to spend the entire morning worrying that something might actually come up.

"So the inn had nothing to do with it. Which makes sense, because you'd think their first reaction if somebody got poisoned would be to call an ambulance," one of the officers said, a section chief from prefectural homicide named Hozumi. He had a thick head of black hair, with a few white streaks through the bushy mustache beneath his hawklike nose.

Everyone was taking the autopsy report from Tokyo very seriously. Yet, while their initial assumption that Tsukahara had slipped and fallen to his death by accident had been thrown out the window, they lacked any evidence indicating murder. Without any evidence of murder, there was no official homicide task force.

"Have we entirely ruled out the possibility of this being an accident?" Hozumi asked the room.

"I think it's safe to say there is a zero possibility he developed acute carbon monoxide poisoning on top of that seawall," the forensics chief said. "I looked over the initial report from the team that examined the body as it was found, and there were no traces of anything having been burned, nor is it particularly easy to poison oneself by burning charcoal outside."

"Is it possible he breathed in enough carbon monoxide to poison himself somewhere else, then went to the seawall, where he expired? I've heard of delayed symptoms in these cases."

"Er, regarding that," Isobe said, gingerly raising his hand. "I had one of my men talk to an expert yesterday." He turned and glared at a young officer sitting in the corner of the room.

The officer stood and pulled out a notepad. "I spoke with Professor Yamada at the medical university, and apparently there have been instances where someone with light symptoms becomes confused, occasionally suffering severe mood swings and other personality changes. This can happen particularly in cases where carboxyhemoglobin concentration is above ten percent. However, the autopsy report showed a concentration so far above ten percent that it would be practically impossible for him to have moved to another location on his own. It was Professor Yamada's opinion that he likely expired in the place where he was poisoned."

"In other words," Hozumi said, "he got poisoned someplace else. Anyone have any ideas on how somebody could've poisoned him intentionally?"

"The most orthodox method of carbon monoxide poisoning would be to situate oneself in a small, confined space, like an automobile, and burn charcoal. There was a bit of a boom in suicides using this method after an Internet post labeling it a 'painless suicide' gained some traction."

"Which reminds me," Hozumi said, his mustache twitching. "Did the autopsy report also mention sleeping pills? Is it possible that our perpetrator here forced the victim into the car, force-fed him some pills, then burned some charcoal?"

"Then, after ascertaining he was poisoned, they dropped him from the seawall," Isobe concluded. "After which the perpetrator could simply drive off. I suppose that would make sense."

Hozumi nodded. "It does. Unfortunately, there's no evidence to support that. So it's still impossible to say whether the carbon monoxide poisoning was done intentionally by a third party or was the work of the victim himself."

"Absolutely, sir," Isobe quickly agreed.

"And there were no records of unusual calls having been made from the victim's phone?"

"That's correct. We checked with the phone company too, just in case someone erased his history. There was nothing."

This meeting is all kinds of wrong, Nishiguchi thought. So far, it seemed, the only people saying anything substantive about the case were from the prefectural police. Motoyama, Chief Okamoto, and even Hari police commissioner Tomita were sitting like obedient dogs, waiting for scraps at the table.

"What's this about the victim taking a detour to see the house of someone he arrested?" Hozumi said suddenly, turning toward the Hari contingent. Nishiguchi stiffened in his chair.

"Ah, right," Motoyama said. "You have a report for us, Detective Nishiguchi?"

Nishiguchi stood, opening his notebook. "The victim visited a house in East Hari, part of a summer home development. The house was purchased by one Hidetoshi Senba, and was his primary residence for some time, until he put it up for sale and moved to Tokyo for work reasons. There, he was arrested for murder by Detective Tsukahara. We've requested the case files from Tokyo, and they should already have been sent to Chief Isobe."

Isobe opened the folder on the table in front of him and showed it to Hozumi.

"So a man from the countryside goes to the big city and stabs a former hostess . . . that's so straightforward it's a little sad," Hozumi said, his lack of interest evident.

"I spoke with the widow over the phone," Isobe added. "She said he frequently wondered about the people he'd arrested. It's not inconceivable that he decided to drop in on Senba's old residence while he was in the area."

Hozumi rubbed his jaw and nodded. "He wouldn't be the first detective like that. Nor would this Senba guy be the first perp to hold a grudge against his arresting officer. Find out where he is and what he's up to."

"Right away," Isobe said, turning to one of his men and passing the order down with a nod of his head.

"Well, Commissioner?" Hozumi said, turning to the ever-taciturn Tomita. "I'll talk to the chief back at the Shizuoka PD, but it looks like we've at least got a case of an abandoned body. That should be cause enough to set up an investigative task force here."

Tomita looked like he had been daydreaming. He jerked upright in his chair and, mouth hanging half open, rapidly nodded his head. "Right, right, of course. Might be a good idea," he said.

"Then let's get that started today. We'll get all of Isobe's men over here, for starters. We can add more as needed. Sound good?"

"Right, understood. We'll help however we can."

Nishiguchi gave a light sigh, watching the commissioner kowtow.

His cell phone buzzed once in his jacket pocket—an incoming e-mail. Sliding it out of his pocket, he held it underneath the table and opened his mailbox, and his pulse quickened when he saw who it was from: Narumi Kawahata.

TWENTY-TWO

Kusanagi parked his beloved Nissan by the side of the road and checked the GPS screen. Houses stood on both sides of the winding single-lane road, small fields and patches of forest between them.

"It should be around here somewhere," he muttered. The houses had been built a distance from the road, making it hard to check the names and numbers.

"I'll get out and look," Utsumi offered from the passenger seat.

Kusanagi pulled out the ashtray and stuck a cigarette in his mouth. He liked being in his own car, where no one could tell him not to smoke. He cracked open the window, and warm air spilled in.

The two detectives were in Hatogaya, a small city north of Tokyo, where Masatsugu Tsukahara had lived.

"There's something there," Tatara had announced when Kusanagi went to see him at the police station in Shinagawa. "Hidetoshi Senba's a part of this," he had explained after Kusanagi shot him an uncomprehending look.

"I went drinking with Tsukahara just before he retired. I remember asking him which case he remembered the most. I was just making conversation. I figured since Tsukahara had a nearly photographic memory, he'd tell me he remembered them all the same or something like that. Except, that's not what he said."

Tatara paused, remembering. " 'Hidetoshi Senba,' that's what he said after thinking about it for a little while. Of course, I had completely forgotten the name, so I had no idea what he was talking about. It was only when he mentioned the former hostess that things started to come trickling back. It was a quick case, with no trouble in court at all, so I asked him, why that one?"

But Tsukahara hadn't answered Tatara's question. He just shook his head and told him he was only kidding.

"There are plenty of detectives who remember every case they've been on, big or small. I'll bet most of them couldn't tell you why, either. So I didn't press him on it. But now that we know he paid Senba's old house a visit, I'm starting to think there was more to it. I need you to look into this."

Kusanagi tried to go straight to the source and set up a meeting with Senba by himself, but his whereabouts proved hard to pin down. Utsumi had found out that when he got out of prison, an acquaintance had gotten him a job working at a recycling center in Adachi, but the company had gone out of business soon afterward. No one knew what happened to Senba after that.

Which left Tsukahara as their only lead. If he was that obsessed with Senba, it was possible they'd been in contact. Kusanagi would've preferred to check his notebooks or phone, but both of those were being held at the Hari Police Department.

Utsumi came jogging back to the car. "I found it, just a little up ahead. There's a place to park."

"Thanks," Kusanagi said, releasing his parking brake.

Masatsugu Tsukahara's house was a simple, wooden, two-story affair. His widow, Sanae, let them in, showing them to a room with a view out on a small rear garden. There was a small alcove for the family altar in the room, with pictures of people Kusanagi assumed were Sanae's and her husband's deceased parents. He wondered how soon Tsukahara's photo would be joining them.

"The mortician will be releasing the body to me tomorrow," Sanae said, her voice as thin as her features.

Kusanagi expressed his condolences before breaking the news that there was an increasing possibility that her husband's death had not been a simple accident. Sanae didn't seem surprised.

"I thought it might've been something like that the moment I heard he died. It just didn't make sense, him getting drunk and falling off some rocks. . . ." She shook her head. "That wasn't him."

Though her tone was soft, it held absolute conviction.

"Do you have any idea why your late husband might've gone to the house of a man he once arrested, one Hidetoshi Senba?" Kusanagi asked.

She frowned and shook her head. "The local police called and asked me the same question when they found out, too. I know he often thought about his old cases, but I never heard the name Senba from him myself. To my knowledge, they never corresponded."

"Did your husband ever keep case files around the house?"

She shook her head again. "He got rid of all of those when he retired. I remember him saying he didn't need them anymore. Since he wasn't a police officer anymore, keeping them would be an invasion of privacy."

Kusanagi nodded, a picture of the old, steel-eyed detective forming in his mind.

"But there's a chance he might've left something in the study. Would you like to take a look?"

"If I might, yes," Kusanagi replied immediately.

The study was a small room on the second floor. A wooden desk sat near a window, with a bookshelf beside it. Most of the books were historical fiction. There wasn't a single mystery in sight, let alone crime fiction or anything to do with the police. On the lowest shelf sat a thick phone book.

With Sanae's permission, he opened the drawer on the desk, but found nothing bearing any relation to the case.

The phone rang downstairs, and Sanae excused herself to go answer it.

Kusanagi pulled the phone book off the shelf.

"Something catch your eye?" Utsumi asked.

"Well, people usually put these directories by the landline phone— but there isn't even a cordless phone up here."

"Good point."

"Also, this is the phone book for Tokyo, and from last year—well after he retired. Why do you think he needed this anymore?"

Kusanagi rested the phone book on the desk and began leafing through the pages, noticing several had been dog-eared. He opened them to find that most were pages showing budget hotels in To-kyo's Taito and Arakawa wards. In particular, there seemed to be a lot of them with addresses in South Senju, near the Namidabashi Bridge.

Kusanagi exchanged a glance with Utsumi, then he smoothed out the dog-eared pages and closed the book. He'd just put it back on the shelf when he heard footsteps coming up the stairs.

"That was the Hari Police. They called to tell me someone from the prefectural police would be coming to pay me a visit tonight to ask some more things about my husband. What should I tell them?"

"Everything you told us. Just the facts should be fine," Kusanagi said.

"Of course. So, did you find anything?"

"Unfortunately, no," Kusanagi said, shaking his head and standing. "Sorry for the trouble. Just one more thing: I was hoping I could borrow a photograph of your husband. Something that shows his face clearly."

"Why didn't you tell the widow about the telephone book?" Utsumi asked shortly after they got into the car and began driving. Kusanagi was surprised she'd been able to resist the urge to ask so long.

"Because I don't know that it has anything to do with the case.

It's never good to bring unsubstantiated evidence to the bereaved. That's one of the golden rules of police work."

"But you think it does have something to do with our case, don't you?"

"Maybe. What do you think?"

"I think it does."

Kusanagi glanced over at his passenger. "That was quick."

"Well, you have to wonder why Tsukahara would have that phone book after retirement. If it was to look up cheap motels, then I can only think of one possible reason."

"And that is?"

"He was looking for someone," Utsumi said immediately. "Tsukahara was looking for someone without a permanent address. And why would this person not have a permanent address?"

"Because he was unemployed with a criminal record, which prevented him from renting?"

"Think I'm jumping to conclusions?"

"Perhaps. I can't say whether Senba was the one staying in a budget hotel or not, but it's very likely that Tsukahara was doing a little sleuthing in his retirement. Old habits die hard."

If Tsukahara had been on the trail of Senba, then they could pick up where he left off, Kusanagi thought.

"Can I ask you something?"

"What?"

"Are you going to tell the local police about this? If you do, they might help us find Senba."

"They don't know Tokyo like we do."

"So you're not going to tell them about this, or what the director said about Tsukahara remembering Senba's case?"

Kusanagi frowned. "You're awful feisty all of a sudden. Do you have a problem with not telling them?"

"Are we under orders from the director to offer all possible assistance to the prefectural police?"

Kusanagi sighed. "Haphazardly feeding them information isn't going to help solve this case."

"What do you mean?"

"I called the Green Rock Inn last night to talk to Yukawa."

"You called the inn? Why not his cell phone?"

"I tried that first, but he didn't pick up. Apparently, his phone got busted in an experiment—something about shoddy waterproofing. Anyway, I talked to him, and of course he knew about the death, but he didn't know any details beyond the basics. So I explained to him what happened, and how I got put on the case."

"The professor must've been surprised."

"Not really. In fact, not at all. He didn't know that the dead man was a former detective, but he had suspected murder."

"Really? Why was that?"

"The sandal. They found one of the sandals Tsukahara had been wearing on the rocks. But according to Yukawa, the seawall was pretty high—it would've been hard to climb up with sandals on. He said it had bothered him, but he trusted the local police to do their jobs, and didn't want to be a nuisance—his words. So he said nothing." Kusanagi rolled his eyes.

"How like him. Did he say he would help with the investigation?"

Kusanagi put his foot on the brake and slowed down as the light ahead of them turned yellow. They pulled to a stop just before the line, and he turned to face Utsumi. "What do you think he said?"

Utsumi's eyes drifted as she thought. " 'I've had enough of helping with police investigations, thank you very much.' Something like that?"

"That's what you'd expect, right? That's what I expected, at least. But instead, he said he'd do what he could."

Utsumi blinked. "Really?"

"I was surprised too. I almost wanted to ask him why, except I was afraid that might make him change his mind."

"Good call," Utsumi said. "But what does this have to do with not passing along our information to the prefectural police?"

The light turned green, and Kusanagi turned his eyes back to the road. "Just before he hung up, Yukawa said this might be a 'particularly thorny' case. I asked him what he meant, but he didn't give me a straight answer. That's when I knew he'd noticed something other than the sandal. Maybe he hadn't figured it out entirely just yet, but there was definitely something that grabbed his interest about the case."

"He does have a keen eye—maybe he saw something?"

"Something or some*one*. He's got a good eye for people, too, and I'd bet his willingness to get involved is because he knows a person with the key to cracking this puzzle. Which is why I decided to bypass the prefectural police and go straight to Yukawa." Kusanagi glanced over. "Well? Think I'm barking up the wrong tree?"

"No, I think you're right to get Yukawa on board. His insight has helped solve more than a few cases in the past. But I think not sharing information with the prefectural police is a separate matter, no?"

"It's not that I'm not sharing anything with them. It's more case-by-case. Think about it—to the local police, Yukawa is just another civilian. They don't know about his reputation, or even his nickname of Detective Galileo. It would never occur to them to ask him to help with their investigation. Yukawa's powers of perception might be unparalleled, but he can't use them without access to information, and we're the only ones who can give him that. Which means that, with all due apologies to the prefectural police, getting valuable information to Yukawa has to be a top priority. Agreed?"

Kusanagi waited until, out of the corner of his eye, he saw Utsumi nod.

"Besides, given Galileo's predilection for staying completely silent until he's satisfied with his conclusions, we're probably the only ones with the patience to use him in the first place."

"Exactly. We're the hands and the feet of the operation, and he's the brain. As per usual."

It was about twenty minutes later when Kusanagi pulled his car to a stop.

"You have everything we need on Senba, right?" Kusanagi asked. "A photo too, I hope?"

"Yes, though it was taken before he got out of jail."

"That'll do. Take this with you, too." Kusanagi pulled the photo of Tsukahara out of his jacket pocket. "Good luck."

He handed the photo to Utsumi, who stared blankly at it.

Kusanagi pointed out the front window. "Hop to it, recruit. This is the spot."

A sign at the intersection just ahead of them read "Namidabashi Bridge." Billboards and advertisements for cheap hotels were clustered thickly on the streets around them.

"Oh. Right," Utsumi said, grabbing her shoulder bag and opening the door.

"No matter who you're talking to, give them a good look at Tsukahara's face."

Utsumi nodded and pushed the door firmly shut.

TWENTY-THREE

It was a little after three in the afternoon when Nishiguchi brought Isobe and two of his men to the Green Rock Inn. He'd called ahead, so the Kawahatas and Narumi were waiting for them in the lobby when they arrived. They had nervous looks on their faces that only worsened when they saw Isobe's scowl.

Isobe began by questioning them in detail about the night that Tsukahara had disappeared. They must've been sick of telling the same story over and over again, but they answered every question thoroughly, and plainly. Nishiguchi had heard it so many times that he stopped paying attention about halfway through and instead stared at Narumi.

"Well then," Isobe said after they had finished. "Could you show us the room where Mr. Tsukahara was staying?"

Setsuko stood. "I'll be happy to take you. Right this way."

"I'll go too," Shigehiro said, tapping with his cane as he followed Isobe and his men toward the elevator.

"Sorry to have to bother you so much about this," Nishiguchi said to Narumi once they were alone. "The investigation's really scaling up, now that they think it wasn't an accident. And we're getting more and more new people showing up at the department and telling us what to do."

Narumi smiled weakly and shook her head. "It's okay. I should apologize to you for sending you that e-mail. I know you're busy."

Nishiguchi waved a hand dismissively. "Not at all. I mean, I am busy, but it's not like they give me anything important to do. Anyway, what did you want to ask?"

"Well," Narumi said, wetting her lips while she considered her words for a moment. "Remember when you came to borrow our guest ledger because you wanted to find out why Tsukahara chose our inn? Well, I was just wondering if you ever found out."

"Right, that. Actually, I was hoping we could borrow those ledgers for a bit longer. I still haven't gotten through all of them."

"So you haven't found anything yet?"

"Not really. At least, no one who stayed here in the last two years seems to have any connection to Mr. Tsukahara. Maybe he chose the place on a whim. You're listed on the local tourism association's Web site."

"Oh," Narumi said; her eyes went down to the floor.

"Is something bothering you?" Nishiguchi asked.

"Not really," Narumi said, a vague smile on her lips, "but you know we have a university professor staying with us: Mr. Yukawa. Well, he got a phone call the other day. I wasn't trying to eavesdrop, but he was standing at the counter and talking in a really loud voice, so . . ."

Nishiguchi frowned. He knew Yukawa was staying there, because it was on the case file. He might've caught a glimpse of the professor the other day, but he wouldn't be able to identify him in a lineup. Was it possible that Yukawa was somehow involved?

"Anyway, it sounded like the call came from someone in the Tokyo Police Department," Narumi said.

Nishiguchi stiffened. "Are you sure?"

"It was just something he said. 'Why does someone from Tokyo care about a case way out here?' He lowered his voice after that, so I didn't hear anything more, and when I asked him about it, he said the call was from an old college friend. But he didn't tell me what they talked about."

"So this university professor and some detective from Tokyo are old friends?"

"Even if they are friends, isn't it weird for someone from the Tokyo Police Department to call him all the way out here? Mr. Yukawa doesn't have anything to do with the case, right? I started to wonder, because he was asking about us: about the Green Rock Inn, my parents, and me."

Nishiguchi smiled. "I'm no expert on how they do things in Tokyo, but I doubt there's any connection. I'm guessing this detective, or whoever it was, found out that a friend was staying out here and called to get his take on the case. Something like that."

"I don't know . . ." Narumi said, still frowning.

"Well, I wouldn't be worried about it if I were you. It's not good if one of your guests dies suddenly, but it's not your fault, or your parents'. As far as the law's concerned, you're just an onlooker. There's no need to worry," Nishiguchi said.

He finished talking just as the elevator doors opened. Nishiguichi turned in time to see Isobe come out, his men trailing behind him. Isobe was wearing his customary scowl, but he didn't look any more disgruntled than he had before going up to the room.

Behind him, Nishiguchi heard Narumi say, "Welcome back," to someone in the lobby. He turned back around and saw a tall man wearing glasses in the process of taking off his shoes. *Professor Yukawa, I presume.*

Noticing the new arrival, Isobe turned to Setsuko, asking her a quick question before muttering, "Perfect timing," and stepping toward the entrance. "Sorry, might I have a word?" Isobe said, flashing his badge at Yukawa.

"Yes?" Yukawa said, giving him a cold stare.

"I was hoping you could tell me about your whereabouts three nights ago. If you remember."

Yukawa glanced at Narumi for a moment before saying, "From

around eight o'clock to after ten, I was at a bar near the harbor. I ordered edamame, shiokara squid, and shochu on the rocks. Kuro Kirishima, I believe the brand was. At first I was joined by Mrs. Kawahata"—here he indicated Setsuko with a wave of his hand. "And later I was joined by her daughter." He nodded in Narumi's direction.

This was exactly what it said in the police report, of course.

"Did you see any unusual vehicles on your way to or from the bar?"

"Define *unusual*."

"For instance, a vehicle parked by the side of the road with some-one inside."

Yukawa shrugged. "Not that I noticed."

"I see, well, that will be all. Thank you for your cooperation," Isobe said with a nod of his head.

"Do you mind if I ask a question?"

"What's that?"

"Did you find the source of the carbon monoxide?"

Isobe's eyes went wide. "How did you . . ."

"It was easy enough to surmise after seeing the forensics team in here last night. Did you find the source?"

"Well, I'm sorry, but I can't say. That's confidential information," Isobe replied, his scowl deepening.

"Of course, I completely understand," Yukawa said with a cheery smile and headed toward the elevator.

TWENTY-FOUR

Kyohei was almost through the current level of his video game when someone knocked on his door. The momentary distraction broke his focus, and the zombies started pouring out of the woodwork.

"Crap!" he yelped, mashing the controller with his thumbs, but it was too late. Lightly insulting music played, and the meter showed his remaining lives lost a bar.

"That's *so* not fair," he said, glaring at the screen before turning toward the door and shouting, "Come in. It's not locked."

The door opened slowly, and Yukawa poked his face through.

"Oh, hey, Professor," Kyohei said, setting the game controller down. "What's up?"

"May I come in?"

"Sure."

Yukawa walked in, an unreadable expression on his face. He was wearing a dress shirt and his jacket, and had a bag in his hands.

"All done with work?" Kyohei asked.

"For today," Yukawa said, walking over to the window. "Not that I have anything to show for it. It was all preparations *before* preparations for the actual test. You know the expression 'Too many cooks in the kitchen'? Well, that applies here tenfold, and they're not even cooks. More like nosy customers who think they know something about soufflés. That chief technology officer wouldn't know a constructive comment if it . . ." Yukawa trailed off before looking up like he'd suddenly remembered where he was. "Ah, sorry. Didn't mean to be a raincloud."

"No problem," Kyohei said. "Sounds like work sucked."

"Yes. Sucked. A little. Of course, working with other people always involves a certain amount of stress."

"I get that. Even when I'm playing games with my friends, if there's someone I don't get along with very well, I don't like doing co-op mode."

"Pardon? Co-op?"

"Like cooperative—when you play a game with three or four people. Everyone has their own controller and you try to beat the game together."

"Indeed," Yukawa said, looking between Kyohei and the TV screen. "Are you good at games?"

"Pretty good."

"You sound confident," Yukawa said, staring at the screen. "Show me."

"Now?"

"Yes. The game you were just playing."

"I don't like playing with other people watching. Especially grownups."

"None of those adolescent hang-ups of yours. It's a game, play it," Yukawa said, sitting cross-legged on the floor behind Kyohei and folding his arms across his chest.

Kyohei shrugged, picked up the controller, and restarted his game. It took him a few minutes to get over being acutely aware of Yukawa's presence behind him, but once he did, his usual focus returned.

He paused the game after making it through the level he'd died on earlier and looked over his shoulder. "Well, that was it."

Yukawa nodded deeply. "You do appear rather skilled."

"'Appear'? What's that supposed to mean?"

"I don't know how difficult the game is, nor do I have anyone to compare you to. Thus, I lack sufficient data to properly assess your skill."

"You try playing then, Professor," Kyohei said, handing him the controller.

A bewildered look came over Yukawa's face. "I'll pass."

"Why?"

"I prefer my trials and errors in the real world."

"Oh, come on, give it a shot. Or maybe you're chicken." Kyohei grinned.

"I'm not 'chicken.'"

"Then play. None of these adult hang-ups of yours." Kyohei nudged Yukawa in the shoulder with the controller.

Yukawa grabbed it, a reluctant look on his face. "You're going to have to tell me how to play."

"It's easy, just go with the flow," Kyohei said, starting the game over.

"Hey, wait! You can't just throw me to the wolves—" Yukawa squawked as his eyes widened behind his glasses and he stared at the screen.

"Not wolves, zombies," Kyohei said, but the physicist's thumbs were already furiously working the controller. Every muscle in his body was tensed.

Yukawa burned through his allotted three lives in less than a minute. Kyohei rolled on the tatami mats, laughing out loud.

"Wow, you *really* suck! Even my mom's better than you. What was that? I've never even seen anyone bomb so hard."

Yukawa set down the controller, his face expressionless. "That was very informative. As far as this game is concerned, you possess a much greater amount of skill than I do."

Kyohei propped himself up on his elbows. "Sorry, Professor, but I'm not sure you're the one I want grading me on games."

"Speaking of which," Yukawa said, suddenly pointing to a stack of thin notebooks on the table behind them. "What's that?"

Kyohei sat further up and made a bitter face. "Japanese and math."

"Summer homework?"

"Yeah, and that's not even all of it."

Kyohei pulled a cardboard box on the floor closer to him. The package had arrived the day after he got to the inn. It held a few changes of clothes, his games, and all of his dreaded homework.

"I have to do this life schedule thing. It's where you plan out every day, and then you write down whether you did what you said you were going to do. It's a total drag. I also have to do a book report. And then some self-study project . . . I'm not even sure what to do for that. I don't get why they make us do all this stuff anyway. It's supposed to be vacation, right? Don't they know what *vacation* means?"

Yukawa picked up the book of math drills and flipped through the pages. "Looks like you haven't even started yet. Are you sure you'll finish on time?"

"Probably not. I'll get home and Mom will yell at me the day before school starts and I'll do it then. It's easier that way, because in between the yelling she helps me by doing some of the problems."

"I wouldn't call that helping. I'd call that getting in your way," Yukawa said. "She's impeding your academic progress."

"Yeah, but if I didn't do my homework, I'd just get in trouble at school."

"Then get in trouble. You'd learn a valuable lesson."

"Easy for you to say," Kyohei grumbled, reaching out to snatch the book of drills back from Yukawa. Just before his fingers touched the book, Yukawa pulled it away.

"How about I help you with your math? We can probably finish this workbook in two or three days that way."

Kyohei sat up straight. "You're going to do my math?"

"I said help, not do. What I'm offering is instruction. I will teach you how to properly approach the problems, so you can do it yourself."

"You mean like a tutor?"

"I suppose you could call it that."

"Blargh," Kyohei said, making a face. "I didn't come all the way out here just to study."

"You have to do it sometime," Yukawa said, opening the book of drills. " 'Find the sum of the angles of an eighteen-sided polygon,' " he read. "Someday, you're going to have to be able to answer this question on your own. Graduate without learning how to do that, and you'll get yourself into trouble later. The obvious solution is to learn how to solve it now. Besides, I've already helped you complete one of your homework requirements."

"Huh? What's that?"

"The rocket we used to see the bottom of the ocean. That was a perfect self-study project. I still have all the data, you only need to collate it and write it down."

"Hey, you're right. But it was kind of you who did the experiment, Professor. Isn't that cheating?"

"I'm startled at this sudden ethical rigor from someone whose mom does his math homework. Besides, you were a full participant in the rocket experiment. That's not cheating."

"Cool! One down," Kyohei said, pumping his fist enthusiastically.

"You're on a roll. How about another?" Yukawa said, lifting up the book of math drills.

Kyohei wrinkled his nose and scratched his head before shrugging. "Fine. It'll be more fun with you teaching me anyway."

"I guarantee it. Which brings me to a question I had for you. In exchange for me helping you with your studies, I was hoping I could ask a favor."

"Sure. What?"

"Are you familiar with a master key? It's a key that opens all the locks in a hotel or inn such as this."

"You mean the one in my uncle's room? I've seen Narumi going there to grab it."

"That would be the one. I'd like to use it, if I can. Just for a little while, of course."

"Sure, I'll go ask for it," Kyohei said, standing. Yukawa put a hand on his shoulder, stopping him.

"You don't have to get it right now. And I don't want you to ask for it," he said, wetting his lips and lowering his voice, "I want you to steal it."

TWENTY-FIVE

Nishiguchi parted ways with Isobe and made it back to the Hari police station just after eight o'clock in the evening to find it bustling with activity. Apparently, whatever strings needed to be pulled to set up a special investigative task force had been pulled, and everyone with a free hand had been deputized. Officers were carrying computers and office supplies into the main conference room.

Someone tapped him on the shoulder, and he turned to see Hashigami with a gloomy look on his face.

"Stand around like you don't have anything to do and someone's going to put you to work, Nishiguchi. You haven't eaten yet, have you? Let's go."

"You sure we shouldn't stay and lend a hand?"

"There'll be plenty of time for that once the prefectural guys get here. Let's live a little while we can."

Hashigami walked out of the police station without waiting for an answer, so Nishiguchi followed. They went to a small place near the station and Nishiguchi ordered the yakiniku dinner set, fuel for the long slog ahead.

"Well, this case has gone from a simple accident to a full-blown disaster," Hashigami grumbled. "That director from Tokyo threw us a curveball. The prefectural guys can't stop dropping comments about how we screwed up the initial investigation. I mean, who would look at that and say it was something other than an accident? You can bet we'd get in trouble if we called for an autopsy on every single one of our cases." He stabbed at his baked fish with his chopsticks.

"Where did they send you today?" Nishiguchi asked.

"East Hari. I spent the whole day walking around with Shizuoka Prefecture detectives, showing them around."

"Up at that summer colony? Marine Hills, was it?"

"We went there too, but we spent most of our time doing questioning at a different development, where Senba's wife's family lived— the place is a parking lot now."

"Senba's wife was from East Hari?"

"Apparently so," Hashigami said, setting down his chopsticks and pulling his notebook from the jacket he'd draped over the chair next to him. "According to the files we got from Tokyo, Senba was originally from Toyohashi City, down in Aichi. He came up to Tokyo when he got a job, and married a girl from the same company when he was thirty."

Hashigami opened his notebook and showed Nishiguchi a page that read, "Etsuko, maiden name: Hino."

"Wait, so his wife already had her family house in East Hari, but they bought a summer home there too?"

"Not quite. By the time they got married, her old house had already been taken down. She only lived in East Hari through high school. After that they moved to Yokohama. Right after she got married, they lived in Tokyo. When Senba turned thirty-five, he quit his job and started his own company doing electrical repairs. They were living in Meguro Ward at the time. Business went well, and at the age of forty-six, he bought the summer place in Marine Hills. I guess his wife always dreamed of living in a place where she could see the same ocean she looked out on as a child, so he bought it for her—that's what he told the detectives after his arrest." Hashigami put down his notebook and picked up his chopsticks.

"Huh. He doesn't sound like such a bad guy, except for the murdering part," Nishiguchi commented between bites.

"Well, things took a turn for the worse, obviously. He might've been flush enough with cash at one point to buy a summer home, but with a small business, one misstep can ruin everything. Turns out they'd gone out on a limb on a new project, and it became an albatross around their neck. Pretty soon they were drowning in debt and had to file for bankruptcy. He got to keep the house in Meguro and the summer home down here, but then his wife got sick. Cancer."

Nishiguchi frowned. "You weren't kidding about that turn for the worse."

"Some guys just run out of luck," Hashigami said, picking at his stew. "They sold the place in Meguro to pay the medical bills, and moved to East Hari. So his wife's dream came true, though not quite in the way they'd hoped, and it didn't last long. She died right after they moved down here, and then it was just him."

"Not the easiest place to live by yourself," Nishiguchi said, remembering the abandoned summer home.

"No, it's not," Hashigami agreed. "He stuck it out for a while, though. Until things got bad. So he headed back up to Tokyo and started doing work for other electricians. That's right around when he got arrested."

Nishiguchi nodded. "I read the file."

"I guess he was broke, and lonely, and things just kind of fell apart. Not that it makes what he did any better, but I feel some sympathy for the guy."

Nishiguchi's chopsticks stopped in midair. "You think Tsukahara sympathized with Senba, too?"

Hashigami mulled it over for a moment, then said, "Why not? He was the arresting detective, so he was probably the one who wrote that report about Senba buying the place in Marine Hills. He might have thrown that detail in there to make things go a little easier for the guy in court."

"Hmm. You suppose it's possible Senba didn't bear Tsukahara much of a grudge?"

"Could be," Hashigami agreed. "There were still a few people left that knew his wife's family in East Hari, and they told us that after Senba and his wife moved to Marine Hills, they came over to pay her old neighbors a visit every now and then. They all seem to think Senba was the nicest guy you could know. More than a few of them wondered why he did it, if there wasn't some bigger reason for the murder. Come to think of it, I could see how that curiosity might've brought Tsukahara back to visit."

"So Hidetoshi Senba and the current case are . . . ?"

Hashigami shook his head. "Entirely unrelated. The prefectural guys lost interest pretty quick, too. Guess we were barking up the wrong tree."

TWENTY-SIX

A game show was on TV, with celebrities trying to complete various hazardous challenges to the laughter of a studio audience. Kyohei wasn't particularly interested in it, but he sat with his arms resting on his knees and pretended to enjoy the show. Aunt Setsuko arrived with a tray of cut pears, which she placed on the low table beside him. "Dig in," she said.

"Thanks," Kyohei said, ignoring the tiny fork she placed next to the plate and grabbing one of the slices of pear with his fingers.

He'd eaten dinner with his aunt and uncle and had stayed on in their small apartment inside the inn afterward. Uncle Shigehiro was sitting nearby, reading a book and drinking tea. Narumi had eaten with them but left as soon as dinner was done.

"What did you get up to today, Kyohei?" his uncle asked. "I didn't see you outside of your room much."

"Summer homework, mostly. And I played some video games after."

"Homework? Good boy."

"Well, I only just started. But the professor helps me out when I don't get anything."

"The professor?"

"He means Mr. Yukawa," Setsuko said as she stood and went off to the kitchen.

"Oh, right. I wonder how long the professor's planning on staying," Shigehiro said.

"He told me he couldn't go until he was done with his research, but he couldn't get anywhere with it because the DESMEC people were a bunch of idiots."

"That so? Well, I suppose he is a professor at Imperial University, so at least we don't have to worry about him running out of money." Shigehiro ran a hand through his thinning hair before looking at Kyohei. "Did he say anything about what happened?"

"What do you mean?"

"I mean, is he upset about that guy dying, or was he wondering about how he might've died, or anything like that?"

"Not to me. He did say it was hard to relax with the police coming and going all the time."

"Yeah," Shigehiro said and gave a long sigh. "Bad luck for you too, huh. This is supposed to be your time in the sun, and I haven't even had the chance to take you swimming yet. Sorry about that."

"I don't mind. The ocean will always be there next time."

"Yeah," Shigehiro said again, when the cordless telephone began to ring. He moved to get it, but it stopped ringing almost immediately. Setsuko must've picked it up at the front desk.

Kyohei looked at the time. It was almost nine. The game show was finished. Kyohei held the remote control in his hand and wondered what kind of an excuse he could come up with for staying a little bit longer. Uncle Shigehiro would go take his bath anytime now; he only had to hold out until then.

He flipped through the channels until he found a show starring a popular actress he'd heard about. He'd never seen the show before, but he immediately put down the remote and settled in as though he'd been waiting for it to start.

"You like these shows?" his uncle asked after a few minutes.

"I guess," Kyohei said without taking his eyes off the TV. He hoped his uncle wasn't a fan.

The cordless phone began to ring again, except with a different ring tone than before.

"Who could that be?" Shigehiro wondered, not moving to pick up the phone.

The sound of hurrying footsteps came down the hallway and Aunt Setsuko came in.

"It's your father, Kyohei," she said, picking up the phone. "Hello? Are you still there? I'll hand you over to him." She held the phone out to Kyohei.

"My dad?"

"He's calling from Osaka."

Kyohei put the phone to his ear. "Hey."

"Hey, how's it going, Kyohei? You doing okay out there?" his father asked in a cheery tone.

"Yeah, everything's fine."

"Great, great. Hey, I heard from your uncle that some pretty crazy stuff was going on. Why didn't you tell your mom when she called the other night?"

Kyohei hadn't told her because he didn't want to have to explain the whole thing, but he resisted the urge to tell his father that. "I dunno," he said. "I guess it just didn't seem like that big of a deal."

"I'd say someone dying is a pretty big deal. You okay?"

"Yeah, why wouldn't I be?"

"I was just thinking it must be pretty hard to relax with the police crawling all over the place. You getting outside, doing your homework?"

"Yeah, everything's fine, really. I've been having a good time, and I even got some of my homework done already."

"Well, that's good. Just, if you don't feel comfortable being there, you be sure to tell me, okay?"

"Yeah, sure thing," Kyohei said, though he wondered what his dad would do if he did say that he was uncomfortable. Would he have him come down to Osaka? Wasn't he out here with his aunt and uncle because he couldn't go in the first place?

"Okay, well, I guess you'll be out there for a little while still, then?"

"Yeah."

"Well, that's good. Mind handing me to your uncle? Oh, wait, your mom wants to talk to you."

"I don't need to talk to Mom. We just talked yesterday."

Kyohei handed the phone to his aunt. Setsuko exchanged a few words with his father before hanging up.

"He sound worried?" Shigehiro asked.

"Not too bad. He has a pretty one-track mind, and right now it's on his work." Setsuko turned to Kyohei. "You're welcome to stay here as long as you want, of course, but if you'd rather be with your dad, just let us know. I'll have your uncle give him a call."

"Sure," Kyohei said.

"Right, well, it's time for me to get into the bath," Shigehiro said, finally standing.

Setsuko went back into the kitchen, leaving Kyohei alone in the room at last.

He opened the door to make sure no one was out in the hallway, then went back into the room and opened the drawer next to the television. The drawer was empty except for a single key attached to a thin wooden block with a ring at one end. He took it out and put it into his shorts pocket.

Turning off the TV, Kyohei left the room and ran down the hallway, leaving his slippers behind to avoid making too much noise. Dashing through the lobby, he pressed the button for the elevator and the door opened right away. Kyohei jumped inside, his heart racing.

Up on the third floor, he knocked on the door to the Sea of Clouds Room. He heard someone undo the latch on the door, and then he was face to face with Yukawa.

"Got it," Kyohei said, showing him the master key.

"Good work. How much time do I have?"

"I should try to get it back before my uncle gets out of the bath, so about twenty minutes."

"That should be more than enough. Let's go," Yukawa said, stepping out of his room in his socks.

Yukawa walked past the elevator and took the stairs up one story to the fourth floor. But then he turned and went in the opposite direction Kyohei had expected him to go.

"Where are you going, Professor?" Kyohei asked. "The Rainbow Room is down that way."

Yukawa stopped. "The Rainbow Room?"

"Didn't you want to see the room that belonged to the guy who died?"

Yukawa had said he wanted the master key because there was a room he wanted to see. Kyohei had assumed it was the room where the guy who had fallen on the rocks had been staying. He had wanted to see it himself, especially after the police put up a line of "do not cross" yellow tape across the door.

Yukawa shook his head. "We don't need to see that room."

"So what room do we need to see, then?"

"Come with me and find out."

Yukawa walked a little bit further, stopping in front of a room with a sign that read "The Ocean."

"This room?"

Yukawa nodded and pulled something out of his pocket. "Put these on," he said.

They were white gloves, a bit baggy on Kyohei's hands.

"Sorry I didn't bring any smaller ones. Try not to touch anything—actually, let me rephrase that. Under no condition should you touch anything in the room."

"What the heck are you planning to do in there?"

A thoughtful look came to Yukawa's face and he said, "A little investigation."

"An investigation? Of what?"

"Call it a physics investigation. This building has an extremely fascinating structure, one that might yield valuable insights in my research."

"So why didn't you just ask my uncle to let you see it?"

"So he could tell the police, and have them waste my time questioning me about every single little detail? No thank you. The key, please."

"Being a scientist must be tough," Kyohei said, handing him the key.

"There's no easy path to the truth," Yukawa said, unlocking the door and opening it. He groped for the light switch, turned it on, and stepped inside. Kyohei followed. The air conditioner hadn't been running, and the room was hot and stuffy.

Yukawa stood by the entrance, scanning the room with his eyes, before kneeling. He ran his gloved hand over the tatami mats on the floor, then turned his hand over to examine his fingers.

"What are you doing?" Kyohei asked.

"Nothing. I was thinking the mats might be a little dusty since the room hasn't been used for a while, but it looks like they do a good job keeping the place clean."

Yukawa walked in toward the back of the room and opened the curtain. Kyohei looked through the window from behind him. He could see the backyard from here.

"You set off some fireworks with your uncle, you said?"

"Yeah, some rockets."

"How many?"

"I dunno. About five?"

"Do you remember if these windows were closed?"

"Yeah, they were closed."

"Are you sure?"

"Yeah, totally sure. My uncle and I checked before we set them off, just in case one of the rockets flew into a room by accident."

Yukawa nodded. "How about the lights?"

"Huh?"

"When you were checking to make sure that the windows were closed, were the lights in this room turned on?"

"Oh." Kyohei scratched his head. "I don't know."

"This room was empty that night, which means that if you looked up at it from the backyard, the windows should have all been dark."

That made sense to Kyohei, too, but he hadn't thought about it at the time, and now he couldn't remember. "I got a feeling some of the lights might've been on, but I'm not sure which room," he told the professor.

Yukawa nodded and closed the curtains. He began to circle the room, examining the walls. Occasionally, he knocked on the wall with his knuckles. He appeared to be checking the sound.

"It's quite an old building. I wonder when it was built."

"I'm not exactly sure, but more than thirty years ago," Kyohei said. "It was my uncle's father who built it, and my uncle took it over about fifteen years ago."

"Fifteen years? How old is your uncle?"

"His late sixties, I guess?"

"Your aunt looks much younger than that."

"She said that in a couple years she'd be sixty if you rounded to the nearest decade."

"I suppose that would make her fifty-three or fifty-four, then. She doesn't look it," Yukawa said, then turned to Kyohei as though he had just thought of something. "How old is your father?"

"Forty-five."

"That's quite a gap between siblings."

"That's because my aunt's mother died when she was really little. My dad's mother was my grandpa's second wife."

"Half-siblings. I see," Yukawa said, adjusting his glasses.

"Also, my aunt left the house when she was still pretty young, and went to live by herself in Tokyo. That's why my dad said he never really felt like he had a sister when he was growing up. She was more like an old cousin or something."

"Your dad isn't one to pull punches, I gather. At any rate, that means that your uncle was already into his fifties when he took over the inn. Any idea what he did before that?"

"He worked at some engine company."

"Engines?"

"Yeah, he kept getting transferred all over the place, too, and leaving my aunt behind. When they were in Tokyo, it was pretty much just my aunt and Narumi in the house."

"So they were based in Tokyo before coming here?"

"Why do you want to know that?"

Yukawa shrugged. "No particular reason." He turned and opened up the closet, revealing a stack of white futons. After staring at them for several seconds, he pulled the futons out and climbed into the closet, where he began rapping on the wall with his knuckles and rubbing it with his fingers.

"Professor?" Kyohei said, suddenly growing uneasy.

Yukawa stepped out of the closet. He replaced the futons and shut the door. "Right, let's go."

"You're all done?"

"I saw what I came to see, and everything was exactly as I expected." Yukawa reached for the switch, but the second before the room plunged into darkness, Kyohei caught the look on the professor's face. He looked more grim than Kyohei had ever seen him before.

TWENTY-SEVEN

Kusanagi stopped his car by the side of the road in Asagaya to take the call from Utsumi. It was creeping up on ten o'clock at night.

"You could've called a bit earlier," he said by way of a greeting. "It's been hours since I dropped you off."

"Sorry, I lost track of time with all the walking around."

"What, you've been beating the street this entire time?"

"Pretty much," she answered, sounding chipper nonetheless. Seemingly boundless energy was one of Utsumi's strong points. "I think it's safe to say I hit pretty much every budget hotel in Sanya."

Kusanagi was impressed. "Well, I hope you found something with all that."

There was a pause, then, "I'd say I did, yes."

"Good," Kusanagi said. "Where are you now?"

"Walking toward Asakusa."

"Asakusa? What's there?"

"A good place for dinner. I haven't had anything to eat yet."

"Great, give me the name. I'll meet you there. Dinner's on me."

"Really? Then maybe I should suggest a different place—"

"Don't get greedy."

Kusanagi punched the name of the place into his car's GPS and pulled away from the curb.

Utsumi's favorite spot to grab a late dinner in Asakusa was right next to the Azuma Bridge, a little place on a narrow alleyway wedged in between the main road and the Sumida River. Lucky for Kusanagi, there was a parking lot just across the way.

The two sat down at a table fashioned from the cross-section of a large log. They both ordered Utsumi's recommendation: the cow tongue platter.

"Well, let's hear it," Kusanagi said, pulling an ashtray over and lighting a cigarette.

Utsumi pulled a navy-colored notebook out of her shoulder bag.

"Well, basically, you were right. Tsukahara was looking for Senba—no fewer than nine places told me that a man in his sixties had been around showing people a picture of him and asking questions. I didn't quite get confirmation that the one asking the questions was, in fact, Tsukahara, but the description matched."

Kusanagi looked up at the ceiling and blew out a stream of smoke. "That sounds about right," he said. "So we know where Tsukahara was. What about Senba? Did Tsukahara ever find him?"

Utsumi looked up from her notebook and shook her head. "I don't think he did. Not with the number of hotels he ended up asking at."

"And nobody said they'd seen Senba around?"

"I showed the picture to everyone I talked to, but nothing."

Kusanagi frowned. "Yeah, that would've been too easy."

Their dinner arrived. Each one of them had seven pieces of cow tongue on a large tray, surrounded by a small bowl of grated yam, a bowl of boiled rice and barley, salad, and oxtail soup.

"This looks fantastic," Kusanagi said, snuffing out his cigarette.

"You didn't think we'd find Senba there, did you?" Utsumi said, staring at him.

"I had my doubts," Kusanagi admitted. "Even if Senba was out looking for places to stay, Sanya probably wouldn't be his first choice. It's a tourist dive for backpackers from overseas. You can't stay there too long without some kind of income. Maybe Tsukahara didn't know how the area had changed because he was off the force for a while. Or maybe he knew, but he went to check anyway. Classic old-school detective, leaving no stone unturned." Kusanagi took a bite of his cow tongue and whistled. The combination of texture and taste was sublime. "That is good. Dammit. Now I want a beer."

"Where would he have gone, then? An Internet café?"

Kusanagi nodded, pouring his grated yam over the rice and barley. "That's where all the drifters, young and old, wind up these days. Cheaper than budget places in Sanya, and they've got showers. Wow, this yam rice is amazing too."

"Okay," Utsumi said, "I'll try the Internet cafés tomorrow, then. We still haven't figured out why Tsukahara was looking for Senba in the first place, though."

Kusanagi sipped his oxtail soup, gave a little sigh, and reached for his jacket on the chair next to him. He pulled his notebook out of the inner pocket and flipped through the pages.

"Well," he said, "while you were out tromping around, I went to Ogikubo and checked the records from the time of Senba's arrest. I found out that Tsukahara's partner on the case was a sergeant by the name of Fujinaka. He's still with the Ogikubo department, though out on medical leave. I got them to call him up, and he agreed to meet me, so I went to his place—a swanky apartment on the thirtieth floor of one of those towers. Sounds like his wife hit pay dirt with a massage business. I guess not every detective lives in a rundown place in the suburbs."

Fujinaka was in his midfifties but skinny, which gave him the feel of a much older person. The medical leave was due to heart trouble.

"I remember the case well," he had told Kusanagi. He was well spoken and had sounded almost like a schoolteacher. "They had me partnered with Detective Tsukahara from the beginning of the case, but I wasn't able to assist with much of it, as I recall." Fujinaka had smiled.

"And you weren't there when Tsukahara took Senba in?" Kusanagi had asked.

"That's right. I was on the other side of town, much to my chagrin. If I'd been with Tsukahara, I would have gotten the chance to see him chase that fellow down," Fujinaka had said. Not *I would've gotten the chance to take him down myself*, Kusanagi noted. The deference Fujinaka showed his ex-partner was impressive.

"You said you weren't able to assist much during the solving of the case," Kusanagi had said next. "Did you do any follow-up work with Tsukahara?"

"Nothing much, beyond being his guide to the streets around here. It was a very clear-cut case, Detective. The murderer's confession was believable; all the details checked out. In the end, there was really only one question."

"What was that?"

"The body was found on the street in Ogikubo, a typical residential area," Fujinaka had told him. "According to Senba's testimony, he had spoken with the victim in a nearby park, and she had laughed at him and walked away. In a rage, he had run after her and stabbed her."

"I read that in the report. Where's the question?"

Fujinaka had straightened in his chair and said, "The question is, why did it happen there? The victim, Nobuko Miyake, lived on the other side of Tokyo, in Kiba. And Senba lived in an apartment in Edogawa Ward, less than ten kilometers away from her. So why did they meet up at a place that was inconvenient for both of them?"

"There was something about that in Senba's testimony, wasn't there? Didn't he call Ms. Miyake, who told him that she was in Ogikubo and if he wanted to talk to her, he'd have to come all the way out?"

Fujinaka had nodded. "He also said that he didn't know why Ms. Miyake was out in Ogikubo—that he'd been too preoccupied with the money she owed him to care. So we tried to piece together where she'd been before the attack. We walked all over town, asking around.

The arrest was quick, but everything after that—well, truth is, we never came up with much of anything to explain what she was doing out there. That's the lingering question."

"It doesn't seem that important," Kusanagi had said.

"That was my opinion as well, given that we had a confession and everything checked out. I could live with a few mysteries. But Tsukahara wasn't satisfied. Not only did he come with me on all the questioning, but he also did a lot of looking into the victim's past on his own. He paid me a visit after the case went to court and Senba had been sent to jail, and I could tell it still didn't sit well with him. I remember thinking that was the difference between a dyed-in-the-wool detective and, well, someone like me."

Kusanagi finished recounting his visit with Fujinaka and took another bite of his meal.

Utsumi picked up her chopsticks, which she'd set aside while Kusanagi was talking. "It sounds like Tsukahara had more suspicions concerning the victim than the murderer."

"That was my takeaway, too," Kusanagi agreed. "What I want to know is, why was Tsukahara so dogged about that point? Sure, it's important to know the background to the case, but it's rare that everything is revealed, even after a successful investigation. He had to have a reason for being so concerned with what the victim had been up to before the murder took place."

"Any ideas?"

"Only that he'd convinced himself that the only way to know the whole truth of what happened was to find out why she was there. I think he started to suspect that part of Senba's confession was less than true—maybe something he saw when he was writing up the case report."

"What do you think he saw?"

"I don't know. It could've just been a hunch, a gut feeling he got during the questioning."

"If he thought Senba was lying, why didn't he press him on it?"

"Probably because he lacked leverage. If there's nothing contradictory in the confession, and all the details check out, what's there to say? I read all of the records from the questioning, and there really weren't any head-scratchers in there, save the location. Senba's claim that he didn't know why she was out there is entirely believable."

Kusanagi took another mouthful of the cow tongue, now gone cold, and gave his yam rice a stir. He'd gotten so lost in talking he had forgotten to enjoy his meal.

"Why don't we do a little investigating into Nobuko Miyake then?" Utsumi suggested.

Kusanagi took a final sip of his oxtail soup and nodded. "My thoughts exactly. I'll start tomorrow. Not that I have any illusions that this will go smoothly. After all, Tsukahara already tried, and we know he didn't find what he was looking for."

"I'll keep looking into Senba."

Kusanagi raised an eyebrow. "Just going to wander into every Internet café you can find, showing photos to people?"

"Is that a problem?"

Kusanagi frowned and shrugged. "It's not that, but . . ."

"But what?" Utsumi asked, an unspoken challenge in her eyes.

"I was just thinking there might be a quicker way. Instead of stopping in at every Internet café, looking for a drifter, why not go to a place where drifters tend to gather?"

"They gather?"

"Even people without a place to live or steady work need a community—in fact, they probably need it more than the rest of us. That's how a lot of them survive on the streets."

Utsumi thought for a moment, her face hard, then her eyes opened wider. "Soup kitchens!"

"Bingo," Kusanagi said with a grin. "I know a few volunteer groups that run soup kitchens on a regular basis."

"Good idea," Utsumi said. "I'll start there first." She scribbled something in her notebook.

"Now I just have to figure out where *I'm* going to start," Kusanagi said with a groan. "The victim's from Chiba originally, but she didn't keep in regular contact with her parents or other relatives. I'm guessing that, as a former hostess, wherever she used to work has long since shut its doors. And even if it hasn't, they don't have very good long-term memory at those places. I doubt they'd remember a girl who worked there decades ago."

The police had done an inquiry into Nobuko Miyake's financial situation at the time, given the motive for the crime, but found only a mostly empty bank account and a long history of late, usually minimum payments on credit cards. They also uncovered more than a few people who'd loaned her money in the past.

"What about asking at the place where the victim and Senba went to get a drink the night before? Didn't the proprietor there know Senba?"

"Could be," Kusanagi agreed. "Still, it's been fifteen years. I hope it's still open."

"There's a better chance that it is than wherever she used to work."

"Agreed. I'll start there, then. Pretty sure the place was in Ginza. Good idea, recruit."

Utsumi smiled. "I guess that makes us even."

"Don't let it go to your head," Kusanagi said, lighting a fresh cigarette.

They walked out of the restaurant and were standing in front of the parking lot when Kusanagi's phone began to ring. He looked at the display and saw the call was coming from a public phone.

"It's probably him," he said to Utsumi before answering it. "Hello?"

"It's me, Yukawa. Can you talk?"

"Just finished dinner. Utsumi's here too. Something up?"

"There's been a bit of a development. I can't go into details yet, but I'm pretty sure I've identified someone with a deep connection to the case."

Kusanagi's grip on the phone tightened. "A suspect?"

After a pause of several seconds, Yukawa said, "I'll leave the choice of words up to you."

"Okay. So who is it?"

There was another pause before Yukawa said, "The owner of this inn."

"What? You mean the place you're staying? What was it called again?"

"The Green Rock Inn. The proprietor's name is Shigehiro Kawahata. He worked at a company in Tokyo before taking over this place from his father. I'd like you to look into him—no, wait, not just him. You'd better look into his entire family."

TWENTY-EIGHT

"Good morning." Yukawa walked in just as Narumi was placing dishes on his breakfast tray.

She turned and smiled. "Did you sleep well?"

"I slept, but I wouldn't say well. Might've had a bit too much wine last night." The physicist's face was drawn tighter around the eyes than usual. She poured him some tea, and he nodded in thanks, reaching for the cup.

"Are you going to see the boat today as well, Professor?"

Yukawa raised an eyebrow at her. "What do you mean by 'as well'? Is someone else going?"

Kneeling by the low table, Narumi straightened her back a little. "Our group has been invited to an informational meeting on the research boat."

"Your group? Oh, right. Save the Cove." Yukawa took a sip of his miso soup. "I can't see what good seeing it will do you, though."

"I think it will be very interesting to see what kind of equipment DESMEC plans on using in their survey. That's a big part of what this is all about."

"You mean you want to see whether their devices are going to disturb the ocean floor, is that it?"

"Yes."

"Then you're wasting your time," Yukawa said. "I can tell you right now the ocean floor *will* be disturbed. All seeing the boat is going to do is get you angry. Unless of course you're really willing to put scientific development and humanity's future on the scales against environmental protection."

"We're certainly open to that, but I think we can do better than either-or. Why can't we have both?"

"Development and protection?" Yukawa chuckled.

"What's so funny? You think I'm being idealistic."

"I see no harm in pursuing ideals," Yukawa said, his smile fading. "But I have a hard time taking you seriously because I don't get the sense you have much respect for science."

Narumi glared at him. "Why not?"

"You may be an expert in environmental protection policy, but when it comes to science, you're an amateur. How much do you actually know about undersea resource development? If you truly want to come up with a solution that allows both, you'll need to have the same amount of knowledge and experience with both. It's arrogant to think that knowing only one is sufficient. Only by respecting the other side's work and way of thinking can you open a path for compromise." Yukawa turned back to his tray and poured a dollop of sticky natto beans on his rice. "Don't you agree?"

Narumi frowned. "So, what," she finally said. "You think we shouldn't go see the boat?"

"I don't think it will do you any good, unless you radically change the way you're thinking about this problem," Yukawa said, using the tips of his chopsticks to deftly dissect his broiled fish. "But, if you have it in your heart to truly understand the other side, then I think going to see the boat is a great idea. With the right frame of mind, you can glean a lot from observing. And I'm sure that having a firsthand appreciation for the various technologies that have been developed for undersea resource development will serve you well someday."

Narumi felt her hands clench into fists. Ever since she had heard about the plan to visit the boat, her head been filled with ways to find problems with the development. It had never once crossed her mind to try to appreciate the technology for what it was.

"Kyohei tells me that your father used to work at a company in Tokyo?" Yukawa asked, changing the subject.

"Yes?" Narumi said, lifting an eyebrow.

"What was the company called?"

"Arima Engines."

"A leading manufacturer of engine components. With him for a father, I'd think you'd have a healthy appreciation for technology."

"I don't see how the two are related, honestly."

"It's related because it's part of your experience. Observation won't get you anywhere if you don't bring all of your experience to bear." Yukawa's eyes shifted to look behind her and his face brightened. "Good morning!"

Narumi turned to see Kyohei walk into the dining room. He was carrying a cup of yogurt in his hand.

"Morning, Kyohei."

Kyohei looked between her and Yukawa, then asked, "What are you two talking about?"

"Narumi was considering joining me today on an expedition of sorts. I was just giving her some pointers," Yukawa said.

"An expedition? Can I come too?"

"It's on a boat," Yukawa said.

Kyohei's face fell. "Oh." He pulled a cushion over and sat down next to them.

Narumi stood. "I'll see you later, then," she said to Yukawa.

"I thought you might have reconsidered going."

"After you've given me such wonderful advice? I wouldn't miss it for the world."

Yukawa smiled at that, but said nothing.

Narumi started to leave, then a thought occurred to her. "What exactly did you talk about with your friend from Tokyo?"

Yukawa's chopsticks stopped in midair. "You're referring to the phone call?"

"Yes. He was calling about Mr. Tsukahara, I'm guessing. Detective Kusanagi, wasn't it?"

"You're curious."

"A little, sure. He was our guest. And I heard that Mr. Tsukahara used to be a homicide detective."

Yukawa looked up at her. "Curious and well informed. That bit of information hasn't been in the newspaper."

"An old classmate is a local detective. He's been on the case from the very beginning. He was here around lunchtime yesterday—I think he was still in the lobby when you came back."

"Ah, I do recall a young detective there."

"So how did you learn about Mr. Tsukahara being a detective? Your friend?"

"Indeed," Yukawa replied. "Kusanagi is a homicide detective himself, so he knew Tsukahara, even though they were many years apart."

Kyohei sat looking between the two of them, a mystified look on his face. He didn't appear to be following the conversation.

"So what does Tokyo think about what happened?" Narumi asked, ignoring her cousin for the time being. "And why did Detective Kusanagi call *you* about it, Professor?"

A wry smile came to Yukawa's lips. "Well, I could tell you why Kusanagi called me, but it's a bit of a long story. Suffice it to say he just called to see how things were going. Of course, Kusanagi often has ulterior motives for the things he does. Actually, *often* isn't quite right. *Always* is the word I was looking for. He always has an ulterior motive."

Narumi furrowed her brows and shook her head. "I don't follow."

"I rarely do myself," Yukawa said with a smile. "At any rate, with regards to what Tokyo thinks about this case, I'm afraid I can't say, because they didn't tell me. Still, I get the feeling that there are concerns. For example, there's the question of why Mr. Tsukahara came to Hari Cove. Was it to attend the hearing on undersea resource development, or did he just stop by the hearing, having some other, primary reason for being here?"

"Like what?"

"Maybe your classmate hasn't told you, but just before Mr. Tsukahara attended the hearing, he paid a visit to some summer homes in East Hari. Apparently, a murderer who Mr. Tsukahara once arrested had a house there."

"A murderer?" Narumi tensed. "Who?"

"I didn't get the name. I'll ask next time I hear from him, if you really want to know."

"No." Narumi shook her head. "It's okay."

"Very well. As for me, I hope that they clear this case up quickly. It's hard to focus on my work with the local police nosing around and friends from Tokyo calling me all the time. Do you know what accounts for most research delays? Interruptions that have nothing to do with the research whatsoever."

He directed the last half of what he said toward Kyohei.

Out of the corner of her eye, Narumi saw Kyohei nod, as though the professor had spoken some deep truth. Shrugging, she left the dining room and headed back toward the kitchen.

TWENTY-NINE

At the Hari Cove police station, the investigative task force was meeting. An investigator from the local prefectural headquarters stood and opened his notebook. "We visited Mrs. Tsukahara last night at her home to ask if she'd noticed anything unusual about her husband's behavior in the past few months. She repeated what we already have on file about movies he likes, books, and his occasional travel. She also mentioned that she couldn't be entirely sure how he spent most of his days, because her job as a dressmaker kept her out of the house. We did confirm that there hadn't been any altercations with anyone from his past or present, nor was the couple experiencing any financial difficulties. She also claims there was never any possibility of an affair."

Section Chief Hozumi butted in with a chuckle. "Well, if his wife says so, it must be true."

"Er, right," the investigator continued, "we're going to be checking on that with his former colleagues, of course. Regarding Hidetoshi Senba, she again confirmed what we already know, that Tsukahara tended to remember everyone he had ever caught, but rarely talked about them. Senba was no exception. We also checked the study, with the widow's permission, but didn't find any materials relating to past cases, Senba's included. It's worth noting that detectives from the Tokyo PD had spoken to her before we arrived, but she said she told them nothing she hadn't told us, nor did they take any evidence with them." The investigator gave a sort of half-bow to the room and took a seat.

The conference room was lined with desks. In the middle, with their backs to the wall, sat the detectives from the prefectural homicide division. Commissioner Tomita and Chief Okamoto from Hari sat near Hozumi. Neither man looked particularly comfortable surrounded by detectives from the prefectural police.

Facing them sat several dozen investigators, their desks neatly arranged side by side—the official task force for what they were calling the "Hari Cove abandoned body case."

Nishiguchi sat toward the back of the room, listening to the proceedings and occasionally taking notes. It was his first time being involved in such a large-scale operation, and he hadn't quite grasped yet how all the parts were supposed to work.

Sitting next to Hozumi, Isobe leaned forward in his chair and scanned the faces in the room. "Any results from East Hari?"

An investigator from prefectural homicide sitting next to Hashigami stood and related what Hashigami had told Nishiguchi the day before—that Senba's late wife's old neighbors didn't have a bad word to say about the man. He also noted for the record that, though Senba's sentence had been served, no one had seen him in East Hari after his arrest.

Isobe turned to Hozumi. "Well? Is Senba still important to our case?"

Hozumi made a sour face. "It's hard to say. No one's been able to track him down, right?"

"Not yet. He had some relatives down in Aichi, but they say they haven't heard from him since he went to prison."

"No doubt they want to keep it that way, too." Hozumi tugged at his mustache. "From looking at the report, it doesn't seem likely

Senba bore a grudge against the victim. Still, just in case, we should probably do some questioning around Hari Cove in case anyone has seen someone matching Senba's description."

"Will do," Isobe said, turning back to the room. "Any suspicious vehicles?"

Another investigator stood, but the report he gave was largely unhelpful. No one had spotted any unusual activity in the area, vehicular or otherwise. They'd compiled a list of people who said they had seen cars parked that evening, but nothing to link any of them to the murder.

Isobe groaned and turned back to Hozumi. "Well?"

Hozumi folded his arms across his chest. "Well, I suppose there's not much to do but see if we can verify who all those cars belong to, one by one. If someone put him to sleep and poisoned him in a car, that could've been done a considerable distance away from where the body was found. We should probably widen the area of our search."

"Got it," Isobe said quickly.

Nishiguchi sighed and sunk lower in his chair. He had no idea which way the investigation was going to go, but it was a sure bet it wouldn't involve him. At least he had something to show for the whole thing: his reunion with Narumi Kawahata. Once things settled down, he planned to invite her out to dinner. He'd already started wondering what restaurant he should pick.

THIRTY

By the time the Save the Cove group got to Hari Cove Harbor, the DESMEC undersea resources survey boat was already at the wharf. Narumi's eyes widened. The boat was much bigger than she'd expected.

"That's not a boat, that's a ship," Sawamura muttered.

Sawamura parked his truck next to the lone car already in the lot, and everyone got out and headed for the wharf. In addition to Narumi and Sawamura, there were five others in the group who'd been sitting in the back of the truck, among them the couple that had joined Narumi at the bar after the hearing.

The survey boat was even more impressive up close. Narumi guessed that it measured at least a hundred meters from bow to stern. Size-wise, it could easily compete with a luxury yacht, but from the dirt and wear on the hull of the ship, it was clear not much effort had been put into keeping up its appearances. This was a working ship, complete with a cargo crane sticking off of the deck.

"I'm impressed they got it into the harbor," Narumi said.

"The harbor is naturally quite deep. I hear that's one of the reasons DESMEC chose it," Sawamura explained.

Two men walked over and greeted them. She recognized one of them as Kuwano, from DESMEC's public outreach office, the emcee on the first day of the hearing. The other, slightly younger, turned out to be one of his subordinates.

"Thanks for coming today," Kuwano said, smiling broadly. "We hope you'll take this opportunity to get a good look at what we're doing here."

On board, they were first shown to the pilothouse, where Kuwano began rattling off facts about the boat's size, tonnage, maximum speed, and range until Sawamura interrupted him, saying, "We really don't need to know anything that's not directly related to the undersea resource development you're doing."

"Right, of course," Kuwano apologized.

They walked through the engine room, communications room, and chart room next. The only thing Sawamura showed interest in was a door marked "Salon," which he specifically requested to see.

Inside, they found a table, a sofa, a large flat-screen TV, and a media cabinet. The room was large enough for a dozen people.

"This looks like an excellent use of our tax dollars," Sawamura said.

"On long surveys, people might have to spend several months in cramped quarters," Kuwano explained. "Without a little entertainment, well . . ." His voice trailed off.

Next, they were taken to the research rooms, five in all.

Kuwano stood in front of a row of monitors and control boards. "Room one contains controls for the various sonar systems on board, including our multibeam echo sounder, as well as a side-scan sonar, and the remote control for our winch," Kuwano explained, a distinct gleam of pride in his eyes. "In order to mitigate the noise from water turbulence, all of the actual sonar equipment is in a special sonar dome positioned toward the center of the hull—"

"How many times do I have to tell you people?" a voice coming from behind a large jumble of machinery echoed loudly in the small room. Kuwano froze mid-explanation, his mouth hanging open.

He blinked and looked around before finally closing his mouth again.

"Listen," the voice continued. "I told you there are two ways to wind the coil. *Two ways.* I even remade the program with that in mind."

Narumi peeked around the machinery and saw Yukawa standing across a desk from a DESMEC employee. The desk held a laptop computer, stacks of files, and what looked like blueprints spread out between them.

"I know that, which is why I tried to contact you, but I couldn't get through to your cell phone," the employee was explaining.

"It broke. Cell phones break. It happens. Why didn't you call the inn?"

"I did call the inn. But they told me you weren't staying there. Something about you canceling at the last minute?"

"Yes. I'm staying in a different inn, as I informed DESMEC that day."

"Well, nobody told me. Why'd you change your reservation anyway?"

"I fail to see what business it is of yours."

"Er, right, yeah," the man said, grinning sheepishly.

Narumi felt a hand on her shoulder and looked around. It was Sawamura.

"Let's go."

She nodded and followed him out. Kuwano showed them the remaining research rooms, then brought them to the upper deck, where he began explaining the various observational equipment on board. A lot of the technical jargon was over Narumi's head, but Sawamura looked like he was following, and kept asking questions.

"With the free-fall grab, after it sinks down to the seafloor and gets a sample, the weight detaches so it can rise back up, correct? What happens to the weight? Is it just abandoned?"

"Yes, but the weight itself isn't anything that can cause any harm down there."

"How can you say that for certain?" Sawamura asked. "I mean, you *are* introducing something to the environment that wasn't there before. Especially now, when in so many areas there is widespread pressure to stop dumping into the ocean, I wonder about a plan that involves intentionally abandoning foreign objects on the seafloor."

Kuwano frowned. "The relative safety of this method has been globally recognized—"

"But this is our ocean. Who cares what they might think in France or the United States? This is a decision we need to make here, in Japan."

Kuwano grimaced and fell silent. Narumi felt a touch of sympathy for the man.

Though she might not have caught all of the technical details, it was clear that the DESMEC researchers had been using all of the technology at their disposal to assess and approach this development of a previously untouched and largely unknown part of the world. At times during the explanation, she had even been genuinely impressed by the technology. Maybe Yukawa was right about having to be able to see things from both sides.

Kuwano moved on, explaining a few of the other monitoring devices before he checked his watch. "That about wraps up everything we have to show you. I want to take you to the conference room and show you some footage we have of one of our test surveys, but it will take a little while for us to get ready. Feel free to walk around in the meantime. Just, please let one of us know if you plan on leaving the deck." He bowed curtly and left them.

Though they had been given free rein of the deck, there wasn't much to do up there. Sawamura sat and began furiously jotting down notes, but most of the others just started milling, unsure what to do. The couple went over by the railing to look down at the water. They were laughing about something. Narumi shrugged and began walking around the deck, looking at some of the devices that had already been explained to her.

She stopped by two long cylinders that looked like torpedoes with propellers attached to one end. Kuwano had mentioned these too, but she hadn't quite caught everything he said.

"Proton magnetometers," said a voice from behind her. She looked up to see Yukawa walking over. "You drag those along several hundred meters behind the boat. They're able to pick up extremely faint magnetic abnormalities caused by things like undersea hydrothermal ore deposits." He stood next to Narumi. "You have a nice tour?"

"Yes. I heard you arguing with someone downstairs. Was there some mistake?"

Yukawa grimaced. "Just an incompatibility between the mount they prepared and my coil. For every advance we make, we find two or three new problems. I can understand if delays are an issue of physical phenomena getting in the way, but human error can be a particularly aggravating source."

"That doesn't sound good," Narumi said. "How are we supposed to feel safe entrusting our ocean to people who make those kind of mistakes?"

Yukawa's eyes narrowed at her, but then he reluctantly nodded. "Unfortunately, I can't think of any good reason you *should* feel safe. I'll mention this next time I talk to DESMEC." Yukawa turned and looked out over the ocean. "Tell me," he said after a moment, "why does a girl from Tokyo care so much about the ocean out here?"

"Why shouldn't I? It's beautiful."

"I agree. I was just wondering if you had some deeper reason."

"I think the beauty of the ocean is deep enough."

Yukawa smiled. "You were fourteen or fifteen when you moved here, right? Didn't you ever want to go back home?"

"Not at all."

"Really? I'd think that for a teenager, the city would have a lot more stimulation to offer. Where were you in Tokyo?"

"Oji."

"Ah, up north."

"Yeah. Not exactly a stimulating part of town."

"A little sleepy, true, but a short train ride from places like Shibuya or Shinjuku."

Narumi stared at Yukawa's face for a moment, then slowly shook her head. "Not every teenage girl dreams of going shopping in Shibuya. Some of them like little country towns with beautiful views of the sea."

Yukawa adjusted his glasses with the tip of his finger and stared back at her.

"What?" she asked after a moment.

"I don't think so," Yukawa said, shooting her an intense look before adding quietly, "That's not you."

Narumi's eyes went a little wider. "Why not? And how would you know what kind of a person I am anyway?" she asked, her voice a little louder than it should be. She could feel the blood rushing to her face.

"Narumi?" Sawamura came striding over. "What is it?" he asked, looking between her and the physicist.

"Sorry," Narumi muttered. "It's nothing."

Sawamura gave Yukawa a quizzical look. "What did you say to her?"

Yukawa maintained a cold silence for a few moments more before saying, "I didn't mean to give offense, but if I did, I apologize."

Narumi stared at the deck in silence.

"Right. I'll see you later," Yukawa said, walking off.

"What's his problem?" Sawamura spat after he left. "You okay? What did he say to you?"

Narumi realized she couldn't stand there frowning forever. She flashed Sawamura a smile. "It was really nothing. Sorry, didn't mean to worry you."

"Hey, if you're fine, I'm fine," Sawamura said, the concern plain on his face.

"Thanks for waiting," Kuwano announced brightly on the deck behind them. "We're all ready, so if you'd please come to the conference room. We have cold drinks for you!"

THIRTY-ONE

Kusanagi stood outside a restaurant that served okonomiyaki pancakes a short walk from Azabu Juban Station. The name on the sign read "Flower," making him wonder if the name of the place wasn't a play on their specialty's main ingredient. The entrance was up a flight of stairs on the second floor.

As he stood looking up at the sign, a young man came out of the door—an employee, by the red apron he was wearing. He flipped over a small placard on the door so the side facing out read "Closed" and went back in.

It was just after two in the afternoon. A couple, the restaurant's last customers, came out and walked down the stairs. Kusanagi waited for them to leave before going up. He opened the door, hearing a small bell jingle above his head.

The employee he'd seen on the stairs looked up from the cash register. "Oh, sorry," he said. "Lunch's all over."

"I know. I'm not a customer," Kusanagi said. "Is Mr. Muroi here?" He looked around the place while he talked. The tables all had hot plates in the middle so customers could cook their own okonomiyaki. A white-haired man was sitting at the nearest one, facing away from the door, reading a newspaper. When he heard Kusanagi, he looked around. He had his fair share of wrinkles, but his skin was tan, making him look young for his age. He, too, was wearing a red apron.

"Who're you?" the man asked.

Kusanagi flashed his badge as he walked over to the table. "Mr. Muroi?"

The man blanched. "Yeah. What do you want?"

"I was hoping I could ask you a few questions about your time at Bar Calvin."

"Calvin? That's ancient history. Haven't been there in over a decade."

"I know. I spoke to the manager last night."

Calvin was a bar on a side street off of lower Ginza. The interior featured gaudy décor, with expensive-looking leather upholstery on the sofas, reminiscent of Japan's economic boom days back during the bubble.

Bar Calvin was where Hidetoshi Senba and Nobuko Miyake had shared a drink the night before he killed her. Masao Muroi was the bartender who served them, and his statement led to Senba's arrest.

When Kusanagi told him what he wanted to ask about, Muroi's eyes went wide.

"Now that's *really* ancient history. What could you possibly—" Muroi started. Then he quickly folded his paper and sat upright in his chair. "Wait a second. Is Senba out already? You think he wants revenge?"

Kusanagi chuckled. "I wouldn't worry about it. Senba's been out of prison for quite some time now. You haven't seen him?"

"No. Okay. Wow. I didn't realize he'd already done his time."

"Did you know the two of them well?" Kusanagi asked.

"I wouldn't say 'well,' but, yeah, I knew who they were. That night was the first time they'd been to Calvin in a while. I was pretty surprised when I heard what happened the following day."

"The case report said they weren't exactly getting along very well that night."

"Well, they weren't fighting or anything. But it was kind of an odd scene," Muroi said, hesitating a bit before adding, "I mean, you don't normally see a guy crying like that."

Muroi asked Kusanagi whether he'd had lunch yet, and when he said he hadn't, Muroi offered him some okonomiyaki and wouldn't take no for an answer.

"I was born up here," Muroi told him. "But when I was in middle school, my family moved down south to Osaka. There was this fantastic okonomiyaki place down the street from us there, and it was always my dream to have a restaurant like that of my own." Muroi stirred a bowl of batter while he talked. His hands moved with an effortlessness that bespoke long years of practice.

"How many years were you at Bar Calvin?" Kusanagi asked.

"Twelve, exactly. They took me on as a bartender when I was in my midthirties. I'd done my time at a few other places before then, but Calvin was the best. Still, I didn't want to be someone else's employee the rest of my life, so about ten years ago I left and started this place. I know it don't look like much, but I've done all this without needing to borrow a single yen," Muroi said, pouring the batter out on the hot plate in front of them. There was a loud sizzle as drops of oil began to dance on the plate.

"I understand Hidetoshi Senba used to be a regular there? Around what time was that?"

Muroi folded his arms across his chest. "I wonder," he said. "I don't think I'd been at Calvin a decade around the time he started coming, so I'd say that was about twenty-two, maybe twenty-three years ago?"

"Right," Kusanagi said, doing some calculations in his head. "So about six or seven years before he was arrested."

"Yeah, sounds about right. Senba was a big spender back in those days. Had his own company and all. But, after a certain point, he stopped coming altogether, and when I saw him next, well, it was clear he'd fallen on hard times. Cheap clothes, you know the look. That was the night."

"What about Nobuko Miyake? Was that her first time to Bar Calvin in a while, too?"

"It was, but she hadn't been away as long as Senba. Maybe only two or three years. Nobuko stopped coming when she quit her hostessing job. She used to bring customers from her place over for drinks at Calvin afterward. Senba was one of 'em."

"Do you happen to know why she quit?" Kusanagi asked.

Muroi paused to check how the okonomiyaki was coming along before leaning forward in his chair. "Actually, I heard a rumor about that."

"What kind of rumor?"

"I heard she got fired. Something about her causing trouble."

"Any idea what that was?"

Muroi chuckled. "Borrowing cash from customers and not paying them back."

"Yeah, that'd get a hostess sacked."

"She'd have these lines, like she lost her wallet to a purse-snatcher, or one of her customers had rung up a big tab and gone missing and the restaurant wanted her to pay them back, and she'd borrow ten or twenty thousand yen from her regulars, just a little bit at a time, but it started building up, and customers started complaining."

"Do you know how she made ends meet after that?"

"Good question. She wasn't no spring chicken anymore. I figure she had it pretty tough."

Nobuko Miyake had been forty when she was killed. If Muroi's story was true, that would make her thirty-seven or thirty-eight when she got fired. If she had a lot of well-heeled regulars to keep her afloat she might have been okay, but without that, it would've been hard for her to find work as a hostess again.

"She was never too careful with money, so when I heard about what happened, I wasn't too surprised. I'm guessing Senba would've been a prime target for her little loan scheme."

"And you're sure about what you told me earlier?" Kusanagi asked, lowering his voice. "He was really crying?"

Muroi flipped one of the pancakes and said, "It wasn't just me who saw him. A few of the other guys at the bar were talking about it, wondering why he was so worked up."

"But you don't know what they were talking about?"

"Sorry, can't help you there." Muroi shook his head and chuckled. "If it was a pretty young girl who was crying, well, I might have gone up and asked what the trouble was, but when a middle-aged man is crying next to a woman, you keep your distance. I thought maybe that's just what he did when he got drunk, you know."

A scene began to form in Kusanagi's mind: a man and woman meeting again for the first time in a long while. The man, a successful businessman who had lost everything, even his wife. The woman, a former hostess who'd reaped what she'd sowed and wound up broke. What could've possibly transpired between them that he would've cried over their drinks, then run up to her the following day and stabbed her to death?

"What about friends?" Kusanagi asked. "You know anyone close to them? Or maybe another bar they might've frequented?"

"Well, not really," Muroi said, scratching his neck. "It was a long time ago. And we didn't talk all that much."

"Right," Kusanagi said, putting away his notebook in his pocket. It was over twenty years ago, as it was. He hadn't been expecting Muroi to even remember as much as he had.

"All done—eat up while it's hot," Muroi said, spreading some rich, dark sauce on the okonomiyaki before sprinkling it with seaweed and bonito flakes and cutting it on top of the hot plate. "Oh, almost forgot the beer."

"Can't drink while I'm on duty, but I'll definitely help myself to this," Kusanagi said, breaking off a piece of the pancake with his chopsticks and putting it in his mouth. The surface was nicely browned, but the inside was still soft and moist. He could clearly taste each of the ingredients. "That's really good," he said through his first mouthful.

Muroi smiled. "I get a lot of people in here from down south, and they always say I nailed the taste. Okonomiyaki is comfort food down there." Then his face got more serious, and he said, "Actually, that reminds me." His eyes got a faraway look in them.

"Yeah?" Kusanagi prompted him.

"No, it's just," he began, rubbing his forehead and trying to remember something. "I just remembered them talking a bit about comfort food once."

"You mean Senba and Nobuko?"

"Yeah. They were talking about the food from back home. They even brought me something once."

"What was it?"

Muroi folded his arms across his chest and groaned, deep in thought. Finally, he shook his head. "Sorry, I don't recall."

"If you remember, could you drop me a line?" Kusanagi asked, writing down his cell phone number on a piece of paper and placing it next to the hot plate.

"Sure thing. But don't get your hopes up. I can't see how it'll help, even if I do remember. Sorry, I probably shouldn't have said anything."

"Not at all. You never know what you're going to find until you start looking." Kusanagi took another bite of his okonomiyaki, then heard the sound of an e-mail being delivered to his phone. He glanced down at the screen. It was from Utsumi.

He looked at his mail after leaving the restaurant. It read: "Checked Arima Engines. Shigehiro Kawahata was in the records." He called Utsumi.

"Yes?" she answered.

"Good work. How'd you get access?"

"I went to the main office in Shinjuku and asked someone in HR if I could see their employee records."

"And they just showed them to you?"

"They had me sign a piece of paper saying that I wouldn't use them outside of the investigation, and I wouldn't pass them on to any third party. They wanted me to write the name of my supervising officer, too, so I gave them your name."

"Fine. If that's all it took, we got off easy."

"Also, they really wanted to know what our investigation was about."

"Please don't tell me you told them anything," Kusanagi said, a growl in his voice.

"Of course not."

"Well, that's a relief," Kusanagi said. "So he worked there."

"Yes, he was a section chief in the technological services division of their Nagoya branch until he left the company fifteen years ago.

"Nagoya? So he wasn't in Tokyo?"

"That's what it said in the records. Except, his residential address was in Tokyo."

"What's that supposed to mean?"

"I don't know. He was listed as living at an address near Oji Station. There was a note on it indicating that he was in a subsidized apartment that belonged to the company."

That probably meant his family was living in Tokyo while he was on an extended business trip in Nagoya. It wasn't that unusual in the tech industry.

"Anything else in there other than his address and workplace?"

"I have an employee number—which is determined by the year the employee enters the company, I'm told. I got the name of the school he graduated from, and a home phone number as well."

"Was there anyone who entered the company the same year as Kawahata and came from the same school?"

"Unfortunately, no," was Utsumi's reply. "But I did copy the records for about fifty people who entered the company around the same time. Also, I got the records for the four people who were working beneath him during his last year. Incidentally, all of their addresses are in Aichi Prefecture, near Nagoya."

"Got it. I think our first stop should be the subsidized housing. If it even still exists, that is."

"It does. Though it's getting pretty old."

"Okay. Meet me at Oji Station, then."

Kusanagi hung up and began walking with long strides toward the subway. As he made his way down the steps into the station, he reflected on his phone call with Yukawa the night before. The physicist had tantalized him by throwing out a possible suspect, yet not even hinting as to what he was thinking. He wouldn't even tell him why he wanted him to look into the Kawahata family. That was all par for the course, but it was what Yukawa had said before he hung up that stuck with him the most.

"I trust you, and I'm telling you this because I think it will lead to the resolution of this case. Please understand, I'm not acting as an official informant to the police here."

Kusanagi failed to see the distinction Yukawa was trying to make, but he grunted over the phone to show he understood.

"I'm almost a hundred percent certain that the Kawahata family is involved with this case," Yukawa continued. "But I need you to refrain from telling that to the police here. In fact, I'd prefer if we could uncover the truth of this on our own. If the local police tried to force the truth out into the open, I'm afraid there might be some . . . irreparable collateral damage."

This also made little sense. Kusanagi had asked him what he meant by "irreparable collateral damage," and Yukawa had told him, "If this case isn't handled properly, there's a good chance it will seriously disrupt a certain person's life. I'd like to avoid that, if at all possible."

But Yukawa wouldn't say who that person was. He had continued, his voice lower, almost solemn. "I know this is asking a lot, but I promise, if I do uncover the truth, I'll tell you straight away. And what you do with that knowledge will be entirely your decision."

Something very unusual was going on, that was certain. Kusanagi had learned a long time ago that asking a lot of questions at this point would do no good. Instead, he had agreed to look into the Kawahata family and hung up.

Now he was left in a bit of a bind. They'd received hardly any information about Shigehiro Kawahata from the local police. The local police didn't consider him involved enough that there was any need to share more information with Tokyo. Nor could he ask directly about Shigehiro or his family without raising a lot of uncomfortable questions and potentially directing suspicion toward the proprietor of the Green Rock Inn. Doing that would constitute a breach of his agreement with Yukawa.

He had been wondering exactly how they were going to start this investigation when, that morning, Yukawa had called him again with the name of the company where Shigehiro used to work. He had sent Utsumi off to Shinjuku right away.

It was an interesting case, Kusanagi thought as he sat in the gently rocking subway car. A man dies out in the countryside, but the key to finding out why is far away in Tokyo—and the task force officially assigned to solving the case hasn't a clue.

Kusanagi looked out the window at the sliding gray walls of the subway tube, picturing his physicist friend's face and wondering just who it was he'd met out in Hari Cove.

THIRTY-TWO

Kyohei's eyes opened wider behind his goggles as he watched the little fish dart from behind the shadow of a rock. It was only the length of his fingertip, its scales a bright, shimmering blue. He reached out for it, but it was far too swift, so he settled for following its quick, jagged movements with his eyes until it disappeared behind another rock. He waited a while for the fish to come back out, but he was running out of air, and his snorkel was entirely submerged.

Kyohei returned to the surface, taking off his goggles and rubbing his face. Swimming on his back, he paddled with his legs back toward shore. He'd always been a good swimmer.

He switched to walking when he reached the shallows. The beach had been busy when he went in, but now only a few other swimmers remained. Most of the tents and beach umbrellas had been cleared away. Kyohei recovered his sandals from where he had thrown them and slipped them on before braving the hot sand above the waterline. His uncle Shigehiro was asleep on a beach chair beneath the lone remaining umbrella, a magazine spread open on his belly.

He called out to him, and his uncle's eyes opened immediately.

"Hey there, Kyohei. Ready to head home?"

Kyohei nodded and pulled a bottle of water out of the cooler next to the beach chair. "Yeah, I'm pretty pooped. Hungry, too."

"Right," Shigehiro said, sitting up and checking his watch. "It's after three already. Let's get home. I think we have some watermelon in the fridge."

"Cool," Kyohei said. "Hey, guess what I saw? A blue fish. It was really bright, about this big." He held his fingertips apart to indicate the size.

"Yeah, there's all kinds in there," Shigehiro said, not sounding particularly interested.

"I wonder what it's called."

Shigehiro shrugged and got off his beach chair. "You should ask Narumi. She knows that kind of thing."

"But you were born here. You never learned the fish?"

"Not really. I was only here through high school, and besides, no one in the family was a fisherman."

"Mom says you went to college in Tokyo and became an elite businessman."

Shigehiro laughed. "She's just pulling your leg," he said. "No, your uncle was just a regular old employee. Now get changed and let's go."

"Right," Kyohei said, picking up the plastic bag with his clothes and towel in it. When he got back from the changing rooms, Shigehiro pulled out his cell phone, pressed a few buttons, and put it to his ear.

"It's me. Yep, he's all done. See you at the same place as before."

He hung up and closed the beach umbrella. It and the chair were rentals. Only the cooler was theirs. Kyohei picked it up and started to walk. His uncle followed behind him, having a little difficulty because his cane kept sinking into the sand.

Today was the first day the police hadn't come up to the inn, which meant it was finally Kyohei's chance to get that ride to the beach he'd been promised. His uncle wasn't much interested in swimming, so he'd sat on the beach watching their stuff and chatting with Kyohei whenever he took a break from the waves.

They got back to the road and waited in front of a small convenience store until Setsuko arrived in the white van with "Green Rock Inn" written across the side. Shigehiro got into the backseat, struggling a bit to lift himself up. Kyohei took the passenger seat, like he had on the way down.

"Well? You have fun?" his aunt Setsuko asked.

"Yeah. And now I won't have to put up with any crap."

"Oh? From who?"

"The kids at school. If you don't go swimming over summer break, the ones that did won't let you forget it. It's so lame. I mean, I guess I could just lie, but it's better if I actually go."

"That's why you wanted to go? Whatever happened to swimming for the sake of swimming?" his uncle asked.

"Oh, I wanted to go swimming, sure. But it's also important *where* you go swimming. I mean, if you just go to the local pool, that doesn't count."

His uncle grunted at that, and his aunt laughed.

They passed by Hari Cove Harbor. The big DESMEC survey boat he had seen there this morning was still at the dock. When he turned to look back at the road ahead, he spotted someone walking by the side of the road.

"Hey, it's the professor," he said, and pointed out the window.

Yukawa was walking with a light-colored jacket slung over his shoulder, a briefcase in one hand.

"Oh, you're right," Setsuko said, slowing down as they got near. She opened her window. The physicist didn't seem to even notice them. He was looking down at the road beneath his feet, a preoccupied frown on his face.

"Mr. Yukawa?" Setsuko called out.

He smiled and stopped, and Setsuko stopped the car next to him. "All finished with work?"

"For today," Yukawa said, his eyes going to the passenger seat.

Kyohei took off his seatbelt and leaned over toward the window on the driver's side. "I went down to the beach with my uncle today!"

"Ah, finally made it, did you? Good."

"If you're heading back to the inn, would you like a ride?" Setsuko asked. "We're on our way back ourselves."

"You don't mind?"

"Not at all."

Yukawa hesitated just a moment, then went around to the side of the van, opened up the sliding door, and got in the backseat next to Shigehiro, nodding in greeting as he sat down.

"Those guys from DESMEC give you more trouble today?" Kyohei asked, twisting around to see him.

"Only the usual annoyances. That organization is too complicated for its own good. Too many captains and no one's holding the steering wheel."

"That doesn't sound good with a big boat like that," Kyohei said, his eyes going a little wider.

"It's a metaphor," Yukawa explained. "I mean that there're so many people giving directions no one knows which way to turn. Not to change subject, but does this van belong to the inn? I saw the lettering on the side."

"Yeah," Shigehiro said. "We used to use it to pick up guests at the station, but they rarely ask these days. So we mostly just use it when I need a ride someplace."

"You don't drive?"

"Well, used to, but not anymore, not with this leg. Too hard to step on the brake."

"Right, of course," Yukawa said, looking around the inside of the van. "I was just wondering if the police gave you any trouble about the van."

"Why would they?"

"Well, it's just that I heard from the DESMEC folks that the police were asking everyone about cars parked in the area on the night Mr. Tsukahara went missing. They were checking vehicle owners, and even searching inside cars. It was quite the ordeal."

"Oh, that," Shigehiro said. "Yeah, the other night when those fellows from forensics came up to the inn, I'm pretty sure they checked the car then. Not sure what they were looking for, though."

"Probably anything that could be a source of carbon monoxide," Yukawa replied. "When those detectives from the prefectural police came to the inn the other day, asking after my alibi, I asked one of them whether they had found the source, and he became noticeably flustered. I'm guessing they found something that indicated Mr. Tsukahara died of carbon monoxide poisoning. But they didn't know where, or how, thus the car-searching business."

"What's carbon monoxide?" Kyohei asked. "Is that like carbon dioxide?"

Yukawa looked a little surprised at the question, but then he nodded and glanced toward Shigehiro. "Actually, your uncle might be able to give you a better explanation of that than I can." He looked toward Shigehiro. "Narumi tells me you used to work at Arima Engines?"

Shigehiro chuckled. "A long time ago, yes." He looked at Kyohei. "Well, what do you know about carbon dioxide?"

"I know it's causing global warming, right?"

"That's right. It's the gas generated when something burns. But when something burns badly, it produces a different kind of gas—that's carbon monoxide."

"And you die if you breathe it in?"

"If you breathe enough of it, sure."

"That's pretty scary. But what's that got to do with cars?"

"Well," Shigehiro said, wetting his lips before continuing. "Cars have tailpipes for exhaust, right? There's carbon monoxide in the exhaust from cars."

"Really?" Kyohei looked at Yukawa.

"Couldn't have said it better myself," Yukawa said, nodding to Shigehiro.

The old man chuckled and shook his head. "I haven't forgotten everything—not yet, at least."

"However, I might've added one thing," Yukawa said, looking back toward Kyohei. "That is, I think there was another reason, besides the exhaust, that the police were interested in cars."

"What's that?"

"Well, like your uncle said, carbon monoxide is generated when something burns badly. What's meant by 'badly' here is something burning without sufficient oxygen. You've heard about not using gas heaters in a room for a long time without opening the doors every once in a while? Well, picture burning something like charcoal in an even smaller space, like the inside of the car. That would generate a lot of carbon monoxide. I think the police suspect that that's how Mr. Tsukahara was poisoned."

Kyohei nodded, but immediately another question popped into his head. "Wait, but if that's how he died, how did he end up on the rocks?"

Yukawa's eyes narrowed, but then he smiled and shrugged, giving Kyohei's uncle a glance before saying, "That, unfortunately, I can't explain."

Shigehiro was silent, looking out the window. Kyohei looked over at him, but his uncle must've been grumpy about something, because he was frowning. He glanced over at his aunt and was surprised to see a deep frown crossing her face as well.

THIRTY-THREE

A pretty girl with a deep brown tan carrying a bowl filled with tropical fruit smiled out of the poster. She was framed by palm trees, and behind her, a pure blue sea stretched out to the horizon. Below her, a printed note read, "We will be closing for the season on August 31. Thanks, The Management."

It said "closing for the season," but everyone knew Hari Cove Pizza would never be opening its doors again.

Narumi and the rest of the group had come here after their tour of the DESMEC survey boat. Someone had suggested they get tea, but there really wasn't any place in town like that, so they ended up here. Narumi remembered when the pizza shop first opened—a garishly painted new arrival in a sleepy town that hadn't quite woken up to the tourist industry and the money it could bring. There were tables inside with views through plate-glass windows and more tables outside on a large deck where you could sit and enjoy your pizza and your beer while feeling the sea breeze on your face. When they first opened, the season ran from the day the beach opened in the early summer all the way through September. The operating season had gotten shorter every year since.

"They didn't do it the right way," Sawamura said, sitting down across from Narumi. He was looking up at the poster, too. "You can't just build some fancy place in the middle of nowhere and expect people to come. If you want to get customers—regulars, I mean—you have to get the town involved." He shook his head. "All this town has, the only thing that'll last, is the ocean. The people at town hall don't get that. If they've got time to court DESMEC's business, you'd hope they'd spend a little more energy trying to develop our tourism industry."

"With what?" asked one of the men, a social studies teacher at the local middle school. "I totally agree that the ocean here is a fantastic resource, but we can talk about it all we want and people still won't come. There are too many other places just like this."

"I don't think other places are like Hari Cove," Narumi said.

"Oh, I agree, but people who aren't from here don't understand that. And to someone from the city, one beautiful ocean view is the same as any other. What's important is name value. Everyone goes to Okinawa because everyone wants to say they've been to Okinawa. No one gets jealous when you tell them you went to Hari Cove. It just doesn't feel like a fabulous vacation without the name."

Narumi frowned. "You're awfully hard on your own hometown," she said.

"I'm just trying to be analytical. When I came back to Hari Cove after spending a couple years away, I was surprised, and not in a good way. Let's be honest, it doesn't look like a tourist destination. Everything's falling apart. The hotels look run down. Go to Okinawa, you're treated to luxury. Here, you blame yourself for wasting your precious vacation time."

"Hey—" Sawamura stood from his chair and grabbed the high school teacher by the collar of his shirt. "That's enough of that."

The teacher blanched but said, "I'm just telling the truth. What's wrong with that?" His voice was a little high-pitched.

"Stop it," Narumi said, standing up and putting a hand on Sawamura's arm. "Calm down, Sawamura. You'll get us kicked out."

Sawamura shook his head and looked around the room. They were the only customers. The waitress was standing behind the counter, a worried look on her face.

Sawamura let go of the teacher's collar and sat back down. The teacher gingerly drank his water. His face was pale.

"It's good to talk about these things, but let's keep our tempers down," Narumi said.

The two men nodded.

"Sorry," the teacher apologized first. "I could've chosen my words a little better."

"No, I'm sorry." Sawamura lowered his head. "I shouldn't have grabbed you like that."

An audible sigh of relief passed over the table, and the waitress, who had been standing frozen the whole time, went back to her cleaning.

"I understand what you're saying," Sawamura continued. "It's true, the shops and the hotels are worse for wear. But nobody here thinks that's okay. We *want* to rebuild, to renovate. We just don't have the money. It's hard enough making it day-to-day. Even up at Narumi's place—"

The social studies teacher blinked and looked toward Narumi. "Oh, that's right, your parents run a hotel. Sorry, I forgot. I didn't mean any offense."

"It's okay. In fact, we've been talking about closing shop ourselves," Narumi admitted.

The tension had gone out of the air, replaced now by a kind of sullen silence.

"Time to head out," Sawamura said after a while, and everyone nodded.

Outside, Narumi got into Sawamura's car—he was driving a hatchback today instead of his usual pickup.

"Sorry about that," Sawamura said, pulling out of the parking lot. "I was out of line."

"I've never seen you lose your temper like that," Narumi said with a smile.

"I just didn't like the way he was talking, to be honest. You know deep down he wants this undersea resource development deal to go through. His family owns a lot of land in town. But you saw the equipment on that survey boat. Let them loose on the ocean with that stuff, and you can kiss your pristine environment good-bye. And if they go on and build a refinery too, well, there's your freshwater pollution. Makes me sick just thinking about it."

"Yeah," Narumi agreed, but inside, she was having a kind of awakening. Ever since talking with Yukawa, she'd been starting to see the value in a more neutral stance. If they could redirect the energy they'd spent on trying to find fault with the other side and put it toward finding a new direction that worked for everyone, they could all benefit.

Narumi shook her head, surprised at her own thoughts. It was Yukawa's fault she'd even started down this path. Then she remembered what he'd said when they met on the boat, about her not looking like the type to choose the ocean over the city. *What did he mean by that?*

"So, have you given any thought to what I said the other day?" Sawamura said, after they had driven a while in silence.

"Sorry?" Narumi said. She knew what he was talking about but played dumb.

"About you being my assistant at the home office. Did you think about it?"

"Oh, I'm sorry," she apologized. "It's just been so busy, I haven't really had time to sit down and mull it over. Could you wait just a little longer?"

"That's fine by me. It's not like I'm going to be asking anyone else. I don't see the point if it's not you."

There he goes again, saying things that can be taken two ways, Narumi thought. Sometimes she wished he could be a little more straightforward, like Yukawa.

They crested the hill, and the Green Rock Inn came into sight.

"What are they up to?" Sawamura muttered.

Out in front of the inn, Yukawa and Kyohei were using sticks to draw something in the dirt. Kyohei looked up when he heard the car approach. "Hey, Narumi!" he called out.

Yukawa looked up, his eyes even colder than usual.

Sawamura pulled the car up and stopped right beside them, opening his window. "How's it going?" he called out.

"Did you see what you wanted to see on the boat?" Yukawa asked.

"And more. Now I'm even more convinced we need to keep a close eye on them."

"Probably a good idea," Yukawa agreed. Then he lifted an eyebrow. "New car?" he asked.

"Old one, why?"

"Oh, nothing much, I just thought you drove a truck."

"Yeah, that belongs to the shop. My folks run an electronics store."

"I see. That pickup was the truck you used when you went to look for Mr. Tsukahara, wasn't it?"

"Uh huh," Sawamura said, his voice low. "What about it?"

"Nothing, I was just wondering what you had planned to do if you found him that night."

"What do you mean? I planned to take him back to the inn."

"How?" Yukawa asked. "Only two people can sit in the truck, and Mr. Kawahata was sitting in your passenger seat, wasn't he?"

"Well, yeah, but what else was I supposed to do?" Sawamura protested. "I had to take him with me or I wouldn't have known what the guy looked like, and the truck was the only vehicle I had."

"They have a van at the inn. I just got a ride in it. You could've used that," Yukawa suggested.

"Well, thanks for the advice, buddy. I guess I just didn't think of it at the time. Okay? I'm sure I could've figured out something if we'd found him, which we *didn't*. Mr. Kawahata could've gotten out and waited while I took them back one at a time, if it came to it."

Yukawa nodded, though by his expression he wasn't convinced. "That's true, I suppose there were options. You could always have put someone in the flatbed, too."

Sawamura looked up at him through the window. "If you have a point, I suggest you get to it. I haven't had the best day."

"No, no, sorry to trouble you," the physicist said. "Nice chatting. Now I need to get back to teaching my young assistant." He walked back over to Kyohei. Sawamura glared after him.

"Sawamura?" Narumi said. "What's wrong?"

"Huh?" He turned back to her. "Oh, nothing. Is he always like that?"

"He's a little eccentric. I wouldn't pay him too much mind."

"Yeah, probably good advice. Anyway, good work today. Let's get together soon and write up that report."

"Absolutely. Thanks for the lift," she said, getting out of the car.

Yukawa and Kyohei were standing around a design Yukawa had drawn in the dirt, deep in discussion. Narumi waited until Sawamura had driven off, then walked over to them. "Mr. Yukawa," she said, "if there's something you want to say to Mr. Sawamura, you should just come out and say it."

"Don't step on that," he said.

"What?"

"The diagram. Don't step on it. I'm showing Kyohei why the area of a circle is the radius times the circumference." Yukawa pointed at Narumi's feet. A large circle had been drawn in the dirt, with thin lines that radiated out from the center, dividing it into sections.

"I totally didn't ask him to teach me this," Kyohei said, looking put out.

"Simply plugging numbers into a formula is just mindless calculation. What we're doing here? This? This is *geometry*."

"Why were you asking him about his car?" Narumi asked. "You don't think he's involved with what happened to Mr. Tsukahara?"

"I said nothing of the sort. I was just asking a few simple questions."

"Yeah, but—"

"Don't worry. He—Mr. Sawamura, was that his name? He had nothing to do with Mr. Tsukahara's death. He has an alibi, doesn't he? He was with you when Mr. Tsukahara went missing from the inn."

"Well, he was, but—"

Yukawa looked down at his watch, then turned to Kyohei. "I just remembered something I have to do. We'll resume after dinner."

"What do you have to do?"

"There's someplace I have to go while there's still light. If I can get a taxi—" Yukawa plucked his jacket off the handles of a nearby bicycle and got on. "I'll eat dinner at six thirty," he said to Narumi, before wheeling off down the road.

THIRTY-FOUR

"Did you say Kawahara?"

"Kawahata, ma'am," Kusanagi repeated. He was speaking to a woman in her midforties.

"Oh, Kawa*hata*. No, sorry, doesn't ring a bell." She frowned a little and put a hand to her cheek.

"This would've been about fifteen or sixteen years ago. I believe you were living here at the time?" Kusanagi asked.

"Yes, that's right. This is our seventeenth year. You know, I think that makes us the longest tenants left! But I'm sorry, I don't know any Kawahata."

"They were in apartment 305. Does that sound familiar?"

"Three oh five? No wonder I don't know them. We hardly ever see the people on the different floors unless they're on the same staircase, and that unit's on the other side of the building."

The woman had been thrilled at first when she heard Kusanagi was a detective, but over the course of the questioning, she'd rapidly lost interest.

"Thank you for your time," Kusanagi said. He started to bow, but the door was already closing in his face.

The Arima Engines company housing was an old apartment building on a small, lightly trafficked street. It was four stories high, without an elevator, and just over thirty units in total.

Kusanagi and Utsumi had split up to ask at each of the apartments whether anyone knew Shigehiro Kawahata or his family, but the results so far were anemic. Most of the people who had lived here at the same time as the Kawahatas had already moved on.

Kusanagi was making his way down the staircase, scratching the back of his head with his pen, when Utsumi called out from the sidewalk below him. "Kusanagi!"

"Hey. You find something?" he asked, his tone making it clear he wasn't expecting that she had. He walked down to the bottom of the stairs so they could talk without shouting.

"Well, I found the current address of the people who used to live in apartment 206 from the woman who lives in 106. They built a house and moved out eight years ago. The name's Kajimoto, and they live near Ekota Station."

"Over in Nerima? You know when the Kajimotos moved into the apartments?"

"Not exactly, but when they moved out, they had mentioned that they'd been here for almost twenty years."

"Well, then they overlapped with the Kawahatas for sure, and 206 is on their stairwell," Kusanagi said, snapping his fingers. "Okay, let's get to Ekota."

Kusanagi hailed a cab. They had only just pulled away from the curb when Utsumi's cell phone rang.

"Hello," she answered, "Utsumi speaking. Yes, thanks for this morning. What, you found someone? Could you put me on the phone with them?" There was a pause. "Okay, I'll call back again later. Thank you so much for your help." She hung up and turned to Kusanagi. Her face was a little flushed.

"Who is that?"

"A volunteer group with offices in Shinjuku. They run a few soup kitchens and homeless shelters. I stopped by there on my way to

Arima Engines and left a copy of Hidetoshi Senba's photograph so they could show it to their staff."

"And?" Kusanagi prompted, hope stirring in his chest.

"Well, one of the women who works for them said she'd seen Senba several times at one of the soup kitchens."

"Around when?"

"She said the last time was over a year ago. I didn't get to speak with her directly—she was out. Back in an hour or so."

"Can you stop the car?" Kusanagi said to the driver. The driver hurriedly pressed down on the brake and pulled over to the side of the road.

"What's wrong?" Utsumi asked.

"Nothing's wrong. This is our best lead yet. I want you to go to that office right now and wait for this woman to get back. Driver, open the door. She's getting out."

THIRTY-FIVE

It was already past five in the evening, but the temperature hadn't dropped a single degree, and the asphalt was steaming from the heat of the day.

Nishiguchi was in East Hari, along with a police sergeant named Nonogaki, looking for the restaurant where Tsukahara had eaten lunch. Noodles had been found in his stomach during the autopsy, but noodles hadn't been served at the Green Rock Inn that evening. The degree of digestion suggested some time had passed. The noodles had an unusual characteristic, too: in addition to the expected wheat flour and salt, there were traces of three kinds of seaweed—the same three kinds commonly found in seaweed udon, a Hari Cove specialty.

Nishiguchi had been on a wild goose chase, making the rounds of all the warehouses and garages in the Hari Cove area where someone could have been poisoned with carbon monoxide, when the orders came to find out where Tsukahara had eaten lunch. Nishiguchi sighed, anticipating another afternoon spent as a tour guide to whomever the prefectural police sent down—a police sergeant named Nonogaki, as it turned out.

Nishiguchi called ahead and found three small restaurants in East Hari that served seaweed udon. They struck out at the first and were now walking over to the second, working up a sweat in the lingering heat.

The second restaurant was on a road that ran across the shoulder of a small hill, sloping downward toward the ocean. There was a gift shop out front and a small dining area in back. Some benches on the opposite side of the road provided a spot to sit and look out at the view.

A middle-aged woman was running the shop by herself. There were no customers. Nishiguchi showed her the picture of Tsukahara.

"Yeah, he was here," she answered with a shrug.

The police sergeant from prefectural homicide pushed past Nishiguchi with an intense look on his face and immediately began questioning the woman, asking if there had been anything unusual about Tsukahara's behavior, if he had made any phone calls, if he looked like he was waiting to meet someone, if he had been in a good mood. The woman just shrugged again and said there were some other customers at the same time, so she never really got a good look at him.

"Was there nothing about him that left an impression at all?" Nonogaki asked, his tone indicating that he'd already given up.

"Well, no, not really. Though he did go and sit on the bench out front when he was done eating."

"One of the benches across the road? What then?"

"That's all, just sat on the bench and looked out at the ocean. Then he walked off. Back toward the station, I guess."

"Around what time was that?"

"Oh, I don't remember exactly. Probably a little after one."

Tsukahara had taken a taxi from East Hari Station at one thirty, heading for the community center. That meant he had gone to see the house in Marine Hills first, then come here for lunch before heading for the station.

They thanked the woman and left.

Nonogaki sighed loudly. "Well, that was a bust. The victim ate seaweed udon for lunch. Big deal."

"If you'd like to ask around a bit more, I'm happy to help," Nishiguchi offered.

Nonogaki made a sour face and groaned. "Time-wise, he would've had to go straight to the station after leaving here. I don't see what more questioning would get us," he said, taking out his phone.

While Nonogaki talked with his supervisor, Nishiguchi went across the road and stood next to the bench. He could see the rooftops of several old houses lower down the hill. The trees poking up between the rooftops were a deep green. Nishiguchi came out to East Hari every now and then. The place hadn't changed in decades, and nature felt even more untouched here than over in the cove area. Of course, that meant there hadn't been much economic development either. He wasn't sure whether that was good or bad.

On another road about ten meters further down the hill, he saw a man standing and looking out over the ocean. He was carrying a suit jacket over one shoulder, and when he turned, Nishiguchi caught a glimpse of his face. Nishiguchi's eyes widened.

"Hey," Nonogaki said, walking up behind him. "I gotta get back to headquarters. Got a meeting with Isobe's team. What're you going to do?"

Guess I'm not invited, Nishiguchi thought. "I think I'll do a bit more questioning around here," he said. "I know a few people in town."

"Home-court advantage, right. Well, it's all yours." Nonogaki thrust his phone back into his pocket and walked off without so much as a glance behind him.

Nishiguchi waited for the sergeant to disappear down the road, then took a flight of concrete steps that led down the hill. The man from before was still standing on the road, apparently deep in thought.

"Excuse me," Nishiguchi said when he got closer, but the man didn't seem to hear him. "Excuse me," he repeated, a little louder this time.

The man slowly turned. There was a deep, thoughtful furrow between his eyebrows. He looked put out at the interruption.

"You're Mr. Yukawa, aren't you?"

"Yes?" the man said, looking at Nishiguchi's face for a moment before blinking, as though he'd just realized something. "We met the other day at the Green Rock Inn. You're a detective."

Nishiguchi introduced himself and Yukawa nodded, then pointed a finger at him. "You're not just any detective. You're Narumi's classmate."

"That's right. Did she mention me?"

"It came up in conversation."

This was news. Nishiguchi was acutely interested in specifically how his name had come up and was wondering how he might ask Yukawa this, when the physicist added, "She only mentioned you were classmates. We didn't get into details."

"Oh, right," Nishiguchi said, his heart sinking just a little. "You have a friend in the Tokyo Police Department yourself, don't you?"

"If you want to call him that, sure."

"He's not your friend?"

"I'd call him more of a nuisance. Do you know the kind of ridiculous questions I've had to answer, just because I happened to stay in the same inn as the victim?"

"What do the police in Tokyo think about the case? Did they say anything?"

"To me?" Yukawa said with a chuckle. "I'm just a civilian."

"But your friend—"

"As I'm sure you are well aware, detectives play by their own rules. While he may relish using friends or family as informants when it suits him, it would never cross his mind to share information with me. Not that I would necessarily want him to."

Nishiguchi nodded, wondering how much of the physicist's glib answer he could take at face value. "Right," he said after a moment. "So, what are you up to?"

"Nothing in particular. Just looking out at the sea."

"Why *here*? There are plenty of fine views of the sea back in the cove, and East Hari's a bit of a hike."

"I'm quite aware of that. It took a whole twenty minutes to get here. Do you know today was the first time I took a taxi since I arrived?"

"You're not answering my question," Nishiguchi said. He wasn't going to let the eccentric physicist push him around.

Yukawa took off his glasses and pulled a cloth from his pocket, with which he began slowly wiping the lenses. "Because I heard the view from here was exquisite," he said after a moment. "In fact, East Hari is supposed to have the best ocean view in the entire area. I read it on the Internet." He put his glasses back on.

"Do you remember what site?" Nishiguchi said, taking his pen and notebook out of his pocket. "If you could tell me, I'd be interested in checking it out."

"Actually, I do. It's a blog called *My Crystal Sea*. I believe your former classmate Narumi runs it, as a matter of fact."

"What?" Nishiguchi said, so surprised he nearly dropped his pen.

"Detective Nishiguchi, was it?" Yukawa said, facing him directly. "Can I ask you something? I couldn't help but notice Narumi's peculiar dedication to the ocean here, but I was wondering, has she always been like that?"

"Well, maybe not when she first came here, not like she is now," Nishiguchi said. "She only started working with Save the Cove this summer. Though, now that I think about it, I used to see her out on the observation deck by our school, just looking at the water. I caught her out there more than once."

"Interesting," Yukawa said, a thoughtful look on his face.

"What? You think what she's doing is wrong?"

"Not at all. It's quite admirable. Not many people have such dedication."

"Well, I'm glad you say that, because I'm a big supporter of Save the Cove, even if it might be getting in the way of your work."

"Not in the least. I always appreciate a lively debate," Yukawa said, smiling a little. "Now, if you don't have any more questions, I think I'll be off."

Nishiguchi watched Yukawa walk away, then he cleared his throat and stashed away his notebook and pen. He hadn't written a word.

THIRTY-SIX

The alarm on Kyohei's phone rang. He checked the time and turned it off. Six thirty. He looked at his open notebook lying on the floor next to him. He hadn't gotten anywhere with his Japanese homework, just written out a few kanji he had to learn and that was it. Yukawa was helping him with math, but the rest was up to him. He had given it a halfhearted attempt, but it was impossible to focus. His hand kept reaching for the game controller. He had managed to resist that urge, but he made the mistake of turning on the TV for some background noise and got sucked into watching an anime. It wasn't even one he liked, but he watched the whole thing, all thirty minutes. Finally he switched the TV back off, but he still didn't feel like studying. He just sat there, waiting for the alarm to ring.

Kyohei left the room and went down to the first floor. He checked the lobby on his way to the dining room and saw Yukawa standing with his arms crossed, staring at the painting of the ocean on the wall.

"Still looking at that painting, Professor?"

"I was just wondering when it was hung here."

Kyohei shrugged. "It's been there forever, I think. I'm pretty sure I remember it from when I came two years ago."

"I don't doubt it," Yukawa said with a chuckle and checked his watch. "Shall we?"

Narumi was just laying out Yukawa's dinner in the dining room. It was seafood, as usual. She had placed a tray for Kyohei across the table. Tonight's meal for the family was meatloaf.

"Looks delicious as always," Yukawa commented as he sat down.

"I'm sorry, I know there's not much variety."

"Not at all. There's a different fish every day. It's given me a new appreciation for seafood."

"Oh yeah," Kyohei suddenly said. "I wanted to ask you, Narumi. I went swimming today and I saw this really cool fish. It was tiny, and bright blue."

"Bright blue? About yea big?" She held her fingertips roughly two centimeters apart.

"That's right." Kyohei nodded. "It looked like a tropical fish it was so bright."

"Sounds like a damselfish," she said.

"A damsel? Like a damsel in distress? I always pictured them in white dresses, not blue."

Narumi laughed. "Well, this one is officially called the neon damselfish. We get them a lot around here. It's usually the first really impressive thing people see when they come here to try diving or snorkeling. I remember when I saw my first one. I thought it looked like a swimming jewel."

"Yeah, I tried to catch it, but it was too fast."

"I'd like to see the person who could catch one of those with his bare hands. You know, in the winter they turn black."

"That's too bad. But not like it really matters. I wouldn't go swimming in the winter."

Kyohei turned to his plate and picked up his fork and knife. The surface of the meatloaf was nicely browned, and when he cut it with his knife, sauce and juices oozed out along with a gush of steam.

"Your dinner doesn't look too bad either," Yukawa commented.

"Trade you for a piece of sashimi," Kyohei said.

"It's not a bad offer. Let me think on it. While you're here—" Yukawa picked up his chopsticks and turned to Narumi. "I had a question for you."

"Yes?" she said, straightening her back a little.

"That painting in the lobby. Do you know who the painter was?"

Narumi took a deep breath. She shook her head. "No. Why?"

"I was just curious. I spoke with Kyohei before about it, and we were wondering where it had been painted. The ocean doesn't look like that from around the inn."

Narumi brushed her hair back behind her ears and wrinkled her forehead in thought. "I don't know. It's been here for a long time. I guess I never really paid much attention to it."

"A long time? From before you moved here, then?"

"Yes. I think Dad said that someone gave it to Grandpa. I don't think he knows who painted it, either."

Narumi picked up the long-handled lighter from the tray and went to light the small burner in front of Yukawa.

"Don't bother, I'll get it myself," Yukawa said. "You can just leave the lighter there."

Narumi looked a little surprised by this, but she put it back. "Enjoy your meal," she said, preparing to leave.

"Actually, I know where that view is from," Yukawa said to her turned back. "That's the ocean from East Hari. I went and checked it out today."

Narumi stopped in her tracks, her entire body motionless. Then her head turned back around, slowly, like a robot badly in need of oil.

"Oh?" she said weakly, an unnatural smile on her face. "East Hari?"

"You really didn't know?" Yukawa asked.

"Like I said, I never really thought about it."

"I didn't think you'd need to think about it, being as familiar as you are with the sea around here. Enough to make your own Web site."

"Well, I don't go to East Hari much."

"Really? I thought you had something on your blog about the views from there."

Narumi's eyes flared. "I wrote nothing of the sort," she said sharply.

Yukawa chuckled. "It's nothing to get angry about."

"Who's angry?"

"Well, if you didn't write that on your blog, I must've been mistaken. I should apologize."

"No need to apologize. Was there anything else?"

"No, I'm fine," Yukawa said, pouring beer into his glass.

"Enjoy," Narumi said and left, her shoulders a little slumped.

"So you really found the spot?" Kyohei asked Yukawa. "You know where the painting was painted?"

"More or less," Yukawa said, pouring some soy sauce into a little saucer in front of him. He grabbed a clump of wasabi in his chopsticks and began dissolving it into the soy sauce. His motions were clinical, a scientist stirring a solution in a petri dish.

"You went all the way out there just to check the view? It bothered you that much?"

"It didn't bother me. It excited my curiosity. And I believe there is no greater sin than to leave one's curiosity unsatisfied. Curiosity is the fuel that powers the engine of human advancement."

Kyohei nodded, wondering why the physicist always made a big deal out of every little observation.

Yukawa picked up the lighter on his dining tray. He pressed on the switch and with a click, a thin tongue of flame extended from the end. Kyohei had a lighter just like it back home. They bought it for barbecues, except they had only actually used it once. His parents were usually too busy for barbecues.

Yukawa used it to light the small cylinder of waxy fuel inside the burner on his table.

"You know what the container on this burner is made out of?" Yukawa asked.

There was a white bowl-shaped saucer sitting on the burner. Kyohei stared at it and said, "It looks like it's made out of folded paper."

"That's right, it is paper. They call these containers paper pots. But don't you think it's strange that the paper doesn't burn?"

"It's probably coated with something, right?"

Yukawa used his fingers to tear a small piece off of the edge of the paper pot, then picked the piece up with his chopsticks and lit the lighter in his other hand. When the flame touched the piece, it didn't burst into flame, but instead slowly shriveled into black ash. Yukawa didn't stop until it looked like his chopsticks were going to catch on fire.

"Regular paper would have burned up the moment the flame touched it. So yes, it has some flame-retardant coating on it. But it wasn't impervious to the fire, either, which makes me question your theory."

Kyohei put down his fork and knife and came around to Yukawa's side of the table.

"So why doesn't it burn?"

"Look inside the paper pot. There's veggies, and fish, yes, but there's also a little soup. Soup is water. Do you know what temperature water boils at? They teach that in fifth grade, don't they?"

"Yeah, sure. A hundred degrees Celsius. We did an experiment on that last year."

"I'm guessing you put water inside a flask, heated it, and checked the temperature?"

"Yeah. When it got close to a hundred, the water started to bubble."

"And what happened to the temperature afterward? Did it keep going up?"

Kyohei shook his head. "No, it just stopped."

"Correct. At one hundred degrees Celsius, water becomes a gas. Conversely, as long as water remains a liquid, it can't get any hotter. In a similar fashion, as long as there is soup inside this paper pot, you can heat up the bottom as much as you want and it will never burn. That's because paper burns at around 230 degrees Celsius."

"I get it," Kyohei said, folding his arms across the chest and staring at the burner.

"Time for our next experiment."

Yukawa moved his beer glass and picked up the round paper coaster from underneath it.

"What would happen if I put this on top of the fuel cylinder in the burner?"

Kyohei looked between the coaster and Yukawa's face. It felt like a trick question. Hesitantly, he said, "It'll burn?"

"Probably, yes."

Kyohei rolled his eyes. "Where's the experiment in that?"

"Patience. How about this?"

Yukawa picked up a pot sitting next to him on the table and poured some water onto the coaster until it was drenched. Some of the water dripped on the tatami mat below the table, but the physicist didn't seem to care.

"Now what would happen if I put this on the cylinder?"

Kyohei thought for a moment. This time, the problem didn't seem so straightforward. "I know," he said. "It would burn, but not right away."

"Why not?"

"Because the paper has water in it. So it won't burn until the water's completely gone. After the water dries up, it'll catch on fire."

"I see," Yukawa said, his face expressionless. "Is that your final answer?"

Kyohei nodded. "Final answer."

"Right," Yukawa said, throwing the drenched coaster on top of the burning fuel. The coaster fit perfectly over the foil packaging around the cylinder, like a lid on a box.

Kyohei stared at the coaster. The middle was starting to get darker. He expected flames to burst up any moment, but after a while, he noticed that nothing had changed.

Yukawa took the coaster off of the fuel cylinder. The fire had gone out. "Hey," Kyohei said, giving the physicist a quizzical look.

"The important detail here is the container around the fuel. Whether you're a fuel cube or a piece of paper, you need oxygen to burn. But when I put the coaster on the fuel container, like a lid, oxygen could no longer get into the fire. Now, if the coaster weren't wet, it probably would've burned before the fire went out, and oxygen would've come back in. However, because it was wet, it didn't burn right away, like you theorized. And wet paper is much better than dry paper at blocking the passage of air."

Yukawa picked the lighter back up and relit his fuel cube. Again, he put the wet coaster on top of it. He snatched it off a moment later, but the fire had already gone out.

"It's like magic," Kyohei said.

"Haven't you ever learned that when oil in a frying pan catches on fire, you shouldn't pour water on it? The best thing to do is to throw a wet towel over it and cut off the supply of oxygen. Things need oxygen to burn, and without oxygen, fires go out. And if there's some oxygen, but not a lot, it will burn incompletely."

"Like what we were talking about today in the car?"

"That's right," Yukawa said, lighting the fuel block for third time. "Burning fuel without sufficient oxygen in the air creates carbon monoxide."

Kyohei thought back to their ride in the van, wondering why his uncle and aunt had looked so put out.

"Aren't you going to eat?" Yukawa asked. "Your meatloaf's getting cold."

THIRTY-SEVEN

Kusanagi was at a coffee shop near the north exit of Ekota Station. It was a small place, with room for only three at the counter by the windows looking out toward the street. He sat on the chair in the middle of the counter, drinking water and biding his time. His coffee cup had been empty for the last ten minutes.

When the hour hand on his watch reached seven, he stood and went outside. He walked down the winding one-way street lined with small shops, noticing signs for ramen and a couple of bars. Eventually he emerged onto a slightly wider street, though still too narrow to warrant a center dividing line.

Past the shopping district, he came into a more residential area. He advanced slowly, taking care not to miss his turns. This was already his second visit to the house, but he'd gotten lost the first time and didn't care to repeat the experience. He used landmarks to guide him. The streets in the residential area were even more tangled than the shopping district, with nary a right angle in sight. He sympathized with the local police—the officers on patrol had their work cut out for them.

It was with some relief that he spotted the white tile building illuminated by a streetlamp: the residence of one Osamu Kajimoto.

He pressed the button by the door, and Mrs. Kajimoto answered the intercom as she had earlier that day. He'd known Mr. Kajimoto wouldn't be home, but he'd dropped by to leave a message and impress her with the importance of his visit.

The front door opened and a skinny man in a short-sleeved polo shirt greeted him. He had big eyes and a long face that made Kusanagi think of horses.

"Mr. Kajimoto? Sorry to bother you this time of the evening."

"Not at all," Kajimoto said, welcoming him inside, a curious look on his face. All Kusanagi had told the wife was that he wanted to talk to them about their old company apartment in Oji.

He was led into a living room that was spacious; however, every flat surface was covered in clutter, making the room feel much smaller. Kusanagi complimented them on their nice home.

"It's falling apart around us," Kajimoto said, though he didn't sound displeased. "I'll have to put some work into it one of these days."

"You moved here directly from the company apartments?" Kusanagi asked, getting right to it. "How long were you in Oji altogether?"

"Quite some time. Eighteen, nineteen years. We married young."

"You were in apartment 206, correct? I was wondering if you happen to remember the person living in apartment 305, a Mr. Kawahata?"

"Kawahata?" Kajimoto said, slowly nodding. "Yeah, there was a Kawahata there. You remember him, don't you?" he asked his wife, who had taken a seat in one of the dining room chairs.

"The Kawahatas lived there almost as long as we did, as I recall," she said.

"Yeah. They had already been there for five years when we moved in. But he got married late, and was a lot older than us. Mostly you just get the young newlyweds in company housing."

"According to our records, you overlapped with them about ten years at the apartments. Did you socialize at all?"

Kajimoto folded his arms across his chest and thought. "Well, there was a big cleaning day every year, and occasional apartment meetings, so I saw him there, but we weren't particularly close." He turned a curious eye toward Kusanagi. "Um, did something happen to Mr. Kawahata?"

Kusanagi gave a thin smile. "I can't get into the details, but we're looking into people who moved from the Oji area to other areas during a certain time frame, and Mr. Kawahata moved during that period."

"Oh, I see. So you're not just looking into Mr. Kawahata, then?"

"That's right. He's the—" Kusanagi paused to count on his fingers. "—twentieth person I've looked into so far, and that's just me."

Kajimoto leaned back and shook his head. "Sounds like quite the job, Detective."

"It's not all car chases and handcuffs like you see on TV," Kusanagi agreed. "Anyway, was there anything about Mr. Kawahata that left an impression on you? Any trouble or anyone else in the apartments?"

Kajimoto gave it a moment's thought, then said, "No, he wasn't really the kind to start trouble, at least as far as I knew."

Mrs. Kajimoto frowned and turned to her husband. "Weren't they the ones who were hardly ever there?"

"Yeah?"

"Yes, I'm sure of it. I remember he got assigned to an office somewhere down south."

Kajimoto pondered that, then nodded. "Yeah, now that you mention it, that's right. Mr. Kawahata did get transferred—he was down in Nagoya."

"Ah, we do have records that say he had been assigned to your company's Nagoya branch at the time of his retirement."

"Well, that makes sense," Kajimoto said, then he laughed. "If you knew that, you could have saved me the trouble and told me, Detective."

"Sorry, I forgot until your wife mentioned it," Kusanagi lied. "So it was just his wife and daughter in the apartment most days, with Mr. Kawahata coming home on the weekends, something like that?"

"That sounds about right," Kajimoto said.

"No, dear, it wasn't like that," his wife butted in. "It wasn't like that at all. You remember."

"What *was* it like?" Kusanagi leaned forward.

"Nobody was in their apartment those last one or two years. Not him or his wife or his daughter."

It was a little after eight o'clock when Kusanagi finally left the Kajimotos' house. He thought back over their conversation as he made his way back down the winding streets toward Ekota Station. The biggest surprise of the evening had been the fact that none of the Kawahatas had been living at the apartment for a year or two before they officially moved out.

"It's not as though they were completely absent," the wife had told him. "Occasionally I'd see Mrs. Kawahata come in to freshen the place up or pick up some things. I talked to her on one occasion, and she said that they were staying at a friend's house—something about their friend being overseas on work, so they were watching the house while they were away. She said it was more convenient for them, because the house was much closer to her daughter's school."

Kusanagi wanted to know who this friend of theirs was, and where their house was, but Mrs. Kajimoto didn't know or didn't remember. She did, however, recall the name of the private school where the Kawahatas' daughter was going. It was a school for girls, wellknown enough that Kusanagi had heard of it.

He decided that he would pay a visit to the school to check out their yearbooks the following morning. He knew from Yukawa that the Kawahatas' daughter's name was Narumi. If he could find some of her classmates, he might be able to find out whose house they had been living in.

He managed to reach the station without getting lost. There was still no word from Utsumi. He was about to call her when his phone rang—but it wasn't her. He quickly answered. "Kusanagi speaking."

"Hey," Director Tatara said in a deep voice. "You have a moment?"

"Yes, sir."

"I was just meeting with a friend of mine—he's a regional director from Tsukahara's last posting."

"Yes?"

"Well, apparently someone from the prefectural police paid them a visit today. I'm sure you can guess why."

"They were asking about Tsukahara? Did they want to know if anyone had a grudge against him, something like that?"

"And whether he had ever mentioned Hari Cove, yeah. They're going down through a list of everyone connected to the victim, looking for loose ends."

"Something wrong with that?"

"Not with that in particular, but there's something I don't get. They weren't asking anything about Hidetoshi Senba. Do the guys down in Shizuoka not think Senba's case is important? You told them what I said, right?"

Kusanagi frowned. He hadn't expected Tatara to get back to them so quickly, nor could he think of a good excuse off the top of his head.

"What?" Tatara said when Kusanagi didn't immediately reply. "You haven't told them?"

Kusanagi took a deep breath and said, "No. Not yet, sir."

"Why not?"

"A conjecture, sir."

Kusanagi tensed; his hand on the phone was sweating. Unconsciously, he braced himself, as though he were about to get physically smacked.

All he heard on the other end of the line was a long sigh. Then Tatara said, "This conjecture of yours is based on some information from a source?"

Tatara was sharp. He was talking about Yukawa, clearly.

"Yes, sir," he replied. "Valuable information."

"Valuable enough to help us identify a suspect?"

"Probably, yes. But it's going to take a bit of doing before we're ready for that."

"On your part, I take it? And you don't want the guys from the prefectural police involved?"

"I think this would go more smoothly if we handled it ourselves, yes."

Tatara fell silent. Kusanagi felt a bead of sweat trickle down beneath his armpit. He tensed again, ready for the shouting to start.

But when Tatara spoke again, he was calm. "What's Utsumi up to? She with you?"

"No, I have her tracking down Senba right now."

"Any leads?"

"An eyewitness who saw him." He explained about the soup kitchen in Shinjuku.

"All right," Tatara said. "I left this in your hands, so we'll play this the way you want to. But I need you to promise me you'll tell me the exact moment you have everything you need to pin down a suspect. Got it?"

"Understood, sir."

"Great, then get to it," Tatara said, hanging up.

Kusanagi took a deep breath and pressed the buttons on his phone, feeling his shirt cling to his skin with sweat.

"I was just about to call you," Utsumi said when she answered. She sounded chipper. Maybe she'd found something.

"Where are you? Still in Shinjuku?"

"No, Kuramae."

"What are you doing out there? You get something from the woman with the volunteer group?"

"I did. Ms. Yamamoto—that's her name—told me that Senba used to come by their soup kitchen every week until last winter or so. She said she remembered him in particular because he carried himself with a little more composure than their usual customers."

"Until last winter . . . so she hasn't seen him this year?"

"That's right. She thought he might have passed away."

"Why'd she think that?"

"He wasn't doing so well the last time she saw him. She said she referred him to a doctor that gave the homeless checkups for free."

"Did he go?"

"I had Ms. Yamamoto call the clinic, but they never saw anyone by the name of Senba. He might've gone under an alias, so I thought I'd pay them a visit tomorrow and show the doctor his photo."

"Right. So, why Kuramae?"

"Apparently, there was one other person who knew Senba—he used to work with Ms. Yamamoto, but he transferred to a different volunteer group this year. Their office is in Kuramae. They run a soup kitchen on Sundays in Ueno Park."

"And you think Senba might've switched from Shinjuku to Ueno?"

"I did, so I had Ms. Yamamoto call him, but unfortunately he hadn't seen Senba in Ueno Park either."

"Okay. So wait, why are you in Kuramae?"

"Well, he hadn't *seen* Senba, but he did meet someone looking for him."

"What? When?" Kusanagi gripped the phone tighter in his hand.

"Back in March."

Kusanagi took out his notepad and pen and crouched on the ground. Holding his phone to his ear with his shoulder, he spread the notebook out across his knee. "Tell me where the office is. I'm coming too."

He hung up and hailed a taxi. The ride to Kuramae took about half an hour. The office was on the second floor of a small, brown building just off Edo Street, near the Sumida River.

He pressed the buzzer outside the door and heard someone moving inside. The door opened, and a short man in his forties peeked out. "You the police?"

Kusanagi nodded and looked into the room. Utsumi was sitting in front of the desk, buried in files.

The man introduced himself as Tanaka. "Please, come in."

Kusanagi made his way in between the cardboard boxes on the floor, and asked Utsumi, "Did you go over everything?"

"Most of it, yes. Mr. Tanaka identified Tsukahara as the man who came looking after Senba."

"Did he say anything about why he was looking for Senba?" Kusanagi asked Tanaka.

"No. I figured he was with a collection agency. We get a few of those. A lot of the homeless are people running from debt."

"Mr. Tanaka tells me that Mr. Tsukahara came here at the end of March, and then again two or three times after that. He would always stand a little ways away from the soup line, just watching. But he never saw him after May—is that right?" She turned to Tanaka, who nodded.

"Nobody much liked the look of him. We were happy when he stopped coming. Did something happen? What's this investigation about, anyway?"

Kusanagi chuckled and waved his hand. "It's nothing big," he said, watching Utsumi stand up out of the corner of his eye. "We may have some more questions for you later on, but I think we're good for now. Thank you for your time," he said, heading for the door.

The left the building together and walked down the street a little way until they found another coffee shop—the same chain as the one in Ekota Station.

The two exchanged reports, and Kusanagi mentioned his conversation with Tatara.

"Did you tell him what Yukawa said about being careful how we solved the case?"

"No. I don't think there are many other people in the department who would appreciate the subtleties involved there. And I think Tatara understands what we're up against. If Yukawa's getting involved on his own accord, we don't want to do anything to hold him back. So, what's your next step? I was going to look into where Mrs. Kawa-hata and Narumi were living those last few years in Tokyo," Kusanagi said, taking an unenthusiastic sip of his coffee.

"Well, something occurred to me when I was talking to Mr. Tanaka."

"And that is?"

"Well, I'd say it's certain that Tsukahara was searching for Senba—we have sightings of him from two places at two different times now. But I'm thinking a detective like Tsukahara wouldn't have stopped there. He was probably making the rounds of several places." Utsumi turned almond-shaped eyes toward Kusanagi. "But then he stopped coming in May. What if he stopped coming because he found Senba?"

Kusanagi set his coffee cup down and shot her a penetrating look. "What if he did? Is there something there that we can work with?"

"When Senba was spotted in Shinjuku, he was emaciated. It was clear at a glance that he was sick. If Mr. Tsukahara found him in April, I doubt he looked any better."

"He might even have been dead."

"Last night, I went through the database of unidentified bodies found in the greater Tokyo metropolitan area this year. There wasn't anyone who matched Senba's description, but I'll check again. It gets more difficult if he wasn't dead. What if Tsukahara had found him at death's door? What you think he would've done in that situation?"

Kusanagi leaned back in his chair and let his eyes wander as he thought. "I suppose he'd have taken him to a hospital first. He'd get him checked out, and if he needed it, hospitalized. There are hospitals that specialize in the homeless."

"Offering free or very low-cost services, yes."

"Right. There's about forty or so just in Tokyo."

"Yes, except it's doubtful he would have been able to get care, even at one of those hospitals. They require a residence card, and Senba didn't have one of those after he got out of prison. I checked his records. If they went to the hospital, Tsukahara must have paid the fees."

"Possibly. It sounded like he was pretty bad off."

"He might've required hospitalization."

"Which would mean paperwork."

"That's right. Except, when a homeless person with no registered address needs hospitalization, the hospital typically tries to register them for public assistance to defray costs. In order to do that, they need to issue a residence card under the hospital's address. But his records showed no sign of that having happened, either."

"So what did happen?"

"Well," Utsumi said. "I'm thinking it was either a hospital that didn't require public assistance, or"—she leaned forward, a gleam in her eye—"someplace that owed Tsukahara a favor."

THIRTY-EIGHT

At the Hari police station, the overall mood of the investigative task force was dark, and with every successive report, the mood in the conference room darkened further. Everyone could see that the proceedings lacked one important element: results. Hozumi from prefectural homicide stared glumly at the reports on the desk in front of him. They were essentially a detailed and objective account of how little the task force had achieved after days of questioning. They included Nishiguchi's report on the restaurant in East Hari where Masatsugu Tsukahara had eaten seaweed udon the day he died—more information that offered no hope of resulting in a lead.

Nishiguchi sat toward the back, keeping one eye on the proceedings while he ruminated on his exchange with Yukawa in East Hari. Nishiguchi had checked the blog *My Crystal Sea*, where Yukawa claimed he'd seen Narumi extolling the virtues of the view, but there was nothing in there about the view from East Hari. In fact, East Hari wasn't mentioned at all.

Did that mean the physicist had intentionally lied? And if so, why?

The meeting dragged on. Now they were getting into the reports on the method of the killing and possible murder scenes. They still hadn't found the place where the victim was poisoned. If the murderer had somehow lured the victim into a car, drugged him with sleeping pills, then arranged to kill him by carbon monoxide poisoning inside the vehicle, he or she could have done the deed anywhere. Afterward, they could have dropped him off the seawall when no one was looking—an easy feat to pull off after sundown, in the countryside, where there would be no witnesses.

Just in case a car hadn't been used, they looked into unused storerooms, cottages, and empty homes in the area as well. Yet they had found nothing with any connection to the case. There was a room in one hotel, closed now for several years, with scorch marks on the floor. However, given the accumulation of dust, it was unlikely anyone had been there within the last month, if not longer. The marks were probably something left by vandals.

"How about the victim's background. Anything on that?" Hozumi asked, his voice thick with fatigue.

"I have a report from our Tokyo task force," Isobe said, standing with some papers in his hand. The Tokyo task force was a small squad that had been sent to look into Masatsugu Tsukahara's personal life and connections.

Isobe cleared his throat and began. "The victim, Masatsugu Tsukahara, retired from the Tokyo Police Department last year. Before he retired, he was part of the Department of Regional Guidance, and we spoke with three of his colleagues there. . . ."

Isobe delivered his report with uncustomary vigor, but the news clearly wasn't what Hozumi had been hoping for. Tsukahara had been devoted to his work, committed to crime prevention with impressive determination, and displayed an uncommon attention to detail. He wasn't very social, but once he got to know someone, he would do anything for them. In other words, he wasn't the type who made many enemies.

He was never at the center of any drama in the workplace, and his transition to retirement had gone smoothly. All his former colleagues agreed that no one had been rubbed the wrong way, and nothing critical had been left undone.

Hozumi frowned and stretched, putting his hands behind his head as he leaned back in his chair. "Doesn't look like much is going to come from that direction, then. How about this other guy. Senba, was it? Anyone seen him?"

"We were thinking of expanding our questioning in East Hari a little further east," Isobe offered, though it didn't sound like he had much hope that would result in much.

"And we still don't know if this guy's even alive?"

Isobe winced. "Tokyo said they'd let us know if anything turns up."

"What about the connection between the victim and Hari Cove? Anything other than Senba we can go on?" Hozumi asked the room, irritation creeping into his voice.

"Tokyo says that no one remembers hearing the victim talking about Hari Cove. Which means the only thing we have that might have brought him here was the hearing on the undersea development project. I think we have a report on that—hey, Nonogaki," Isobe called out, looking around. Nonogaki stood from one of the tables toward the front of the room.

So that's where he got to after we finished, thought Nishiguchi. He hoped Nonogaki had more to show for the day than he did.

"Right, so, attendance vouchers were required to get into the hearing, and we confirmed that the voucher in the victim's possession was genuine. In order to get a voucher, it was necessary to send an application to DESMEC by mail, along with a self-addressed stamped envelope. Also, not everyone who applied actually got in. They received about twice as many applications as they had spots for, so the winners were decided by lottery. I talked to DESMEC, and they confirmed that the victim was one of the winners."

"And?" Hozumi prompted, a look in his eyes that said there had better be more.

"The dates for the hearing were set in June, and they started accepting applications to attend in July. Announcements were posted in the Yomiuri, Asahi, and Mainichi papers, as well as on DESMEC's Web site. The victim sent in his application on July 15, which we determined by checking the postmark on the envelope he'd used to send it in. Interestingly, the watermark showed that he'd mailed it from the Chofu Station Post Office."

"Chofu?" Hozumi raised an eyebrow. "That's in Tokyo, right? Er, out on the west side, was it?"

"Someone get a map of Tokyo," Isobe barked.

One of the young detectives on Isobe's team dashed up to the front table with a Tokyo-area road map in his hand and opened it for Hozumi. In the back, Nishiguchi looked up Chofu Station on his phone. It *was* to the west, about fifteen kilometers out from Shinjuku.

"The victim's residence is in Hatogaya, Saitama, which as we know is north of Tokyo," Nonogaki continued. "That address was written on the back of the envelope, and matches the address that DESMEC had on file from their application lottery. But we're still not sure why the envelope was posted from Chofu." Nonogaki took a seat.

Hozumi looked at the road map a bit more, then he frowned. "Could be there was no particular reason. He probably had something to do in Chofu and threw the letter in a mailbox along the way."

"That's a possibility," Isobe said. "But we spoke to the widow on the phone, and she said she couldn't think of any reason why her husband would have gone to Chofu. They had no friends or relations out there, and it's also quite a haul from their home in Hatogaya. The victim didn't own a car, so he must've gone by train. That means he would've had several chances along the way to post a letter much closer to home."

Hozumi's silence seemed to indicate that he didn't think Isobe was full of it, for a change. Eventually, he lifted his eyes from his desk and looked around the room. "Anyone else have any opinions on this?"

After several seconds of silence, a deep voice said, "Sir," and

Motoyama raised his hand. "We might not know why the victim went to Chofu, but isn't it possible that he was in Chofu when he found out about the DESMEC hearing? What if someone he met there told him about the hearing, and he decided he had to go, filling out an application on the spot? Then he could've put the application in the mail when he got back to the station on his way home."

Hozumi nodded. "That works. That just leaves us with the question of why he went to Chofu."

"I can get the Tokyo task force on that," Isobe offered.

"Do that. Probably best to have someone meet with the widow directly and ask her again, too."

THIRTY-NINE

Kusanagi whistled as his eyes followed the polished curves of the navy-blue hybrid. It was a two-wheel drive, got 15.8 kilometers to the liter, and cost a cool six million yen.

If I had that kind of money to drop on a car, I'd think about moving first.

He tried opening the driver's-side door. It had a good weight to it and shut with a nice, solid sound.

"Feel free to get in," said a voice from behind him. He turned to see a woman in a light gray suit with short-cut hair smiling at him.

"That's okay, I didn't come to see the car, actually," Kusanagi said. He looked down at the badge on the woman's lapel. "Ms. Ozeki?"

"Yes," she said, still smiling. "And you are Detective . . . ?"

"Kusanagi," he said, quickly flashing his badge.

Her eyes widened for just a moment, and she said, "Right this way," leading to him to a table with some chairs.

"Would you like something to drink?"

"No, that's fine. Save it for the customers."

"It's quite all right," she said. "Some coffee? Or iced tea?"

"Iced tea, then."

"Great," she said, bowing curtly before walking off.

At least she seems cooperative, Kusanagi thought, sighing a little as he checked out the catalogs featuring the latest models on the table.

It was a little after one in the afternoon. Kusanagi had come to a car dealership in Tokyo's Koto Ward to talk to one Reiko Ozeki, Narumi's former classmate.

Earlier that morning he'd visited Narumi's old middle school and taken a look at the yearbooks. Kusanagi then tracked down three of the girls who'd been in tennis club with Narumi and set out to pay each of them a visit. The first was out when he dropped by. At the second house, the girl's parents told him she'd gotten married and moved up north to Sendai. At the third house, he had found Ozeki's parents. Her mom had been kind enough to call her at the car dealership so she would know he was coming.

Reiko returned with a tray and a glass of iced tea, which she placed in front of him before sitting down with her own glass.

"Sorry to bother you at work like this," Kusanagi apologized.

"My mom called back after you left, you know," Reiko said. "She wanted me to find out what kind of investigation it was. She loves those mystery shows on television."

"Can't say I watch them."

"She was very excited about meeting a real detective. Which, I guess I am too, a little." She smiled and drank some of her tea. "So, what kind of investigation is this?"

"Unfortunately, I'm not allowed to talk much about it."

"I was afraid of that. Too bad," she said, still smiling.

"Actually, I came to talk to you about your middle school. You were in tennis club, correct?"

"Oh, wow, that was a long time ago. Yes, I was."

"Do you remember a Ms. Narumi Kawahata?"

Reiko's smile grew brighter and her eyes sparkled. "Narumi? Of course I remember her. Boy, it's been ages since we talked."

"Were you in touch after graduation?"

"Oh sure. She didn't go to my high school, though. Her family had to move away. But we talked on the phone now and then. It's been about ten years, I think." Reiko looked off, reminiscing, before quickly turning back to Kusanagi, her mouth open. "Wait, was Narumi involved in something?"

"Not at all," Kusanagi said, remembering to smile. "My case doesn't directly involve her, actually. I had a few questions about the place where she was living."

"You mean her house?"

"Yes. At the time the Kawahatas' address was in Oji, but I understand that Ms. Kawahata commuted to school from a different house. Were you familiar with her living arrangements?"

A wrinkle formed between Reiko's eyebrows as she thought. Kusanagi knew it was a long shot. She might have forgotten in the last fifteen or so years, if she even knew in the first place.

He was on the verge of telling her it was okay and leaving, when Reiko looked up. "Well—"

"You remember where she lived?"

"I went to her house a few times. I know it wasn't in Oji."

"Where was it?"

"I don't remember the place exactly. Except, I remember the station we got off at."

"Which was?"

"Ogikubo."

Ogikubo, where Nobuko Miyake was murdered. Kusanagi's heart thudded in his chest. He made an effort not to let it show on his face. "Ogikubo, right. Do you remember anything more? For example, what direction you walked from the station?"

Reiko frowned and shook her head. "It was a bit of a hike. Narumi used her bike to get to the station from home, I remember that," she said, not sounding particularly confident.

"Did she live in a house or an apartment?"

"A small house, I think."

"Do you think you could show me on a map?"

"Sure, one moment." Reiko stood.

Kusanagi watched her walk off and drank some of his tea. He loosened his necktie and tried to cool off a little.

Reiko returned a few moments later, carrying a laptop computer. "It'll be quicker if we check on this," she said, going online and pulling up a map of the area around Ogikubo Station.

"Do you have any idea where the house might have been?" Kusanagi asked.

Reiko started the screen for a while, but then shook her head. "I'm sorry. I don't think so. I was always following Narumi, so I never really paid attention to the route."

That was unsurprising. At least Kusanagi wasn't leaving empty-handed.

"I was thinking," Reiko said. "You could ask Narumi yourself. I have her number. At least, that is, if she hasn't moved."

"Oh, no, that's fine." Kusanagi shook his head. "We're just starting by talking to people here in Tokyo. I'll be speaking with Ms. Kawahata at some point, and I do have her number. She's currently in Hari Cove, I believe."

"That's right. Her father's from there originally, right? That's where they went after Tokyo."

Kusanagi nodded. "Actually, I wanted to ask, do you remember if the move was a sudden decision, by any chance? Had they known about it for some time before?"

"Well, for us, it did seem pretty sudden. I mean, Narumi thought she'd be going to high school with us. And we knew about the family business, but she said she wouldn't go, even if they left—even if it meant staying in Tokyo all by herself. That's why we were all so surprised when she just up and left for Hari Cove."

"Did you talk to her about that on the phone?"

"No, not really. I think there must've been something going on, you know, something personal." Reiko's eyes narrowed as she looked at the detective. "You said this didn't have anything to do with Narumi, right? Does her moving have something to do with your case?"

"No, not particularly."

"Well then, I have no idea what you're after. Could you at least tell me what kind of case it is? This is really going to bug me."

"I'm really sorry," Kusanagi said, bowing his head, "but it's against the rules." He stood from the table. "Thank you again for your time and for your help."

"Was it? A help, I mean."

"Absolutely." Kusanagi began to walk toward the door, but stopped halfway and turned around. "Actually, there's one more thing I'd like to ask you. A favor. I am going to go talk to Ms. Kawahata, eventually, but if you could, please don't mention this to anyone. Word travels fast, and there's a chance she might hear about it before I get a chance to sit down with her."

Reiko nodded, then a mischievous smile came to her face. "I can tell my mom, right? She knows I'm meeting with you, after all."

"I'd prefer it if you didn't, honestly."

"What? You know she's going to give me a thorough questioning when I get home."

"Well, you'll just have to think of something to tell her," Kusanagi said.

"Something to tell her. Right." Reiko frowned.

He walked out through the sliding doors onto the street. He was pondering his next move, when a voice from behind called out, "Detective?"

He turned to see Reiko running over to him. "I just remembered something. I went over to her house once in early April. There was a park really nearby, and we all went there to see the cherry trees."

"A park with cherry trees? Are you sure?"

"Yes—that was the only time we went cherry blossom–viewing in middle school, so I remember it really well."

Kusanagi give it some thought, then nodded and smiled at her. "Thank you, that's very—"

"Helpful, I know. You're sure I can't talk about it?"

Kusanagi shook his head. "Sorry, no."

"Right," she said. She wished him good luck with the investigation, then went back to the showroom. Kusanagi watched her leave, then set off again, taking big strides in his excitement.

Both Ogikubo and a park featured prominently in the crime scene details surrounding Nobuko Miyake's death. It was looking more and more like the Kawahatas were involved with the Senba case after all.

He was just thinking he should call Yukawa and tell him, when his phone began to buzz. He checked the display. It was Utsumi. She had gone to talk to Tsukahara's widow to see if she might know where he would've taken a homeless man to receive medical care.

"You get anything?" he asked, picking up.

"I can't say for sure, but what I did hear is very intriguing."

"The widow told you something?"

"No, not from her, it was from the prefectural detectives."

"What, you ran into them?"

"They were at the house when I got there. Two guys, both in homicide. They let me observe."

"What were they there for?"

"They wanted to know if Tsukahara had any connections out in Chofu."

"Chofu? This is the first time I've heard anything about Chofu."

"Yeah, me too. Apparently he mailed something from the post office by the station." She explained the attendance voucher and the hearing in Hari Cove.

"What did the widow say?"

"She gave it some thought, but in the end, she said she didn't know. She thought he might've gone there while he was still on duty, but he never talked about work at home."

He pictured Sanae Tsukahara's face, that look of determination in her eyes. If she had never asked her husband about his work, it wasn't due to a lack of interest. It was because she knew there were things she was better off not knowing, just as there were things he was better off not having to share.

"The prefectural guys want to know anything else?"

"Nothing new. They asked again whether she'd thought of any connection to Hari Cove, things like that. Of course she had nothing for them."

"Did they ask you anything?"

"They wanted to know why I had come to visit the widow."

"You tell them about the hospital?"

"Should I have?"

Kusanagi grinned. "What'd you say?"

"I told them I came to borrow family albums—that I was looking for a photo that might show Tsukahara in Hari Cove."

"Did they buy that?"

"It took the wind out of their sails a little. They knew that the Tokyo Police Department was involved, but I don't think they were very impressed with that particular line of inquiry. Nor with the fact that Tokyo had put a single detective on the case—young and female, at that. Incidentally, there weren't any photo albums in the house. Someone from the prefectural police took them all the last time they visited."

Utsumi spoke very matter-of-factly, and Kusanagi had to strain to detect the slight hint of irritation in her voice.

"Don't let it get to you," he said. "Besides, you got something out of it."

"It didn't get to me. And I'm glad you think the trip was useful."

"Of course it was. If Tsukahara mailed his application from Chofu, it probably means he was out there meeting someone with a deep connection to Hari Cove."

"I agree, and I'm already on it. Sorry to tell you after the fact."

Kusanagi steadied his grip on his phone. "You're going to Chofu?"

"I went back home and got my car—the plan is to check in with every hospital in the area."

"Good call. Shizuoka prefectural police will start asking questions around there sooner or later, but you've got a leg up on them with the hospital lead. Make it count."

"Will do. How are things on your end?"

"Well . . ." He licked his lips. "I've got a few leads. I'll tell you about them when you're done. I don't want to distract you while you're on the beat."

"Now you're getting my hopes up."

"As they should be. Later," he said, and hung up. Normally, he would've told her about the house in Ogikubo by the park—except he didn't feel ready yet. He was still turning it over in his mind, trying to figure out what it all meant.

FORTY

Yukawa had placed three paper triangles on the table. He'd stacked three sheets of paper and cut them out at the same time, so they would be identical. First, he stuck two of the triangles together to make a parallelogram, then he added the third to form a trapezoid.

"See? Put the three inside angles together, and you get a straight line. In other words, 180 degrees. This is the basis for the rest of our calculations. You can make a square by putting two triangles together, which means that the sum of its inside angles is two times 180, so 360 degrees. Similarly, with a pentagram . . ."

Yukawa was going out of his way to make everything clear, but to no avail. Kyohei's mind was off in a different place. Last night, before he went up to bed, he wandered down to check in with his uncle and aunt and heard hushed voices spilling out into the hallway by their apartment. He couldn't catch everything they said, but one thing he heard crystal clear:

"He knows. That professor knows."

It was Uncle Shigehiro's voice.

Kyohei had crouched, frozen in place. Gradually, he forced himself to turn around and walk quietly back down the hallway, straining to step quietly across the old floorboards.

He'd gone straight up to his room and crawled into his futon. A horrible, black premonition pushed down on his chest, and it felt like his heart would never stop racing. He was being kept in the dark, but he wasn't stupid. Something was happening, something bad. Why else would his uncle talk like that, in a voice that made him sound like a horrible person saying horrible things?

At some point, Yukawa had stopped talking. Kyohei looked up. The physicist was resting his chin on his hands, staring at him as though observing some experimental test subject.

Kyohei scratched his head and looked down at the table. Yukawa had drawn several diagrams in a notebook spread out on the table. The most recent one was a shape with nine sides.

"I asked you how many triangles you can divide a nonagon into, but from that look on your face, I don't have my hopes up for an answer."

"Uh . . . right . . ." Kyohei hurriedly picked up his mechanical pencil, but he wasn't even sure where to begin.

"Pick one corner, then draw lines from that corner to every other corner, except the ones right next to it. That means you can only draw six lines, giving you seven triangles. The sum of their inside angles is seven times 180 degrees, so 1,260 degrees." Yukawa reached across the table and wrote the calculation in the notebook. He wrote upside down so Kyohei could read it, the pencil moving even faster than Kyohei could have written it right side up.

"What's the matter?" The physicist raised an inquisitive eyebrow. "You aren't focusing at all today. Something on your mind?"

"No," Kyohei said, unable to come up with a good excuse. When his phone began to ring, he reached for it, thinking, *Saved by the bell*. But he didn't recognize the number on the display.

"Aren't you going to answer that?" Yukawa asked.

"My mom told me never to answer the phone if I don't recognize the number."

"The number wouldn't happen to be . . ." Yukawa said, rattling off ten digits in rapid succession, ". . . would it?"

Kyohei jerked in his seat. "Yeah. How'd you know?" He held up the phone to Yukawa.

"It's for me," Yukawa said, snatching the phone from Kyohei's hand and answering it as though he'd done nothing out of the ordinary at all. "Yeah," he said. "No problem. You find anything out after that?" He stood and left the room, still talking.

Hey, that's my phone, Kyohei thought, standing with a scowl. He went over to the door and opened it a little. He could see Yukawa standing with his back to the room, phone pressed to his ear.

"I see. Ogikubo? Yes, that's probably it, then. I knew it had something to do with the family. Right, good idea."

Kyohei slid the door shut and stepped quietly back to his spot at the table. His knees were trembling, just like they had the night before. His uncle's voice echoed in his ears.

"He knows. That professor knows."

FORTY-ONE

When a guest stays six days, it starts getting hard to come up with a new menu for dinner, Narumi thought with some guilt as she laid out a meal almost exactly the same as the one from the night before.

Yukawa walked into the dining room. "Evening."

"Hello, Mr. Yukawa. Did you go out to the survey boat again today?"

Yukawa nodded, sitting cross-legged on his cushion by the low dinner table. "I finally have things up to speed to start some tests. Makes me wonder when I'll be able to go back to Tokyo, though."

"You'll be here a while longer?"

"It's hard to say. If DESMEC would stop wasting everyone's time, this should really only take a few days."

There was a sound at the door, and Kyohei strode in. As usual, he sat down across from Yukawa. He was carrying a tray with some pork cutlets and rice.

"Once again, you've got quite a feast for yourself."

"I'm always willing to share," Kyohei said.

Yukawa snorted and looked up at Narumi. "I have a request. Starting tomorrow, can I have the same dinner as him?"

"Oh, but that's the family dinner, you don't want that—"

"Actually, I *do* want that. And don't worry, I won't ask you to lower your rates or anything."

Narumi rested her hands on her knees and hung her head. "I'm sorry. You must be sick of the same thing every night. I'm really trying my hardest."

Yukawa chuckled dryly and waved his chopsticks in front of his face. "I'm not upset. The seafood here is remarkable. It's just, it's possible to grow tired of restaurant food, and start wanting something a little more like home."

Narumi looked him in the eye. "You mean like your wife cooks?"

Yukawa shrugged. "Unfortunately, my wife doesn't cook anything, because I'm not married. When I speak of home cooking, I mean things that I make at home. Although I've no doubt the home-cooked meals from your kitchen would be several grades superior. Do you do the cooking here?"

"I help, but it's my mom who does most of it. When we're busier, we have a cook who comes."

"Your mother?" Yukawa said, sticking his chopsticks into some jellied fish. "Well, she has quite a bit of talent. Did she study somewhere?"

"She worked at a restaurant when she was younger. I think as a sort of apprentice."

"Someplace in Tokyo?"

Narumi shrugged. "I think so."

"Oh, I know that story," Kyohei butted in. "She met Uncle Shigehiro at a restaurant, right?" He looked to Narumi for confirmation.

"Right," she admitted. "But I don't know any embarrassing details, if that's what you're after."

Yukawa shrugged. "It was before you were born."

"They made lots of local dishes there, that's what Uncle Shigehiro said," Kyohei added.

"Local to where?" Yukawa asked.

"I mean they caught lots of fish from the sea here in Hari Cove and made it like they do here, except they were serving it at the restaurant in Tokyo. Get it? That made it taste different from the other places. My uncle told me all about it."

"Was that so?" Yukawa asked, looking at Narumi.

She shrugged, unsure why the physicist's eyes put a knot in her stomach.

"Well, it sounds fabulous. Local food away from home. A welcome taste for people in the big city, no doubt. That must've been what attracted your father. Sounds like destiny to me."

"Sounds like you've been watching too many movies," Narumi said, shaking her head.

"I wouldn't be surprised if a lot of people from around here ended up at that restaurant, along with your father. They must've had quite the reunion, familiar friends around familiar dishes."

"I don't know. I guess," Narumi said, standing. "My parents never really talk about it." She tried to smile, but her cheeks were tight and her face drawn. "Enjoy your meal," she managed, and fled the room.

Back in the lobby, she stopped when she saw the painting on the wall, remembering what Yukawa had said to her the night before. He knew the painting had been made in East Hari. And now he was asking more questions. She regretted having mentioned that Setsuko had ever worked at a restaurant.

She wondered what Yukawa knew. How much had he realized? And what had he been discussing with his detective friend, Kusanagi? The sound of the telephone ringing on the front counter stopped her on the way to the kitchen. She tensed, a bad feeling welling up inside her as she remembered the last call she had taken from the Tokyo Police Department. Her throat felt tight. She coughed once to clear it before picking up the receiver. "Hello, Green Rock Inn."

"Hello? I'm sorry, but is this the Kawahata residence?" The voice belonged to a young woman. She sounded very polite.

"Yes, it is, may I ask who's speaking?"

There was a pause, then the woman said, "Yes, my name's Reiko Ozeki. Is Narumi home?"

Narumi immediately began flipping through faces in her head. It took about three seconds before she remembered.

"Reiko! Hi, how are you? It's me."

"I thought it was you! Your voice hasn't changed at all. It's been so long! How have you been?"

"I'm doing okay."

The unexpected call from an old classmate lifted Narumi's spirits for a moment, but then another premonition crept in. *It's been ten years. Why would she call now?*

"It's been so long, and I've been thinking I should give you a call, but I just never found the time. It's been busy at work. You know, I'm working at a car dealership now."

"Wow, sounds great," Narumi said, bristling. *You never found the time before, so why have you found it now?*

"What've you been up to? I guess if you're still at your parents' house, you're not married?"

"Nope. I'm here, helping out with the inn."

"Oh, that's good. Hey, have you heard? Naomi's got two kids already. And her husband's a *total* loser."

They began talking about some of the other girls who had been in their tennis club, feeding each other with gossip and recent news. It was fun enough, but a voice inside Narumi's head kept repeating the question, *Why now?*

She listened politely until Reiko asked, "So, how've things been with you? Anything new?"

"What do you mean, anything new?"

"I mean anything. You know, any fun surprises, random encounters?"

What are you getting at? Narumi thought, but she said "No, nothing really. Just life, you know."

"Oh," Reiko said. "Well, that sounds just like me, then. Oh, hey, look at the time. I'm sorry. You must be busy. I hope I didn't interrupt your work too much."

"No, it's fine. I was just wrapping up for the night."

"Look, I'll call again soon. Hey, can you give me your cell phone number?"

They exchanged numbers and Narumi was half expecting her to hang up, when Reiko asked, somewhat hesitantly, "That was Ogikubo, right?

"Huh?" Narumi tensed. "What about Ogikubo?"

"Your house. You lived near the station, didn't you?"

"Yeah, but what about it?"

"Oh, it's nothing. Just, talking about old friends made me remember, but I wasn't entirely sure, you know? Sorry. Anyway, talk again soon."

"Yeah, thanks so much for calling," Narumi said, waiting until she heard her hang up before she put down the phone. Her hand was shaking.

There was no doubt about it in her mind: someone had come asking Reiko questions. They wanted to know about Narumi's middle school, about where she had been living. Whoever it was must have left an impression for Reiko to call like this out of the blue.

The police, Narumi thought. *They're looking into my past. Into Ogikubo.* Her legs shook beneath her until it was too much for her to stand, and she had to crouch, steadying herself with one hand on the old front desk.

FORTY-TWO

By the time he reached Azabu Juban Station, it was a little after nine o'clock. *There won't be too many customers left by now,* Kusanagi thought. Flower restaurant closed at ten.

He approached the building and looked up the outside staircase. A young man and woman were just coming down the steps. He waited for them to pass by before climbing the stairs.

Kusanagi opened the door and looked inside. The young man at the cash register looked up, then swallowed whatever he was about to say.

"Sorry, it's me again," Kusanagi said.

The young man nodded and looked into the back. Muroi was just coming out, wearing a red apron.

"I'll be free in just a bit, if you don't mind waiting," he said.

"Not a problem," Kusanagi said, sitting down at the nearest unoccupied table.

There were three groups of customers still seated. They looked mostly like businessmen, sharing the day's news over beer and whiskey sours.

Kusanagi reflected on his last conversations with Yukawa. He'd spoken to the physicist twice today. The first time, he called in the early evening, using a number Yukawa had given him for the phone of "someone who is the most likely to be with me." It had rung a few times before Yukawa had answered.

Kusanagi told him that while Shigehiro Kawahata had been posted in Nagoya, his wife and daughter had been living in a house in Ogikubo—the very same town where Senba had murdered Nobuko Miyake.

"Very interesting indeed. That puts the Kawahata family and Senba at the same spatial and temporal coordinates," Yukawa had mumbled, half to himself.

"That may be," Kusanagi said, "but I still have no way of finding out what the family was up to back then. You think you have a chance of finding some connection with Senba?"

"Hard to say, but I'll give it a try," the physicist had responded. "Given that Senba's wife and Shigehiro Kawahata are from the same area originally, it might be that they just happened to run into each other at some point. But given that Shigehiro wasn't in Tokyo at the time of Senba's crime, it might be that the connection lies not with Shigehiro, but with his wife, Setsuko."

"That's a possibility. So, what's Mrs. Kawahata like?"

"Well, if you're picturing some old lady in the countryside, you couldn't be further from the mark. She doesn't wear much makeup, but she's no bumpkin. Looks a lot younger than her age, too. I hear she left home young and was living on her own in Tokyo before she got married."

The description did overwrite the mental image that Kusanagi had of Setsuko Kawahata. He also sensed that the physicist was driving at something. "A young, attractive woman living on her own in Tokyo . . . you think she might've been involved in the sex industry?" Kusanagi asked.

"I don't get those vibes, but I'd say there's a high possibility she was involved in some kind of customer service."

"Okay, well, find out what you can," he had said and hung up.

Then, about two hours ago, Yukawa had called him back. "It was a restaurant," he said as soon as Kusanagi picked up.

"What was a restaurant?"

"Setsuko worked at a restaurant in Tokyo before she got married. That's where she met Shigehiro Kawahata. Also, it specialized in Hari cuisine. Shigehiro probably went there for a taste of home."

"And walked away with a lot more," Kusanagi had said, when a light went off in his head, and he gasped out loud.

"What?" Yukawa asked.

Kusanagi licked his lips before saying, "Every once in a while, I get flashes of inspiration too."

"This sounds interesting."

"I'll tell you when I know for sure," Kusanagi said, giving the physicist a taste of his own medicine for once. He would've gone straight to Flower, but knowing it would be crowded, he'd decided to wait until closer to closing time.

Muroi walked over to the table, unfastening his apron. "Sorry to keep you waiting," he said.

"Not at all. Sorry to bother you again," Kusanagi replied. "There was something from our discussion yesterday that I want to check with you."

"What, exactly? We talked about a couple things, as I recall."

"You mentioned that the late Ms. Miyake and Senba used to talk about food from back home. You think they might've been talking about Hari cuisine, by any chance?"

"Hari?" Muroi put a hand to his forehead and thought for a moment, then he slapped his knee. "Yeah, there was a Hari place in Ginza they talked about going to. That's where they got the present they brought me! It was dried noodles or something."

"Seaweed udon, maybe?" Kusanagi asked.

"Yeah, that was it. The noodles were pretty standard, except for the flakes of seaweed in them," Muroi said, his face brightening.

That was confirmation enough for Kusanagi. Senba had been a regular at the restaurant where Setsuko worked. Not just Senba, but the late Nobuko Miyake, too, which meant Setsuko had probably seen her as well.

Just then, a text came in to Kusanagi's phone. It was from Utsumi. He pulled up the message, and his eyes widened.

Found out where Senba is being hospitalized. Coming back now.

FORTY-THREE

Narumi hesitated as she walked. She knew she had to do something, but she wasn't sure what. She poked her head into the kitchen. Setsuko was standing there, sharpening a knife. The clock on the wall showed it was already after ten.

"Mom?"

Setsuko almost jumped. "Hey, there. You startled me."

"Where's Dad?"

"Hmm? The bath, probably."

Perfect.

"There's something I wanted to ask you," Narumi said hesitantly.

Setsuko put down a knife. There was no astonishment in her eyes, just cold resolve, as though she already knew what her daughter was going to say. "Yes?" she said, her voice barely a whisper.

"I just got a call from one of my friends back in middle school. It wasn't about much, but at the end, she asked me about Ogikubo."

Setsuko's eyes narrowed. "Ogikubo?"

"Yeah. She just sounded like she wanted to make sure that's where we lived. She didn't say why. But I think I know."

"And?"

The look of defeat on her mother's face made Narumi's chest ache. It was a sure confirmation that her suspicions were right, and any hope she might have clung to was false.

Desperately trying to keep any hint of tears out of her voice, she said, "Well, this is just a guess, but I think someone came to talk to her. Someone wanted to know where I was living in middle school. Probably the police."

"Why do you think that?" Setsuko asked with an uncomfortable smile. "Maybe she just called you on a whim?"

Narumi shook her head. "I don't think so. The timing's too perfect."

"What do you mean by that?"

"I heard from Nishiguchi that Tsukahara, the man who was killed, used to be a detective with the Tokyo Police Department. A homicide detective."

The smile faded from Setsuko's face.

Narumi continued. "And I heard something else from Mr. Yukawa about Mr. Tsukahara being spotted at a resort development in East Hari, where a murderer he arrested once used to live—I'm pretty sure he heard it from his friend in Tokyo homicide. I'm also pretty sure who the victim of that murder was."

"Narumi," Setsuko said, a severe look on her face. "We promised never to talk about that."

"I think we're past that point now, Mom. I don't know what's going on, but the police in Tokyo are moving on this. They're looking into our family. Please, you have to tell me the truth. I know you know something. Why was Mr. Tsukahara here? What happened that night? *What did Dad do?*"

A look of anguish passed across Setsuko's face. She lowered her eyes.

"Please," Narumi said.

Setsuko looked back up, but before she spoke, she glanced over Narumi's shoulder, and her eyes went wide. Narumi turned, almost fearfully. Her father was standing in a T-shirt and exercise shorts, a towel draped around his neck.

"Keep it down," Shigehiro said, languidly, "or they'll hear you all the way to town." He walked in, leaning on his cane. He pulled a bottle of tea out of the refrigerator, poured some into a nearby cup, and drank it down with gusto. He appeared so calm that Narumi thought for a moment he actually might not have heard what they were talking about.

Setsuko was still silent, her eyes fixed firmly on the floorboards.

Shigehiro finished drinking his tea, then took a deep sigh. "Guess that's it, then," he said.

Narumi glanced at her father. "What's it?"

"Shigehiro—" Setsuko began.

"You be quiet," Shigehiro said in a gravelly voice. He turned a gentle smile to Narumi.

"There's something we need to talk about. Something very important."

FORTY-FOUR

Kusanagi arrived at the restaurant and found Utsumi sitting at one of the tables in the back. He waved off the hostess, who had come to greet him, and walked in.

Utsumi had been fiddling with her phone, but she put it away when she saw him approach. "I'm sorry," she said. "I wasn't thinking and sat in the no-smoking section. You want to move?"

"No, we're fine right here," he replied. "You get precedence tonight. You've been out questioning people all day."

The waitress came up, and without looking at the menu, Kusanagi ordered coffee. Utsumi already had a coffee on the table in front of her.

"So, let's have it. How'd you find him?"

"The traditional method. I started asking at every hospital in the Chofu Station area. I could eliminate any place that was outpatient only, which didn't leave too many. When I showed Tsukahara's picture to the receptionist at the fifth hospital, she told me she'd seen him visit several times."

"Good work. Where was this?"

Utsumi produced a brochure from the Shibamoto General Hospital.

"It's a medium-sized place. Notable because it has a hospice center."

Kusanagi had been about to take a sip of his coffee, but he put it back on the table. "Senba's in hospice? What is it, cancer?"

"The director of the hospital and his appointed physician were both out today, so I couldn't get the details. But one of the nurses confirmed that Senba's in hospice care. That would indicate late-stage cancer, or something close to it. She couldn't tell me more."

"Did you see him?"

Utsumi shook her head. "They don't let anyone in other than family after 6:00 p.m. In this case, they'd been considering Tsukahara family, and the nurse mentioned that he'd paid for the hospitalization."

"Was there some connection between Tsukahara and the hospital, then?"

"I'm not sure. One of the nurses did see Tsukahara speaking with the director on several occasions, and she thought they might be friends."

Kusanagi took a sip of weak coffee and grunted. "Well, you might be right about Tsukahara having some pull there. The question now is, why did he go to such lengths to take care of Senba?"

"A very good reason," Utsumi agreed, a hard light in her eyes.

Kusanagi crossed his arms and leaned back in his chair, looking at her. "You're thinking something, aren't you? You've got an idea, vague though it might be."

"I'm guessing you do too, Detective Kusanagi."

Kusanagi snorted. "Okay, stop acting all important and get on with it. What's your amazing theory?"

"There's nothing amazing about it. It's just what Tatara said. Tsukahara had Senba's case on his mind. The case might have been officially closed after the arrest, but there was some deeper truth that remained uncovered, and Tsukahara knew it."

Kusanagi rested his arms on the table and looked up at the younger detective. "A deeper truth, eh? So let's hear it."

Utsumi hesitated for a moment before brushing back her hair and shaking her head. "I don't believe in wild speculation without solid evidence."

Kusanagi chuckled and scratched his lip beneath his nose. "That's probably a good policy, but maybe I can give you a little help on the evidence front." He glanced around and said, more quietly, "I found out where Mrs. Kawahata and her daughter were living. The exact address is still a mystery, but I know the station they lived near: Ogi-kubo."

Utsumi's eyes gleamed.

"The Kawahatas were involved in that case sixteen years ago—there's your deeper truth. As to how they were involved, well, I have a guess," Kusanagi said, adding with a grin, "Of course, that would be wild speculation."

FORTY-FIVE

Kyohei was busily removing a mountain of mud with his hands. He attacked it with vigor, both arms flailing, yet no matter how hard he worked, the mud only piled higher and higher, outpacing his efforts.

The pile was towering over his head when it started to change shape into a more familiar, humanlike form. *It's going to chase me.* Kyohei ran—or tried to run, except his feet wouldn't budge. He crouched, and the mud-man peered down at him. *Don't look at his face.* Kyohei shut his eyes. Then he felt it pressing into him, the mud-man's face pushing into his own until it became difficult for him to breathe. Still, he kept his eyes shut.

I won't open my eyes, I won't—

Finally he couldn't stand it any longer, and he let his breath out. The feel of the mud against his face changed, turning to something softer.

Fearfully, he opened his eyes to see he was in his room. His head had slipped from the pillow, and he'd been sleeping with his face buried in the folds of his futon.

What a crazy dream.

He got up slowly. His pajamas were clingy with sweat.

Still a little groggy, he grabbed his phone off the table and checked it, a little surprised to see it was almost eleven in the morning. He hadn't slept in like this once since coming to Hari Cove.

He got dressed and stepped out of his room. He was hungry. He made his way down the elevator to the first floor and was heading for the dining room when he stopped. He had almost forgotten what time it was. Yukawa would have finished his breakfast ages ago. He cut across the lobby and made for the family apartment, when he heard someone talking. Kyohei stopped again, remembering the overheard conversation from the night before.

Stepping quietly, Kyohei approached the door. He was about to put his ear up to it and eavesdrop when he heard a voice say, "And how did that happen?" Kyohei almost jumped. The voice sounded exactly like someone he knew very well, someone who couldn't possibly be inside the apartment.

"I'm sorry about all of this, really, I am," he heard Uncle Shigehiro say.

"It's not me you need to apologize to," the familiar voice said. Now Kyohei was almost entirely sure who it was. He opened the sliding door.

Shigehiro and Setsuko were sitting down side by side, both of them looking surprised. The man standing facing them turned around. It was Kyohei's father. He was wearing jeans and a T-shirt, and his travel bag was on the floor next to him.

"Kyohei! How long have you been there?"

"I just came in. Why are you here, Dad?"

"Why? I'm here to come get you."

"Already? You're all done in Osaka? Where's Mom?"

"No, the work's not done. Your mom is still down there. We're going to go join her."

"What? I'm going to Osaka too?" Kyohei asked, confused.

"Yeah. We're not so busy anymore, so it's not like you'll be stuck in a hotel all day. And it's about that time when you start getting serious about your summer homework, isn't it? I can help you if you're down there with me."

Kyohei stared at his father's face. Something was wrong. There must have been some reason he came to pick him up early. Kyohei wondered what it was but didn't ask. He was scared to hear the answer.

"Are we going to Osaka right away?"

"Well, no." His father looked back toward Shigehiro and Setsuko, before returning his gaze to Kyohei. "Not right away. We won't be leaving until tomorrow morning."

"Tomorrow?"

"Yeah, there's a few things we need to settle here first. Anyway, I've got you a room at a different hotel, so you can move there for the night."

"Why? I can't stay here?"

"Sorry, Kyohei," Aunt Setsuko said, smiling. "It's probably better for you to go. We're a little busy here tonight."

"Sorry," his uncle echoed.

Kyohei grunted and shut the door. He walked down the hallway out into the lobby, where his eyes rested on a train schedule posted on the wall, and he stopped short.

When would you have to get on a train from Osaka to make it to Hari Cove by this time of day? He didn't know for sure, but it must've been a really early bullet train, like the very first one of the morning. *Why was Dad in such a rush to get here, and why are they kicking me out?*

FORTY-SIX

Utsumi drove a dark red Mitsubishi Pajero. They'd been told to avoid using personal vehicles for investigations, but this was one regulation the usually straight-laced junior detective didn't seem to mind ignoring. Kusanagi frequently ignored it himself, which was why he never said anything to her. In fact, today, she was giving him a ride.

They got off the freeway at the Chofu exit and drove to the hospital. There were two buildings: a square cream-colored one and a longer gray one. Utsumi told him the gray one was the hospice center.

She parked in the lot out front and they went in through the main entrance to the hospital. The air conditioners were running, and the inside of the building was cool. There were about a dozen people sitting on the long benches in the waiting room, though it was difficult to tell how many were patients and how many were just visitors.

Utsumi walked up to the information counter. She'd called ahead to confirm that the hospital director was in today.

The woman at the desk made a phone call, spoke a moment, and handed the receiver to Utsumi. She took it and turned around to face Kusanagi while she talked, a curious look on her face. Finally, she hung up, and after exchanging a few words with the woman at the front desk, Utsumi walked back over, looking relieved.

"The director says he'll meet with us. He's up on the second floor."

"Was there a problem? You were on the phone for a while."

"He said he was busy, and we should come back if it wasn't an emergency."

"What did you tell him?"

"I told him I wanted to talk to him about Masatsugu Tsukahara. He knew immediately who I was talking about and asked if anything happened to him."

"So he doesn't know about the murder."

"Apparently not. When I told him Tsukahara had passed away, he said he wanted to hear everything, and we should come up right away. He sounded shocked."

"I'd imagine so," Kusanagi said. "Let's get up there."

They took the stairs up and walked down the hall until they found the director's office. Kusanagi knocked on the door, and a man's voice from inside said, "Come in."

The director was an older man wearing glasses and a white doctor's coat. He had a large build, with white streaks running through his short-cropped hair. Kusanagi showed his police badge, and they exchanged cards. The hospital director's name was Ikuo Shibamoto.

Shibamoto motioned for the detectives to sit down on a sofa and took a seat across from them. "I was very surprised to hear that Mr. Tsukahara passed away. When did this happen?"

"The body was found roughly five days ago in a place called Hari Cove."

"Hari? What was he doing out there?"

"He was discovered having fallen on some rocks by the ocean. The exact details are still unclear."

"I see," Shibamoto said, looking down for a moment. "What is it you wanted to ask?"

Kusanagi straightened a little in his seat and looked the director straight in the eye. "We understand that you have a Mr. Hidetoshi

Senba in your facility. And that it was Mr. Tsukahara who checked him in and paid for his treatment. Is this correct?"

Shibamoto looked a little bewildered, but when he spoke, his voice was steady. "That's right."

"When did he check Mr. Senba in?"

"Around the end of April."

Kusanagi nodded. That fit with Tsukahara's absence at the soup kitchen in Ueno from May onward.

"Pardon the intrusion, but what was your connection to Mr. Tsukahara, Director?"

Shibamoto was silent for a moment, collecting his thoughts. "About twenty years ago, we had a bit of difficulty concerning malpractice at the hospital. Someone on the staff leaked word that one of our doctors had made a mistake, a patient had died, and that there had been a hospital-wide effort to conceal what happened. Typically, it's very difficult to prove malpractice, but in this case, every new piece of evidence that came to light was stacked heavily against the hospital. The doctor tried to assert his innocence, but the defense was a mess, losing critical pieces of evidence and the like, until the hospital was pushed into a corner. The director of the hospital at the time was my father, and the investigation took a toll on him.

"Masatsugu Tsukahara came to their rescue. He did the rounds, questioning everyone at the hospital until he found the informant, a nurse who'd been present at the surgery. It turns out that she'd fabricated the malpractice claim, trying to get back at the hospital for years of poor treatment.

"Her motives were infantile, yet her actions put the entire hospital in a very precarious position. If the truth of the matter hadn't come to light, even if we'd been found not guilty of malpractice, the stain on our image would've been difficult to remove," Shibamoto explained calmly.

"So when Mr. Tsukahara came to you with an ill homeless man with no residential card, you felt obligated to take him in?"

Shibamoto frowned for moment, but it soon faded. "If it hadn't been Mr. Tsukahara who brought him, it would've been difficult to convince us to make the exception, yes."

"How did Mr. Tsukahara explain the request to you? Did he mention his connection to Senba at all?"

"Not in much detail, no. He only said Senba was someone he had known for a long time."

"And Mr. Tsukahara covered all of his hospital expenses?"

"The patient was penniless."

"How is Mr. Senba's condition? I've heard he's in hospice care?"

A wrinkle formed between Shibamoto's eyebrows, and he frowned. "We're generally not supposed to talk about the condition of patients in our care, but I'll make an exception, given the circumstances. As you said, he's in our terminal care ward. Mr. Senba has a brain tumor."

That was a surprise. Kusanagi had been expecting some other kind of cancer.

"Malignant, I assume?" Utsumi asked.

Shibamoto nodded, his face hard. "At the time when Mr. Tsukahara brought him here, he'd already deteriorated quite a bit. He could still walk, though he required a cane. His health was in bad shape, and he was emaciated. Mr. Tsukahara said that one of his friends, another homeless man, had been taking care of him, but if he'd found him even a week after he did, it might have been too late."

"And there's no hope for recovery?"

Shibamoto shrugged. "If there were, he wouldn't be in hospice care. Surgery isn't an option. His disease is so far progressed that there would be no point."

Kusanagi sighed and leaned forward. "Is he conscious?"

"It depends. Would you like to see him?"

"If possible, yes."

"Wait a minute," Shibamoto said, standing. He walked over to his desk and picked up the phone. After exchanging a few words, he turned to look at the detectives. "The nurse says he's doing well today. You can meet him now if you'd like."

"Please," Kusanagi said, standing.

Shibamoto nodded and spoke a few more words on the phone before putting it down. "We have a visiting room on the third floor of the hospice ward. Please wait there."

Kusanagi and Utsumi thanked him and left. The hospice center was newer and wrapped in a deeper silence than the hospital. They took the elevator up to the third floor and followed the map they found posted on the wall. A nurse in a pink uniform was standing outside the room.

"You're from the director's office?" the nurse asked.

"Yes, thank you for letting us see him."

Kusanagi went to show his badge, but the nurse smiled and raised her hand to tell him there was no need. "Please wait here. I'll bring Mr. Senba."

The nurse walked off, and Kusanagi and Utsumi went inside the visitors' room. There were two small tables, with folding chairs on either side. No one else was in the room.

Kusanagi sat down on the nearest chair and looked around. The room was devoid of décor and had only a single round clock on the wall. He could hear the sound of the second hand ticking.

"It's quiet," he said. "Almost like time moves at a different pace here."

"I'm guessing that's on purpose," Utsumi said.

"Why do you say that?"

"Well . . ." She hesitated for a moment before continuing. "When you consider that everyone here has a limited amount of time left . . ."

Kusanagi grunted and leaned back in his chair.

They sat in silence until they heard a sound approaching: something rubbing against the floor outside. Eventually, Kusanagi realized it was the sound of wheels rolling across the tiles.

The noise stopped, and the door opened. The nurse reappeared, pushing a wheelchair in front of her. Sitting in the wheelchair was an old, emaciated man. His wrinkled skin clung to his bones, and the shape of his skull was clear beneath his wispy hair. His neck made Kusanagi think of a plucked chicken, and his hands where they emerged from the sleeves of his billowing pajamas looked like withered twigs.

Kusanagi and Utsumi both stood. The nurse pushed the wheelchair in front of them and put on the brake.

The old man remained facing the back wall, unmoving, except for his eyes, which twitched a little in their sunken sockets. Kusanagi knelt down and peered into those eyes. "Hidetoshi Senba?"

The man's narrow jaw moved. "Yes," he said. His voice was raspy but firmer than Kusanagi had imagined it would be.

Kusanagi showed the old man his badge. "We're detectives from Tokyo homicide. I believe you know a Mr. Masatsugu Tsukahara?"

Senba blinked a few times, then said, "Yes."

Kusanagi kept looking straight at him when he said, "I'm afraid Mr. Tsukahara has passed away."

Senba's sunken eyes opened wide, staring out into space. Though his face was pale, the skin around his eyes reddened as his mouth cracked open. "When? Where?"

"Several days ago, in a place called Hari Cove."

"Hari . . ." Senba croaked, opening his eyes, then narrowing them. The wrinkles on his face shifted each time he moved. Then he groaned, a low, guttural sound that might've been a quiet scream. But he hardly moved. He was still facing the blank wall in front of him.

"The investigation is still ongoing, but there is a possibility that Mr. Tsukahara was murdered. I was hoping you might have some information that could help us."

Senba's eyes turned toward Kusanagi, not quite focusing.

"Mr. Senba. Do you know why Mr. Tsukahara went to Hari Cove? That's near where your wife's family lives, correct? Do you think there could be a connection?"

Senba's mouth twitched, as if he was muttering.

Kusanagi was about to repeat his question when Senba turned his head a little and raised his left hand—a signal for the nurse to put her ear by his mouth. She nodded once or twice, then said, "Wait just a moment" to the detectives and left the room.

Senba sat in his chair, his eyelids closed. Kusanagi waited in silence.

When the nurse returned, she was carrying a piece of paper. She exchanged a few words with Senba, then held the paper out to Kusanagi.

It was a clipping from a newspaper article. The date read July 3. It was a call for applications to attend a hearing on undersea development in the Hari Cove area.

"The sea in Hari," Senba suddenly began to speak. "The sea is a treasure to me. I wanted to know . . . to know what was going to happen to it, so I talked to Mr. Tsukahara." He spoke slowly, mustering the strength for each word. "Mr. Tsukahara said . . . that he would go. He said he would hear what they were going to do. That's why Mr. Tsukahara went to Hari Cove."

"That's all? Is there another reason why Mr. Tsukahara would have gone to Hari Cove?"

Senba shook his head, his face quivering. "No other reason." Then he tilted his head again and raised his right hand. The nurse quickly undid the stopper on the wheelchair with her foot.

"Wait, I have a few more questions—"

"I'm sorry, Mr. Senba is tired now," the nurse said, pushing the wheelchair out of the room.

Kusanagi exchanged glances with Utsumi and sighed.

They were outside the hospital, heading for the parking lot, when Kusanagi's phone rang. It was from a public phone. *Yukawa.* He answered it.

"So, did you find out who did it?" Kusanagi asked.

"In a manner of speaking."

"What manner of speaking?"

"I was just told to leave the Green Rock Inn. It sounds like the Kawahatas are going to be leaving for some time."

"Wait, they're not—"

"They're turning themselves in to the police."

FORTY-SEVEN

Nishiguchi paced like a caged animal at the zoo. He glanced down at his watch. Only two minutes had passed since he'd last looked at it. He scratched his head and pulled his handkerchief out of his pocket to wipe the sweat from his forehead. He had already loosened his tie, and his jacket was sitting back in the lobby of the Green Rock Inn.

It was a little after one thirty in the afternoon, and the sun was nearly at its zenith, blazing down from the nearly cloudless sky, baking the pavement beneath. He wanted to go back inside, where the air-conditioning would at least keep him cool, but then he'd have to be with the Kawahatas, and that was even more uncomfortable than this heat.

Soon he heard the sound of engines coming from up the hill, and several police cruisers arrived, followed by a van. They all had their lights blinking, but no sirens were on.

The lead cruiser pulled in while the rest remained parked alongside the road.

Isobe and two of his men got out. Nishiguchi bowed to them.

"Where's the suspect?" Isobe asked.

"Inside."

"He's saying he did it?"

"Not quite. He is saying it was his fault, though."

Isobe frowned at that. "Any accomplices?"

"The wife helped get rid of the body."

"And the daughter?"

"She . . . it seems like the daughter didn't know anything."

Isobe snorted to indicate he wasn't buying any of it. He barked an order to his men, and the three of them headed for the door. Nishiguchi followed along behind.

The call had come from Narumi about an hour earlier. Nishiguchi had been eating lunch at a small police station to the east of East Hari. He'd spent the entire morning walking around, looking for people who'd seen Senba or Tsukahara, only to end up with empty hands and an emptier stomach. It was clear they were just making him walk around to prove there were no gaps in their questioning dragnet—busywork for a young officer.

Still, his heart had leapt a little when he saw the call from Narumi. The way his day had been going, an opportunity to talk to her was like a ray of sunshine through the clouds. But her voice was far darker than he had anticipated. She said she wanted him to come to the inn. She had something to tell him, but it didn't sound like good news. He told her he'd be there right away and hung up. When he arrived at the Green Rock Inn, Narumi was waiting for him with her parents, all of their faces long.

When he asked them what had happened, Shigehiro Kawahata stepped forward and announced he was turning himself in for allowing Masatsugu Tsukahara to die, and trying to hide that fact by abandoning the body.

Nishiguchi had been taken aback. He hurriedly pulled out his notebook to write the words down, but his hand was shaking so badly he couldn't write straight. It was hard enough to write the date.

Shigehiro spoke in a calm, orderly manner, and through his confusion, Nishiguchi slowly understood what the man was telling him.

He immediately called his supervising officer, Motoyama, and was told to wait there.

When Isobe and his men walked in, the Kawahatas stood up from their bench in the lobby. Shigehiro bowed his head deeply. "I'm sorry for causing everyone so much trouble."

"It's okay, you can all sit down," Isobe said, taking off his shoes and stepping up into the lobby. His men followed suit.

Nishiguchi paused, unsure whether he should follow, and ultimately remained standing by the entryway. He looked up with a start to realize that Motoyama and Hashigami had arrived and were standing next to him.

"We'll get the story in more detail down at the station," Isobe said, looking down at the family, "but if you just give me a general idea?" Next to him, Nonogaki took out a notepad and prepared to take notes.

Shigehiro looked up. "It was my fault, all of it. I was lazy, and Mr. Tsukahara paid a horrible price for it."

"Sorry?" Isobe asked. "Lazy?"

"I knew the boiler and the building were getting old, but I did nothing about it. I was wrong. That's why this . . . accident happened."

"You're saying it was an accident?"

"Yes, an accident. I should've told the police right away, but then I . . . I'm so sorry." He bowed his head deeply once more.

A perplexed look passed across Isobe's face, and he scratched his head. "I think you should start by explaining exactly what happened."

"Right, of course. Well, like I said in an earlier statement, that night I was outside in the backyard with my nephew setting off some fireworks.

"A little while before that, Tsukahara came down to the kitchen and asked if we had any good strong drink. When I asked him why, he said that he always had trouble sleeping on trips. I know I shouldn't have, but I gave him a sleeping pill I'd gotten from a doctor friend years ago. It was only one, I swear. Anyway, Tsukahara thanked me and went back to his room. Right after that, I called Kyohei and told him to come on downstairs so we could set off some fireworks in the backyard."

Later, at around eight thirty, Shigehiro had gone back inside to call Tsukahara's room and ask when he wanted his breakfast in the morning, but Tsukahara didn't pick up. So he went back out to the backyard and resumed the fireworks. They finished a little before nine. He tried phoning Tsukahara again, but there was no answer. He went to check the baths, found them empty, then went up to the Rainbow Room on the fourth floor, where their guest was staying. He found it unlocked, with Tsukahara nowhere in sight. Eventually, Setsuko came back from town in Sawamura's truck, and he told them about their missing guest. Sawamura said he would help check the area around the inn, so with Shigehiro in the passenger seat, they drove around, but found no sign of Tsukahara—all of this was exactly as Shigehiro had said in his earlier testimony.

What he didn't say, however, was what had happened next.

After Sawamura went back to town, Setsuko took another look around. It was then that she noticed some light spilling out of the doorway on the fourth floor, the door to the Ocean Room. She opened the door and noticed a faint smell of something burning. When she went inside, she was astonished to find Tsukahara lying there on the floor. He wasn't breathing. Panicked, she called Shigehiro. Shigehiro took stock of the situation and hurried down to the basement, where he discovered that the boiler had stopped.

The boiler room in the basement was connected by a single pipe to the chimney on the roof of the inn, bringing the exhaust from the boiler up through the walls and outside. The pipe ran past some of the guest rooms, including the Ocean Room, where it passed just behind the main closet. It had never been a problem, except the gradual deterioration of the building and an earthquake several years earlier had resulted in a crack in the back wall of the closet. The pipe itself wasn't airtight. The Kawahatas had noticed an occasional smell of soot in the room before, and generally avoided using it for that reason.

Tsukahara, sprawled on the floor in his yukata, was dead, except his skin color looked unusually healthy. Having worked many years at an engine manufacturer, Shigehiro realized immediately it was carbon monoxide poisoning.

As to why Tsukahara had been in the Ocean Room in the first place, he could only guess. He thought maybe he had heard the sounds of fireworks going off in the backyard and come to take a look. In order to make things easier when they did cleaning, they rarely locked the unused rooms. To Tsukahara's misfortune, he'd already taken the sleeping medicine he got from Shigehiro. Shigehiro thought he must've fallen asleep while he was watching the fireworks and never noticed the smell of gas in the room.

"I know I should have alerted the police immediately, but I didn't. I don't know what came over me," were the words Shigehiro Kawahata used. He had suggested to Setsuko that they move the body somewhere else. Carbon monoxide poisoning wasn't something readily apparent, so if Tsukahara were wounded in some other way, Shigehiro figured the police might never look any closer.

"I suggested we throw him over the seawall. My wife resisted. She said we should call the police. But I pressured her." Shigehiro sat with his head hanging, his hands clenched into fists on his knees.

Setsuko looked like she might say something, but Isobe held up a hand to stop her.

"If you would, ma'am, please hold your testimony until later when we're all back at the station. I'd like to hear everything your husband has to say first. Mr. Kawahata?"

Shigehiro coughed once before resuming his story. "My wife and I carried the body. It wasn't easy, with my injury and all, but we got him into the van. Then we took him down to the seawall and, after we were sure no one was looking, we threw him over. I put an overcoat on the body before we dropped him so it would look like he had gone out for a walk. I threw the sandal down too. Then the two of us went back up to the inn. Our daughter and our only other guest, Mr. Yukawa, came back right after that. That's it. That's everything." When he had finished speaking, he lowered his head again slowly.

Isobe nodded, rubbed the back of his neck for a moment, then turned to Nonogaki. "You get all that?"

"Yes, sir."

"Detective," Shigehiro said, looking up. "I hope you understand, it was all my fault. My wife was just doing what I told her to. Please—"

Isobe held his hand out in front of Shigehiro's face to silence him. "That's enough of that," he said in a low, cold tone. "I think we get the general picture. We'll speak to both of you individually down at the station. We'd like your daughter to come down too."

Narumi nodded silently.

"Okay, this hotel is off-limits to anyone not on the task force," Isobe said in a loud voice. "We'll take all the keys. And, didn't you have a relative staying here? A boy?"

"His father came to pick him up this morning."

"His father?" A cloud passed over Isobe's face. "So he took the kid back home?"

"No, they're still in town."

"Good. Give me the number. We need to talk to the kid, too. Also, where is your other guest, this Yukawa fellow?"

"We had Mr. Yukawa move to a different hotel. We told him something came up and we had to leave town for a few days."

"You know which hotel he's staying at, then? We'll get that number from you too."

Isobe told his men to take the Kawahatas down to the station. Then he picked a few other detectives to close off the crime scene and had someone give forensics a call.

Nishiguchi stood and watched as the three Kawahatas were shepherded into three separate police cruisers. He wanted to call out to Narumi and tell her not to worry, but she was surrounded by officers, and he couldn't get close enough to talk to her.

FORTY-EIGHT

Kyohei looked up from his notebook at the sound of a phone buzzing. His father swore under his breath and checked the display before answering it. It was the fourth call in less than an hour—probably Mom again.

"What? Look, I told you I don't know anything. . . . Yeah, we're at the hotel. We checked in, now we're just waiting. I said we're waiting. Look, given the circumstances, the police are definitely—" He stopped speaking for moment and looked around, then continued in a quiet voice. "The police are definitely going to want to talk to Kyohei. . . . No, what good would you coming here do? That would just make things even more confused than they already are. . . . No, we can't. We absolutely *can't* delay the opening." Still holding the phone to his ear, he stood from the table and walked away.

Kyohei drank his orange juice through a long straw. They were sitting in the hotel lounge. The only people in the pool were a little kid wearing a floatie and a woman—probably his mother.

Kyohei's father stood in a corner of the lounge, still talking. From the way it sounded, he'd left everything in Osaka up to Kyohei's mom. Kyohei knew it was no little thing getting a new store open. He could imagine his mother fretting up a storm. *"How dare they pull a stunt like this when we're up to our necks in work!"*

At first, his father had been mum about why he'd suddenly come to pick Kyohei up, but after they left the Green Rock Inn and checked in at this resort hotel, he had told him the truth. The guest, Tsukahara, had died because of a boiler malfunction at the inn. His aunt and uncle had tried to dispose of the body to hide that fact.

"They should've just called the police right away, but because they didn't, well, now they're in a bit of trouble. They might even have to spend some time in jail," his father told him with a dark face.

Kyohei thought back to the way his aunt and uncle had been acting in the days after Tsukahara went missing: the strained conversations, the dark looks in the car. Suddenly it all made sense.

Kyohei slurped at his drink, becoming aware of someone standing next to him. He looked up. "Hey, Professor!"

"They send you here?"

"Yeah, with my dad. Did they put you up here too?"

"This is the hotel where DESMEC made my initial reservation. I hardly imagined I'd be taking them up on it under these circumstances."

Kyohei looked up at him. "You knew what happened, didn't you?"

The physicist pushed his glasses up with the tip of his finger. "Knew what?"

"About the accident at the inn. That it was my uncle's fault."

"Accident?" Yukawa raised an eyebrow. "I had some theories. How long will you be staying here?"

"I don't know. We might head out tomorrow, but Dad says we might leave later tonight if we can."

"I see," Yukawa said, nodding. "That's probably for the best. This isn't a good place for you to be."

"Why not?" Kyohei asked.

"I should think you'd know that better than anyone else."

Kyohei looked up at Yukawa, but then he saw his father putting his phone in his pocket and turning back around. Yukawa nodded and walked away with long strides.

"Who was that?" Kyohei's father asked him.

Kyohei didn't answer. His eyes were on Yukawa's back, watching him leave.

FORTY-NINE

No matter which way they asked the questions, Narumi's story remained the same. She'd been with her friends at the bar that night. She was still there when she heard that Mr. Tsukahara had gone missing. After going home, she'd gone to her room and hadn't come out until the following morning. She hadn't heard anything about a boiler malfunction.

"So last night was the first time you heard the truth?" Detective Nonogaki asked.

"How many times do I have to tell you? Yes."

Nonogaki crossed his arms and frowned. "It's just, I have a hard time believing you didn't notice anything strange."

"What can I say? It's the truth," Narumi said, looking down at the floor.

She was sitting in a conference room down at the Hari police station, empty save for herself and the detective. She imagined her mother and father in tiny questioning rooms in some other corner of the station, getting the full shakedown, and it made her chest ache.

Her father had told her he'd be turning himself in the night before. When she asked what happened, her father had glumly replied

it was an accident. Except when he should have called the police—
he'd tried to hide it and only made everything worse.

"I know the police will figure it out sooner or later, and frankly, I
can't go on like this, it's too painful," he'd told her. "I'm sorry. They'll
probably arrest your mother, too, but as long as I make it clear that I
forced her to help, she'll get off easy."

Narumi was shaken and confused. It terrified her to picture her
mother and father trying to hide the body. Except, in the middle of
that nightmare, a part of her mind was relieved. As long as Tsukahara's death had been an accident, the fault of an old inn and an old
innkeeper, then there was a light in the darkness.

Or was there? Was her father telling her the truth? Had it really
been an accident? Was this just another attempt to pull the wool over
everyone's eyes? Narumi didn't give voice to her doubts. It'd been
hard, but she'd decided to take her father's confession at face value.
And if she was being honest, she wanted it to be true.

Setsuko hadn't said a word the entire time. Narumi didn't think
it was just because her father told her to be quiet. She sensed that Setsuko had her own version of what happened but that she had decided
to let her husband handle this his way.

Narumi didn't ask many questions after hearing her father's confession. She kept it simple. What would they do with the inn? And
with Kyohei? Her father had already figured it all out. For one thing,
he said with a lonely laugh, they would definitely be closing down
the inn.

She'd barely slept that night. She feared the coming dawn, the day-
light that would see her parents being arrested. At the same time, a
different worry played through her mind. Would this really be the
end of it? The call from her middle school friend, Reiko, still bothered her. What if the police in Tokyo were still investigating, still
digging up the past?

"Well, did you?"

Narumi blinked, suddenly aware that Nonogaki was asking her a
question. "I'm sorry, did I what?"

"I was asking you if you played any sports when you were younger."

"Oh, right. I played tennis in middle school."

"Tennis, okay," he said, giving her a look-over. "You were a diving instructor too, weren't you? You're pretty tough for a girl."

"I wouldn't know about that," she said, a little coldly.

Nonogaki slowly tapped his finger on the table. "I just don't think those two could've pulled this off by themselves. Your dad's got his leg, and your mom's pretty short, and frankly, she doesn't look like she has much lifting power. We're supposed to believe they carried a body down from the fourth floor and tossed it over the seawall? Doesn't seem very likely. What do you think? You think they could pull it off?"

"That's what they said, so they must have, yes."

"Yeah, they did say that," Nonogaki said, stretching his neck. "But there's no way. No way at all."

Narumi shrugged.

Nonogaki rested his elbows on the desk and looked her in the eye. "I can understand why your parents would want to protect their only child. They can live with turning themselves in, but they don't want to see their baby behind bars."

"What are you talking about?"

"You know what I'm talking about. You're going to let your aging folks go to prison while you live a life of ease? That the plan?"

Narumi's cheeks tightened. "You're suggesting I helped?"

Nonogaki smiled. "We're not idiots, you know. All we have to do is get them to try and reenact how they pulled it off, and it'll be pretty clear their story's full of holes. They're protecting someone, and it's not hard to guess who."

Narumi shook her head. She felt her face burning. "I didn't do *anything*. That's the truth. If I had helped them, I would tell you. I wouldn't just stand by while they took the blame!"

Nonogaki shook his head and picked at his ear with his fingertip. *Act all you want, you won't fool me*, his look said.

There was an abrupt knock at the door, and it opened slightly. Someone outside called for Detective Nonogaki.

Nonogaki stood, his chair making a loud noise as he pushed it back, and he walked out, a sour look on his face. He slammed the door behind him.

Narumi put a hand to her forehead. She knew they were going to ask her questions, but she hadn't anticipated becoming a suspect. She imagined that they were grilling her parents now too, trying to get them to admit that she'd helped. But she had to admit that what the detective said made sense. It would've been next to impossible for the two of them to manage a grown man's body.

The door opened again, and Nonogaki came back inside, his expression a little different than it had been a moment before. His brow was still furrowed with consternation, but now his eyes looked a little twitchy, like he was excited.

He sat back down in his chair and began tapping his finger on the table again, only to a much faster rhythm. Finally he stopped and looked up at Narumi. "You said you got to the bar around nine o'clock?"

"Yes," she replied, returning his gaze.

"And you were there when Mr. Tsukahara died. Are you sure you arrived at nine?" Nonogaki asked again, irritation in his voice.

"Yes, very sure," Narumi answered, growing bewildered.

"You said that this man, Sawamura, gave your mother a ride home, right? What time did he get back to the bar?"

"He came back a little before ten o'clock. I thought he'd been gone a long time for just having given my mom a ride home, which is when he told me that a guest had gone missing from the inn—why are you asking me this?"

Nonogaki looked like he was about to say something, then shook his head. "It doesn't matter," he muttered under his breath. "You'll find out soon enough."

"Is it my parents?"

"No, it's Sawamura. One of the guys went to talk to him, and it sounds like he's claiming he was the one who helped them get rid of that body."

"What?" Narumi said, sitting upright in her chair.

"They're bringing him in for questioning now, but from the sound of it, his story's a lot tighter than the one your parents have been telling. I think we might just have figured this out," Nonogaki said, sounding a little relieved. Apparently, Narumi's interrogation was over.

FIFTY

Isobe was quick to claim the right to question Sawamura, sensing an opportunity to earn some points with upper management. He brought along his own men, of course, but surprisingly, chose Nishiguchi to take notes. Nishiguchi walked toward the interrogation room, wondering why he'd been picked, but he didn't have to wait long to find out.

"Nishiguchi here is from town," Isobe said. "He knows your family's appliance shop, and he knows about the Green Rock Inn. He was classmates with the Kawahatas' daughter and knows the parents, so he knows what kind of folks they are and what they're liable to do or not do. Keep that in mind when you tell us exactly what happened."

In other words, he brought along Nishiguchi for some local cred. However, Nishiguchi didn't think any of that was really necessary. He could tell by the look in Sawamura's eyes that the man was ready to talk.

"I've no intention of hiding anything," he began. "Yes, Mr. Kawahata turned himself in, and I didn't, which is a little awkward, but if he'd told me beforehand, I would've been here with him."

"Okay, well, why don't you tell us what happened, in as much detail as possible."

Sawamura took a deep breath. "As I think you're already aware, I was with Narumi and the others at a bar that night. We ran into Narumi's mother out front, and I offered to give her a ride home in my pickup truck, which I'd left parked out in front of the station."

"And you had no idea what was going on at the Green Rock Inn at that time?"

"Of course not. I was with the other people in Save the Cove the entire day."

"Fine," Isobe grunted. "Go on."

"When we got to the inn, Mr. Kawahata was out in the lobby, just standing there. His wife asked him what was wrong, and he said he'd let one of the guests die."

Nishiguchi paused his typing and looked up at Sawamura, but a glare from Isobe sent him back to his keyboard.

"So what you're saying is that at the time you got there, it was already over?"

"That's right. Mr. Kawahata said he'd found their guest lying on the floor in one of the rooms and knew immediately that the cause had been a boiler malfunction."

"And what did Mr. Kawahata say he would do about it?"

"Well, he said we needed to tell the police."

Isobe raised an eyebrow. "And yet he didn't. Why not?"

Sawamura took a quick, pained breath before saying, "I stopped him."

"Why?"

"Because . . ." He paused, chewing his lip before continuing, "If word got out about what had happened, it would destroy Hari Cove. People would think everything in town's falling apart, and what's left of our tourism industry would die."

"I see. You're one of the activists working against the undersea development, aren't you? That why you took such an, er, proactive stance?"

"I just wanted to save our town."

"Right. So, what did Mr. Kawahata have to say about your idea? He changed his mind on the spot?"

"No, he was torn at first. But I told him this wasn't just about his inn. I told him if word got out about this, it would affect the entire town and everyone living in it, so he asked me what he should do. That's when I told him we should move the body to a different place."

"So it was your idea?" Isobe asked, leaning forward and speaking clearly to drive home how important this particular point was.

"That's right. And it was my idea to drop him on those rocks."

"And the Kawahatas went along with this idea?"

"Not at first, no. They seem very troubled about it. But I told them that if we spent too much time up there, making it look like it had happened somewhere else would no longer be an option. That got them moving."

According to Sawamura's story, he carried Tsukahara entirely by himself. Putting the body on the flatbed of his truck, he drove down to the seawall with Shigehiro. With his leg, Shigehiro hadn't been much help when it came to dropping Mr. Tsukahara over the seawall, either.

After bringing Shigehiro back to the Green Rock Inn, Sawamura went back home, dropped off his truck, then headed to the bar. He managed to act like nothing happened in front of his friends, but he admitted he hadn't really been able to follow the conversation at all.

"That's what happened. I know there are criminal charges for abandoning a body, and I won't deny my guilt. So please—" Sawamura took another breath before continuing, "please let Narumi go. She knew nothing of any of this. She had nothing at all to do with it."

As he listened to this final, impassioned plea, it dawned on Nishiguchi why this man had been so eager to admit his culpability. He must've heard that Narumi was a suspect—and hoped he could get her off the hook.

Because any man who spends enough time around her starts to love her, Nishiguchi thought, glancing at Sawamura out of the corner of his eye as he typed.

FIFTY-ONE

My aunt's cooking is way better than this, Kyohei thought as he bit into the fried scallop. The food was piled high on a fancy plate, but from the taste it could have come from any restaurant chain back in the city. What was the point of coming all the way out to the ocean to eat *this*?

Kyohei had come to the hotel restaurant with his father. It looked like they would be spending the night after all. He'd assumed that meant they'd be leaving first thing in the morning, but his father said, "With what's going on with your uncle, I might have to stick around and do some paperwork and things. You know how it is." He gave Kyohei a smile. "Hang in there, buddy."

Kyohei had nodded, but he didn't agree that delaying their departure for Osaka constituted "hanging in there." It would be worse to leave without knowing what was going to happen to his aunt and uncle.

They'd just finished dinner when his father's phone rang. He looked at it and frowned as he lifted the phone to his ear. Covering his mouth with his hand, he spoke quietly for a few moments before hanging up. He was still frowning.

"What is it?" Kyohei asked.

"The police say they want to talk to you," his father said, a wrinkle forming across his brow. "They say a detective is waiting in the hotel's tea lounge. They want you to come out once you're finished eating. You okay with that?"

"Yeah, sure, fine," Kyohei said, eating the rest of the scallop and taking a bite of his tomato salad. He hadn't eaten much, but he already felt full.

There were two men waiting for him in the tea lounge, Detective Nonogaki and Detective Nishiguchi. He had a feeling he'd seen both of them around, but this was the first time he'd ever talked to either of them.

Kyohei sat down across the table from the detectives. His father took the seat next to him. Nonogaki asked if they wanted anything to drink, but Kyohei's father said no, so Kyohei shook his head.

"How's it going?" his father asked. "Are they still in questioning?"

Nonogaki sat up a little in his chair. "I'm afraid these things are never so simple. Frankly, they never are when a death is involved. And . . . well, there were several aspects to what the Kawahatas told us that don't exactly mesh. I'm sorry for the trouble, but you understand we need to do things by the book here."

"I'm sorry, mesh? What doesn't mesh?"

"I'm afraid I'm not at liberty to talk about that. Let's just say that people other than Mr. and Mrs. Kawahata were involved."

"Accomplices? You don't mean Narumi—"

"No, not her," the young detective named Nishiguchi blurted out. Nonogaki gave him a glare, and he went back to taking notes.

Nonogaki turned a cold smile onto the father. "We actually aren't here to answer your questions, sir, so if you don't mind?"

"Right, of course," Kyohei's father said, then gave Kyohei a look to see if he was ready. Kyohei nodded and turned back to the detectives. The one named Nonogaki was staring right at him. His face reminded Kyohei of a fox.

"You remember lighting fireworks with your uncle? It was about six days ago," the detective asked.

"I remember," Kyohei said.

"Was that your idea, the fireworks?"

"No. I was watching TV in my room, and Uncle Shigehiro called me from downstairs."

"Around what time was that?"

"Eight o'clock . . . I think."

The detective's questions were all pretty much what he had expected. They didn't care about him, they wanted to know about Uncle Shigehiro. What time did he go back inside? What time did he come back out to set off more fireworks? How late did they stay out? Kyohei hadn't been checking his watch that night, of course, so he only had a vague idea. When they asked him if anything unusual had happened, all he could do was shrug and say no, they'd just lit some fireworks. Still, that appeared to satisfy the detectives.

He told the detective that after the fireworks, he'd gone to his aunt and uncle's apartment, eaten some watermelon, and fallen asleep watching TV. At that point in his story, Nonogaki turned to look at Nishiguchi and nodded.

"Thanks for your time," Nonogaki said, standing. "If we have some more questions for you later, we'll get in touch." He gave a little bow with his head and walked off toward the exit. Nishiguchi hurried after him.

Kyohei's father gave a little sigh and stood.

"Dad?" Kyohei asked, still in his chair. "It *was* an accident, right?"

His father got an angry look on his face. "Of course. What else would it be?"

"I . . . I don't know, I just, you know. I wondered why they're so serious."

"It's like the detective said. When somebody dies, even if it's an accident, they have to check every little detail. Don't worry. Your aunt and uncle *did* do something bad, and they'll definitely get punished for it, but it won't be too harsh."

Kyohei's head drooped. His father took it for a nod and walked off with another, "Let's get going." Kyohei stood to follow him, but in his head he could still hear Yukawa's voice echoing.

"This isn't a good place for you to be. I should think you'd know that better than anyone else."

FIFTY-TWO

"Good thing the kid could talk. Some kids these days, the things they say, you wonder if they're even speaking the same language," Nonogaki said as they left the lounge. "Other than hiding the fact that Sawamura helped them, it sounds like the Kawahatas' story checks out. That just leaves their guest, Yukawa. Who, it turns out, is at this hotel, too. Too bad his phone's busted or we'd be done with all this by now."

"I'll ask which room he's in," Nishiguchi offered.

Nishiguchi headed toward the front desk. Over the last few days, he'd gotten so used to taking orders from the guys in prefectural homicide that it was second nature now.

He found Yukawa's room number quickly and called from the front desk, but there was no answer. Only after Nishiguchi frowned and put the phone back down did the desk clerk speak up.

"If you're trying to reach Mr. Yukawa, he asked that any calls for him be directed to the bar on the tenth floor."

"Oh, thanks," Nishiguchi said, resisting the urge to add, "You could have told me sooner," and went back over to Nonogaki.

"This physicist guy is the one here doing research on the undersea development project, right?" Nonogaki laughed. "They haven't even started mining yet, and he's already living large in the resort hotel bar?"

Nishiguchi kept his opinion to himself.

There were only a few patrons scattered throughout the large bar. The side facing the sea was all glass, but they could see nothing because the sun had already set and it was pitch black outside. Nishiguchi imagined the bar probably got pretty busy on the nights when they had fireworks shows.

Yukawa was sitting at a table against the window. His glasses were resting on the table in front of him. Next to them was a bottle of red wine and a single wineglass. He was listening to something on a pair of headphones.

Yukawa slowly looked up at the two detectives when they approached. He noticed Nishiguchi and removed the headphones from one of his ears. "Is he a detective too?" he asked, indicating Nonogaki with his eyes.

Nonogaki introduced himself and sat down across the table from Yukawa. "Could we have a moment?"

"What if I said no?"

Nonogaki frowned, and Yukawa's lips curled upward. "I'm kidding, of course. Are you going to keep standing?" The question was directed at Nishiguchi, who quickly sat.

"You should order something," Yukawa suggested. "It's a little odd drinking alone," Yukawa said to Nonogaki, removing his headphones completely.

"We're fine. But please, go ahead."

"Right, well then," Yukawa said, picking up his wineglass and taking a leisurely sip.

Nonogaki cleared his throat and announced, "We've arrested Mr. and Mrs. Kawahata."

Yukawa set down his glass. "Okay."

"You're not surprised?"

"Well, this morning they did tell me they wanted me to move to another hotel, and they didn't ask me to pay for my stay, which gave me fairly good warning that something was up. Later I heard rumors that a number of police cruisers were spotted up at the inn, so I assumed there'd been an arrest. On what charges were they arrested?"

"Right now, professional negligence resulting in death and the abandonment of a corpse."

Yukawa picked his glasses up from the table and wiped the lenses with a paper napkin. "Right now? Do you mean to suggest that the charges might change?"

"I can't say. We're still in the process of looking into everything—a process that includes talking to you."

"I see. So, what should I say?" Yukawa asked, putting on his glasses.

"Just the facts as you saw them. I know you've given a statement already, and you're probably tired of repeating it, but I'd like you to begin with your first day at the Green Rock Inn."

The physicist snorted. "I *am* sick of it, but here goes," he said, and began his story, the same one he had been telling from the very beginning. There was nothing in Yukawa's account that contradicted Sawamura's confession. Nishiguchi was relieved. If Yukawa was telling the truth, the chance of any blame falling on Narumi was slim.

"How was Sawamura when he came into the bar?" Nonogaki asked.

"How do you mean?"

"Well . . ." Nonogaki paused. He had probably been hoping for something like "He looked nervous," but suggesting that would make it a leading question. "Anything is fine. Whatever you sensed at the time."

Yukawa shrugged. "Then I suppose I should say I sensed nothing. It was my first encounter with the man."

"So when you went back to the inn, did you notice anything unusual about the Kawahatas' behavior that night or the following day?"

"Nothing that I noticed," Yukawa replied simply. "I didn't speak directly with him that much, however. And most of my meals were served by the daughter, Narumi. She's not involved with this, is she?"

Nishiguchi resisted the urge to blurt out *Of course not.*

Nonogaki ignored the question and stood up from the table. "Thank you for your time. We'll let you get back to your wine."

"What? That's all?"

"That's all," Nonogaki said, already turning to leave. Nishiguchi was standing up when Yukawa asked, "Did they try to reproduce what happened?"

Nonogaki stopped and turned. "Excuse me?"

"You mentioned negligence. I'm assuming that meant that there was an accident of some sort at the Green Rock Inn, probably involving carbon monoxide poisoning. I would expect that forensics would be trying to reproduce what happened by experiment."

"Carbon monoxide poisoning? I don't know what you're talking about," Nonogaki said.

"Oh? Then whence the negligence?" Yukawa asked, scratching his chin.

Nonogaki's eyes widened and his nostrils flared. He took a deep breath, said, "Thank you for your cooperation," and strode swiftly out of the room.

Nishiguchi nodded to Yukawa and started to follow Nonogaki. Behind him, he heard Yukawa said, "They're not going to be able to reproduce it, you know. The carbon monoxide."

Nishiguchi stopped. "Why's that?"

But Yukawa didn't respond. Instead, he slowly poured himself another glass of wine. Nishiguchi was about to ask again when the physicist said, "I know the men and women in your profession have something they call detective's intuition." He picked his wineglass up and swished the liquid around, staring at it. "Well, you might say I have physicist's intuition." He took another sip.

Nishiguchi shook his head. It didn't sound like Yukawa was making fun of him, but he didn't understand what the man was driving at. Unable to think of anything to say, he turned and left.

Outside, Nonogaki was talking on his phone. He hung up, a sour look on his face, and pressed the elevator button.

"Glad we won't have to talk to him again. Are all scientists like that?"

"He's particularly eccentric, I hear."

"Right, well, I won't miss him. And it looks like the case is closed anyway."

"Was there some new information?"

Nonogaki nodded. "Tokyo found Senba. He's hospitalized out in Chofu. Turns out that the victim used to pay him visits out there. So, our prime suspect's not a suspect at all."

The elevator door opened, and the two detectives got in.

There had been a number of question marks left over after the Kawahatas gave their first testimony, but after Sawamura turned himself in, the remaining contradictions had disappeared. That only left the question of why Tsukahara had come out to Hari Cove in the first place, but from what Nonogaki said, it sounded like they had an answer for that now, too. Maybe the case really was closed.

But what Yukawa had said as he was leaving the bar stuck in Nishiguchi's mind.

While they were questioning the Kawahatas down at the police department, forensics had indeed been up at the Green Rock Inn, trying to reproduce what had happened the night Tsukahara died. The first report to the task force had confirmed the cracks in the wall of the Ocean Room and the presence of exhaust from the boiler pipe. Next, all they would have to do would be to make the boiler malfunction and see if it pumped enough carbon monoxide into the room.

But it had been hours, and the only word from the team was, "We don't know what happened."

FIFTY-THREE

Narumi opened the window and felt a warm breeze blow in, carrying the scent of the sea. Outside, the seawall and the road floated in the light of the streetlamps overhead. Everything else, including the ocean beyond, was lost in inky blackness.

She pulled out her phone and checked the time. It was almost 9:00 p.m.

She heard someone running up the steps, and the door opened. Wakana Nagayama came in, carrying a bag from the convenience store in one hand and a cooler in the other.

"Hey, thanks for waiting. Well, they had *absolutely* nothing down there. I got some sandwiches and some rice balls, and, yeah, that's about it. Oh, and some instant miso soup and a few snacks to go with the beer." She laughed, emptying the contents of the bag on the table.

"Thanks and sorry for the trouble," Narumi said.

"Don't mention it," Wakana said, dismissing her with a wave of a deeply tanned hand in front of a deeply tanned face. "That's what friends are for, right? Helping each other out. And I'm honored you chose me to mooch off of, really, I am. I know the place isn't much, but you're welcome to stay here as long as you need, babe."

"Thanks."

"So, what'll it be? If you want some of the miso, I'll go downstairs and get some water on," she said, picking up a cup of instant soup.

"No, I'm fine for now. Got anything to drink?"

"Oh ho ho, if it's drinks you're after, you've come to the right place," Wakana said, opening the cooler. "We've got beer, we've got wine coolers, we've got everything. What'll it be?"

"Any tea?"

"Coming up," Wakana said, pulling out a plastic bottle of green tea.

Narumi took a sip, feeling the cool liquid trickle down her throat as she looked out the window. She reflected back on the events of the day. None of it felt real.

They had released her from the police station a little after eight o'clock. Sawamura's confession had cleared her of any suspicion, but that hadn't stopped them from asking her a million more questions and making her wait around for no reason whatsoever. In the end, she'd spent most of the day there. By the time she walked out, she was so exhausted she wanted to collapse in the parking lot and take a nap right there on the asphalt.

She couldn't even go home and crash, because the Green Rock Inn was off-limits. Worse, the detectives had practically ordered her to call them once she knew where she was going to be staying, so that was hanging over her the whole time. They wouldn't tell her anything about her parents, either.

After agonizing over it for a while, she'd finally called her friend who worked a part-time job at a marine sports shop. Wakana was studying at a university in Tokyo and came back to Hari to work during the summer. Narumi had taught her when she tested for her scuba instructor's license two years ago.

She'd told Wakana over the phone what had happened, and Wakana had come to pick her up right away. On the way back to her place, Wakana hadn't asked any questions. She'd just wanted to be sure that Narumi was okay, confirming Narumi's suspicion that she'd made an excellent choice of friend to turn to.

She looked up and noticed that Wakana was drinking tea too.

"You can have a beer, you know," she said. In addition to her skills as a diver, Wakana was an accomplished drinker.

"It's okay," she said.

"Don't go dry on my account. I won't last a day if I have to deal with a grumpy Wakana!"

Wakana grinned. "Well, if you put it that way." She put her bottle of tea back in the cooler and pulled out a beer, cracked it open, and took a long swig. "Ah, that's nice," she sighed.

Narumi smiled at her friend and found herself wondering what Yukawa would say if he saw Wakana—maybe the same thing he had said to Narumi about not seeming like the country type. Thinking of Yukawa made her think of the Green Rock Inn. She wondered what would happen to it now. Her father had talked about selling it, but who would buy a rundown inn where someone had died? It would cost money to tear it down if they just wanted to try to sell the land. And Narumi still had to find a place to live. Wakana had offered her flat for as many days as she needed it, but Narumi knew there was a limit to that. Ultimately, she guessed she would be going back to Tokyo. She looked up. "Can I borrow your van?"

"My van? Sure, but if you want to go someplace, I'm happy to drive you."

"No, it's okay, I'm just going home quickly."

"To the inn?"

"I need a change of clothes and my makeup. And money. The detective said it was okay as long as I told the guard."

"All right. I guess that makes sense. I don't think many of my clothes would fit you anyway," she said, putting down her beer can and standing.

Wakana's room was on the second floor of the shop. They went down the stairs, through the dark shop interior, and outside. The van was parked right in front. Narumi took the keys from Wakana and got in. Though the make was different from the one that they had at the inn, she was used to driving vans. "Drive safely," Wakana said as she pulled out.

She drove along the empty coast road and started up the slope past the station. Pretty soon the inn came into view. There were several red flashing lights out front, like the kind they put up at construction sites. The young officer in uniform was sitting on a folding chair out front, but he stood when he saw the van approach.

Narumi stopped the van and explained herself to the guard. He opened the front door, talked to someone inside, then told her she could go in. A middle-aged, overweight officer was standing inside the lobby. He had the TV on, tuned to a show with some comedians talking loudly.

"You mind if I go with you?" the officer asked. "If someone finds out I let you go in by yourself, I'll get in trouble."

Narumi nodded and went inside. The police officer turned off the television and followed her in.

In her room, she pulled a large traveling bag out of the closet and started cramming whatever clothes she could find into it.

"So, what's your plan? Kind of a tough situation, huh," he said. Narumi shrugged and didn't say anything.

"Sorry, I shouldn't have asked," he continued. "A long time ago, I was stationed at the police box out by the train station. I was there for twenty-some years. Hari Cove was bustling back then, you know. This place was pretty busy too. But it's hard these days, with the economy in the tank. Who has the time or the money to fix every little thing that goes wrong in these places? I sympathize with your pops, I really do. Just a stroke of bad luck, that's what it was. Well, that and throwing out the body. If he hadn't done that . . ."

Narumi had stopped listening to him halfway through his monologue, but he didn't seem to mind. Her bag packed, she left the room. As soon as they were back in the lobby, the policeman turned the TV back on and sat down on the wicker bench without so much as a nod in her direction.

When she opened the front door, she heard voices talking outside. It sounded like they were arguing.

"I'm sorry, but those are the rules," the young officer from before was saying. "No one not associated with the investigation is allowed inside."

"Like I said, I'm associated. I was staying here until just this morning."

"That's not associated enough."

"How associated do I have to be? Where's the cutoff? Explain."

It was Yukawa, staring the young officer down, a scowl across his face.

"Mr. Yukawa?" she called out to him.

"Just the person I wanted to see," he said. "Can you please ask this fellow to let me inside, just for a little? I've tried talking with him myself, but it's absolutely no use. He speaks in riddles."

"You're the one speaking in riddles," the officer retorted. "And how complicated is 'no'? Please, go home," the officer said, stepping inside the inn and shutting the door behind him.

Yukawa put his hands to his hips and sighed. "Well, that's just great."

"Why did you want to see inside?"

"Because forensics was in here trying to re-create what happened and I thought I would check and see if I could tell what they were up to. You see, I have a theory that their experiment didn't go well."

Narumi stared at the physicist's face for moment, then blinked. "Didn't go well? Why not?"

In lieu of an answer, Yukawa pushed his glasses up with one fingertip. "And to think I walked all the way up here for this," he said, then turned and began walking down the hill.

"Wait, I'll give you a lift," Narumi said, running over to the van.

Yukawa got into the passenger seat, and they took off. The resort hotel where he was staying was less than ten minutes away.

They rode in silence. Narumi was still wondering what he meant about forensics, but she had a feeling there was no point in asking him again.

The hotel came into view, but before they reached the front, Yukawa said, "Let me off here."

"Why? I can drive you up to the door."

"No," he said. "Kyohei and his father are staying here too. They might see you."

"Oh . . ." Narumi pulled over to the side of the road. "Yeah. Probably a good idea not to get into that now."

"Also, there were a few things I wanted to ask you," Yukawa said. "You don't have to answer if you don't want to."

Narumi looked over at him. Her heart thudded in her chest. "Yes?"

"Do you think Mr. Tsukahara's death was an accident?"

Narumi tensed. "If it wasn't an accident, what was it?"

"I'm asking the questions. Here's another. Did your parents tell you it was an accident?"

"My father did. He explained it to me."

"And you believed his explanation?"

"Should I not have? Where are you going with this?"

"Just wondering if there was any doubt in your mind, even a little. No, that's not entirely true. I'm sure there were quite a few things that didn't fit right. Just like I'm sure you have at least two good reasons why you would have believed your father anyway. The first would be, you trust him. The second is, you *want* to believe. In fact, both reasons might apply."

Every word the physicist spoke felt like a physical thing, probing something deep inside her chest. But not too deep, or too painful. These were quick, calculated thrusts.

"Okay, so maybe there were a few strange parts in my father's story. But maybe he just doesn't remember what happened, and I don't think little contradictions necessarily add up to a big problem. You have to remember, he's turning himself in. He knows he did wrong. Why sweat the details?" Narumi said, a little defensively.

"True. You may be right. So, different subject. How well did you know the very unfortunate Mr. Tsukahara?"

"How well? I barely know anything about him. Except that he used to be a detective in Tokyo."

"You may recall I have a friend in Tokyo homicide. If I asked him, I could get in touch with Mr. Tsukahara's widow. If you wanted to write an apology on behalf of your parents, I could make that happen. If you wanted it."

Narumi felt a shiver run down her spine. It hadn't occurred to her until now that she owed Tsukahara's widow an apology. "I think I'd like all the questioning to be finished before I decide what to do," she said at last.

"Understood. I'll tell my friend. Thanks for the ride," Yukawa said, opening the door, but he didn't get out. Instead, he turned back around and said, "What are you going to do next? Are you going to stay in Hari Cove?"

Narumi hesitated. She couldn't be sure exactly why he was asking her. "I haven't thought about it yet. I don't even know what I'm going to do tomorrow."

"But the ocean will still need saving, won't it?"

"Of course."

"And how long will you be the one saving it?"

She stared back at him. "How long?"

"Are you going to stay here, watching over these waters until the day you die? Are you not going to marry? What if you met someone but he had to go far away? What would you do then?"

"Why are you asking me these things?"

Yukawa stared at Narumi through his glasses. "Because I feel like you're waiting for someone. I feel like you're trying to protect Hari Cove until someone *specific* comes back."

She could feel the blood drain from her face. She knew she should say something, but the words wouldn't come. Yukawa pulled a small notepad out of his pocket.

"'Welcome to *My Crystal Sea*. The ocean is Hari Cove's most valuable treasure. For now, I am one of its protectors. Please, come see our beautiful sea. I'm waiting for you'—these words are at the top of your Web site. Am I overthinking it if I said it sounded like you were talking to a specific person?"

Narumi sighed. "Yes, you are completely overthinking it." Her voice was trembling.

"Well, I guess I was wrong then. Good night—oh, except there was one more thing I wanted to ask."

"What now?"

"It's nothing much," Yukawa said, pulling a digital camera out of his pocket. "I'll be leaving Hari Cove pretty soon myself. I wanted to take a picture of you to remember you by."

"A picture of me? No thanks."

"It's okay, I won't post it online or anything," Yukawa said, clicking the shutter. The flash briefly illuminated the inside of the van. He looked at the display on the back of the camera and nodded. "Good shot." He turned the camera so Narumi could see. She looked startled in the image. Her eyes were wide open.

"Good night," Yukawa said, getting out. He walked off toward the hotel without turning to look back. Narumi watched him walk away before she slowly pulled away from the curb.

FIFTY-FOUR

It was already past midnight by the time Kusanagi came home to a depressingly muggy apartment. He tossed his jacket on the bed and turned on the air conditioner. Pulling off his necktie, he grabbed a beer out of the fridge and drank, feeling the cool refreshment spread from his throat down through his body all the way out to his fingertips. Breathing out a long sigh, he collapsed onto his low sofa.

He undid a few buttons on the shirt and reached over to pull his jacket off of the bed. Fishing his phone from his jacket pocket, he pulled up the address book until he found the entry for the Hari Cove Resort Hotel.

Yukawa had called Kusanagi to tell him that the Kawahatas were kicking him out because they were going to turn themselves in, and apparently, they had. Kusanagi didn't hear about it until the evening, when he got a call from Tatara.

"They're saying it was an accident. The boiler malfunctioned, and then they tried to hide the body, but there are still a lot of things in their story that aren't adding up." The alarm in Tatara's voice was obvious. "They're supposed to give me a call when they know something, but I'd like to share what we have if it'll help. How are things going with you?"

Kusanagi told him about meeting with Senba, and Senba having no idea why Tsukahara might've been killed.

"Right," Tatara said. "Well, might as well let Hari PD know."

"Yes, sir," Kusanagi replied, still wondering whether he should tell Tatara about the possibility that the Kawahatas had been involved in the Senba case decades before. He had decided not to. All he could do was pray that it didn't come back to bite him.

Kusanagi called Hari and talked to Detective Motoyama about finding Senba in the hospital. The detective thanked him, but he didn't sound entirely grateful. The reason why became immediately clear.

"It looks like we've finally nailed this one," Motoyama told him. "We found the guy who helped the Kawahatas move the body—he's a friend of the daughter. His story checked out, so we're calling this one a wrap."

He'd sounded genuinely relieved, a feeling that Kusanagi couldn't share. Everything he'd seen up until that point indicated that this wasn't a case they could write off as a simple accident.

He discussed it with Utsumi, and she agreed.

"Sounds like we have to go back to the very beginning," she had said.

The two of them headed for Ginza to find the restaurant where, thirty years earlier, Shigehiro and Setsuko had first met. They found it, but not before Kusanagi walked enough that his feet were swollen and painful and his shirt was drenched in sweat, sticking to him in all the wrong ways. This might be the key that unlocked the truth about everything—but it felt like failure.

Kusanagi sighed again and called the number for the Hari Cove Resort Hotel. It was a long time before someone picked up, and another minute after he asked the receptionist to connect him to Yukawa before the physicist finally answered the phone.

"It's me, Kusanagi. Were you asleep?"

"No, I was waiting for you to call. I figured you'd have something to tell me."

"How are things on your end? It sounds like they're getting ready to wrap this case up over there."

"I'd say your assessment is correct. Unless there's some dramatic change, I doubt the police will take one step further on this case. That is, they can't. They're effectively blind."

"But you can see?"

"All I have is conjecture. You're the one who has to tell me if I'm right or not. Isn't that why you called?"

Kusanagi grinned and opened his notebook. "I found the restaurant where Setsuko Kawahata was working. It's moved since then, but it's still in business. Same owner, too."

"And you had a chat with him?" Yukawa asked.

"That I did."

"About what?"

"The good old days."

The restaurant was on a small alley off of the Ginza. To the side of a white wooden lattice door hung a modest sign that read "Haruhi." The place was practically designed to avoid attracting passersby.

"You must have a lot of regulars," Kusanagi had asked the owner.

"About seventy to eighty percent, yep," the owner, a Mr. Tsuguo Ukai, had replied. "And the people they bring with them wind up becoming regulars, and that keeps us gratefully in business."

Ukai had perfectly white, neatly trimmed hair and looked sprightly for a man in his seventies. He said he still handled all of the buying for the restaurant himself.

When Kusanagi and Utsumi had arrived, it was a little after closing time, and there was still one customer at the bar, finishing his drink and chatting with Ukai while he cleaned up. They had to wait for the customer to leave before they could really start asking questions.

Other than the chairs at the counter, there were only three tables in the place. Kusanagi had guessed the max capacity was somewhere around thirty. Besides himself, the owner employed two cooks and a server.

Ukai had left Hari to become a chef while still in his teens. After working at a few famous places in the city, he had started Haruhi, a Hari cuisine specialty restaurant, at the age of thirty-four. In the beginning, he didn't hire any help. It was just him and his wife.

"Our old shop was about a block down from here, along Sony Street. Small place—couldn't fit much more than ten people. But we had some loyal customers, and that let us move up here once we'd saved enough."

The move had been about twenty years ago.

"So when Setusko worked for you, that was at the old place?"

Ukai nodded. When they'd arrived, the detectives had told him they'd come to talk to him about Setsuko. They said that they were looking into someone else and trying to establish a better picture of their friends and associates.

"Yeah, I think she started working for us about two or three years after we opened. Eventually the work got too much for just the two of us. We started asking around, and one of our regulars said that he knew this nightclub hostess who liked to cook and had just quit her job, so he brought her by. I liked her well enough, but my wife, she loved the girl. Turns out she'd left the nightclub world and had no plans to go back, so she was only too happy to accept our offer. And it was a great deal for us. She was good with her hands and sharp as a tack. Learned recipes quick, too."

She'd only stayed there three years, though, because she got married—to one of the regulars, no less.

Ukai remembered Shigehiro Kawahata well.

"His family ran an inn down in Hari Cove, as I recall. He was a big-city businessman through and through, but he got a longing for home now and then. That's why he came. They used to come by together after they got married, too. Had a kid real quick, and they were pretty happy. I wonder what they're up to these days. They sent me New Year's cards for at least ten years after they left."

"Were any of your regulars besides Mr. Kawahata on close terms with Setsuko?" Kusanagi had asked.

"Oh sure, there were a few. She was young, and, well, she used to be a nightclub hostess, so you can imagine she was great with customers. I'm guessing that more than a few of our regulars came here just for her," Ukai said, his eyes twinkling.

"How about this man? Did you ever see him here?" Kusanagi had asked, showing him the photograph of Senba from around the time of his arrest. "He might've been a little younger than in this photo."

"Oh!" Ukai had said, his eyes going wide. "Of course I remember him. That's Mr. Senba. He's the one I just mentioned."

"Excuse me?"

"The one who introduced Setsuko to us. Yeah, he was a regular, too. Something about his wife being from Hari, I think."

Kusanagi and Utsumi had exchanged looks.

"Did she know Mr. Senba because he was a customer at the bar where she worked?"

"That's right. He started his own business and was always out on the town. He would drop by every once in a while with one girl or the other on his arm, getting drinks after work and such. We used to stay open a lot later in those days."

Kusanagi had shown him the photo of Nobuko Miyake. Ukai had stared at the photo for a while, thinking, before he said, "Isn't that Nobuko?"

"That's right," Kusanagi said.

"Yeah, she was a beauty, though I guess age caught up with her," he'd said with a nod. "Well, it was thirty years ago I'm thinking about, so she's probably a grandma by now."

"The photo's from about fifteen years ago."

"Right, right. Nobuko worked at the same bar as Setsuko." He'd chuckled and shaken his head. "We were all a lot younger then, that's for sure."

"But Mr. Senba and Nobuko stopped coming after a while. I always wondered what became of them. You don't happen to know, do you, Detective?"

"No, I'm afraid not," Kusanagi had lied. "That's why we're out here asking all these questions."

"Mr. Senba didn't do anything, did he?"

"No, no, nothing like that," Kusanagi said. "I was wondering, though—do you think Senba and Nobuko ever had a serious relationship?"

"No, I don't think so," Ukai had said simply. "The way I saw it, the only one Mr. Senba had a thing for was Setsuko. He came here because his wife was from Hari, but he never brought his wife. I don't think he wanted her meeting Setsuko, if you know what I mean. Of course, that might just be my imagination running wild."

Ukai had told him he had some photos from back in the day, so they'd had him show them. The photo right in the middle of the front page of the neatly kept album showed a man sitting in front of a small counter with a woman on either side. The photo was about thirty years old, but the man was clearly Ukai. His build and his hair had hardly changed in the intervening decades.

"That's Setsuko on the right," Ukai had said.

She was a young girl, with large eyes and a memorable face. She had sharp features and might've looked a little aggressive without her round cheeks and big smile. She was wearing a kimono patterned with autumn leaves.

"She's beautiful," Kusanagi had said, and Ukai broke into a grin.

"Wasn't she? You see why she was so popular. That foliage-print kimono of hers was like her trademark, too. My wife gave that one to her."

The woman standing on the other side of Ukai in the photograph was a slender beauty, too, though much older than Setsuko.

"That's her, my wife," Ukai had explained. "She was three years older than me, and a hard worker. If she wasn't around, well, Haruhi wouldn't be here either. I doubt I ever would've tried starting a place without her."

She had passed away the year before from pancreatic cancer.

Kusanagi finished relating what he'd learned from the old chef at Haruhi, but Yukawa was still silent.

"Hello?" Kusanagi said. "What do you think?"

He heard Yukawa sigh on the other end. "So that's what it was," he muttered.

"What's what it was?"

"I'm sure you've realized by this point what interested the retired detective, Tsukahara, about Senba's case so much. And how the Kawahatas were involved. Given what you just told me, there's no possible way you *couldn't* know."

"Well, I do have a vague idea."

There was an awkward silence. Kusanagi imagined he could see Yukawa's wry grin.

"I can understand," Yukawa said after a moment, "how you wouldn't want to make any rash suppositions, given your position in the police department, so allow me to say it on your behalf. Senba was wrongfully accused. He was not the killer, he was covering for someone. How am I doing so far?"

Kusanagi frowned. In truth, he did feel uncomfortable revealing his hand to Yukawa, but at the same time, he knew it was useless to try and obfuscate the facts. Yukawa knew better than anyone else how willing the truly devoted were to assume guilt in order to protect the ones they loved.

"It's a bit of a stretch, though," Kusanagi said.

"I don't think so. Tsukahara continued investigating the case even after Senba confessed. Since it was his arrest, in ordinary circumstances, he wouldn't want to uncover any unpleasant truths. The deed was done. But Tsukahara wasn't satisfied. Why? Because Senba was found guilty with the truth only half uncovered, and Tsukahara couldn't abide by that. That's why Tsukahara looked for him once Senba got out of prison, and went so far as to put him into a hospital. He hoped to get the truth out of him. I think that was partly because he felt responsible for the wrongful sentencing—even if Senba set himself up."

Kusanagi gripped his phone in silence. It mirrored his own thoughts exactly.

"Kusanagi?" Yukawa said. "I have a request."

FIFTY-FIVE

Kyohei woke to the sound of his father talking on the phone. He rubbed his eyes and looked up. Hs father was standing facing the window. The curtain was partway open, and sunlight was streaming through. It was the beginning of another beautiful day in Hari Cove.

"No, we don't need to tell the clients anything like that," he was saying. "Yeah, yeah, that'll work. I'll probably have to come out here a few more times. Sure, there'll be a trial. Yeah, you too." He shut his phone.

"Morning," Kyohei said to his father's back.

His father turned around, smiling. "You're awake?"

"That Mom?"

"Yeah. We're leaving after lunch. We'll probably get to eat dinner with Mom tonight."

"We don't have to stay here anymore? Won't the police have more questions?"

His father gave a thin smile and shook his head. "No. I called them while you were still asleep. They said they don't have any more questions for you. And if something comes up, they can just talk on the phone. I gave them my number."

Kyohei got out of bed. "Are Uncle Shigehiro and Aunt Setsuko going to jail? Can't we do something?"

The smile faded from his father's face. He groaned and scratched his head. "We'll do everything that we can. I'm going to get them the best lawyer I can find. But I don't think they'll get out of going to jail entirely. Especially not your uncle."

"Is it that bad, what they did?"

His father frowned. "Like I said, if they'd told the police when the accident happened, it wouldn't have been such a big deal. That's the way it works. We all make mistakes. What's important is how we deal with them. What your uncle did—well, that was *not* the right way. And it's going to cause all of us a lot of trouble."

To Kyohei, it sounded like his father was less concerned about the *rightness* of what Uncle Shigehiro and Aunt Setsuko had done and more concerned about the trouble it would cause him. "But," Kyohei said after a moment. "He'd be in even more trouble if the accident was on purpose, right?"

Kyohei's father leaned back and shook his head. "You bet it would! An accident on purpose isn't an accident: in this case, that would be murder. It's an entirely different thing. You might not just get prison for that, you could even get the death sentence," he said, looking down at his watch. "Hey, it's getting pretty late. I'm not that hungry, but we should get breakfast."

Kyohei looked at the alarm clock. It was almost 9:00 a.m.

Breakfast was served in the same tea lounge where he'd talked with the detectives the day before. There were a bunch of plates laid out on a large table, and his father told him he could pick what he wanted.

"But only take as much as you can eat. If you're still hungry, you can always get more," his father said, but Kyohei didn't think the advice was necessary. For one, he wasn't some stupid little kid who grabbed too much food. For another, none of the things on the table really looked that good.

Back at the table, he chewed on some bacon and drank his juice and looked around. The place was pretty empty. Yukawa was nowhere in sight.

After breakfast, they were heading back up to the room, when Kyohei called out to his father, who was walking ahead. "Can I go take a look at the ocean?"

"Sure," his father said. "Just don't go too far away from the hotel."

"Okay."

Kyohei went back to the lounge and out to the pool. There was a door here that went out to the beach. The beach was ostensibly private, which was apparently a selling point for the hotel, except it really didn't mean anything with so few people around.

He looked around but didn't see Yukawa, so he went back to the hotel. At the front desk, he asked the receptionist if she could tell him Yukawa's room number.

"Did you have something for him?"

"I needed to tell him something," Kyohei explained.

"One moment," she said, making a phone call. However, after a few moments, she hung up without saying a word.

"Looks like he's not in," she said, typing something into her computer. "Oh," she said. "He left a message saying that he would be out today. He'll be back tonight."

"Tonight?" Kyohei's shoulders sagged. He'd be gone by then.

"You could leave him a note if you like. I'll be happy to give it to him when he returns."

Kyohei shook his head. "That'll be too late," he said and walked off toward the elevators.

FIFTY-SIX

"We found no issues with Sawamura's statement," Nonogaki said. "The people at the bar confirmed the time of his arrival after he disposed of the body, and the timing fits with the distance between the Green Rock Inn and the place where the body was found. There were, of course, no witnesses to any of this, but given the time and the location, that was to be expected. That's all I've got for now," he added crisply and took a seat.

The mood in the conference room in the Hari Police Department, where the investigative task force was meeting, was considerably different from what it'd been several days before. In particular, Commissioner Tomita and Chief Okamoto looked relieved that the days they would have to spend with the Shizuoka prefectural police breathing down their necks were numbered.

Among the detectives from prefectural homicide, however, there were a few glum looks. A closed case was a closed case, but the trail that had begun with an abandoned body had led them not to a homicide but to professional negligence resulting in death—a far less satisfying outcome.

Shigehiro and Setsuko Kawahata had both acknowledged the

details of Sawamura's story. They claimed they had lied because they didn't want to burden one of their daughter's friends, but now that he'd confessed himself, there was no longer any reason to hide the truth.

Physical evidence in support of their story was piling up, too. An examination of Sawamura's pickup truck revealed several hairs in the flatbed. Though they were still running DNA tests, from the shape and composition of the hairs, it looked extremely likely that they belonged to Masatsugu Tsukahara.

The sleeping pill that Shigehiro had given to Tsukahara matched ones they found in the drawer of the living room table. They had gotten confirmation from the doctor who gave Shigehiro the pills as well—prescribed five years earlier for mild insomnia.

Yet there were still a few unanswered questions, the most pressing of which being exactly how Tsukahara had died.

The chief forensics officer stood and reported that his team had been up at the Green Rock Inn again that morning attempting to reproduce the conditions on the night of Tsukahara's death.

"Basically," he explained, "there were no major malfunctions in the boiler itself. However, we did find that by blocking the air duct leading down to the boiler, we could create a low-oxygen burn. The suspect was not clear on how the air duct might've been blocked, but we did find a cardboard box nearby that could've done the trick if, say, it had been standing near the vent and fallen over, blocking it. We furthermore went on to check the carbon monoxide concentration in the Ocean Room on the fourth floor in the event of a low-oxygen burn in the boiler. In our tests yesterday we were able to achieve a maximum concentration of one hundred ppm, with an average between fifty and sixty ppm. In addition, we discovered that the boiler was fit with a detection device designed to automatically stop improper burns after thirty minutes. However, a burn of that length is insufficient to produce the level of carboxyhemoglobin found in the body."

"So what happened? Do we have an explanation for any of this?"

Chief of Homicide Hozumi asked, his eyebrows knitting in frustration.

"We think that other conditions may have played a factor."

"What other conditions?"

"The weather on the night in question, for one. If a strong wind blew, pushing smoke back down the chimney, carbon monoxide levels could rise dramatically. We estimate concentration in the room could have reached as high as a thousand ppm."

"Okay," Hozumi said, nodding. "So would it be fair to say that, basically, we're still looking at negligence as the root cause of the accident, but the fatality was due to a number of coincidental factors?"

"That's correct. Of course, we're still running tests."

"Right, carry on," Hozumi said, his earlier consternation gone.

Things were drawing to a close, Nishiguchi thought. If the conditions leading to the death were so specific it was impossible for even forensics to re-create them, it made the possibility that Shigehiro had intentionally caused the poisoning extremely slim.

But what Yukawa had said the day before still bothered him. How had he known that forensics wouldn't be able to re-create the accident? Could it be because the physicist knew how it was done?

Motoyama stood and began giving his own report on news they'd received from Tokyo concerning Hidetoshi Senba. Hozumi was chatting and laughing with Isobe. Most of the other ranking officers weren't even listening. It was clear that the room had lost interest in Senba and their suspect's past.

And once the case was closed and a little time had passed—

I'll go pay Narumi a visit, Nishiguchi thought. The presence of an officer might comfort her. He could be with her the entire time while the trial was going on.

A smile slowly spread across Nishiguchi's face as the cloud over his thoughts lifted.

FIFTY-SEVEN

Kusanagi waited by the exit at Shinagawa Station for a full five minutes after Yukawa's train was supposed to arrive before he saw the physicist walking toward the ticket gate. He was wearing a light-colored jacket and carrying a large document case under one arm. Kusanagi raised a hand in greeting, and Yukawa nodded back.

"Looks like you got yourself a tan," Kusanagi said by way of greeting.

"I had to do more outside work than expected."

"Glad to hear you're keeping busy," Kusanagi said. He had a vague grasp of what Yukawa had been doing out in Hari Cove, but he didn't need to know the details. Yukawa stopped, looking at the long line of taxis waiting in front of the station.

"Something wrong?" Kusanagi asked.

"No, I was just amazed at how one's perception of certain things can change in just one short week. For instance, train stations. I never realized how vast the stations in Tokyo are."

"Got the country-living bug?"

"Hardly. No, in fact I've only reaffirmed that I don't belong out there. I'm much more comfortable in a crowd. And look at all those wonderful taxis. Speaking of which, where's your car?"

No sooner had Yukawa spoken than a red Pajero pulled up and parked alongside the curb. They ran over and got inside—Kusanagi in the passenger seat, Yukawa in the back.

"Long time no see," Utsumi said as she pulled away from the curb.

"Kusanagi tells me you've been out pounding the pavement on this one—unofficially, no less."

"Sounds like you've been doing your share of unofficial work too, Professor. Just can't stay out of trouble, can you?"

Yukawa was silent for a moment, considering his reply. "No, I wouldn't put it quite that way," he said. "If trouble had been my concern, I had plenty of opportunities to avoid it. Even if you'd asked me point-blank to help you with your investigation, I could've always refused."

"That's my first question," Kusanagi said. "Why are you being so helpful?"

"I believe I already told you."

"Only something vague about a certain person's life being 'seriously disrupted.' So who's this mystery man . . . or woman?"

Yukawa made an audible sigh. "I'll have to tell you at one point or another, but I'm not sure it will mean much when I do. The Kawahatas turning themselves in has made an already complicated situation worse. I might've been overly optimistic."

"Lead me on, why don't you."

"You're right, I'm sorry," Yukawa apologized. "I will tell you everything. Just not right now."

"Aren't you going to have to show your hand today?" Utsumi asked.

Yukawa thought for a while, then said, "I'm not coming with you today to lay any mysteries bare. I'm just looking for confirmation. If I get that, then many things may indeed become clear. But don't think that this will solve everything. In fact, it's more likely that we'll end up a good distance away from anything like a solution."

"Leaving us unable to prevent a certain person's life from being seriously disrupted, maybe?"

Yukawa shook his head at Kusanagi and said, "I don't know."

For a while after that, the three of them rode in silence. Utsumi took them up on the freeway and exited at the Chofu interchange.

A few moments later, they pulled in to the parking lot at the Shibamoto General Hospital.

Yukawa stopped as they walked into the hospice. He looked around. "It's so quiet," he said.

"Yeah, Utsumi has a theory about that," Kusanagi said. "She says it's so the patients don't notice the passing of time."

Utsumi sighed. "It was more of an idea than a theory," she added.

"I'd say it was a rather astute observation," Yukawa said.

They took the elevator to the third floor. The nurse in the pink uniform was standing outside the visitors' room, just like she had the day before.

"Sorry to bother you again so soon," Kusanagi apologized. She smiled and asked them to wait as she walked off down the hall.

The director of the hospital had been unenthusiastic about giving Kusanagi permission to bring another visitor to see Senba when he'd called the hospital that morning, and he took some persuading. As they waited for Senba, Kusanagi was full of questions, though he decided it would be better to follow Yukawa's lead. He was the man on the ground in this case, and he knew Hari Cove. If there was any key to tying together all the disparate threads of this investigation, Hari Cove was where they'd find it.

Kusanagi heard the sound of wheels rolling across the tiled floor and stiffened in his chair. Senba arrived, wrapped like a mummy in beige pajamas. He was facing straight ahead, a look of deep alarm floating in his sunken eyes. Kusanagi assumed it was because he thought they were going to ask him about Tsukahara again. He glanced sideways at Yukawa, curious to see how the physicist would act toward a man in his final days.

Yukawa's eyes were fixed firmly on the old man. His face betrayed no emotion or surprise. Either he'd seen terminal cancer patients before, or he'd made an accurate assumption about the state Senba would be in.

"Should I introduce myself?" Yukawa asked.

It took a moment before Kusanagi realized the question had been directed at him. He turned to Senba. "Thanks for talking to us yesterday. I brought someone else who wanted to meet with you. This is my friend Yukawa. He's not a police officer, he's a scientist. A physicist."

Yukawa held out his business card, but Senba's arm didn't move. The nurse took the card for him and held it up in front of his face.

Senba's eyes moved across the card. His lips parted, and he made an inquisitive grunt.

"I suppose you're wondering why a physicist would want to talk to you," Yukawa said. "As a matter of fact, up until this morning, I was in Hari Cove." His voice was low, but it echoed in the quiet room.

Senba's eyelids twitched.

Yukawa opened his document case and pulled out a single file and turned the cover so Senba could see it.

"I'm involved in a project investigating the potential development of undersea resources in Hari Cove. I attended the hearing the other day. You're aware of the development project? I heard you sent Mr. Tsukahara to the hearing in your stead."

Senba gave a jerky nod.

"The sea in Hari Cove . . ." Yukawa began, speaking slowly, ". . . is beautiful. Enough to make you catch your breath. I saw the crystals on the seafloor. There's no other word to describe them but *miraculous*. They are a true miracle, Mr. Senba, and they've been well looked after. I shouldn't be surprised if the sea there today looks exactly as it was the last time you saw it."

Senba began to sway, almost noticeably. His cheeks tightened and his lips trembled. For a moment, Kusanagi read his expression as fear, but he soon realized he was mistaken. The old man was trying to smile.

"We don't know what's going to happen with the development project. Except, even if it does go ahead, it won't be for some decades. We can expect that technologies to preserve the environment will have advanced significantly by that point. I tell you this as a scientist who is committed to preserving the beauty of the cove and will do anything in my power to keep it unblemished. This is my promise to you."

Senba nodded slowly. The hospital director had told them that the patient occasionally slipped out of consciousness, but he seemed to be fully alert at the moment.

"There's something I'd like you to see," Yukawa said, pulling a sheet of paper out of his case.

Kusanagi glanced at it from the side. It looked like a printout of a photograph, showing a painting of the ocean. Distant clouds floating in a blue sky reflected off the surface of the water. In the foreground, the coastline traced a gentle curve, and near the rocks, waves sent up a white spray.

Yukawa turned the picture toward Senba, and the reaction was instantaneous. It was as if something buried deep within him suddenly came welling up to the surface, charging his body with electricity. His skin blushed ever so slightly, and his clouded eyes became red. He groaned.

"This painting is on the wall at a small hotel called the Green Rock Inn. Perhaps you've seen it? It shows the view of the ocean from East Hari. I believe you lived there with your wife just before she passed. I should think the ocean looks much like this from her house. In fact . . ." Yukawa leaned forward, placing the photograph closer to Senba. "I wouldn't be surprised if you or your wife had painted it. Then, after she died, and you left the house in East Hari behind, you held onto it as a memento, a treasure. Something you would only give to the most important person in your life. Am I right?"

Senba's eyes widened, and his entire body went stiff. His breathing had grown ragged, making him shudder at regular intervals.

The nurse looked at him, worried, but when she looked like she might step in, Senba raised his left hand to wave her back. Mustering his strength, he took a deep breath. A look of determination came over his face.

"That . . . that's not true," he said in a thin voice. "I've never seen that painting before. Not . . . not in my entire life."

"Are you sure? Please take a close look," Yukawa said, holding the photograph even closer.

"No!" Senba batted at it with his other hand, knocking the paper out of Yukawa's grasp. It fluttered and fell to the floor.

"I see," Yukawa said calmly. "I have another photograph I'd like to show you." He pulled another piece of paper out of his case.

Kusanagi peered over his shoulder at it. This time, it was a picture of a young woman. She looked like she was sitting behind the wheel of a car. She had a look of surprise on her face, as if she wasn't expecting her photograph to be taken. She was attractive, with a healthy tan.

"I told you earlier that the cove is being well looked after. This is the woman who's doing that. I'm going back to Hari Cove today. Isn't there anything you'd like me to tell her for you?" Yukawa showed the photograph to Senba.

Senba's face twisted halfway between tears and a smile. His many wrinkles froze in curved lines down his face, and his lips fluttered.

"Well?" Yukawa asked again. "Don't you have any message for the woman responsible for protecting your home?"

Senba's emaciated body convulsed. But then his throat moved like he was trying to swallow something, and the spasms subsided. He straightened his spine, and thrust out his chest, his sunken eyes fixed on Yukawa.

"I don't know this woman, but tell her . . . thank you," he said forcefully.

Yukawa blinked and a smile came to his lips. He looked downward for a moment, then back up at Senba. "I will tell her you said that. You can keep the photograph."

He handed the two photographs to the nurse and turned to Kusanagi. "Let's go," Yukawa said, walking straight out the door.

"You're done?" Kusanagi asked.

Yukawa only nodded.

Kusanagi looked over at Utsumi, then stood. He bowed his head to Senba and the nurse, and thanked them.

Outside the visitors' room, the three walked toward the elevator in silence broken only by the echoes of their footsteps. While they were waiting for the elevator, they heard the sound of the door to the visitors' room open. The nurse came out, pushing Senba in his wheelchair. She saw them and nodded in their direction, but Senba's head was bent over and he wasn't moving. The two photographs were clutched in his hands.

"You said that Nobuko Miyake met with Senba the day before she was killed?" Yukawa asked after they reached the parking lot. It was the first thing any of them had said since they left the hospice.

"That's right, at a bar they used to frequent."

"Any idea what they were talking about?"

Kusanagi shrugged. "I don't know, the good old days? Except the bartender back then said that he saw Senba crying."

"Crying," Yukawa echoed, almost as if he had expected this. "Right."

"You mind telling us what this is all about?"

Yukawa checked his wristwatch and opened the door to Utsumi's Pajero. "Let's talk in the car. We'll get sunstroke standing out here, and, as I just said to Mr. Senba, I need to get back to Hari Cove."

Kusanagi nodded to Utsumi, and she pulled the keys from her bag.

"Why do you think Nobuko Miyake went to Ogikubo?" Yukawa asked from the backseat as they drove.

Kusanagi looked around. "That's exactly the question Tsukahara was asking after he arrested Senba. He never found out the reason himself, but I think it's pretty clear at this point: she went there to meet with Setsuko Kawahata."

"I agree, that's the most obvious explanation. So why did she go to meet her?"

"Well, maybe when she was talking about the old days with Senba, she remembered Setsuko, and wanted to catch up. . . ." Kusanagi said before his voice trailed off. He shook his head. "No, that's not it."

"It's not," Yukawa agreed. "First of all, it would've been difficult for her to find out where Setsuko Kawahata was living, since the house she was staying at wasn't her official address. She could have gone back to their mutual friends from their nightclub days and found out that way, but that would've taken quite a bit of time. So she would've had to have had a pretty good reason for wanting to see her—more than just wanting to catch up."

"We know that Nobuko was in financial straits," Utsumi said. "Maybe she went to borrow money?"

Kusanagi snapped his fingers and pointed at her. "That's it. She got the idea when she was talking to Senba. Right?" He turned back to look at Yukawa.

"I can't think of any other reason myself," he said, "but that raises a new question. Why did Nobuko believe Setsuko would give her money? If they were that close, wouldn't she have gone to see her before then?"

"That's true, and as far as I'm aware, Setsuko and Nobuko weren't all that close," Kusanagi said, crossing his arms.

"They weren't close, but she was sure Setsuko would give her money—absolutely sure. What does that suggest?" Yukawa asked.

"She had something on her," Utsumi suggested. "She knew her weak spot."

"A weak spot, yeah," Kusanagi nodded. "In other words, she was collecting hush money."

"Correct," said the physicist. "Nobuko learned something from Senba about Setsuko Kawahata, a secret that only she and Senba knew until that moment. Then Nobuko went to use that secret as leverage to pry money from her. That accounts for the special trip out to Ogikubo the very next day."

"But things didn't go the way Nobuko planned," Kusanagi said, continuing the story. "Instead of money, Setsuko killed Nobuko to keep her quiet. Which means we're talking about a pretty damn big secret. Come on, Yukawa, I know you know. Spit it out already."

Yukawa leaned back into his headrest, his eyes going up to the roof of the car. "The woman in the photograph I showed Senba just now is one Narumi Kawahata—Setsuko's daughter."

"And you said she's been looking after Hari Cove?" Utsumi asked.

Yukawa nodded. "Yes, passionately. There's a deep pathos in the way she goes about it, with almost painful dedication. But why is she so committed to a town, and a coast that's not even her birthplace? And why did she so readily agree to move out there, when just the year before, she told her friends that she wanted to stay in Tokyo, even if it meant living by herself? I can only offer one theory that accounts for these mysteries. She needs to have believed in her heart that it was her duty. Not a civic duty, mind you, but a duty she owed to another person. A paying of a debt."

"Yukawa," Kusanagi groaned, "you're not thinking what I think you're thinking, are you?"

"At first, I thought that Senba was taking the fall for Setsuko when he confessed. Except, at the time it happened, it's likely they hadn't seen each other for over a decade. Even if they'd once been intimate, it's hard to imagine he'd accept a murder sentence to save an old flame. No, there was something bigger driving him. This realization brought me to another, completely different idea. Senba wasn't protecting Setsuko. He was protecting her daughter—their daughter."

"So Narumi Kawahata is Senba's daughter."

Yukawa looked out at the street straight ahead and breathed a deep sigh. "That's the secret that Senba and Setsuko had to keep. The secret that drove their daughter to murder."

FIFTY-EIGHT

With the nurse's assistance, Senba lay down on his bed, still clutching the photographs in his hand. Sometimes lately, he couldn't make his fingers grasp things like he wanted them to, but not today.

The nurse told him to call her if he needed anything and walked out without asking any questions, for which he was grateful.

He heard someone cough. Probably Mr. Yoshioka. He had a brain tumor too. There'd been three people in their four-person room up until the week before. Now, as of two days ago, the bed right next to him was empty.

He felt a dull pain in his head, and his field of vision narrowed. Darkness crept in around the edges, until he had to hold the photographs directly in front of his face to see them.

He looked at the girl, with the look of surprise on her face. She was sitting behind the steering wheel of a car. Her chestnut-brown skin shone in the photograph.

She looks just like her mother, Senba thought. Lately, he had a hard time telling his dreams apart from reality, and occasionally he would get confused, but there were a few memories he had been holding onto with particular tenacity. Setsuko was one of them. He could close his eyes and be instantly transported back decades.

Senba was still in his early thirties. He was working for a company selling electronics, wearing a suit, carrying his attaché case as he flew around the country. His sales numbers were the best in the company, and he got special dispensation when he took customers out to party in Ginza. Their best customers he took to luxury nightclubs, sometimes more than once a week.

It was at one of those clubs that he met Setsuko. She had a pretty face but an at-home feel to her. She wasn't pushy with her conversation and mixed drinks without a lot of small talk.

She reacted differently one night when Senba brought up the topic of local cuisines—he caught a sparkle in her eyes, which he remembered. The next time he had a chance to talk with her alone, he asked her if she had an interest in cooking.

Her answer was as clear as could be: *absolutely*. She confided in him that what she really wanted to do was quit her nightclub job and work at a restaurant. Not as a waiter, but as a cook. Except, she said, she probably lacked the experience she would need.

Senba immediately thought of Haruhi. He had been to Hari several times to visit his wife's hometown, which was enough to pique his interest when he found the little restaurant. The food was excellent, and Senba quickly became a regular. The proprietor was a short man with a beautiful wife, and they ran the whole place by themselves. He'd heard them say on occasion that they were looking for extra help. He mentioned it to Setsuko, who was interested, so he took her over one night after the nightclub had closed.

The proprietors loved Setsuko the moment they set eyes on her, and one month later, Setsuko was working there. Within three months, the regulars were calling her by her nickname, Setchan, and after half a year had passed, the owners couldn't imagine running the place without her. Every night, she wore her trademark foliage-patterned kimono. To Senba, she looked ten times more alive than she had when she was working as a hostess.

Haruhi was open late those days, and Senba would almost always drop by after he'd seen his clients off for the evening. He enjoyed closing off his nights in Ginza with a cup of warm sake, a bit of Hari-style hors d'oeuvres, and Setsuko's smile.

The food at Haruhi was always good, but that wasn't the only reason he went. No matter how tired he was or how pressed he was for time, he always stopped by to see Setsuko. He wasn't sure exactly when it had started, but it was clear she had a hold on him. He thought she noticed, too, and when their eyes would happen to meet, he felt a connection there.

But he lacked the courage to do anything about it. He was married, after all, and he told himself he should be happy just getting to sit across the counter from her like this. Occasionally, Senba would bring a hostess he knew well along with him to Haruhi, as a kind of camouflage and a way of restraining his own feelings. The hostess's name was Nobuko Miyake.

Senba wasn't the only customer who came there to see Setsuko. Some of them made open passes at her, which she brushed aside with finesse. But there was one customer whose advances she didn't seem to mind. That was Shigehiro Kawahata.

Senba had seen him at the restaurant several times before. They would usually nod to each other, but they had hardly ever exchanged a word. Senba got the sense that Kawahata came there even more often than he did.

"He's a good man," the owner's wife would say. "Hard worker, gentle, and *single*. A perfect catch, if you ask me." Setsuko seemed to agree. She would laugh and shake her head while jealousy burned inside Senba's belly.

Then one night, after work was done, Setsuko invited Senba out for a drink out of the blue. He was a little surprised, but happily agreed. They went to a wine bar that stayed open all night. Setsuko was in unusually high spirits. She suggested they drink champagne, and when that was done, they ordered a bottle of wine. She drank quickly, and the bottle was gone before they knew it. He asked her why the good mood, and she said it was nothing, she just felt like tying one on that night.

She was considerably drunk when he brought her home, and he was laying her down on her bed when she wrapped her arms around his neck. When he looked down and saw the tears glimmering in her eyes, he lost what self-control he still had and returned her embrace, his lips pressing against hers. Setsuko was still lying in bed the next morning when Senba left. Her eyes were closed, but he didn't think she was asleep.

It was the only time they slept together. The next day, when he saw her at Haruhi, she acted the same as she always had. The events of the night before might as well have been nothing more than a dream.

He heard shortly thereafter that Kawahata had proposed to Setsuko, and she'd said yes. Only then did he understand what their night together had meant. She'd had something she needed to get off her chest, and that was him.

Setsuko quit Haruhi a short while thereafter. Senba heard about the wedding, raised a glass to her happiness, and tried to forget. But when he later heard that Setsuko had already been pregnant at the time of the ceremony, he became unsettled. He checked his calendar over and over, making sure of the date.

As the days passed, he grew increasingly suspicious that the child was his. When he heard that Setsuko had given birth to a baby girl, it took considerable effort to keep from dashing over to the hospital.

His own wife was in frail health and had been told she should avoid childbirth. He'd known this when they got married and had never thought of having children of his own. But now that it had happened, he couldn't get it out of his head.

After agonizing over it for days, Senba contacted Setsuko. He needed to know the truth.

It was his first time seeing her in a while, and though her skin practically glowed, her face had changed. She looked like a mother.

Her voice was softer, too. She hadn't brought the baby with her, dashing Senba's secret hope that he would get to meet his daughter.

They spoke briefly about their lives for a while, before Senba asked his question point-blank: are you sure Kawahata is the father? Setsuko didn't seem taken aback in the least. "Of course he is," she said. Her calmness struck Senba as unnatural, and when he saw the hard look in her eyes, he knew that she was lying.

But he didn't press her further. Instead, he made a request. He wanted a photograph of her child. Setsuko hesitated. Why would he need a photograph of someone else's baby, she wanted to know. But Senba was firm. He promised that, if she gave him just one photograph, he wouldn't speak of the matter again.

Finally, she relented, and on another day, they met in a different place, and she gave him a photo of Narumi cradled in her arms. Narumi's eyes were big and her skin porcelain white. Just looking at it brought tears to his eyes.

"Thank you," Senba said. He looked at Setsuko and saw that her eyes were red, but she held back her tears in front of him.

Senba promised he would tell no one, that he would keep it a secret to his death. Then he said, "Just give her the happiest life you can." Smiling, Setsuko told him that had been her plan regardless. Senba had laughed a little at that and agreed it had not been the most helpful advice.

The photograph became Senba's most prized possession, a secret treasure he could allow no one to see. He put it inside a plastic case and hid it toward the back of a drawer in his study.

He no intention of ever seeing Setsuko again after that. He still longed to see his daughter's face but kept that desire buried as deep as he could. Thankfully, he'd just started his own company, and there was plenty of work to keep him busy and keep his mind off things that didn't matter now.

For the next dozen years or so, he rode the waves of the economy. At first, his new venture was successful, but their time in the sun was very short. Before he knew it, he was left with nothing but an incurably ill wife and a small summer home in East Hari.

Yet, some good came of those days spent in East Hari. By losing everything, he was able to reflect back with unusual clarity on the path he had walked. He felt a resurgence of gratitude toward his wife. All of his successes had been thanks to her unflagging, unquestioning support. In his heart, he apologized to her many times about his one infidelity.

His wife did not have long to live. Senba stayed by her side at all times and tried to give her all she asked for. Not that she asked for much. She said she was happy just being able to look out over the sea where she had grown up. One day, she announced that she would like to paint the sea, and so he went and got her some supplies. She placed a canvas out on the porch of their cottage and began applying paint to it, a little each day. When he saw the finished painting, Senba was shocked. He'd never known his wife had any artistic talent.

After she passed away, he went back to Tokyo. He had no intention of starting over. He just needed a way to pay the bills. An old friend gave him an introduction and helped him land a job at a home appliances wholesaler.

It was around this time that he met a face from the past: Nobuko Miyake. He had spent many an evening with her when she was a hostess, but he had not seen her since his company folded. She invited him out for a drink.

He accepted lightly, never questioning her motives. He even thought it might be fun to remember the good old days. They ate dinner, then went to their old hangout, Bar Calvin. Nobuko had always been good at getting men to talk, and after two or three glasses, Senba had pretty much told his entire life story. He watched as she went from interest to disappointment, right around the part where he made it clear he was no longer the high-roller she once knew. As though she couldn't already tell from the clothes he was wearing. Senba realized she'd been hoping to borrow money.

It was then that he made the mistake he would regret for the rest of his life. He pulled out his wallet to buy some smokes, and the photograph fell out—the picture of Setsuko's baby. Nobuko picked it up and asked him who it was.

He told her it was a friend's child, but his words didn't sound convincing even to him. Setsuko's face wasn't visible in the photo, but when Nobuko said she remembered the foliage-patterned kimono the woman was wearing, Senba stiffened in his chair and fell silent.

She asked him to tell her the truth, promising she wouldn't tell a soul. Senba feared she would make assumptions anyway and spread the word around if he said nothing, so he told her on the condition she keep her promise. As he talked, he felt her warming to him, and this put him at ease. Maybe, he thought, she was a friend after all. Maybe he could trust her to keep his secret.

When he had finished, Nobuko told him to hold on a moment, and she left the table. When she returned after a few minutes, she placed a piece of paper with an address and a phone number on the table in front of him.

She told him that was where Setsuko was living. She had called Haruhi and pretended to be one of Setsuko's nightclub friends to get the information.

Nobuko suggested he go see her. Surely she wouldn't mind a single meeting. But Senba shook his head. There was no need. He'd put all of that away for good and had no intention of dragging it back out now. But even as he said it, tears came to his eyes.

As it turned out, Nobuko had another reason for looking up Setsuko's address.

Two days later, he saw on the morning news that she'd been killed. When he learned where it had happened, the blood drained from his face. After going back and forth on it for hours, he called Setsuko, half worried he might already be too late. In his heart he was already sure she'd stabbed Nobuko. But when she answered the phone, he was relieved to hear her sounding calm. She was a little surprised when he told her who he was, but she didn't sound unhappy to hear from him. Senba explained what had happened the other night and why he had called. Halfway through his explanation, Setsuko sounded noticeably disturbed. She hadn't seen her daughter yet that morning, she told him.

She said she should go check on her, so Senba hung up and waited by the phone for a terrifyingly long time. Anxiety rose in him until he felt nauseated, and he couldn't sit still. When Setsuko finally returned his call, her voice was filled with despair. Her daughter had killed Nobuko, she said through tears. The bloodied knife was still on the table in her room.

Senba made up his mind about what he was going to do. He told her to bring him the knife. Setsuko sounded hesitant, but they chose a place and a time, and he hung up.

He looked around his apartment. There was nothing he worried about losing, with one exception. He bundled up the painting of the sea his wife had made in her last days and, tucking it under his arm, he left.

Setsuko was there when he arrived at their rendezvous point. From the way she acted, he guessed she'd already figured out his plan. She told him she wasn't sure she was doing the right thing, but he told her that as a mother, protecting her daughter had to be the right thing.

He gave her the painting in exchange for the knife, and asked her to keep it for him until the day came when they might meet again. As he was about to leave, Setsuko told him to look at the café across the street. He did so and saw a slender girl with long black hair sitting at the table by the window. To his astonishment, she looked almost identical to the sister he'd lost to illness when she was young.

He thanked Setsuko. Seeing his daughter was the one thing he felt he needed to do. Now he would have no regrets.

Senba pulled out a small bag containing several photographs from beneath his pillow. He took out one, the photo of the baby, and compared it to the girl in the photo the physicist had given him. He could still see the baby there in her grown features. He wondered what kind of woman she was. He wondered what her voice sounded like. He would have liked to meet her once again before he died, but he knew that would never happen. He couldn't allow it to. If he did, then all he had endured would be for nothing.

His mind traveled back again to sixteen years earlier, to himself, standing in his old apartment in Tokyo's Edogawa Ward. The police would be arriving any moment. Once they had identified Nobuko's body, it would only be a matter of time before they tracked him down as the man who'd shared a drink with her the night before.

The detective came, a tough-looking man. Senba refused to let him inside, hoping to draw his suspicion. The detective left, but Senba knew he would be lingering in the area, keeping an eye on the apartment. Senba waited a while and then headed out, carrying a bag with the knife he'd taken from Setsuko.

He walked to a nearby river, and began to look around suspiciously— an act for the benefit of the detective following him. It worked. The detective came running down the bank toward him.

Senba ran, going as fast as he could, making an honest attempt at escape. For a moment, he feared he might actually succeed, but the detective's stamina had him beat. He was grabbed from behind and thrown on the ground.

Senba was arrested, put on trial, and declared guilty. And no point did anyone doubt his testimony—save one man, Tsukahara, the arresting detective. Tsukahara wanted to know why he hadn't thrown the bag into the river when he had a chance. He'd run along the waterway and could've tossed the bag in at any time. They might've found the bag later, of course, but it would've bought him some time. As it was, with the knife in his possession, he'd been arrested for suspicion of murder on the spot.

Senba claimed that tossing the knife hadn't occurred to him. He'd been so intent on escape that he'd forgotten the knife was in the bag. Tsukahara never seem satisfied with his answer, but Senba didn't change his story.

Life in prison wasn't easy. But it gave him strength to know that, because he was here, his daughter could live normally. It gave his own life meaning. When he got out, he called on a friend he'd made while serving his sentence. The man got him a job as a waste collector. The salary was pitifully low, and he was forced to live in a tiny, dirty room, but he was happy enough just to be alive.

Yet even this meager happiness didn't last long. The man who had gotten him his job ran off with the company's money. The waste collection service shut down, leaving Senba without a job or even a room to call his own. After that, he was forced to live on the streets. He knew where some homeless people lived, so he turned to them for help. They were kind to him, teaching him everything he needed to know to live outside the framework of society.

He was just getting used to his new life when a new challenge arose. He started finding it difficult to move his arms and legs the way he wanted them to move, and he was afflicted with terrible headaches that kept him from sleeping. Some days, he found it impossible to talk. He stopped being able to go to the soup kitchens he had come to rely on for food. He knew he was sick, very sick. His homeless friends took care of him, but he showed no sign of improvement.

That was when the last person he expected to see in the world found him: Tsukahara. He told Senba he had been searching for him for years. And when he learned that Senba was sick, he pulled some strings and got him into the hospice.

Senba wasn't sad when he learned about the tumor. In a way, it was a relief. He much preferred to die here, in a well-appointed facility. It was all thanks to Tsukahara—which was why he felt so guilty whenever the detective would beg him to tell him the truth about what had happened.

"I know you're protecting someone," Tsukahara told him. "Someone very important to you. Which is why I gotta know, are you okay with it ending like this? Don't you want them to know what's happened to you? Don't you want to see them one last time?"

Every time he came to visit, the detective would sit down on his bed and say the same thing. The secret became harder and harder for Senba to keep, especially when Tsukahara swore to him he would never tell a soul. By the time he relented, it was already difficult for him to speak, and it took a very long time for him to tell the whole story. Tsukahara listened patiently, barely saying a word.

When he was done, the former detective thanked him, and told him his secret was safe.

Nor did Tsukahara ever tell anyone else the truth. He even went so far as to do some sleuthing to find out where Setsuko and her family was living now. Senba felt a stirring of warmth in his chest when he heard they had returned to Kawahata's hometown of Hari Cove.

Tsukahara found something on the Internet, too: mention of a Narumi Kawahata in an article about ongoing efforts to protect Hari Cove's natural environment. Tsukahara learned there would be a hearing in August about the undersea development in Hari Cove she'd been fighting against. He wanted Senba to come to the hearing with him.

"You don't have to meet her. You could just see her from a distance. Don't you want to see the girl you protected for so long? Don't worry, I'll go with you. Hell, I'll push the wheelchair."

Tsukahara's invitation tore at Senba's heart. He wanted to see her more than anything else in the world, yet in the end, it wasn't to be. A man in his condition at the hearing would draw attention. Someone might figure out who he was, causing trouble for Setsuko and Narumi.

Tsukahara went ahead and applied for the hearing without his permission anyway. He came to the hospice one day to show him the letter. He had applied for two tickets, but only received one in the lottery.

"Let's go anyway," he said. "I could wait for you outside," Tsukahara had said.

Senba shook his head. He was grateful for everything the detective had done, but he would not go. Nor could he, physically. His condition had worsened to the degree that a long trip was entirely out of the question.

"It's a shame," Tsukahara had said. It was the last time he'd visited the hospice.

But Tsukahara hadn't given up. He'd gone to Hari Cove by himself, probably to try to meet Setsuko and Narumi. Senba was sure he'd met them. He didn't want to think about what happened to him there, though he had a pretty good idea.

He deeply regretted not stopping Tsukahara from going. He wished he could've reached out and taken that ticket from his hand and ripped it into pieces.

Senba looked down at the photograph of the baby in his hand and whispered, "I'm so sorry." *It's my fault this happened. It's my fault you've had to bear the burden of yet another sin. But don't worry. I'll die before I ever say a word. I only hope that you can forgive your father for being the fool that I am.*

FIFTY-NINE

Shinagawa Station came into view. There were a lot of cars, and traffic was moving slowly.

"You can just let me out here," Yukawa said, gathering his things.

Utsumi pulled over to the side of the road, and Yukawa opened the door. "Thanks for the lift," he said, getting out.

"Hold on, I'll see you to the gate," Kusanagi said, undoing his seatbelt.

"It's fine, it's still a bit of a walk to the station."

"None of that, now." Kusanagi opened his door. "You go on back without me," he said to Utsumi as he stepped out onto the sidewalk.

The two men walked past the line of cars toward the station. It was nearing the end of August, but the heat made it feel like midsummer. Yukawa started sweating, the grime of the city clinging to his face.

"It's still impossible to say what's true and what's not," he said abruptly. "I have my theories, but I would hesitate to even call them conjecture. In the end, it might all just be my imagination. The only reason I think Narumi might have been the one who killed Nobuko is because it answers several questions. I have no concrete evidence.

And there are many things I still don't know. The entire premise that Narumi is Senba's daughter might be flawed. And if it is true, does Shigehiro Kawahata know? What about Nobuko's murder, does he know about that? If so, when did he learn of it? It's all mysteries within mysteries. The only thing that could clear any of it up would be a confession from those involved, but that's one thing I am absolutely positive we'll never get."

"And what about Tsukahara's murder?"

"You mean Tsukahara's 'death due to negligence.' It's the same situation. As long as the Nobuko Miyake case is considered closed, there would be no motive for murdering him."

"But it is possible to connect the Kawahatas with him," Kusanagi said. "Tsukahara was the one who arrested Senba. And Senba knew Setsuko."

"True. But how much does a thirty-year-old connection between a barmaid at a restaurant and one of her customers count for, I wonder."

"It's hard to write it off as coincidence."

"Is it?" Yukawa wondered out loud. "I see coincidences like that all the time. Regardless—" The physicist breathed a deep sigh. "Regardless, as long as Senba isn't telling his story, I don't see a way for us to get to the bottom of this case. And he won't talk. He took a long prison sentence to protect the daughter he loved; he won't throw that away now. He intends to take his secret to his grave, and he won't have long to wait. No, I'm afraid this is one fight your side isn't going to win, Kusanagi."

The physicist's tone of indifference irked him, but Kusanagi couldn't think of a retort. Everything he said was true.

They arrived at the station. Yukawa said farewell and started to walk off toward the ticket gate.

"You're just going to let it go?" Kusanagi asked to his turned back. "You're okay with the way things turned out? What about that person you were trying to protect?"

Yukawa turned. "Of course it's not okay," he said, his voice ringing out over the din of the station. "That's why I'm going back to Hari Cove."

"Wait—" Kusanagi said, but Yukawa just slung his jacket over his shoulder and walked through the gates.

SIXTY

Setsuko was sitting across a small table from Detective Isobe. A younger detective sat next to him, taking notes.

"The temperature in here good for you? Not too cold?" Isobe asked. His face was set in a permanent scowl, but there was a look of real concern in his narrow eyes. Setsuko imagined that the scowl was something of a professional affectation, a look he'd had to wear so often it became his default mode. She'd had customers like that back in the day at Haruhi. They weren't grumpy, they were just too shy to make a kind face.

"It's fine," she said, and Isobe nodded, looking back down at his case report.

The room wasn't bad for an interrogation room. It was well air-conditioned, and the detectives weren't smoking. She'd always pictured these rooms as stark places with frightening décor, like one-way mirrors, but there was nothing of the sort here. Well, except for the bars on the one window.

"So, right, I need to ask you about a few more details," Isobe said, before launching into a long list of questions about the upkeep of the inn, boiler maintenance, whether they had ever considered repairs, whether they knew how much repairs would cost, and other things of that nature. There was no need to lie, so Setsuko just told it like it was.

Maybe we'll get out of this after all, she thought. The police were definitely moving toward wrapping the case up as professional negligence and corpse abandonment. The punishment for that should be relatively light, not that Setsuko feared punishment. She was happy as long as they could keep what happened sixteen years ago under wraps.

"Sounds like things are pretty rough," Isobe said, scratching his head. "I guess it's pretty much the same story for most of the hotels around here."

Setsuko nodded in silence and thought, *If only we'd shut the place down last summer.*

"What I'm wondering mostly now is why Mr. Tsukahara chose your inn. You hear anything about that from him? You served him dinner, right?"

Setsuko shrugged. "I did, but we didn't talk. I just explained the dishes, as usual."

"Right," Isobe said, shaking his head. He didn't seem that concerned either way.

He turned and spoke to the other detective, the one taking notes, and the two left the room. Setsuko's eyes wandered over to the one barred window in the room. There was a blush of red in the sky. Evening was coming.

The sunset had been glorious that night too, sixteen years ago.

It was a Sunday. The day before, Setsuko had met with an old friend and arrived at Ogikubo Station late, a little tipsy. Walking back, she saw a number of police cars near their house but shrugged it off as another car accident. It was nearly midnight when she got home.

She peeked into Narumi's room. The lights were out, but she could see a shape buried under the covers. Setsuko smiled and shut the door quietly.

When the call from Hidetoshi Senba came the next morning, she'd been a little bewildered to hear from him now so many years later, but the call wasn't unwelcome. The surprise mingled with regret in her heart, and, she admitted, a bit of longing.

What he had to say drove all such thoughts out of her mind. Nobuko killed, so close to their home, and her knowing the truth of Narumi's birth.

She hung up and went into Narumi's room. She was still in bed, curled up in a fetal position. She wasn't sleeping, and there were streaks down her cheek. Setsuko understood immediately that she'd been up crying all night.

The knife was on the table next to her bed—a kitchen knife Setsuko often used. It was black with blood. Not just the blade, but the handle, too. Setsuko stood, stunned. Her eyes went to the window, where red streaks of dawn lit the clouds in the distance with an eerie light—an ominous sign, she thought at the time.

Half panicking herself, she began to interrogate Narumi. *What happened? What's this knife? Talk to me, Narumi.* The girl's shock was too deep for her to relate the story with any kind of coherence. Gradually, though, Setsuko learned that a strange woman had come to their house the night before and started saying things to Narumi about her father. Then, after she had left, Narumi had gone to the kitchen, grabbed the knife, and presumably chased her down, though Narumi's account was particularly vague on that point.

There were still many unknowns, but Setsuko didn't hold out much hope of getting anything more from her panic-stricken daughter. She didn't know what to do. She couldn't call Shigehiro. What could he do, way down in Nagoya? And how could she explain any of it to him? No, the only person she could call was Senba. When she did, he was ready with instructions. "Bring the knife," he said. "I have a plan."

Setsuko knew immediately he was going to try to turn himself in and take Narumi's place. She also knew she should probably try to stop him. But when she thought of Narumi, she was ready to do anything to protect her. She would gladly take her place if she could, but ironically enough, Setsuko had an alibi. And she couldn't think of a motive that wouldn't involve revealing the truth of Narumi's birth.

Her mind a whirl, she followed Senba's instructions, leaving the house with the knife. She made Narumi come with her. If she was going to let him go through with this, the least she could do for him was let him see Narumi. He was her true father, after all.

The first thing she noticed when she saw him was how tired and worn he looked. It was clear he'd been through a lot in the many years since they'd last seen each other.

Senba had Setsuko explain the murder in as much detail as she could. Setsuko told him everything she had managed to wring out of Narumi, then, hesitantly, asked him if he was sure he wanted to do this. All he said was, "A parent will do anything to protect their child." His words were like a firm hand pressing against her back, pushing her toward the inevitable.

She saw on the news when he was arrested two days later, chased down by a detective as he was trying to get rid of the evidence. She was surprised he hadn't just turned himself in, but she assumed it was a calculated move to make him look even guiltier. It would certainly mean a stiffer sentence, Setsuko thought, and her heart almost burst.

Nothing in the news or the paper indicated the police had any doubt about his story. The police never showed up at Setsuko's door. Senba's plan had worked.

She then decided it was time to tell everything to Narumi. It was quite a shock to her, and she stayed home from school for four days. But as talk of the case faded from the news reports, things started to return to normal. It was clear that Narumi had begun to understand better what she had done and who had saved her.

There was an unspoken agreement never to mention this to her father. In fact, they never talked about it again, not even to each other. Nor did they forget. It remained an unfading scar on both their hearts, occasionally surfacing as a dull pain that cast a shadow over their

lives. Setsuko could understand why Narumi suddenly became en-
thusiastic about her father's plans to move the family to Hari Cove.

Indeed, their new life in Hari Cove was relatively happy. Narumi
had thrown herself into environmental issues with a passion that was
almost painful for her mother to see. She let Narumi do as she wished,
in hopes it might lessen the burden of her guilt. Nor did she try to
stop her when Narumi hung the painting Senba had given them in
the lobby of the Green Rock Inn.

And so sixteen years passed. She hadn't forgotten Senba, but it was
true that the memories didn't seem as clear now, with the veil of so
many years' worth of history pulled over them. It was Tsukahara who
drew back that veil. She was setting out his dinner when he said suddenly, "He's in the hospital, you know."

Setsuko blinked. "Excuse me? Who is?" Tsukahara wet his lips,
smiling stiffly. "Senba," he said. "Senba is in the hospital."

Setsuko could feel her face tense. Then, in a lower voice, Tsukahara told her he was a former detective, in charge of the murder in
Ogikubo.

Setsuko's heart nearly beat out of her rib cage. She could hear her
pulse in her ears.

"There's no need to be scared," Tsukahara said. "I'm not here to
dig up the past. I do have a request, though."

"What?" Setsuko asked. Speaking suddenly seemed almost impossible.

Tsukahara looked her straight in the eye and said he wanted
Narumi to visit Senba on his deathbed.

"He doesn't have much longer. Maybe not even a month. I want
him to be able to see the person he traded his life to save before he
goes. It's the only way I can think of to make up for the mistake
I made sixteen years ago.

"Please," Tsukahara said, bowing his head deeply.

Setsuko felt her tension ease. *This man's not here to reveal Narumi's
crime. He's here because he sympathizes with Senba.*

Still, secrets were meant to be kept. Setsuko straightened her back and told him she had no idea what he was talking about. She didn't know who this Mr. Senba was, and she certainly didn't think he had anything to do with them.

"I see," Tsukahara said sadly. "That's unfortunate." He said nothing more.

Setting down his food, Setsuko walked out of the room to find Shigehiro standing in the hallway. Startled, she asked him what he was doing, and he said, "Nothing, just walking down the hall."

She couldn't read his expression, but she wondered if he hadn't been listening at the door. She watched him go, leaning heavily on his cane in silence.

After that, Setsuko took Yukawa down to the bar and drank with him a while before leaving. She didn't want to go straight back to the inn, however, mostly because she was worried that Tsukahara might say something again. So she was fretting out in front of the bar when Narumi and her friends showed up. When Sawamura offered her a ride back, she had to accept.

Everything after that happened just like she told the police. She found Shigehiro sitting, dumbfounded, in the lobby of the Green Rock Inn. He told her there had been an accident with a boiler: a guest had died. He wanted to tell the police, and Setsuko agreed, but Sawamura was against it. He thought a different kind of accident would be better for the town's image. They argued about it a bit, but in the end, Shigehiro and Setsuko agreed. Setsuko in particular was eager to do anything that kept the investigators from connecting her family to Tsukahara.

But was it really an accident? she wondered.

Even if he'd overheard them talking that night in the hall, how could Shigehiro have known what they were talking about? Unless, she thought, he'd realized more than she knew about what had happened sixteen years ago.

Despite the fact that he was down in Nagoya, he could have heard about Senba's arrest for the murder of Nobuko Miyake from the news, or through a friend. He'd known both of them well enough back in the day. And if he'd learned that the murder had happened near their home, wouldn't he have put two and two together?

That, and she was pretty sure he knew Narumi wasn't his daughter. *He knows*, she thought, *and he's accepted her as his own anyway.*

Shigehiro was too smart to not connect Setsuko and Narumi to the murder sixteen years ago. And he'd never mentioned it once, which only made Setsuko even more sure he knew. Nor did she think it was entirely coincidence that he started talking about moving to Hari Cove soon after it happened. Had he been protecting the family, trying to make a physical break with their bloodstained home?

Maybe, she thought, when Tsukahara came to the inn, Shigehiro saw him as an envoy come to open the door on a buried past. Maybe he thought that leaving him alive would destroy their own lives. But Setsuko never learned the truth. Nor did she ask Shigehiro. As long as he was silent, so would she be. For the rest of her life, if she had to.

Setsuko knew better than anyone that silence was the only option.

SIXTY-ONE

Kyohei looked up from the hotel bed. His father was on the phone again. He could picture his mother's look of exasperation on the other end of the line.

"Well, what do you want me to do?" his father was saying. "He says he wants to stay here another day. I don't know, something about his homework. I said *I don't know*. Well, you tell him," he said, thrusting his cell phone toward Kyohei. "It's your mom."

Kyohei sighed and took the phone.

"Hi."

"What's this all about?" his mother asked. "Didn't you tell everything to the police already? Why can't you come down right away?" She was talking fast and loud. Kyohei held the phone further away from his ear.

"I've got homework," he said.

"So? Do it down here."

"I can't. I'm getting some help with it here."

"From whom?"

Kyohei rolled his eyes. "Someone I met at Uncle Shigehiro's inn. He's a professor at a university."

"Why is a university professor helping you with your fifth grade homework?"

"I dunno. I was telling him about it, and he said he'd help. He's staying in the same hotel as us—but he's out now. He won't be back until tonight, and I really gotta talk to him."

He heard his mom snort. "Why can't your father and I help you, like we always do?"

"He said it's not good if you do it for me. I have to learn how to do it for myself."

His mother was silent for a moment.

That shut her up.

"Fine, whatever. Give me back to your dad."

Kyohei handed the phone back to his father, then opened the sliding glass door and stepped out onto the balcony. The room was right over the hotel pool. He scanned the chairs around the pool, but Yukawa was nowhere to be found. It was a little after three in the afternoon.

He had almost given up when the woman at the front desk had told him Yukawa would be out all day. But when he got back to his room and started packing up his things, a strong urge had struck him to stay and wait for him, no matter what it took. He needed to talk to Yukawa one last time.

Despite the fact that he didn't even have a good explanation, his father didn't put up too much of a fight when Kyohei pleaded to delay their departure by another day. Maybe, Kyohei thought, he sensed Kyohei's deeper reason for needing to stay.

His father put down the phone. "We're going home tomorrow afternoon, and that's final."

Kyohei nodded.

He figured that since he'd told his mom he was staying to do his homework, he'd better get to it, so he spread his books out on the one table in the room. He didn't feel like playing anyway. He couldn't imagine enjoying anything right at that moment.

"I'm going to go talk to the police," his father said. "I want to check in and see how your aunt and uncle are doing. If they'll tell me, that is."

He returned a little after six o'clock, empty-handed. "I pushed pretty hard, but they wouldn't tell me anything. So I just hung out there for a while," he said.

Kyohei hadn't gotten much done either. His head was whirling too fast for him to focus on his homework.

They decided to eat dinner in the restaurant on the first floor. Kyohei ordered the fried shrimp platter—one of his favorites. It was a big plate, with three giant shrimp on top.

He was about to dig in when he heard a familiar *whiz pop*, and Kyohei's eyes went out to the ocean shore.

"Fireworks?" his father said. "Sounds like someone's shooting off some big ones down on the beach."

Kyohei was about to correct him—the sound was definitely a smaller bottle rocket—when memories of that night came rushing back. He felt a large lump in his throat, heavy, like lead weighing on his chest. Kyohei shook his head and put down his fork and knife.

"What's wrong? You aren't sick, are you?" his father asked.

Kyohei shook his head. "Nah, just full."

"Full? You've barely eaten a thing."

Just then, Kyohei spotted Yukawa walking past the restaurant toward the lobby. He hopped out of his chair and ran toward him, calling out, "Professor!"

Yukawa stopped and turned. A momentary look of confusion passed over his face when he saw Kyohei, then he smiled. "Hey," he said. "You're still here?"

"I didn't know what to do," Kyohei said, the words coming out in a rush. "I couldn't tell my mom or my dad, I wasn't even sure if I should be telling you—"

Yukawa held a finger up to his lips. Then he lowered his hand until he was pointing at Kyohei. "This is about the night you set off the fireworks with your uncle, yes?"

Kyohei nodded, relieved beyond words. He knew that somehow Yukawa would understand.

"Then let's talk about that tomorrow. You should get your rest tonight," Yukawa said, turning slowly and walking off without waiting for Kyohei's reply.

SIXTY-TWO

Narumi scanned all the sites she could find for any follow-up on the incident but found nothing. The only headline about the case read, "Falling Death in Hari Cove Actually a Poisoning—Local Innkeepers Involved in Cover-Up," followed by a short article that told her nothing she didn't already know. It didn't look like the case was getting much attention beyond the borders of their town.

That didn't make it any less of a big deal for her, though. Narumi wondered almost constantly how her parents were doing, with no means of finding out. She tried calling Nishiguchi, but he only apologized. "Sorry, I don't know exactly what's going on either," he said. "I'm sure they're fine, though."

He said they should get together for a drink once things calmed down, and she told him she'd think about it. Going for a drink was the last thing on her mind.

She was listlessly looking through some help wanted ads when she heard footsteps on the stairs outside, and the door opened. It was Wakana.

"Narumi? There's someone here to see you downstairs."

"Me?" Narumi said, putting a hand to her chest. "Is it the police?"

"No, someone who says he wanted to go for a dive. He requested you specifically and said you'd talked about it before?"

"Tall guy? Glasses?"

"That's the one."

"Right," she said, standing up.

She went downstairs to find Yukawa waiting for her. He was looking at one of the stickers they had for sale.

"Hello," she said.

He looked up and smiled. "Thanks for the other day."

"My pleasure," she said. "How did you know I was here?"

Yukawa put the sticker back on the shelf. "I paid a visit to the police department and told them I had a question about my bill from the other night and wanted to talk to the person in charge at the Green Rock Inn. They told me where you'd be."

"That worked?" Narumi shook her head. She half wanted to ask him if he had heard anything about her parents, while he was at it.

"As a matter of fact, I'll be leaving town today," Yukawa said.

"Really? All finished with your research?"

"I think DESMEC can handle the rest. School's starting up soon. Anyway, I figured this is my last chance to see this ocean you're so proud of. I believe you promised to take me diving?"

"I did, but—"

She heard a sound behind her and turned to see Wakana step up. "If you don't mind, I'll take you out," she offered. "Narumi's had a lot going on lately, and she's probably pretty tired. It's not a good idea to dive when you're not at your best."

Yukawa nodded thoughtfully and turned his eyes to Narumi. "I certainly won't force you. Though there were some things I wanted to talk to you about."

Narumi stared at Yukawa's face. There was a serious look to his eyes, more so than usual. And yet, there was a kindness there too. She got the sense that he had something he needed to tell her.

"I'd rather not do all the prep we'd need to go scuba diving, but

I could handle some snorkeling," she said. "And that should be more than enough for you to see the real treasure of Hari Cove."

"Perfect," Yukawa said, picking a pair of goggles off the shelf. "I might have lied when I said I had my diver's license, anyway."

An hour later they were in the ocean, at the very spot that made Narumi a snorkeling fanatic years before. It was a bit of a secret, being a ways away from the main swimming area and most of the popular diving spots. Here, only a short distance off shore, it got very deep very quickly, and the scenery changed dramatically. The seafloor was a beautiful carpet of light, with a hundred gradations of color, and there were fish everywhere.

This is what I've been protecting, she thought. *Just like it's been protecting me.* She wondered what would have become of her if she hadn't found the ocean, and the thought frightened her.

Sixteen years ago, when she moved here, she had no guidepost to live by. She'd begun to seriously entertain doubts about whether she deserved to be alive at all. How could she possibly have a right to a happy life after killing one person and sending another to jail for her crime?

Her hands still remembered what it felt like to stick a knife into that woman's body. She doubted she'd ever forget. And still, she didn't know why she'd done it. It was like her body had been moving by itself. But she did remember how she'd felt just before it happened. She felt like everything would fall apart, their lives dashed on the rocks.

Nobuko Miyake rose in her mind. She could see her frown when she heard Narumi's mother was out, then how she stared at Narumi, a faint smile coming to her lipstick-red lips. "You do look like him, don't you," she said.

"Like who?" Narumi asked. Thinking about it later, she wished she hadn't.

Nobuko had scoffed, her smile turning mean. "Narumi, was it? I bet people tell you all the time that you don't look like your father."

Her eyes opened wider. Nobuko chuckled. "Bull's-eye, hmm? It's okay. I'm the only one who knows the truth."

Narumi felt the blood rush to her head. "What do you mean, the truth? You're crazy," she said sharply.

"There's nothing crazy about it, dear. But my, you do look so much like him. Especially the mouth." Narumi could feel the woman's eyes invading her space, an unwelcome presence lingering over her features.

"Stop. I'm going to tell my father."

The woman made a mock show of alarm. "Please do," she said. "In fact, I'd be happy to tell him the truth myself. I wonder what would happen then? You and your mom would probably get kicked out onto the street, at the very least. Anyway, tell your mother I'll be back. And don't make that face at me, young girl. You'll regret making an enemy of me when the tables are turned—and they will be, very soon."

Narumi was still watching those ruby-red lips when she realized Nobuko had already left. Her head was a whirlwind. She couldn't think straight, and yet, her body knew what to do. She grabbed a knife from the kitchen, then went after her.

She ran mindlessly, and yet, there was one shred of clarity at the bottom of her murky consciousness. It was the realization that the woman was telling the truth. She wasn't her father's daughter. It confirmed a doubt she'd been holding inside for years.

It started one night when her father came home from a school reunion, unusually drunk. He couldn't even walk straight, slumping onto the kitchen table when he sat down and tried to drink some water. Setsuko tried to rouse him but he didn't look like he was listening, until he suddenly turned and slapped her mother full across the face. Narumi was shocked. She'd never seen her father lift a hand against anyone before. Setsuko froze.

"Don't you say anything," he growled in the most terrifying voice she'd ever heard him use. "You don't have the right." Then he opened his wallet and pulled out a photograph, tossing it on the floor. Narumi recognized it: a family picture of the three of them, taken at a studio. "They all laughed. Said she didn't look like me. Of course she doesn't look like me." And then, drunk, her father fell asleep on the spot with her mother standing over him.

The next day, Shigehiro was back to being her gentle father, a kind husband. He apologized to both of them about drinking too much the night before and said he didn't remember a thing. It never came up again, and Narumi never asked her mother about it, but she didn't forget.

Nobuko Miyake brought that memory screaming back to the surface, and with it came the fear that her family would fall apart. She saw the woman walking away, her silhouette floating in the light of the streetlamp. Narumi grabbed the knife tight in both hands and charged. Her mind was a blank. She didn't stop to think—that this was a crime, that people who did this went to prison.

She didn't remember what happened next very clearly. When she came to, she was curled up in her bed. She didn't sleep, she just lay there trembling until morning. When her mother questioned her, she tried to tell her what had happened but couldn't put the pieces together. Her recollection was too vague.

But she did what she was told, and when her mother came back to collect her, she changed her clothes and left the house with no idea where they were going, what they were doing, or what would happen to her.

A few days later, it was announced on the news that the man who killed Nobuko Miyake—a man she didn't know—had been caught. Her mother then explained who he was, and why he'd taken the blame. Narumi was aghast. She didn't want to believe it, she couldn't believe it. And yet, here she was, free and not in prison.

"You can't tell anyone this. Especially not your father," her mother said, her face severe.

Narumi didn't object. Her chest ached when she thought of this man she'd never met serving her prison sentence. But there was blame there, too, for the married man who had a one-night stand with another woman. And for the child born from that union, there was guilt.

Her days were spent struggling with that guilt. She'd put her real father in jail and deceived the man who had raised her. When her father would come home on the weekends, she would feel such a welling of emotion she couldn't look into his eyes.

Which was why she didn't resist when her father quit his job and said he was going to take over the inn. She wanted to leave that place as soon as possible. Her knees felt weak every time she walked past where it happened.

Then, about a month after they had moved to Hari Cove, one of her friends took her to the observation platform on their way back from school. It was the first time she'd really looked out over the ocean, and she was awestruck by its beauty. She remembered then what her mother had said about the painting Senba had given her.

In that moment, she felt like she knew what she had to do with her life. She owed it to her real father. She would protect the ocean that he loved until the day he could see it again.

Yukawa worked his diving fins like a pro, not a bit of wasted movement. Narumi started to wonder if he'd been lying about not having a license. She showed him a couple of her favorite spots, then they went back to the shore and climbed up on the rocks.

Yukawa took off his snorkel mask and smiled. "Amazing. I understand why you're so proud of the ocean here. Makes me wonder how so many people in Tokyo can go off to Okinawa and Hawaii when there's this beauty right here under their noses." He turned to Narumi. "Thank you. When I think of Hari Cove, this is what I'll remember, and that's saying something."

Narumi took off her fins and sat down on the rock. "I'm glad you liked it. But wasn't there something else you wanted to talk to me about?"

Yukawa smiled knowingly and sat down next to her. His eyes were fixed out on the horizon. "Summer's ending soon," he said.

"Mr. Yukawa?"

"My detective friend found Hidetoshi Senba. I met him yesterday, in fact. He's in the hospital with an incurable brain tumor. He doesn't have long to live."

Narumi felt a lump form in her chest, an uncomfortable tightness she couldn't swallow or spit out. Her face drew tight.

"I'm sure you're wondering why a physicist would go so far out of his way. I wonder that myself. It's really none of my concern."

Narumi searched for something she could say that would explain it all away. But at the same time, she realized there weren't any magic words. He already knew everything.

"The man mostly responsible for taking care of Senba was none other than the detective who arrested him sixteen years ago. Tsukahara had retired from the police force, but that one case still bothered him. I'm not sure what the two of them spoke of, but I imagine that Tsukahara tried everything he could to get the truth out of Senba. And I'm guessing he did, in the end, though he didn't feel the need to make that public. Instead, all he wanted to do was fulfill an old man's dying wish to see the daughter he'd traded his life to save."

Yukawa spoke evenly and calmly, giving each word time to make an impact. Narumi remembered when her eyes met Tsukahara's at the hearing, finally understanding that gentle look he had given her.

"I don't think what Tsukahara was trying to do was a bad thing. But it was dangerous. Like trying to open a set of doors on the bottom of the sea. You don't know what's going to happen when you do. That's why no one touches them. And when someone comes along who does, others try to stop them."

Narumi looked over at Yukawa. "Are you saying it wasn't an accident?"

"You think it was?" Yukawa asked, giving her a cold look. "Really?"

"Of course," she wanted to say, but she couldn't make her lips form the words. Her mouth was bone dry.

Yukawa was looking back out at the horizon. "I didn't want to say anything, to be honest. There were a number of things about what happened that bothered me right from the beginning, but I decided to ignore them. That is, until I realized if I didn't take action, it would have a tremendous impact on someone's life, through no fault of his own."

Narumi looked at him, not understanding.

"Tsukahara's death wasn't an accident, it was murder," he said, suddenly turning to face her. "And the murderer . . . was your cousin, Kyohei."

For a second, everything around her went silent. Even the surface of the sea appeared still, completely frozen. Then, sound returned with a gentle lapping of waves. She felt a gust of wind blow between them. She stared at the physicist. *What the hell is he saying?* For a moment, she wondered if she had misheard.

"Of course," Yukawa said, "he didn't do it on purpose. He didn't even understand the meaning of what he was doing at the time."

"What did he do?" Narumi asked, her voice a whisper.

Yukawa looked down in silence for a moment before turning to face her. "I believe I mentioned that the police were having a hard time re-creating the conditions for what happened. There's a simple reason: your father is lying to them. In order to reproduce what happened, one very important condition needs to be met. It's nothing elaborate, nor particularly difficult. But it's impossible if you have a bad leg like your father, which is why forensics hasn't even considered the possibility."

Narumi flinched. "I don't understand."

Yukawa took a deep breath. "It's simple. All you have to do is cover the top of the chimney, which causes the exhaust to flow back down the pipe, eventually resulting in an incomplete burn in the boiler. The carbon monoxide then goes up, and leaks out through the cracks in the pipe into the Ocean Room. I calculated that it would take fewer than ten minutes to reach lethal concentrations."

"When did you know this?"

"I understood the potential when forensics first came to the Green Rock Inn and began sniffing around your kitchen burners."

"But you didn't say anything."

"Like I said, I didn't feel it was my place to get involved."

"What changed your mind?"

"Something Kyohei said. He was watching one of the forensics officers come down the fire escape, and he mentioned there was a chimney up on top of the roof. That surprised me, because you can't see the chimney at all from the ground, so he must have gone up there at some point. It's unlikely to have been the last time he came to the Green Rock Inn, because he would've been much smaller, and it would've been too dangerous. That left the night of the fireworks. From there, it was a process of connecting the dots until I realized Kyohei must have done something—unknowingly, mind you—to the chimney that caused the accident."

"Did you ask him?" Narumi asked.

"No, I didn't want to lead him to the same conclusions I'd reached, not before he was ready." Yukawa smiled. "Although I did have him help me a little. He stole the master key for me."

"Why did you need that?"

"To investigate the Ocean Room. I realized the chimney must pass through the wall in that room, and that was the only door on the floor that was locked. Nothing raises suspicion like a locked door. As I thought, I found cracks in the back wall of the closet. That's when Kyohei supplied the final piece to the puzzle—when he told me he'd gone around the inn before setting off fireworks and had covered up every place and window a bottle rocket might accidentally fly into. That's when I realized why he'd gone up to the chimney."

"He covered it?"

"A slightly dampened cardboard box placed over the top would do the trick. I'm sure those were his instructions."

"My father's instructions," Narumi said.

Yukawa didn't answer. Instead he picked up a small pebble by his foot.

"It wasn't difficult to get Tsukahara to sleep in the Ocean Room. Your uncle could have given him some excuse for why they needed to switch rooms, then moved his things back into the Rainbow Room afterward. The sleeping pill could've been mixed into his drink."

Narumi felt the last shreds of her hope fade as a deep despair settled in. It was impossible to imagine it having been an accident after hearing Yukawa's theory.

"I can't say how serious your father was about killing him, of course," he continued. "He couldn't have been certain that covering the chimney would have the desired result. No, I'd say he was just crossing his fingers—but intent is still intent, which suggests a motive. Which is why I had my detective friend in Tokyo investigate your family." Yukawa stood and tossed the small pebble in his hand into the water. "Once we started down that road, it quickly became clear that we'd have to uncover what happened sixteen years ago. Thus my meeting with Mr. Senba. Who, by the way, didn't confirm a thing."

Narumi noticed she was trembling, and not from the cold. The sun today was bright and strong. Her wetsuit had completely dried out some time ago.

"Are you going to tell the police?" she asked with a shiver.

Yukawa's lips settled into a straight line, and he shook his head. "I can't, which bothers me. In order to prove your father's intent, I would have to tell them what Kyohei did. I don't think he would be punished, of course. But he would have to make a very difficult choice. He would wonder whether he should tell the truth. In fact, I think he's already wondering. I think he knows the meaning of what he did by now."

Narumi caught her breath.

"That said, putting him on the spot right now would only make things worse. Whether he tells the truth or not, he's going to blame himself for what happens as a result." Yukawa looked down at Narumi. "That's why I want you to do something."

Narumi straightened. "What?"

"Kyohei is going to have to live with a very big secret. But someday, he's going to want to know why his uncle made him do what he did. If he comes to you with that, I want you to tell him the truth, the whole truth. Then I want you to let him decide what he should do. I'm sure you know better than anyone what it is to live with the consequences of one's actions."

Every word Yukawa spoke sank deep into Narumi's heart. It made her heart ache, but there was no helping that.

She stood and stared into Yukawa's eyes. "Okay. I will."

"Good, I'm glad to hear that." Yukawa said. "There's something else I want you to do, too."

"I . . ." Narumi began, steadying her breath. "I should turn myself in, shouldn't I?"

Yukawa looked surprised for a moment. Then his smile returned to his lips. "I want you to value life. Yours and others. More than you ever have before."

Holding back tears, Narumi looked off into the distance, out across the sea.

SIXTY-THREE

Tatara flipped through the pages of the report, the wrinkles across his brow frozen in deep lines. Kusanagi sat across from him, rubbing his hands together beneath the conference table. His palms were sweating.

"So basically," Tatara said, looking up with a deep sigh, "we have absolutely no evidence?"

"I'm sorry, sir," Kusanagi said, lowering his head. "As that says, it's very likely that Setsuko Kawahata was involved with the murder of Nobuko Miyake. However, as long as Senba remains unwilling to talk, it will be extremely difficult to prove."

Tatara leaned one cheek on his hand and groaned. "If Tsukahara couldn't crack him, neither can we. Not to mention the Miyake murder was a closed case. We can't do anything about that. Nor should we. You did a good job, though. At least, I've got some closure on this now."

"What about Hari Cove?" Kusanagi asked.

Tatara groaned again and pulled a notebook out of his pocket.

"Yeah, about that, I got a call from the police. Sounds like they're going to write the whole thing off as an accident after all.

The testimony they got left no room for questions, and forensics says the chances of the accident having been arranged are next to nil. They didn't say anything about Tsukahara's connection to the Kawahatas, either. Of course, we haven't told them what we know."

"Well? Should we?"

Tatara's eyes went a little wider. He crossed his arms across his chest and stared back at Kusanagi. "Now? What good would that do? We're not reopening the Nobuko Miyake case."

Kusanagi shrugged. "So what do we do then?"

Tatara picked up the report and slowly tore it in two. "This is the prefecture's call, so we take it. I'll explain everything to Tsukahara's widow."

"Are you—" *Sure*, Kusanagi was about to say, but he swallowed his words.

Torn report in one hand, Tatara stared straight back at him. "I meant what I said. You did good work. Now it's time for you to go back to your regular assignment."

Kusanagi stood, bowed stiffly, and walked over to the door. He stepped outside, glancing back at Tatara before he closed the door behind him. The white-haired director was looking out the window, lines of deep regret on his face.

SIXTY-FOUR

Kyohei paced around the lobby while his father was settling the bill at the front desk. He checked the lounge and the pool, even though he knew it wouldn't do any good. Yukawa was nowhere to be found.

He said we'd talk tomorrow, Kyohei thought, getting angry. Grownups were always breaking promises as if it didn't matter at all. He'd thought the professor was different, though.

"Come on, we're going," his father called out to him. "If we leave now, we'll get to the station right on time. Hurry up." He began walking toward the front entrance, checking his wristwatch.

Kyohei had run out of excuses. Shoulders slumped, he followed his father.

They got in a taxi just outside the hotel. Kyohei looked out of the window. He could see several boats in the harbor. In the distance, the swimming beach shone white under the sun. He spotted the breakwater where he and Yukawa had launched their water rocket. It seemed like an eternity ago.

The taxi got to Hari Cove Station faster than he'd expected. As soon as he stepped out of the door, he started sweating.

"It's hot again," his father said. "Good thing the waiting room's got air-conditioning."

The small waiting room was up some stairs, just before the gate. It *was* cool inside, but that wasn't what made a smile break out across Kyohei's face. Yukawa was sitting in a corner of the waiting room, reading a magazine.

"Professor!"

Yukawa looked up and nodded. "Right on time," he said. "Getting on the next express?"

"Yeah, you too?" Kyohei said, putting down his backpack and sitting next to Yukawa.

"No. I'm going back to Tokyo by bus with the DESMEC crew."

"Oh," Kyohei said, disappointed. He had been hoping they could talk.

"But I did come here to see you," Yukawa said, then he looked up at Kyohei's father. "You don't mind if I speak with him a bit?"

"Not at all," Kyohei's father said. "I'll be outside." He made a gesture of smoking a cigarette.

"First, let me give you this," Yukawa said, pulling some papers out of his jacket pocket. "The data from when we set off our rocket. You'll need this if you're going to finish your report."

"Oh, right," he said, grabbing the papers and looking them over. They were covered with tiny, precisely written numbers. Someone who hadn't been there that day would have no idea what they meant. But Kyohei did. He remembered when the rocket flew right, and when it didn't fly at all. He could draw a picture in his mind of exactly how the water shooting out from the back of the rocket sparkled in the sun over the waves.

"There are some mysteries in this world," Yukawa said suddenly, "that cannot be unraveled with modern science. However, as science develops, we will one day be able to understand them. The question is, is there a limit to what science can know? If so, what creates that limit?"

Kyohei looked at Yukawa. He couldn't figure out why the professor was telling him this, except he had a feeling it was very important.

Yukawa pointed a finger at Kyohei's forehead. "People do," he said. "People's brains, to be more precise. For example, in mathematics, when somebody discovers a new theorem, they have other mathematicians verify it to see if it's correct. The problem is, the theorems getting discovered are becoming more and more complex. That limits the number of mathematicians who can properly verify them. What happens when someone comes up with a theorem so hard to understand that there isn't anyone else who can understand it? In order for that theorem to be accepted as fact, they have to wait until another genius comes along. That's the limit the human brain imposes on the progress of scientific knowledge. You understand?"

Kyohei nodded, still having no idea where he was going with this.

"Every problem has a solution," Yukawa said, staring straight at Kyohei through his glasses. "But there's no guarantee that the solution will be found immediately. The same holds true in our lives. We encounter several problems to which the solutions are not immediately apparent in life. There is value to be had in worrying about those problems when you get to them. But never feel rushed. Often, in order to find the answer, you need time to grow first. That's why we apply ourselves, and learn as we go."

Kyohei chewed on that for moment, then his mouth opened a little and he looked up with sudden understanding.

"You have questions now, I know, and until you find your answers, I'll be working on those questions too, and worrying with you. So don't forget, you're never alone."

Kyohei looked up at Yukawa and took a deep breath. It felt like a little light had flickered back on in his chest. The weight he had felt pressing down on him for the last several days lifted. Now he finally understood why he'd needed to talk to Yukawa so much. It was because he wanted to hear this.

His father came back. "Train's coming pretty soon."

Kyohei stood. He turned back around to face Yukawa. "Thanks, Professor."

Yukawa smiled back. "Be well," he said.

Kyohei followed his father through the ticket gate just as the express train was pulling into the platform. Just before he got onto the train, he took a glance back at the waiting room. Yukawa had already left.

Kyohei sat down in a booth seat across from his father. His father asked him what they'd been talking about, so he showed him the data from the rocket test.

"Wow, that's too complicated for me," his father said, handing the papers back to him.

Of course you're not interested, Kyohei thought. *You wouldn't understand unless you'd done the experiment yourself. That's what science is all about.*

Kyohei looked out the window and watched the scenery going by. The ocean sparkled in the sunlight. Just above the horizon he saw billowing clouds, white like ice cream.

"Don't tell anyone, okay?"

His uncle's voice sounded in his mind. It was the night of the fireworks. His uncle had just told him they should put something over the chimney in case one of the rockets went in. *"I've got this box here. See? The bottom's damp. That's to keep it from catching fire. Thanks, kiddo. I'd do it myself, but my leg . . ."*

When Kyohei came back down, they had set off a few rockets. He'd watched each one shoot off into the night sky. When he glanced at his uncle, he saw that he, too, was looking up, but not at the sky. His eyes were fixed on one of the upstairs windows, and his hands were pressed together, just the way he did when he was praying. Except he didn't look peaceful. There was deep pain in his face. To Kyohei, it looked like he was apologizing to someone.

But who?

And why?

Kyohei shook the memory from his head and looked back out the window. *It's okay*, he thought. *I don't need to know those answers right away. I have time, and besides, I'm not alone.*